Praise for *New York Times* b
author Eileen Goudg

IMMEDIATE FAMI

"Satisfying women's fiction . . . with happy endi̶̶...

—*Publishers Weekly*

"Zesty . . . Once again, Goudge excels at exploring the unconventional ways in which the bonds of family and friends are pulled, twisted, and tested, and her trademark creation of genial, winsome protagonists makes the process delectably entertaining."

—*Booklist*

OTHERWISE ENGAGED

"Creating strong, resourceful heroines is what Goudge does best, and both loyal fans and new readers alike will be thoroughly captivated by the unique adventure Jessie and Erin embark upon."

—*Booklist*

"Fun, romantic, and heartwarming . . . Goudge explores the power of loving relationships."

—*Romantic Times*

More praise for Eileen Goudge and her bestselling fiction

"A gifted writer with an eye for telling detail."

—*Chicago Tribune*

"Goudge keeps you cheering . . ."

—*People*

"A page-turning drama that delivers a little something for everyone . . . Just right for that perfect summer day's read."

—*Bookpage.com*

"Goudge . . . reminds us of the delights to be had in explorations of the improbable."

—*New York Times Book Review*

ALSO BY EILEEN GOUDGE

Otherwise Engaged

Eileen Goudge

Immediate Family

POCKET BOOKS

New York   London   Toronto   Sydney

POCKET BOOKS, a division of Simon & Schuster, Inc.
1230 Avenue of the Americas, New York, NY 10020

ISBN-13: 978-0-7434-8319-3
ISBN-10:   0-7434-8319-7
ISBN-13: 978-0-7434-8342-1 (pbk)
ISBN-10:   0-7434-8342-1 (pbk)

First Pocket Books trade paperback edition July 2007

10 9 8 7 6 5 4 3 2 1

POCKET and colophon are registered trademarks of
Simon & Schuster, Inc.

For information regarding special discounts for bulk purchases,
please contact Simon & Schuster Special Sales
at 1-800-456-6798 or business@simonandschuster.com

Manufactured in the United States of America

To my chosen sisters—
Kathee, Kay, Connie, Brenda, and Catherine—
who've always been there, through good times and bad, and who
know that true friendship is being able to pick up the phone at any
hour and know you'll always find a sympathetic ear.

Acknowledgments

In every fictional tale, there's usually a nugget of truth. This one began with an unusual proposal set forth by a good friend of my husband's, a woman looking for a man she admired and trusted to father her child. Rather than resulting in a baby, this novel was hatched.

Along the way, I was aided in particular by my husband, Sandy Kenyon, who not only made dinner the nights I was burning the midnight oil, but who provided useful material and insights into the life of an entertainment reporter. Thanks to him, I fulfilled a lifelong dream of standing on the red carpet on Oscar night, if only in the pages of this novel. Should it ever happen in real life, I will ditch the comfortable shoes reporters wear and step out in style!

Thanks, too, to Kenny Plotnik and Liz Aiello, of WABC-TV, who allowed me to be a fly on the wall of a television newsroom. Without them and the hardworking team at WABC, who made me feel right at home, I wouldn't have been able to bring my fictional newsroom scenes to life. I also came away with increased admiration for what my husband and his coworkers do for a living.

Last but not least, a big kiss to my wonderful agent and friend, Susan Ginsburg, who proved once more that I couldn't do without her.

Friends are relatives you make for yourself.
　　　　　　　—Eustache Deschamps

Each friend represents a world in us, a world possibly not
born until they arrive.
　　　　　　　—Anaïs Nin

Immediate Family

Prologue

Looks like the gang's all here."

Stevie Light, all five feet two inches of her honing in like a heat-guided missile, managed to jostle her way to the front of the crowd, cameraman in tow, to where the director of the extended care facility, a stout, officious-looking gray-haired woman caught in the glare of a dozen on-board lights was announcing, above the cacophony of shouting voices, "We have no comment at this time, except to say that Miss Rose is doing fine! Her doctors will be briefing you at the press conference later today."

The story had come off the wires no more than an hour ago, and already the place was teeming with news crews and reporters, their vans double-parked along the curb. On the lawn out front, Kimberly Stevens, from KBLJ, was doing her live shot, kittenish blond hair fluttering in the breeze. A short distance away, Mark Esposito, from *Live at Five*, was powdering his nose while peering into a handheld mirror as he awaited his cue. Paparazzi were out in force as well, long-range lenses aimed like snipers' rifles at the third floor: the room where Lauren Rose lay newly risen from the coma she'd been in for the past twelve years.

An event nothing short of a miracle. What were the odds? Stevie wondered. *Less than those of my ever finding my father.*

She turned to her cameraman, but Matt was already heading off to scout for a location for her stand-up. With his scraggly hair and two-day-old beard, torn jeans and tattoos, Matt O'Brien might have been mistaken for a vaguely disreputable onlooker if not for the Betacam propped on one scrawny shoulder, but he was one of the best in the business.

Minutes later, freckled cheeks powdered and lips freshly glossed, she stood before the Betacam's lens as her cue came from the noon anchor, Charlie Karr, and she launched into her intro: "The stunning news came yesterday when doctors caring for Lauren Rose here at the Oak Hills long-term care facility, in Westwood, reported that their patient had emerged from the coma she'd been in for more than a decade. It was back in 1994 that Ms. Rose was a guest at the home of veteran rocker Grant Tobin, when the LAPD got a 911 call in the early hours of the morning saying a woman had been shot in the head. While paramedics labored to save Ms. Rose's life, Tobin was questioned but never charged in connection with the incident he called an accidental shooting, the exact cause of which was never officially determined. Tobin, best known for his chart-topping hits in the seventies with the group Astral Plane, has remained in seclusion ever since. More details on Ms. Rose's condition will become available when her doctors speak at a news conference set for later today. . . ."

Stevie remembered well the day of the shooting. It was her first week on the job at KNLA, fresh from KESQ in Palm Springs and still wet enough behind the ears to believe she'd be doing some real reporting, as opposed to covering water-main breaks and shopping-center openings. The media had gone wall to wall with coverage, news crews camping out in front of Grant Tobin's Holmby Hills estate for weeks on end, the tabloids trumpeting rumors of a lovers' quarrel gone awry and showing photos of Lauren, at the time a beautiful and promising young actress, in various cleavage-baring poses. But the publicity eventually died down when, after a lengthy investigation, no charges were filed.

Now this. It was unclear yet the extent to which Lauren could communicate, if at all. Only one thing was for sure: She was the only one besides Grant who knew what had happened that night. If she were to refute his version of the events, it could land him behind bars.

In her twelve years on the beat, Stevie had covered her share of celebrity trials. And this promised to be as sensational as Michael Jackson's. Just in time for the station's recent slide to second place in the ratings, behind Channel 5, which had KNLA's news director, Jerry Fine, on a tear and those up for contract renewals sweating bullets.

Her live stand-up wrapped and the news conference still hours away, Stevie and Matt headed back to the newsroom. It was in full-tilt mode when they arrived: computer and TV monitors glowing in every pod and those not at their desks dashing about at warp speed. The night-side producer, Liv Henry, was firing questions at April Chu, on the phone relaying breaking news overseas. In its glass-enclosed hub, the assignment desk was busy gathering info from police and fire scanners as well as other media outlets, while in the remote-field room, the live trucks making their way on city streets and freeways were being tracked via microwave uplink.

Stevie banged out her copy, and when Liv had okayed it and the tape had been cut, she headed into hair and makeup for a quick touch-up before taking her place at the anchor desk beside Charlie and Carol. The two anchors had been at it since earlier in the day and looked it . . . until the cameras went up, then suddenly they appeared as fresh as if they'd just breezed in off the golf course—one of the tricks that made them worth every cent of their hefty salaries. Stevie sailed through her report without a hitch, and tossed back to Charlie and Carol, who moved on to the breaking news of the hour: a shooting in Compton that had left one cop dead and two wounded. She hung around the newsroom for another couple of hours after that, tracking down leads and feeding teases for the five o'clock broadcast into the Flashcam, until it was time to leave for the news conference at Cedars-Sinai. Her shift had ended hours ago, but she was so pumped with adrenaline, she didn't feel the least bit tired.

This was what she loved and hated most about her job—the high when she was crashing on a story that, when she came down from it, was like coming off a weekend-long bender. Yet she couldn't imagine any other kind of life. From the time she was a kid, conducting mock interviews using a pencil in place of a microphone, she'd known this was what she wanted. "Curious kids grow up to be reporters," she'd reply, when pressed for an explanation. And if she was more curious than most, was it any wonder? She'd grown up not knowing who her father was. An answer not even her mother could supply.

It was the era of free love, and Nancy was freer than most, moving like a nomad from one place to the next, changing bed partners with the same ease. Stevie would probably never know who, besides her mother, had been present at her conception. It was the one mystery that would never be solved, the one story she'd never break. And the one thing she wanted most in this world.

She and Matt arrived at the press conference early enough to secure places near the front. By the time Lauren's doctor, a beak-nosed neurologist with thinning brown hair, stepped up to the podium, there was barely elbow room to be had in the packed hospital conference room. Dr. Ragione informed them that Ms. Rose was responding to stimuli and showed signs of recovering her speech. She appeared to recognize family members, he said, and was able to communicate through simple hand and eye movements. When asked if there was any indication she could recall the shooting, he replied curtly that it was too early to say at this point.

Stevie did her stand-up on the lawn outside, which Matt fed from the live truck to the control room back at the station, along with footage of the news conference. It was close to seven before she finally packed it in, after twelve hours without a break and only a couple of protein bars gobbled on the run.

She headed for her car, in the parking lot behind the featureless glass cube of a building KNLA occupied on a side street off Wilshire Boulevard. The sight of her lovingly restored '67 Pontiac Firebird, cherry red with cream interior, never failed to boost her spirits at the end of a long day, and today was no exception. It was by far the biggest expenditure she'd ever made and one she was still paying off, but the joy it gave her outweighed her mother's frequent reminders that she could have put a down payment on a house with what it had cost her.

It wasn't until Stevie was tooling along the freeway with the top down, on her way to Ryan's, enjoying the feel of the wind in her hair and the envious looks she never failed to get from other drivers, that she remembered tonight was the night she was supposed to have dinner at her mother's. She groaned aloud. The only thing she was in the mood for was a stiff drink coupled with a foot rub, if her boyfriend was feeling especially generous.

She thought about begging off, but something kept her from reaching for her cell phone. Nancy was always understanding when she had to cancel at the last minute due to breaking news, but the image of her hobbling around in her cast—she'd broken her left foot rock climbing a few weeks back—added an extra helping of guilt. She phoned Ryan instead, letting him know not to expect her.

"Should I wait up for you?" he asked, in a low, throaty voice that had the desired effect of igniting a little trail of fire below her belly button.

She hesitated before replying, "No. I'll stay over at my place." It was closer to her mom's. Besides, she hadn't been home in over a week.

"All the more reason to move in with me," Ryan said, after she'd explained about needing to water her plants and collect her mail. He spoke lightly, but she caught a note of impatience. He'd been urging her to take this next step, reasoning that it was silly to pay rent on her own place when she was almost never there, but so far she'd resisted. Not that she wasn't crazy about him. She had been since the day they'd met, when she'd interviewed him following his Oscar nomination for best documentary. It was commitment itself that caused her to break out in a cold sweat.

Stevie sighed as she hung up. Her friends thought she was crazy, period. Franny, whose biological clock was ticking loudly enough for everyone within a mile's radius to hear, had stated with her usual bluntness that she'd be happy to take Ryan off Stevie's hands if she didn't want him. Emerson, a single mom, had no illusions about romance, but even she thought Stevie was being unnecessarily cautious. And Jay . . . what could you expect from him, with a wife and now a baby on the way? Naturally, he was prejudiced.

But what if she took the plunge and found herself in over her head? Drowning in shattered illusions. Sure, it was all hearts and flowers in the beginning. But things changed. People changed. With all the uncertainty she'd had in her life, Stevie didn't need any more. Also, Ryan wanted a family, and how could she promise him that? All her years growing up, moving from one place to the next, Nancy struggling to make ends meet, selling her pots in local galleries, Stevie had fantasized about her mystery dad swooping in to the rescue. Never mind that he probably didn't even know she existed. How could she bring children into the world when she didn't even know her own place in it?

Fifteen minutes later she was pulling up in front of her mother's cedar-shingled bungalow, on a wooded slope in Topanga Canyon, only to find it dark. Odd. There was no light burning, either, in the converted garage that housed Nancy's studio. Could she have gotten the dates mixed up? No, Stevie thought. She'd spoken to her mother only last night, Nancy informing her that she was making her famous zucchini fritters and asking her to pick up a jar of mayonnaise.

She let herself in with her key, placing the jar in its bag on the painted Tibetan cabinet by the door and calling out, "Mom?" Her heart was pounding and her mouth suddenly parched—too many years of listening to what came in over the newsroom's police scanner. In her mind, an intruder lurked in every darkened hallway and at any given moment a medical emergency was but a heartbeat away.

She found Nancy stretched out, fully clothed, on her bed, eyes closed and her foot in its cast, an abstract montage of doodles drawn on with colored Magic Markers—her mother never met a blank canvas she could resist—propped on a bolster. Stevie let out the breath she'd been holding. Not a 911 call after all; Nancy must have taken a nap and overslept.

Stevie was reaching for the light switch on the wall when Nancy said, "Don't." Her voice was small and pained.

"Are you okay?" Stevie asked, thinking her mom's foot must be bothering her and wondering if that ancient jar of aspirin was still in the medicine cabinet. Her mother didn't reply. The pair of overalls she had on were crusted with bits of dried clay. Her hair that had once been the rooster-red of Stevie's, now faded to the color of

7

old pennies, fell in crinkly waves down her narrow, freckled shoulders. The TV was on, its sound muted, and in the flickery glow her face had the bluish-white cast of someone underwater. When she opened her eyes at last, it was only to stare sightlessly at the vintage Fillmore poster on the wall opposite the bed, with its swirly psychedelic print advertising a long-ago Big Brother and the Holding Company concert. Nancy had been there that night, close enough to feel the sweat off Janis Joplin's brow.

"I was wrong to keep it from you," she said in that same small, pained voice. "I should have told you."

Stevie sank down on the bed, taking her mother's hand in hers. It was cool and dry, with ridged calluses on her palm from her potter's wheel. "Told me what?"

"About your father."

Stevie's heart bumped up into her throat. "But I thought—"

Her mother didn't let her finish. "I was only trying to protect you, you have to believe that." Tears leaked from the corners of her pale blue eyes to trickle down her temples and into her hair. "I was afraid of what would happen if it got out. Reporters hounding us everywhere we went, people staring and making assumptions . . . and worse." She shuddered, closing her eyes again. "But I *should* have told you. You had a right to know."

Stevie stared at her, shock pounding in dull waves against some distant shore inside her head. All this time she'd been led to believe that Nancy knew little more than she did.

"If I wasn't sure at the time," Nancy went on, "I'd know now just looking at you." She turned toward Stevie, a faint, mirthless smile on her lips. "You're the spitting image of him."

Stevie felt the blood drain from her face. Her voice seemed to come from another room as she croaked, "Who?"

Nancy turned her gaze to the TV, where an old clip of Grant

Tobin, in concert with Astral Plane, was playing on CNN—a slightly built young man flashing like quicksilver across the stage, his dark hair whipping about his head, his Rasputin eyes that had captivated a generation afire in his pale, fine-boned face. She lifted a trembling finger to point at the screen.

"Him."

Spring

spring *v.* **sprang,** (spr«AA»ng) or **sprung** (spr«AB»ng) **sprung,**
spring«AC»ing, springs *v. intr.* 1. The season of the year occurring
between winter and summer; a time of growth and renewal 2. To
move upward or forward in a single quick motion or a series of
such motions; leap. 3. To become warped, split, or cracked, as if
with excessive force.

Chapter One

D ammit, guys, where are you?" Franny muttered, wondering what was keeping her friends.

Stevie, at least, had an excuse—her flight had been delayed. And Emerson was back at the hotel nursing a hangover from last night's reception at the Graduate Center. She'd muttered groggily from under her pillow, as Franny was leaving, that she'd get up as soon as the room stopped spinning. Jay, though, was unofficially MIA. Franny had been going it alone for close to an hour, smiling until her face hurt, seemingly the only one at this function who didn't have a spouse, or tennis elbow from whipping out snapshots of kids to show off.

She felt like a crasher at her own college reunion.

She deposited her empty champagne flute on a passing tray and helped herself to another mimosa, sinking down on the wrought-iron bench by the koi pond. Surveying the grounds, with its well-tended lawn and trees, where her former classmates milled about, chatting with each other and nibbling on canapés, she thought: *Who are these people?* Even the radicals who'd tilted at windmills alongside her at the *Princetonian* in their torn fatigues and Doc Marten boots had morphed into lawyers and bankers and hedge-fund managers, all married and with kids. Kids, who to hear them tell it, were the cutest, most gifted children on the planet.

Where had *she* been all those years? Franny wondered. Okay, so she'd been pursuing her career. Albeit not one with a high six-figure salary—unless you were Mort Janklow or Binky Urban, being a literary agent was more about cachet than cash—though there was always the hope she'd discover the next J. K. Rowling. But where was the husband who she'd naively assumed, back when she was graduating, would be standing beside her today? The photos of children to fill up the empty plastic sleeves in her wallet?

Was it some failure on her part?

True, she wasn't drop-dead gorgeous like Emerson; but she wasn't chopped liver, either. "Earthy" was the word most commonly used to describe her, with her profusion of curly dark hair and a body that, while not exactly *Playboy* centerfold material, manufacturers of underwire bras and stretch jeans salivated over. Nor was she all that picky. A guy didn't have to have movie star looks or be at the top of his profession. He didn't even have to be Jewish—her mother, may she rest in peace, would be none the wiser. He just had to be smart and kind and good in bed . . . and to want kids as much as she did.

Just then, she spotted a rangy figure jogging toward her across the emerald expanse of lawn, where it sloped up from the roadway toward the knoll on which the Hartleys' residence—as in Pamela Hartley, née Bendix, who was hosting this event along with her husband—nestled amid the sheltering arms of venerable old elms. She'd have known it was Jay from half a mile away, with his loose-limbed grace and swoosh of wheat-colored hair that flopped over his forehead as he ran. He had on a pair of jeans worn to snow at the knees and his navy blazer that had to be at least ten years old. Which meant that without even trying, he fit right in with the old-money crowd, many of whom were similarly attired; at the same time, reminding her that she was *overdressed*, the only woman here in Prada heels.

He spotted Franny and waved, breaking into a wide grin, oblivious to the female heads turning toward him—part of Jay's charm was that he never seemed to notice the effect he had on women. "Sorry. You wouldn't believe the traffic on the turnpike," he apologized breathlessly when he'd caught up to her. She gave him a stern look, and he confessed, with a shrug. "Okay, I got a late start. Viv was feeling a little under the weather." She'd needed him to pick up an herbal something or other at the health food store, he explained.

Franny didn't doubt it. Since she'd become pregnant, Vivienne had become obsessed with health. She consulted her nutritionist daily and was an authority on homeopathic remedies. If she had so much as a sniffle or a twinge, she was on the phone with her doctor. Jay hadn't known a moment's peace since the pink line had appeared on the EPT stick.

"What she wants to know," he went on, "is how *I* can be so calm about this baby."

Franny scooted over to make room for him on the bench, hooking an arm through his. "Easy," she said, feeling a pinprick of envy, as she always did whenever the subject of his wife's pregnancy came up. "It's like when a building's on fire, there's always this one guy telling everyone not to panic. One of you has to be that guy."

"I guess it helps that I grew up on a farm," he said.

She rolled her eyes. "I'm looking for a husband and you're talking animal husbandry."

"You're in the right place, at least. There's no shortage of candidates," remarked Jay, his gaze falling on a group of men chatting nearby.

"All married. Though from what I've seen," she added, thinking of the family photos she'd dutifully oohed and ahhed over, "they're plenty virile."

"I brought my turkey baster along just in case." Jay's blue eyes twinkled with merriment. All week he'd been teasing her about this reunion being a chance to scout for potential sperm donors.

Franny shot him a dirty look. "Please. You make it sound like I'm shopping for a new car."

"All I'm saying is that there's more than one way to skin a cat, as my ma would say. Anyway, here's to finding Mr. Right." Jay lifted the mimosa he'd snagged off a passing tray.

"Make that Mr. Right on Time." According to the experts, at thirty-six she was already approaching the outer edge of viability, her eggs shriveling as they spoke. If she didn't get started soon, she'd be looking at the front end of baby strollers for the rest of her life.

"What about Stu? Didn't you used to date him in college?" Jay pointed out a stocky, dark-haired man in the requisite khakis and creased linen blazer pacing back and forth nearby, conducting what appeared to be urgent business over his cell phone.

"For all of five minutes," she reminded him. Her short-lived romance with Stu Felder had ended with her informing him, as he was groping her in the library late one night, that she wasn't going to have sex with him, not then or ever. More puzzled than anything, he'd asked if she was into girls; naturally it wouldn't have occured to Stu that it could have anything to do with *him*. "Anyway, if I asked, he'd think it was because I was gay and couldn't have a baby the regular way. Either that, or he'd insist we forgo the turkey baster."

"Would that be so terrible?"

She eyed Stu thoughtfully. "He's okay looking, if that's what you mean. Not my type, though."

"I thought we were talking about sperm donors, not potential partners."

"Yeah, well, shouldn't I at least *like* the person?"

Jay idly rolled his glass between his hands, sunlight sparking off its rim like in a "Diamonds Are Forever" commercial, as he sat leaning forward with elbows resting on his knees. He tilted his head to peer up at her, pushing back the lock of hair forever falling over his eyes—eyes the blue of a prairie sky in haying season, with tiny creases radiating from their corners like sunrays. "You could make it easier on yourself, you know. No hassle, no ties."

In other words, why not save herself a lot of grief by heading straight for the nearest sperm bank? The answer was simple: Bobby. Her brother, who'd jumped to his death on the tracks of a Brooklyn-bound D train, no doubt attempting to escape the imaginary government agents forever pursuing him. The memory brought a dull ache. Poor Bobby; he hadn't asked to be born that way. And what if the same time bomb was lurking in her own DNA? How could she compound that risk with some anonymous donor who might have a family skeleton or two stashed in his own closet?

"No one said it was supposed to be easy," she replied, with an airiness that didn't fool Jay for an instant, from the way he was eyeing her. "Look how long it took *you*." When Jay finally tied the knot, she, Em, and Stevie had all breathed a sigh of relief. They'd been so sick of their girlfriends asking if he was up for grabs, Franny had been ready to marry him herself just to shut everyone up. Abruptly, she rose to her feet. "I have to pee. Why don't you keep an eye out for Em and Stevie? They should be here any minute." She started off toward the house, feeling a little wobbly from the two mimosas she'd downed and trying to walk a straight line. In college, her friends used to tease her about being a cheap date—three beers and she was under the table.

She was on her way back to Jay several minutes later when she bumped into Stu Felder. "Well, well. If it isn't Franny Richman," he greeted her, his swarthy face, with its perennial five o'clock shadow, lighting up. "You haven't changed a bit. Still as luscious as ever."

Franny felt anything but, with her hair frizzing in the damp air and sweat oozing from her armpits. But she smiled anyway. "Hey, Stu. You're looking good yourself. What are you up to these days?"

"Making money." His wry tone kept it from sounding too smug.

"You're in real estate, right?" She'd looked him up in the alumni directory.

"Something along those lines," he replied, just modestly enough to let her know it wasn't houses in the 'burbs he was brokering. "What about you?"

She shrugged. "Making a living." She explained that no one got rich in the book business.

"Married?" When she shook her head, he commented with a wry chuckle, "Thank God. I was beginning to think I was the only one here without a charge account at Toys 'R' Us."

Franny gave a knowing laugh. "Tell me about it."

"So you've never taken the plunge?"

She shook her head again. "Though I'd like at least one kid before it's too late."

He raised an eyebrow. "Don't tell me you're thinking of going the solo route?"

"More than thinking." Franny kicked herself as soon as the words were out. Damn. Why had she opened her big mouth? To Stu, of all people.

"Well, if you're looking for a volunteer . . ." He waggled his brows suggestively. Suddenly she was back in the carrel at Mudd Library, Stu with a hand up her shirt and the other one wriggling its way down the waistband of her pants.

"Thanks, I'll keep that in mind," she replied dryly.

"Why don't we continue this discussion over dinner some night? You free next Saturday?" he asked. She recalled the alumni directory's listing a Manhattan address for Stu, and her heart sank. What had she gotten herself into?

"I'm afraid not." Franny took a step back, her smile fading as the lie rose to her lips. "I have a client coming in from out of town. In fact, my calendar's pretty full at the moment. Plus, I'm up to my ears in manuscripts." She shrugged helplessly, taking another step back. "Listen, I should go. It was good seeing you . . ."

She started to move away, but he took hold of her arm, leaning in so close she could smell his breath. *I'm not the only one who's had too much to drink,* she thought. "You don't know what you're missing." His tone was teasing, but his coolly assessing eyes were those of a man on a mission: Stu wasn't used to losing, and she was no doubt the one deal he hadn't closed.

"In that case, I'll just have to dream on, won't I?" she told him, freeing her arm from his grasp.

Out of the corner of her eye, she spotted Jay walking briskly toward them. From the look on his face, it was clear he'd witnessed enough of the exchange to feel the need to come to her rescue. "I'm not interrupting anything, am I?" he said when he'd caught up to them. His tone was mild, but he flashed Stu a narrow, assessing look.

Stu's grin remained intact. "I was just offering Franny here my services." His tone made it clear it wasn't a business deal they'd been discussing. "But maybe she has a better offer."

"As a matter of fact, she does." Jay looped an arm around her shoulder. "Me."

"Why did you tell him that?" Franny hissed as they were retreating across the lawn. She felt unreasonably annoyed, where moments before she'd been mentally blessing Jay for coming to the rescue. "Now he'll go around telling everyone we're lovers."

Sure, she'd briefly toyed with the idea in college—what straight female wouldn't?—but he'd been involved with Megan Keisser at the time, a leggy blond poli-sci major who'd gone on to marry a state supreme court judge. Franny was glad now that they'd never gone down that road. Lovers came and went, but friends were there to stay. Besides, she couldn't imagine loving Jay more than she already did.

He grinned and puffed out his chest. "Guess it's never too late to be the campus stud."

Franny groaned. "Knowing Stu, he'll have you sleeping with Stevie and Em, too."

"My own harem? Hmmm . . . now there's an idea."

"With Em, you'd have to get in line." As long as Franny had known her, Emerson had had men clustering around her, though since her divorce she'd sworn off on dating. "And it looks like Stevie's down for the count, for now at least." Franny told him the most recent news, that Ryan and Stevie had broken up; Stevie had phoned her the other night in tears.

Jay frowned in commiseration. "Poor Stevie."

"First, she finds out her dad's the infamous Grant Tobin. Now this." Franny sighed, tucking her arm into Jay's and leaning in to him slightly to keep her high heels from sinking into the soft turf. "Though I can't say I blame Ryan. All he did was ask her to marry him. It's not his fault that Stevie's a commitment-phobe."

"From what you're telling me, it doesn't sound like she turned him down flat," Jay said.

"She didn't exactly jump at the chance, either. I guess from Ryan's point of view, no answer is as good as no." Franny shook her head, wondering how someone as smart as Stevie could be so thick-headed when it came to love. "I just wish she'd make up her mind one way or the other and put us *all* out of our misery."

"Maybe it's better to be like Em, and know what you *don't* want," he commented.

"Speaking of the devil, I wonder what's keeping her?" Franny glanced at her watch and frowned. It had been an hour and a half since she'd left Emerson nursing her hangover back at the hotel. Had she decided to skip the brunch altogether? No, that wasn't like her. When she said she was going to be somewhere, you could count on it. If Franny had to use one word to describe Emerson, it was focused. Even with the four vodka gimlets she'd downed at last night's reception, she'd managed to line up two prospective accounts for her PR firm. Unless the roof had caved in at the Nassau Inn and she was buried under the rubble, she'd be here.

At that very moment Emerson Fitzgibbons was circling the block in search of a parking space, her head throbbing in time with the Coldplay tune pumping from the car stereo. Why, oh why, had she had so much to drink last night? Normally all she ever had was Perrier. Otherwise, with all the functions she had to attend, she'd be a lush. She had to stay on top of it at all times, not just for her clients' sakes, but for Ainsley's . . . and her mother's.

The lines in her furrowed brow deepened. No, she wasn't going to think about her mother today. She was taking a weekend off from anything related to Marjorie Kroft-Fitzgibbons.

A cat darted into the street in front of her, and Emerson slammed on the brakes, causing her Lexus to slew to one side and driving a spike of pain through her throbbing temples. God. What if it'd been a child and she hadn't been able to stop in time? It was her worst nightmare, second only to that of something happening to her daughter. It was sheer luck, after all, that anyone made it to adulthood. Wasn't life itself an accident waiting to happen?

It was all she could do to keep from warning Franny to be careful what she wished for. Emerson adored her daughter, but being a single mom was the hardest job she'd ever tackled. Harder than building her own PR firm from the ground up; harder than the clients she practically had to breast-feed and the TV producers, magazine editors, and reporters who made Saddam Hussein look like a pussycat by comparison. Not just in terms of the days she felt like sliced and diced sushi. It was the constant worrying. Was she doing it right? Or was she screwing up her daughter's life the way her mother had screwed up hers?

But on this mild spring day, as she cruised the quiet residential streets bordering the campus, it seemed nothing bad was lurking around the bend. If it weren't for this hangover, she might have gone so far as to say she was having fun. Fun being a relative term, of course—Emerson couldn't remember the last time she'd completely cut loose. But the drive up yesterday with Franny, the two of them gabbing the whole way just like old times, had done more for her than a week at Canyon Ranch. For the past twenty-four hours she'd been free of concerns about her daughter, who was being well looked after by her father, Emerson's ex-husband, Briggs, or her mother, who was no doubt tormenting the new night nurse the agency had sent over to replace the last one who'd quit, the third in less than six months.

And soon there would be Jay and Stevie as well. Emerson recalled the nights they used to hang out together in each other's dorm rooms, drinking cheap wine and staying up until all hours, talking about everything under the sun. As disparate as four people could be, but with a common bond: They were all on scholarship. The only difference was, with her pedigree, no one would have guessed.

She was turning onto the next block, wishing she'd been smart and taken the shuttle like Franny, when she spied a space at last. It was a little tight, but she managed to squeeze into it with only a few inches of her rear bumper jutting into the adjacent driveway.

As she was climbing out of her car, a burly man in sweats came charging out of the house she was parked in front of, shouting, "Hey, lady! What the hell d'ya think yer doin'!"

"Excuse me?" Emerson drew herself up to her full five feet eleven inches, a blond Amazon who appeared even taller in her Christian Louboutin wedges.

"Yer blockin' my driveway!" He waved a hand at the four inches or so of gleaming silver Lexus protruding past the curb. But as she continued to stare down her nose at him, she saw a flicker of uncertainty in his eyes. Apparently he hadn't encountered many blue bloods of the old school, who'd once ruled neighborhoods like this one with a velvet fist. In those days, all it would take was a scornful look, a well-aimed epithet hissed between locked jaws, to level someone of "lesser status." She ought to know. She'd seen her mother do it any number of times. In fact, wasn't it Marjorie she was channeling now, her knee-jerk reaction when backed into a corner? Not because she thought she was better than everyone else, but because it was the only defense at her disposal.

"Is that so?" she replied, eyeing the narrow passage through which he could back out with some maneuvering.

"Don't make me call the cops." A wheedling note crept into his voice, letting her know it was an empty threat.

Marjorie would have made a pointed remark aimed at his impertinence in even owning a house in this former bastion of WASP-dom. What was the world coming to, her tone would imply, when civilized people couldn't walk out their front doors without being accosted by the bourgeoisie? But Emerson was more aghast at her own behavior than his. Why was she acting this way? The man had a perfect right to demand that she move.

The starch went out of her spine and her expression softened into one of appeal. "Listen, you'd be doing me a huge favor if you'd let me park here. If you have a problem getting out, you could always call me on my cell." She handed him her card. "Normally, I wouldn't put you to the trouble, but I'm running late as it is." She cast him a beseeching look.

He hesitated, torn between his manly pride and a desire to play the good guy. Finally, he relented, saying grudgingly, "Awright. But I don't wanna be kept waiting."

"Thanks. I really appreciate it." She flashed him a grateful smile, dashing off before he could change his mind.

The man might have been surprised to learn that there had been a time in Emerson's life when she'd felt like the biggest impostor on the planet. What the rest of the world had seen was a poised young woman with all the advantages—a Park Avenue address, a listing in the *Social Register*, enrollment at one of the city's best private schools—but it was all a sham. Her mother was broke: She owed everyone, from the butcher to the lawyer who'd handled the estate, what little of it there was, after Emerson's father died. If their apartment hadn't been rent-controlled, they'd have been forced to move to one of the outer boroughs—Siberia as far as Marjorie was concerned. The only reason Emerson had gone to Chapin was because Marjorie had pawned jewels, sold paintings, and borrowed from everyone she knew to pay the tuition. Public school, in her view, would've been as unthinkable as living in Queens. The Fitzgibbons would have ceased to exist as far as the old-money crowd was concerned.

It wasn't until Emerson was at Princeton and fell in with Jay, Franny, and Stevie, each of whom had their own hard-luck tale, that she'd been able to let down her guard at last. The night she'd opened up to them, after they'd polished off a fifth of tequila Stevie had smuggled into the dorm, it had been like Noah's floodwaters. Emerson had wept into her pillow while Franny stroked her hair and Jay and Stevie murmured consoling words. Afterward, they'd all told embarrassing stories about their own parents.

Now she hastened her step, eager to join her friends. She hadn't seen Stevie since Jay's wedding. That was what—two years ago? Emerson had still been with Briggs at the time, but now Jay was the only one among them wearing a wedding ring. Her own marriage had crumbled like stale bread, Franny was still looking for love, and Stevie claimed she'd sooner have her eyeteeth pulled than tie the knot.

She was within a stone's throw of the Hartleys' residence when she caught sight of a taxi pulling up to the curb. Out stepped Stevie, in low-rider jeans and a clingy top that showed off her flat, tanned belly and pierced navel. From this distance she looked closer to sixteen than thirty-six, her cropped hair the color of rooster feathers, moussed into spikes, her slender wrists stacked with silver bangles that slid up and down her arms as she heaved her suitcase out of the trunk. She lingered at the curb after the cab had pulled away, her gaze sweeping over the assemblage on the lawn before finally lighting on Emerson.

"Em!" she cried, doing a little jig before racing toward her with a whoop of delight.

On the way to the reunion, Stevie had been in a less than joyful mood. Her flight out of LAX was delayed, and she'd landed at Newark only to find that Avis had no record of her reservation. Apparently there were no cars to be had anywhere, so she'd been forced to take a taxi. Her only bit of luck was the driver's taking pity on her; he informed her as they were pulling away from the curb that he wouldn't charge her the customary return fare for out-of-Manhattan trips.

"You look like nice girl," he said, by way of explanation.

"Actually, I'm not so nice," she replied. *Ask my boyfriend, he'll tell you.* "But thanks anyway."

"You have good trip?" he inquired, as they were easing their way onto the turnpike. She looked up into a pair of faded blue eyes framed in the rearview mirror.

"The plane didn't crash—that's something." She was in no mood for chitchat, but it was already established that she was a nice person. Besides, it was going to be a long trip.

"You live in Jersey?"

"No, just visiting. I'm from L.A."

He wanted to know if she had family in the area, and she told him her only family was her mom, who lived near her. Stevie saw no reason to mention that she had a father, as well. Grant Tobin probably didn't even know of her existence, and judging by the brick wall she'd come up against in trying make contact with him, there was a good chance he never would.

"I have wife in Czechoslovakia." The driver spoke wistfully.

"You must miss her."

He nodded. "A man without wife is no good."

She felt a pang, thinking of Ryan. "I've never been married, so I wouldn't know. But I'll take your word for it."

The faded eyes in the rearview mirror regarded her curiously. "You have boyfriend?"

She stared out the window at the gray industrial landscape oozing past. "I'll have to get back to you on that."

The memory surfaced once more. Thursday she and Ryan had been enjoying a quiet evening out at the Buffalo Club in Santa Monica. When dessert arrived at the table she'd been stunned to see, in place of the crème brûlée that she'd ordered, a lemon tart with the words "Will You Marry Me?" drizzled in chocolate over the top. So stunned that, stupidly, the first thing out of her mouth was, "Wow. How did they squeeze in all those letters?"

Ryan's smile wavered a bit. "It's not brain surgery."

"Still, it must take a steady hand."

"Stevie . . ." His smile gave way to a faintly exasperated look. "Is there something you want to tell me?"

He regarded her with a mixture of hope and wariness. She knew

26

what he wanted to hear—*yes, I'll marry you*—but the words were like a piece of meat stuck in her windpipe, cutting off the flow of air. Was there a Heimlich maneuver for terminal fear of commitment?

She looked down at the table, saying softly, "I love you, Ryan. You know I do. But . . . it's such a huge step."

"We're practically living together as it is," he reminded her.

"Practically" being the operative word here, she thought. "And it's been great!" she said, looking up into the rapidly cooling warmth of Ryan's eyes. "See, that's my point. What we have is so good, why mess it up?"

"I didn't know the M word stood for mess." His voice was cold. His normally expressive face, with its full mouth and wide-set gray eyes as true as the camera lens with which he captured people's lives, set into hard lines.

"I still love you. Nothing's changed," she said.

In the warmth of the restaurant, the chocolate on the tart had begun to weep, tiny tears running down to pool between the letters, causing them to blur. Stevie had wanted to weep herself seeing the crushed look on Ryan's face. How could she not have seen this coming? He'd certainly dropped enough hints.

"So your answer is no." Ryan spoke softly.

"I didn't say that."

"You didn't have to."

"I'm sorry." She reached for his hand, but he moved it out of reach, and she ended up only grazing his knuckles.

He paid the check while Stevie ducked into the ladies' room. They didn't speak again until they were on their way home. When she pointed out that he'd taken the wrong exit off the freeway, he explained curtly that he was dropping her off at her place. She'd planned on staying over with him—most of her clothes were at his apartment, and besides, it was closer to the airport—but from the look on his face, she thought it best not to object.

"Have a good trip," he said woodenly as she was getting out of the car, in front of her condo.

"I'll call you when I get back," she said.

There was a beat before he replied, "You know something? Don't." He sounded more tired than angry. In the glare of the headlights backfiring off her garage door, his face, framed by its tumble of dark hair, was a black-and-white image caught in freeze-frame.

Her breath caught in her throat. "Are you saying . . . ?"

He didn't let her finish. "I think we need some time apart."

Stevie's throat tightened, the crisp, authoritative voice she used to her advantage at press conferences and red-carpet events coming out small, almost childlike. "Ryan, I meant what I said before. I *do* love you. There's no one else I'd rather be with. If you'd just be patient a little longer . . ."

He turned to her. "It's been two years. How much longer do I have to wait?"

"I wish I could tell you. It's just . . . there's a lot going on right now. My father . . ." She let out a breath, spreading her hands in a helpless gesture.

"I know." His tone softened, and he placed a hand over hers.

She felt a flicker of hope. So he *did* understand what she was going through—if only a little. She laced her fingers through his, squeezing tightly. "If it's any comfort, I see us together down the line. It's just that right now I can't handle one more thing."

His fingers disengaged from hers, sliding away like cool water. "That's the difference between us," he said, shaking his head slowly. "You look at it as something to 'handle,' while I see it as something to celebrate. The trouble with us, Stevie, is that we don't see eye to eye."

"That doesn't mean I won't eventually come around to your point of view."

"When will that be?"

"I can't answer that."

"Well, when you have it figured out, you know where to find me. Just don't count on being able to pick up where we left off." He shifted the car into reverse, revving the motor: her exit cue.

Stevie had spent the rest of the night lying in bed, staring up at the ceiling. Until now her condo had been little more than an insurance policy, a place she'd held on to *just in case*. Well, it was no longer an eventuality; the other shoe had dropped with a resounding thud.

Now, in the cab on her way to her college reunion, she ground out the memory like a cigarette, traces of it lingering like smoke before dissolving into the gulf that stretched ahead of her—the gulf that was the Rest of Her Life. She'd deal with it when she got home. For the time being, she planned to enjoy this all too rare visit with her friends. She didn't see as much of them as she'd like, though whenever they talked on the phone, even if it'd been months, there was never any of the awkwardness she'd experienced with other, lesser friends, that little conversational bridge you had to negotiate before you could get back to where you'd left off. With Jay, Franny, and Emerson, it was as if no time at all had elapsed.

It was nearly noon by the time they reached Princeton. After several wrong turns and some backtracking, they pulled up in front of the Hartley's residence. Eyeing the festivities in full swing on the lawn, Stevie was bracing herself for an assault on her jet-lagged senses when Emerson appeared from out of nowhere, a shimmering blond vision in black jeans and a Chanel jacket.

They fell into each other's arms, hugging and laughing with delight, each telling the other how great she looked. Which happened to be true in Emerson's case. After her long trip and the two previous nights in which she'd scarcely slept, Stevie knew she looked like shit.

"Where's Franny? I thought she was with you." Stevie glanced around her.

"She went on ahead. I was feeling a little under the weather," Emerson explained.

"Nothing serious, I hope," Stevie eyed her with concern. She *did* look pale.

"Just hungover."

"You?" Stevie couldn't remember ever seeing Emerson drunk, not even when the rest of them were trashed. Emerson was always the one in control—life's designated driver.

Emerson smiled thinly. "Yes, Virginia, occasionally even Santa ties one on."

They headed up the grassy slope in search of Franny and Jay, Stevie taking two steps for every one of Emerson's long-legged strides. At last, she spotted them over by the gazebo, standing apart from everyone else, deep in conversation as usual—a closed corporation. Stevie wondered, not for the first time, why they'd never become a couple. They were so perfect for each other. Maybe too perfect. Like a coin with two heads or two tails.

With a cry of joy, Franny darted over to throw her arms around Stevie. Jay hugged her hard enough to crack a rib when it was his turn. "We were wondering if you were going to make it," he said.

"Did I miss anything?" Stevie asked.

"Only Stu Felder volunteering to knock me up," Franny reported dryly. She looked, as always, like she'd just climbed out of bed after a night of mind-blowing sex, with her sultry eyes and bee-stung mouth, her corkscrew curls sprouting every which way.

"Uh-oh. Sounds like an offer you can't refuse," Stevie teased.

Franny laughed, and shook her head. "I'd rather die a lonely old maid."

"Where's Viv?" Emerson wanted to know.

"She decided to sit this one out," Jay informed her.

Emerson gave a knowing nod. "Smart lady. There's nothing more boring than being a spouse at a class reunion."

"The fun isn't over yet, kids. There's still tonight's dinner dance at Ivy," Franny reminded them.

"Where's the food? I'm starved," Stevie announced. She hadn't had a thing to eat all day except a packet of pretzels on the plane.

"Follow me, ladies," said Jay, with a courtly little bow.

With that, they all trooped off toward the buffet table, as inseparable now as when they'd been a familiar sight around campus: the tall, clean-cut kid from Wisconsin and his three female sidekicks—a blonde, a brunette, and a redhead.

"To the class of '92," Jay toasted.

They'd all headed back to the city after the weekend's festivities and were now seated upstairs under the domed skylight at Babbo as the glow of sunset faded into dusk. Jay had ordered a magnum of Cristal from the year they'd all graduated, and as they lifted their glasses—all except Vivienne—they reflected on the various roads, both traveled and as yet untaken, that had brought them, over bumpy terrain at times, to this juncture in their lives.

Franny took a careful sip of her champagne. "It was fun while it lasted."

"What, the reunion?" Stevie helped herself to a sourdough roll.

"I was referring to our youth," Franny said.

"We're hardly old!" protested Emerson, looking anything but in a fitted velvet jacket and silk trousers, a pearl choker around her swanlike neck. Everything about her, in fact, was perfection, from her sleek blond hair to her French-polished nails—a *Mayflower* descendant only her best friends knew felt more closely aligned with the *Titanic*.

"I, for one, am celebrating the fact that we're all together," said Stevie. "Who knows when we'll get another chance?"

"You'll all come for the christening, I hope," Vivienne piped.

She glanced around the table wearing a small smile, one hand resting on the barely noticeable swell of her belly. Pregnancy had only added to her luster, making her dark hair and eyes shine and giving her skin, the color of crème caramel, a rosy hue. The little demon inside Franny she did her best to keep at bay delivered a hard, swift jab with its pitchfork. Why Vivienne, and not her? Why was it *always* Vivienne?

It was like when they'd roomed together after college, back when Franny was scraping by as an editorial assistant and Vivienne was making a good living as a model. Franny had been madly in love with the guy she'd been seeing at the time, an up-and-coming writer named Brian Henley whose first novel, a snarky take on the Soho art scene, had just made the *Times* list. She supposed she should have predicted that he'd fall under Vivienne's spell. What red-blooded male wouldn't? Franny couldn't even hold it against Vivienne, who'd done nothing to encourage him, after all. She didn't have to. She was just . . . well, Vivienne. It wasn't long before Brian began dropping by only when he knew Vivienne would be there. After she left for Europe, he'd stopped coming altogether.

Vivienne felt bad about it, she knew. They'd talked about it years later, after Vivienne had become engaged to Jay. She'd confessed that Brian had followed her to Paris, which Franny hadn't known about until then and which, instead of making her see how nobly Vivienne had acted in spurning him, had only brought it all back in a searing rush.

Franny's thoughts were interrupted by their waiter returning to take their orders. After he left, talk turned once more to the reunion.

"It sounds like I didn't miss much," Vivienne said with an amused roll of her eyes after Jay told about getting buttonholed by Winston Hayes III, or Winnie, as he was known in college, who'd spent at least ten minutes regaling Jay with all his accomplishments.

"It was fine, until I ran into this guy I used to date," Franny said.

"Who offered to put a bun in her oven," giggled Stevie, already working on her second glass of champagne. She wore jeans and a hot pink chiffon handkerchief top with a plunging neckline, chandelier earrings swinging from her ears. Franny didn't have to look under the table to know she was barefoot. Stevie, a California girl through and through, was in the habit of slipping out of her shoes every chance she got.

Franny stared pensively into her glass at the bubbles rising in little columns. It was a year ago this month that she'd buried her brother, and all this talk was reminding her of her loss. With both her parents and Bobby gone, there wouldn't be a single family member other than distant cousins to mark her grave with a stone when her time came. "Maybe I should've taken him up on it," she said glumly. "Who knows when I'll get another offer."

"There's always Jay," teased Emerson. She filled Vivienne in on the incident with Stu, which Franny had recounted at last night's dinner-dance at Ivy to a round of groans and laughter.

But Franny wasn't laughing now. Seeing her expression, Jay reached over to squeeze her hand. "I'm sorry. It was stupid of me," he said. "I should've kept my mouth shut."

"It's not *you*." Franny mustered a smile. "I was thinking of my brother."

The table fell silent, Franny's friends eyeing her in sympathy.

"You think someone will be around forever, then one day they're gone. Just like that," she went on. Not wanting to spoil the mood, she was quick to add, "I'm sorry, I don't mean to be a downer."

"You still have us," Emerson said gently.

Vivienne offered her an encouraging smile. "You'll find someone. Look at me. I didn't think I'd ever get married."

Franny refrained from reminding her that it wasn't for lack of opportunity. Vivienne had had suitors on two continents—a prince, a Greek shipping heir, and the head of a vast conglomerate, to name a few. During the years she'd flitted in and out of Jay's life, living mostly in Paris, where she'd been brought up, the product of a French father and a Lebanese mother, he'd have married her a dozen times over if she'd ever settled down long enough for him to ask. It wasn't until he'd started getting serious about someone else that Vivienne reappeared on the scene, this time for good.

"As I recall, it took some convincing," Jay said.

"You didn't have to twist my arm very hard." Vivienne gave a light laugh, bringing a hand to rest on his forearm. She turned back to Franny, her smile falling away. "*Chérie*, what is it? Did we say something to upset you?"

Franny shook her head, embarrassed as she dabbed at her eyes with her napkin. "No, of course not. It must have been the reunion. All that talk of kids and families."

"You know," Vivienne said, as if mulling it over as she spoke. "Maybe there's a simple solution to all this."

"Like what?" Franny smoothed the napkin back over her lap.

"Jay could father your child."

Franny felt the breath go out of her. "You can't be serious," she gasped.

"It makes perfect sense when you think about it," Vivienne went on. "You've known each other forever. You wouldn't have to wonder where your baby got his nose or his chin. Or his medical history." She turned to Jay, who looked as stunned as Franny. "And if Franny gets pregnant right away, our child would have a baby brother or sister."

"Great. And just how would we explain it to our kid?" Jay wanted to know.

"Kids," Emerson corrected.

"My point exactly. It'd be weird and complicated." Jay threw up his hands. "Why are we even discussing it? It's not as if it's going to happen." He cast a frantic look around the table, as if beseeching his friends to toss the cold water of reason on this crazy idea.

"Don't look at me," Stevie said. "This is one subject I'm not remotely qualified to give advice on."

"I *am*. And, trust me, it's not easy being a single mom," Emerson put in.

Franny said nothing. She was lost in thought, hardly daring to believe what she was hearing. Was Vivienne really as serious as she seemed? The French were more open-minded about such matters, she knew, but still it was a stretch. Whatever the circumstances, most wives wouldn't be in favor of their husband's fathering another woman's baby. Nonetheless, the idea had taken root. A picture formed in her mind: all of them gathered around the table at Thanksgiving, she and Jay and Vivienne and their children. One big happy family. She thought of all the holidays and birthdays they'd celebrate together. The baseball games and soccer matches with someone aside from her rooting from the sidelines. The hard times, too, when she'd need all the support she could get.

Who better to father her child than her dearest friend in the world?

Chapter Two

Do I have to kiss Grandma?"

Ainsley peered up anxiously at Emerson as they sat nestled together in the backseat of the cab taking them to Marjorie's. In the late afternoon sun playing hide-and-seek with the tall buildings along Park Avenue, her strawberry blond hair shone like pink gold.

From the mouths of babes, Emerson thought. Ainsley wasn't being rude, just honest.

"Not if you don't want to." Emerson gave her daughter's shoulder a little squeeze. How had she and Briggs managed to produce such a wisp of a thing? The first time Emerson had held her, just after she was born, it was like cupping a butterfly in her hands.

"Grandma's nice, but she smells funny."

"I know, sweetie. She can't help it." Emerson felt sorry for her mother, despite how difficult she could be at times. Before she became ill, Marjorie had always been perfectly turned out, from head to toe, every hair in place. Emerson remembered how, at Ainsley's age, she'd been so proud whenever Marjorie showed up at school; even in a sea of Chanel and Yves St. Laurent, she was easily the most glamorous mom. But these days no amount of perfume could mask the medicinal smell that clung to her. "But you know what? I know she'll love the picture you drew her." Rolled up on Ainsley's lap was a crayon drawing she'd done of Gus, the polar bear at the Central Park Zoo, where her first-grade class had gone on a field trip earlier in the week.

Ainsley's shoulders drooped. "No, she won't."

"Why do you say that?"

"She threw away my duck picture."

"Maybe Natalia did by mistake." Natalia was their housekeeper, whom she paid to clean her mother's apartment as well.

Ainsley shook her head, giving Emerson a look that said she understood more than her mother gave her credit for, insisting, "I found it crumpled up under Grandma's bed."

Emerson didn't see the point in arguing—how did she know it wasn't true? As they made their way past St. Barthomew's, with its courtyard café facing out on Park Avenue, she was recalling her own childhood, how Marjorie would ignore her for long stretches then snatch her up like a doll to be played with and dressed in cute little outfits. But if history was repeating itself, it wasn't all Marjorie's fault. Her illness had taken so much out of her. She doted on Ainsley but just didn't have the strength most of the time to rise to the occasion.

"Hey, I know. How about a frozen hot chocolate at Serendipity?" she suggested, in an effort to brighten the mood. "We could stop there on our way home from Grandma's."

Ainsley perked up. "With everything on top?"

"The works." Serendipity's sundaes could easily feed four people, and despite her best efforts Ainsley never managed to make more than a dent, but that didn't keep her from trying.

"I *guess* that would be okay," Ainsley said, her pixie eyes dancing.

Minutes later the taxi was pulling up in front of her mother's building at Seventy-second and Park. "You know who else will be happy to see you?" Emerson said as they were climbing out.

"Uncle Nacario?" Ainsley asked hopefully.

Emerson nodded, and Ainsley gave a cry of delight, darting ahead of her. Before Emerson had stepped under the scalloped burgundy awning, her daughter was halfway up the carpet that stretched from the curb to the plate-glass door, which a white-gloved doorman was holding open for them. Emerson stepped into the gleaming marble-tiled lobby to find forty-two pounds of wriggling little girl in the arms of the elderly Puerto Rican concierge.

"Ainsley!" she chided, hurrying over to them. "You'll give Uncle Nacario a hernia." To Nacario, she said, with a laugh, "She sometimes forgets she's not a baby anymore."

"And *I* forget I'm an old man." He deposited Ainsley on the front desk with a *whuff* of expelled breath. "Ay, *chiquita,*" he sighed in mock despair, "what your mama been feeding you? I'm away only two weeks, and I come back to find you twice as big." He tipped her a wink, turning back to Emerson. "You were the same at her age. Always wanting me to pick you up or to ride on my shoulders. Carlos"—the doorman when she was growing up, long since retired—"he used to call you my little *sombra,*" he reminded her, the Spanish word for shadow.

Emerson smiled at the memory. Nacario had been more than a kindly concierge; during those difficult years he'd been a surrogate father. She used to fantasize about going to live with him and his big, noisy brood in the Bronx—a home that to this day she'd never set foot in. Not that she wouldn't be welcomed, but the risk was too great. If Marjorie were to find out, it would place him in an tenuous position and maybe even cost him his job.

Now she noted the roundness of the broad shoulders on which she'd once ridden, and the gray that ran like tread marks through his thick black hair. Creases curved from the corners of his eyes to his temples and the flesh around his jaw had begun to sag. The thought of one day walking in and not seeing him at the desk brought a pulse of dread.

"Did you have a nice vacation?" she inquired.

"If you can call putting a new roof on my sister's house a vacation," he said.

"Don't you ever put your feet up?" Emerson said, with fond exasperation.

He gave a good-natured shrug. "With a big family there is no such thing as rest."

"They're lucky to have you."

A chunk of his paycheck every month, she knew, went to his relatives in Puerto Rico—*What is money for, if not to help those less fortunate?* he'd always say. And if riches were measured in loved ones, he was wealthy beyond all measure, with his wife of forty years, three grown children, and twelve grandchildren.

"Now." He bent so he was eye level with Ainsley. "Do you want to know what I brought you all the way from Mayagüez?" Emerson had phoned ahead to let him know they were coming and now he drew something from the pocket of his trousers, which had once produced a seemingly endless supply of riches for Emerson, and pressed it into Ainsley's hand: a carved wooden statuette. "It's the Virgin Mary. If you're ever in trouble, she will help you."

"How would she know?" Ainsley eyed it in fascination, turning it over in the palm of her hand.

"Ah, *chiquita*. The Lady, she always knows." He tapped his chest.

"So what do you make of the new guy?" Emerson asked when she had his attention, giving an upward jerk of her head to indicate the tenth floor, where the recently hired night-duty nurse, whom she had yet to meet, was no doubt being put to the test by her mother. The only information the agency had given her was that he was Nigerian and a licensed LPN. "Should we place bets on how long he'll last?"

Nacario cast her a faintly reproving glance. Whatever his private opinion of Marjorie, he'd always treated her with the utmost respect and insisted that Emerson do the same. His only comment was "Your mother is in good hands, from what I can see."

Moments later Emerson and Ainsley were riding the elevator up to her mother's floor. As they stepped out into the foyer, she took note of the vase of fresh flowers on the reproduction Louis Quinze table against the wall—she would have to remember to once again thank the Townsends, in 10B, who had an arrangement delivered each week and refused to let her share the cost. Letting herself into her mother's apartment, Emerson drew in a breath against the little stitch in her stomach she got each time—however often she visited, it never seemed to get any easier—and, holding tightly to Ainsley's hand, made her way inside.

It was like stepping into a sauna, it was so hot—Marjorie was always cold these days and insisted on keeping every window shut. In the late afternoon sunlight, slanting in through the bank of tall casement windows overlooking Park Avenue, the gracious living room where Emerson had once tiptoed as a child, fearful of toppling some priceless artifact, looked strangely barren. The antiques and fine art had all been sold off, one by one, replaced by factory-made furnishings and castoffs. All that was left from Emerson's childhood was the rather severe-looking portrait of her father that hung over the marble fireplace, and which looked nothing like him. Her memory was of a gentle, soft-spoken man, with white hair like snow melting from the pink dome of his balding crown, who'd taken frequent naps and was always going to the doctor—he'd been quite a bit older than Marjorie, old enough to be Emerson's grand-father, and suffered from a bad heart.

"Hello." A low, musical voice caused her to spin around. A man stepped from the darkened hallway into the light. Tall, around her age, with skin the color of the walnut wainscoting against which he stood. He wore pressed khakis and a short-sleeved shirt that showed off the well-defined muscles in his arms. He smiled, his teeth very white against his dark skin. "I'm sorry. I didn't mean to startle you." He held out his hand. "Reggie Okanta. We spoke on the phone?"

"Yes, of course. Emerson," she said, introducing herself. His handshake was firm but not too firm, his large hand seeming to engulf her none too delicate one. She took in his high, slanting cheekbones and full lips, his eyes the green-gold of stones glinting at the bottom of a creek bed. She felt vaguely flustered for some reason, and it was a moment before she recovered her manners, gesturing toward Ainsley. "And this is my daughter, Ainsley."

"Very pleased to meet you." Reggie bent down to shake Ainsley's hand with the same formality he had Emerson's. "What's that you have there?" He eyed the drawing she clutched in one hand.

Ainsley held it out for him to see. "I made it for Grandma."

Reggie unrolled it carefully and took his time examining it, as if he were a museum curator pondering the work of an emerging artist. "Hmmm . . . yes. I like your bold use of color. Very original. I think this bear would be pleased with how you've drawn him." He spoke with a British-inflected accent that carried lilting overtones of his native land.

"I could make you one, too." Ainsley was staring up at him, enraptured.

"I'd like that very much." Reggie spoke gravely, as if it were a great honor she was bestowing on him.

Ainsley darted over to the cabinet Emerson kept stocked with art supplies for when they visited. "You're good with children," observed Emerson, smiling as she watched her daughter dig out a drawing pad and colored markers. She turned to him. "Do you have any of your own?"

"Just nieces and nephews. They keep me from sleeping as much as I'd like," he added with a laugh, explaining that he was living with his aunt and uncle for the time being, until he finished college. He had another year to go before he could apply to medical school. In the meantime, he was making ends meet working nights.

"That doesn't leave you much free time." Emerson recalled her brutal schedule at Princeton, how she'd had to knock herself out just to pull Bs.

He treated her to another of his dazzling smiles. "Free time is a Western ideal." He'd been brought up to believe that any time spent on furthering oneself was well spent he said.

"I suppose that's one way of looking at it. Still, it can't be easy."

"Your mother's been most helpful. Every night she quizzes me on what I've learned that day."

Emerson could hardly contain her astonishment. "Helpful" wasn't a word she normally associated with Marjorie. "You must be having a good effect on her then. She's usually not feeling up to much these days." She'd have liked nothing more than to continue the conversation, learn more about Reggie, but filial duty tugged at her like an insistent child at her hem. "Speaking of our patient, I should look in on her. Is she awake?" she inquired, half hoping it wasn't the case, which would buy her a few more minutes.

"Yes. In fact, she has a visitor." Reggie gestured down the hallway toward Marjorie's bedroom. "I was just making tea. Would you like some?"

"What? Oh, no thanks." Emerson was momentarily distracted,

contemplating the surprising fact that Marjorie had company. She didn't get many visitors these days.

Leaving Ainsley to her scribbling, Emerson headed down the hall. Marjorie was sitting up in bed when she walked in, propped against a bank of pillows, the room to which she was mostly confined these days spread out around her like a tattered gown from a ball long over, its tufted velvet headboard showing signs of wear, its mirrored vanity cluttered with ancient perfume vials. She'd freshened her face, her wig—stiff blond wings sprouting from either side of her head—framing it like some improbable costume piece. You could see only a glimmer of the beauty she'd once been.

"Darling!" her mother trilled, as if she hadn't seen her in ages. "You remember Mr. Stancliffe?" She indicated her male visitor, seated in the worn plush chair by the bed.

Recognizing him, Emerson felt the stitch in her stomach tighten. How could she not? Her mother had been pushing him on her ever since he moved in upstairs, insisting he'd be perfect for her. How often did a suitable man come along? she'd reasoned. Would it kill Emerson to have a drink with him? She wasn't getting any younger, after all. And she had Ainsley to think of. Emerson had demurred, claiming she was much too busy. Besides, Briggs had been "perfect" for her, too, and look how that had turned out. But her mother had persisted, and finally Emerson had caved in and agreed to meet him for coffee. A perfectly dull date with a perfectly dull man who'd been pestering her ever since with repeated invitations to dinner, a concert, a show.

"Ed." She forced a smile as he rose to greet her. "How nice of you to drop by," she said, with the practiced ease of a seasoned pro.

"I was in the neighborhood." He grinned at his own joke, looking not the least bit surprised to see her. Was he in on the setup? Knowing her mother, it wouldn't surprise her.

Marjorie cocked her head, eyeing Emerson with such fervent brightness there could be no mistaking her intent. "Mr. Stancliffe was just telling me he lived next door to the Lyttons on Martha's Vineyard. Isn't that the most amazing coincidence?"

That would be the Lyttons who were second cousins on Emerson's father's side. "I only met them once. To be honest, I thought they were kind of stuck-up," she commented with a shrug.

Marjorie darted her a black look before bringing her bright, fixed gaze back to Mr. Stancliffe. "Nonsense. They're perfectly lovely people. Isn't that what you were just telling me, Mr. Stancliffe."

"Actually, I didn't know them all that well," he confessed, darting Emerson an uncomfortably chummy look, as if they were in solidarity somehow. "Old Mr. Lytton invited me sailing once, but the wind kicked up and we had to call it off. I haven't seen them since then." He'd sold the house when he and his wife divorced, he explained.

They chatted briefly about other things, familiar haunts and acquaintances they had in common. The white-shoe world was like a small town in that way: Everybody knew everybody, and if you went back far enough, chances were they were related to you. Emerson would have been bored silly if she hadn't been seething inside. Just when she'd begun to think that all her efforts with her mother, not to mention the bills she paid, had accrued some sort of interest, she was reminded of what little value her mother placed on *her* wants and needs. It was Marjorie, after all, who'd pushed her to marry Briggs, then insisted she'd be a fool to divorce him when it was clear the marriage wasn't working. And now, not content with ruining Emerson's life once, she was aiming for a second time.

Her thoughts were interrupted by Reggie appearing with the tea tray. She found her gaze straying toward him as he poured the tea, touched that he'd brought an extra cup in case she'd changed her mind. He moved with an almost balletic grace that was soothing to watch. Courteous without seeming subservient, he attended to her mother, making sure she had enough pillows to support her back and that she'd taken her medication.

"You'll see Mr. Stancliffe out, won't you, darling?" Marjorie said when it was time for him to go, giving Emerson a pointed look as she rose to comply.

At the door, when he once more pressed her to have dinner with him, Emerson told him she was sorry but she was devoting all her spare time to Marjorie these days. A devoted daughter who wanted nothing more than to throttle her mother right then.

"How could you do that to me?" she berated Marjorie afterward. "You purposely set me up!"

Her mother, sitting up in bed sipping her tea, appeared unruffled. "Honestly, darling, you're making much too much of it. The man was just being neighborly."

"Then why did I feel like a sitting duck?"

"Don't be so dramatic." Marjorie set her cup down on the night table, wincing at the effort. She was so frail, the tiniest movement was a strain. "Even if I did have an ulterior motive, is it a crime to look out for your only child?"

"You could have at least warned me," Emerson said.

"If I had, you'd have invented some excuse not to come."

"You're damn right!"

"Darling, please." Marjorie squeezed her eyes shut, as if in pain.

Emerson felt her anger deflate, giving way to sadness. All her life, she'd wanted only to be loved for herself, not the ideal daughter she tried to be. Was that too much to ask?

Abruptly, Marjorie changed the subject. "So what do you make of Reggie?"

"He seems nice." Emerson knew better than to reveal more

than that. Marjorie had drummed into her since childhood the pitfalls of becoming too familiar with the hired help.

"He's a hard worker, I'll say that for him. Not like some."

"I'm glad he meets with your approval," Emerson said, with a trace of sarcasm. Her tone softening, she added, "He tells me you've been helping him with his studies."

"You know me, I like to encourage the bright ones." A real lady, Marjorie was fond of saying, knew how to treat the help. "Did he tell you he's studying to become a doctor?"

"He mentioned it, yes."

"Very noble of him, don't you think? All those poor people in Africa dying of AIDS."

"Is that what he told you? That he's going to treat people with AIDS?"

"Not in so many words. I just assumed . . ." Marjorie had the decency to blush.

Emerson suppressed a sigh. "Well, I just hope he sticks around longer than the last one," she said pointedly.

"I wouldn't need anyone to look after me at night if you'd stop being so stubborn and move back in," her mother reminded her for the umpteenth time. "This apartment is more than big enough for the three of us, and it's ridiculous for you to pay rent on two places."

"I can afford it." Emerson's divorce settlement had left her fairly well off even without the money she earned. But that wasn't the point. "Besides, you know perfectly well we'd be at each other's throats."

"I didn't know I was such a chore." Marjorie, wearing an injured look, drew her shawl around her as if she'd been exposed to a sudden chill. "God knows what you talk about with your therapist. All the ways I ruined your life, I suppose."

Emerson sank down on the bed, taking her mother's hand in

hers—it was so light, it might have been made of parchment. "I haven't seen Dr. Shapiro in months." She'd stopped going soon after she'd filed for divorce. "Besides, I have no desire to rake up the past."

"I'm sorry, darling. I don't mean to be so cranky. It's just . . ." In that instant, Marjorie's mask fell away, revealing the frightened woman underneath, a woman terrified of dying and even more terrified of living.

Emerson's heart went out to her. Whatever her mother had done . . . or not done . . . no one deserved this. "Dr. Vanacore says you're responding well to the chemo," she said, with feigned enthusiasm. His exact words had been that the cancer's spread had slowed. Not exactly the news they'd hoped for, but it would buy her mother another six months, a year at best.

Marjorie gave a small, choked laugh. "I'm not sure which is worse, the disease or the cure."

"You're tougher than you think." Whatever her faults, Marjorie had faced her illness, as she had widowhood, with grit and style. If she was bedridden, it was just as well, she'd say. Who wanted to be seen in public wearing last season's styles?

"Let's face it, the sooner I go, the sooner we'll all be put out of our misery."

Emerson winced. "I wish you wouldn't talk that way."

"It'll be a blessing in some ways. These days I can't help wondering what there is left to live for." Marjorie's face crumpled, and all of a sudden she looked a hundred years old.

"You still have me. And Ainsley," Emerson said, wishing her mother didn't have to be reminded of the fact.

Marjorie perked up. "Where is my little cupcake?"

"Drawing a picture for Reggie. I'll tell her you want to see her." Emerson rose from the bed.

"I see he's worked his charms on her, too."

It was Marjorie's way of saying that he'd passed the test, Emerson knew, and she smiled to herself, her step lighter as she set off down the hall, drawn by the low, melodic rumble of Reggie's voice mingling with the high, sweet one of her daughter.

An hour and a half later, having left Ainsley at home with the nanny, Emerson was back on the job, pacing the lobby of the Ziegfeld Theatre with her cell phone glued to her ear. Outside, ticket holders were lined up and limos were pulling up to the curb, while inside a small group of reporters had gathered beyond the velvet ropes. But still no sign of Sally Boyle from ABC or Eric Jameson from Fox News. Where the hell were they? They *owed* her, dammit. She'd delivered her end of the bargain—one-on-one interviews with her star client, Jeffery Kingston. If they stiffed her on this, she'd look like an idiot. New Line Cinema wasn't paying her big bucks for a one-line mention in the *Post*.

Normally at premieres her job was merely to field the press. When it was a picture starring Russell Crowe or Will Smith, they turned out in droves. But who wanted to shoot a cast of little-known actors making their way down the red carpet? She'd spent the better part of the week making calls, using every trick in her arsenal to generate some buzz.

Just then she spotted Franny pushing her way through the crowd. Watching her bypass the ticket-holder line to sail down the red carpet as if she owned it, her bouncing hair and red dress that showed every curve causing more than one photographer's flashbulb to go off, Emerson felt herself relax. *It's going to be okay*, she thought. Franny always had that effect on her. She was the earth mother to Emerson's poor little rich girl.

"Looks like a good turnout," Franny said, when she'd caught up to her.

"I'm still waiting for a few people." Emerson glanced about anxiously. The director and stars had yet to make their entrance, so there was still time. She brought her gaze back to Franny. "You look different. Did you change your hair?" No, that wasn't it. Suddenly it hit her, and she let out a gasp. "Omigod. Are you . . . ?"

"Afraid not." Franny shook her head. "I just got my period." She was trying her best to appear sanguine, but Emerson could see the disappointment on her face. She'd been so sure . . .

"There's always next time," Emerson reminded her.

"If Jay doesn't decide to back out."

"He wouldn't do that." Not to Franny.

"Helping out a friend is one thing, knocking her up is another."

"He knows how much you want this."

"Not enough to let it screw up our friendship."

"As if that could ever happen." Those two were like as peanut butter and jelly.

Franny mustered a smile. "Yeah, you're right. It's just my hormones talking."

"I saw my mother today," Emerson informed her as she was ushering Franny to the taped-off section of seats set aside for reviewers and VIPs.

"How's she doing?" Franny asked.

"Not so good." Emerson didn't want to put a damper on the occasion, so she added with more enthusiasm, "The new nurse, on the other hand, is just what the doctor ordered."

Franny, who could read her like a book, arched an eyebrow. "For you or your mom?"

Emerson felt herself blushing. "He *is* good-looking," she admitted.

"Come on, you gotta give me more than that."

"Think Sidney Poitier in *Guess Who's Coming to Dinner?*"

"Uh-oh. Better watch out, girl, or Momma's gonna *un*invite him."

"The thought had occurred to me," Emerson was quick to add, "But not to worry, I'm keeping it strictly employer-employee."

"Famous last words." Franny flashed her a grin.

Emerson wondered, with a delicious little thrill, if she was indeed in danger of starting something with Reggie Okanta, LPN.

Franny took her seat next to Lois Campanela from the *Daily News*, who was busy chatting up Ben Sokolin from *Variety*. She was careful to lower her voice as she told Emerson about the book deal she was on the verge of closing. "Get this. An unauthorized bio of Grant Tobin." She didn't have to add that, with the resurgence of public interest in the former rocker, it could be a very lucrative one.

Emerson gave a little start. "Does Stevie know?"

"She's the one who hooked me up with him. Apparently she's known him for years."

"So she knew he was writing this book?"

"Before she found out Grant was her dad. Now she has a vested interest in making sure it gets into the right hands."

"Just how much has she told him?" Emerson asked, wondering how well Stevie knew this guy.

Franny shook her head. "She's keeping it under her hat for now, at least until she's met Grant."

"*If* she meets him." So far even Stevie's wiles hadn't been enough to penetrate his fortress.

"She's planning to. Soon."

"What's that supposed to mean?"

Franny shrugged. "She says the less we know, the better."

"Oh, God," Emerson said, groaning.

The two friends exchanged a look. Knowing Stevie as well as they did, they didn't doubt she'd resort to any means necessary. And whatever she had up her sleeve, it was likely to spell trouble.

Chapter Three

Stevie wondered if this was such a good idea. Trying to hold her balance as she sat perched on top of a fifty-pound sack of fertilizer, in the back of a panel truck winding its way up the hill to Grant Tobin's Holmby Hills estate, she was pretty certain it wasn't. But she'd run out of other options, so what choice did she have? Gaining access to the Pentagon would be easier than getting in to see Grant Tobin. After butting her head against the collective brick wall of his lawyer, publicist (a misnomer, since his only job, it seemed, was to keep people away), and bodyguard-slash-houseman, a scary-looking dude covered in tattoos who looked like a former gang member, one of her contacts, a nerdy guy named Sammy Garber who collected celebrity trivia the way other people collected stamps—stuff like where they got their clothes dry-cleaned and where they ordered their pizzas from—had turned her on to the gardener who maintained the estate's grounds. Luckily, Mr. Mori had a soft spot for damsels in distress. Or maybe it was because he was retiring soon. Either way, he'd agreed to smuggle her in past the gates.

Which was how, on this early May morning, while her colleagues at KNLA were at their desks or heading out into the field to cover assignments, she came to be riding in the Trojan horse of Mori and Sons Landscaping, on her way to meet her father for the first time.

The van braked suddenly, sending her sprawling onto its floor. Cursing under her breath, she pulled herself upright, wrinkling her nose at the smelly brown stuff spilling from a tear in the sack. The van picked up speed again, twisting its way up the steep grade, which sent her lurching from side to side with each turn. At last, it slowed to a stop, and she heard Mr. Mori call out a greeting to the security guard at the gate.

Holmby Hills, even more exclusive than Beverly Hills or Bel Air, was nosebleed country, where the megawealthy occupied sprawling mansions set amid acres of well-tended grounds. The reason Grant could afford to live there, she knew, was because, unlike his former bandmates, who'd gone on to inglorious solo careers or playing backup, he'd written most of Astral Plane's hit songs. Songs that provided him with a steady flow of royalties, enabling him to live like a king without his ever again having to pick up his guitar.

The van started moving again, rattling over a pebbled drive. From her narrow vantage point in back, she caught glimpses of well-tended grass and trees flashing by. When the van finally ground to a halt and she lurched out into the cool air, she saw that they were in front of a greenhouse situated some distance from the house. A house that loomed like a fortress, high stucco walls festooned in bougainvillea and banked with windows covered in decorative wrought-iron bars, with a terra-cotta-tiled roof that gleamed like dying embers in the rosy dawn light. She stood gazing at it, her pulse quickening as the full realization hit her that she was at last going to be face-to-face with the man she'd seen only in old concert footage. Then Mr. Mori shooed her away, hissing, "You go now!"

Stevie thanked the old man once more and set off toward the house, dressed in a navy tracksuit, Nike running shoes, and a black baseball cap embroidered with a gold gramophone, a souvenir from last year's Grammy Awards. She crouched low, using the dense shrubbery as cover. The sun was coming up over the distant hills, its pale light glistening on the still damp grass, where shadows stretched like mile markers pointing the way. The only sound was the chittering of birds in the branches overhead.

As she wriggled through hedges and around rosebushes that snagged her clothing, Stevie found herself wondering again what had driven Grant Tobin into seclusion. Was it guilt over the Lauren Rose affair, or being hounded by the press, or both? Whatever the reason, she was determined to find out. It was either that or spend the rest of her life wondering if the man who'd given her life was a would-be killer.

The thought sent a cool trickle down her spine. For all she knew, Grant could be holed up in there with an arsenal of weapons, like those crazy fanatics on Ruby Ridge. What was to stop him from taking a shot at *her*?

She spun it out a little further, picturing herself laid out in her coffin. Would Ryan cry at her funeral? Would he be sorry for ignoring her attempts to get in touch with him? Her throat tightened, and she squinted against the light that had become suddenly too bright.

When she was close enough to the house, she circled it once to get the general layout before stepping onto the shaded walkway that led around in back. The air was still cool, but she was sweating as if it were high noon. Stevie Light, known for having nerves of steel, felt more like a scared kid right now than an ace reporter. As a child she'd dreamed of this reunion and had imagined her father clasping her in his arms, weeping with joy. But what if he turned out to be an uncaring prick? Or worse, a monster.

She stepped through a stone archway draped in honeysuckle and onto a patio sheltered by walls on all four sides, in the center of which glimmered a pool undisturbed by so much as a ripple. It was so perfect, she thought, it might have been a back-lot set for one of those suspense thrillers that lull you down the garden path before scaring the bejesus out of you.

A pair of French doors led into the house, and she noticed that one of them stood open a crack. Glancing around first to make sure she wasn't being observed, she stepped through it into a cool, darkened room. At one end stood a grand piano, gleaming dully in the bands of light that filtered in through the closed shutters. On the wall between sets of bookshelves hung a collection of framed gold and platinum records from the days when Astral Plane had ruled supreme along with Joplin and Hendrix, the Stones and the Grateful Dead.

From down the hall drifted the faint sound of voices—a man and a woman conversing in Spanish. Stevie's heart began to hammer in earnest. But she didn't dare turn back. Who knew when she'd get another opportunity to meet her dad? Cautiously, she crept out into the dimly lit hallway, the soles of her Nikes squeaking faintly against the polished hardwood floor as she made her way toward the circular staircase that led to the floors above. Grant would most likely still be in bed at this hour. That is, unless she'd miscalculated and, contrary to the rumor that he never set foot off this estate, he wasn't home.

After poking her head into several rooms that were unoccupied any time in her recent memory, she found herself peering into a darkened bedroom in which she could make out an unmade bed and clothes strewn about. She was venturing inside to explore it further when a soft moaning sound caused her to freeze in her tracks. That was when she noticed the figure seated crosslegged on the carpet at the foot of the bed: a bony castaway of a man with scraggly gray hair to his shoulders, dressed only in a pair of boxer shorts. His face was in repose, eyes shut, his hands resting lightly on the bony knobs of his knees.

Stevie's heart lurched. She'd read the accounts of Howard Hughes's bizarre behavior toward the end, and that's what flashed through her mind now. She could hardly believe the lithe, dark-eyed young man in the grainy concert footage she'd seen, with his angel's voice and devil's licks, all tossing black hair and twitching limbs, had become this wasted old wreck.

But he looked harmless enough. Not the drug-crazed psycho painted by the press. If he was crazy it didn't appear she was in any immediate danger. Her heart was pounding nonetheless as she sank onto the bed, waiting what seemed an eternity until his eyes opened and his gaze settled on her. She braced herself against the cry of alarm she was sure would bring the bodyguard running, but Grant—if it was indeed him—remained perfectly still. Except for the flicker of surprise that crossed his face, the sight of a complete stranger sitting on his bed didn't seem to faze him.

He broke into a slow, dreamy smile. "Hey there."

"I'm sorry if I disturbed you," she said.

"It's cool. I didn't even hear you come in." His voice made her think of a rake being dragged over a bed of gravel.

"I tried meditating once, but I couldn't sit still that long," she told him.

He shrugged. "You get the hang of it after a while."

An awkward silence fell.

Stevie cleared her throat, and said, "You're probably wondering who I am."

"Oh, I know who you are." He spoke calmly, but his words sent a bolt shooting down through the pit of Stevie's stomach. Had he known all this time? All the years she'd believed her father was ignorant of her existence? Then, in a voice heavily laced with irony, he went on, "You came to see the great Grant Tobin. Well, I hate to disappoint you, but the dude checked out a long time ago."

She eyed him in confusion. "You're not Grant?"

"I used to be. Not anymore."

She understood now. "I'm not who you think I am, either," she informed him.

He cocked his head, eyeing her with new interest. "Okay, then, why don't you tell me why you're here."

She drew in a breath. "I'm your daughter."

Grant stared at her in disbelief. He was clearly a man for whom life bore few surprises—he'd done and seen it all—but this was obviously the last thing he'd expected to hear. After a bit, he let out a raspy chuckle. "Well, ain't that something. Me, a dad." He shook his head from side to side, marveling at the concept. "You sure about that?"

"I'm sure." Now that her eyes had adjusted to the gloom, she could see the resemblance. She had his mouth. His square jaw with its slight underbite—that was hers, too.

"Well, shit." He went on shaking his head, chuckling to himself.

"You never got the letter?"

"What letter?"

"The one my mother sent telling you she was pregnant."

"I get a lot of mail. Most of it I never see." His minions would take care of all that, which explained why he hadn't gotten the letters Stevie had sent, either. "You see, the thing is—What did you say your name was?"

"Stevie." She blushed a little. "I was named after Stevie Nicks."

After a moment she added hesitantly, "You believe me, don't you?"

"Well, Stevie, I can't say that I do, and I can't say that I don't. There was a lot that went down in those days that I don't rightly recall. That's just how it was." His gaze turned inward, his expression briefly clouding over. Then, he stirred and brought his gaze back to her, his lips curled in a small, ironic smile. "So I guess I'll just have to take your word for it."

"How do you know I'm not making it up?"

He eyed her with amusement. "Are you?"

"No, but you must get a lot of crazies."

He regarded her for a moment. "You don't look crazy to me."

"Even though I broke into your house? Well, I didn't actually *break* in. The door was open." She hastened to add, "I tried getting in touch with you, but you have more people than a moat has alligators."

He broke into a grin that showed the trademark gap between his front teeth. "It keeps the press away."

Stevie felt herself grow uncomfortably warm, reminded that in his eyes she would be the enemy. But he didn't have to know what she did for a living, at least not until after they'd become better acquainted. Even so, she felt compelled to say, "It hasn't stopped them." The press was having a field day with this latest, bizarre turn of events in the Lauren Rose affair. Each step in the woman's painstaking recovery seized upon, complete with quotes from unnamed, and often fictitious, sources. Yesterday's tabloid headlines had Lauren providing the district attorney with an account of what had happened the night she was shot that was very different from Grant's. Grant Tobin, meanwhile, was back in the spotlight, too . . . and his head on the chopping block.

He shrugged, wearing an impassive look. "I'm used to it."

Abruptly he unfolded from his seated position on the floor, a bundle of sticks magically assembling themselves into a man standing upright. He yanked open the drapes before crossing the room to where she sat. In the harsh light of day, he looked even older, his face a rutted road in which the ghost of the young Grant Tobin, his flashing dark eyes and the loose-limbed suppleness with which he'd once walked, glinted like shards of broken glass.

"Yeah, I see it now." He put a hand under her chin, turning her head this way and that. "You look a little like my mom."

"Everyone says I look like mine." From her pocket, Stevie produced a faded snapshot of her mother, circa 1970, in a peasant dress and Birkenstocks holding the infant Stevie in her arms.

He peered at it, frowning, then shook his head. "Sorry. Don't take this the wrong way or anything—I'm sure she's a great person—but back then . . ." He spread his hands in a helpless gesture, wearing a vaguely troubled look. "Like I said, I don't remember much."

Stevie smiled to let him know it was okay. Nancy had warned her not to expect too much. She'd been just another groupie, one of hundreds he'd slept with no doubt. The only difference was that she'd come away with something more than bragging rights and an autographed keepsake. Her souvenir had been the six-pound baby girl she'd given birth to nine months later.

Another silence fell, broken when Grant inquired, "Hey, you had breakfast yet?" She told him no. Earlier, she'd been too keyed up to even think about eating, but suddenly she realized she was starving. "Great," he said, looking pleased. "I'll tell Maria to set an extra place. How do you like your eggs?"

Stevie's mind was whirling so, she had to stop and think before she could answer. This whole thing was so surreal. What had started out as *Mission, Impossible* had morphed into *The Twilight Zone*. At the same time something was sliding into place in her like the last, missing piece to a puzzle. Rumors about

Grant's dark side, fanned by the former girlfriends who'd come forward with stories of their own in the wake of the Lauren Rose tragedy, crept into her head, but she resolutely pushed them away. She'd been waiting all her life for this moment; she wasn't going to spoil it.

They lingered over breakfast, talking about everything from Stevie's passion for muscle cars to the current music scene—Grant, she learned, was a fan of Eminem. He told her stories about Astral Plane's glory days in the seventies, when they'd played to sold-out stadiums on two continents. She, in turn, told him what it had been like growing up in Bakersfield, where Nancy's VW bug plastered with left-wing stickers had stuck out like a sore thumb in a town in which pickups with gun racks were the norm. The only tense moment was when she revealed what she did for a living. Which, it turned out, came as no surprise.

Grant said with a laugh, "I may be an old coot, but I *do* watch TV. It just took me a little while to figure out where I'd seen you before."

Luckily for her, he was cool with it. Like a lot of celebrities, Grant could afford to be laid back because he paid others to play the heavy. Like the scary-looking bodyguard-slash-houseman who'd eyed her menacingly when they were properly introduced, then barely spoke a word to her as he was driving her home later on.

By the time he dropped her off at her condo, she was a bundle of mixed emotions. In some respects her curiosity had been satisfied, but she still had more questions than answers. What had Grant been doing with himself all those years he'd been holed up? And was there any truth to the stories told by ex-girlfriends, specifically that he turned into Mr. Hyde when he drank? More importantly, where did she fit in?

Before she'd even changed out of her sweaty clothes she found herself picking up the phone and punching in Ryan's number. He'd been through it all with her, the endless speculating about her father and occasional bouts of weepiness after one too many glasses of wine. How could she *not* share something as important as this with him?

"Red Gate Productions," answered a female voice at the other end.

"Jan? It's me, Stevie. Is he in?" Her words came in a breathless rush.

She'd left so many messages over the past weeks, it was almost a shock when a moment or two later Ryan's voice came on the line. "Listen, can this wait?" he said, sounding harried. "We had to do some recutting, and it's a little crazy right now. The deadline for submission is tomorrow." The life of a documentary filmmaker was always racing to meet a deadline, usually involving some film festival or other. She knew better than to take it personally, but she was nonetheless taken aback. It had been more than a month since they'd last spoken. Didn't he miss her even a little bit?

She swallowed against the knot forming in her throat. "I just thought you'd want to know, I met him—my dad." Ryan was the only person aside from Franny, Emerson, and Jay in whom she'd confided about Grant.

There was a little pause, then he said, "Wow. That is big news. How'd it go?"

"It's kind of a long story. Are you going to be free later on? I was hoping we could meet for coffee."

He hesitated, and in the background she could hear muffled voices calling out to one another. Red Gate's edit bay, in full-tilt mode, easily rivaled KNLA's. "I could probably break away for twenty minutes or so," he said after a bit, "but it won't be until later in the day. I'll give you a call when I come up for air."

Not exactly a declaration of undying love, but it would have to do for now. She consoled herself with the thought that it couldn't be entirely hopeless, or he wouldn't have agreed to meet her.

Stevie showered and changed into her sexiest jeans and a top that showed off every set of crunches she'd sweated at the gym. It wouldn't hurt to remind him of what he was missing. At the same time, a voice whispered in her head: *Are you sure you know what you're doing?* Even if she managed to lure him back, what then? She still wasn't ready to give him what he wanted, and maybe wouldn't be for some time. All she could do was pray that this cooling-off period had made Ryan realize she was worth the wait.

It was late in the afternoon by the time he called back. They arranged to meet at a café near his studio, just off Pico Boulevard. On the way there, cruising along in her Firebird with the top down, Stevie found herself reflecting on happier times. On their first date, Ryan had taken her to a little Mom-and-Pop Italian restaurant that was the perfect antidote to the "in" spots frequented by celebrities, then to the Cinerama Dome to see *Notorious*, one of her favorite old films, which turned out to be one of his, too. Afterward they'd gone for a drive up Highway 1, stopping in Malibu for a moonlit walk on the beach. As they'd strolled along the sand, the incoming tide lapping at their toes, Stevie had felt a sense of possibility she hadn't known with other men. And when he'd paused to kiss her, a kindling, not just in her loins, but in her soul.

"There's something I've always wondered about," she'd said, as they'd strolled back they way they'd come. "Why, in all those old movies, the men are such shits." She was thinking about the character Cary Grant had played in *Notorious*, who'd treated Ingrid Bergman badly throughout most of the film.

"A better question would be why the women put up with it," Ryan had replied.

"Obviously they're gluttons for punishment."

"Or maybe they didn't see an alternative."

"Such as?"

"A nice guy who knows how to treat a woman right."

Looking into his long, angular face, with its intelligent gray eyes and sensitive poet's mouth—not the kind of guy she normally fell for, but attractive in an Adrien Brody kind of way—she sensed it wasn't just talk. He would be good to her, not just until he'd gotten her into bed, but always. Until now, she'd always gravitated toward the bad boys who were good at starting fires but didn't stick around to watch them burn. Maybe because, lacking any blueprint for what a man should be, she'd adopted hers from old movies like the one they'd just seen. But here was one, she suddenly knew without a doubt, who wouldn't be just another footnote in her long, inglorious history with men.

In the weeks and months that followed, her instincts proved correct. He was as good a friend as he was a lover. Even their differences complemented each other's. He was the ballast to her occasional flights of fancy, and she provided insight into some of the more angst-ridden subjects of his films who hadn't enjoyed the normal upbringing he had. He was also romantic where she tended to be practical, often surprising her with thoughtful, quirky gifts, like a pair of vintage platform shoes she'd admired in a thrift shop or tickets to a classic-car show.

Now, as she exited off the freeway onto Pico, she felt as nervous as she had before their first date. By the time she pulled into the parking lot behind the café, her heart was doing a drum riff against her rib cage and her stomach was where her throat should have been. Joe's was where they'd often met after work and where she'd occasionally picked up coffee for Ryan and his crew when he was crashing on an all-nighter, and the familiar place brought a host of memories. She was almost relieved when she walked in to find she'd arrived ahead of him; it would give her a chance to collect herself. While she was waiting, she ordered for them both. She knew how he liked his coffee, black with no sugar.

She was seated at a table by the window, sipping her coffee, when he walked in. Her heart took flight. He'd lost some weight, she noted, which only accentuated his soulful eyes and angular frame—he looked like a starving Eastern European poet.

"I can't stay long," he said, sinking into the chair opposite hers.

They might have been any couple, except for the catch in her throat and his smile that didn't quite reach his eyes.

"I know." She drank in the sight of him, storing it up for later on.

He blew on his coffee, taking a careful sip. "You look good," he said.

"So do you."

It was all she could do to keep from reaching for his hand. A hand he was now forking through his hair, a nervous habit of his. His hair had grown out since she'd last seen him, enough to curl over the collar of his faded chambray shirt. He was in need of a shave, too, but she thought it made him look sexy and a little bit dangerous.

"So tell me. What's he like?" He leaned back in his chair, a genuine smile softening his stark features.

She told him about the strange morning she'd had. "It was weird. Almost like he was glad to have the company, and not just because I was his kid."

"From what you've told me, it doesn't sound like he gets too many visitors."

She nodded thoughtfully. "It was kind of like visiting someone in prison. Though I don't know of many where they serve caviar with the scrambled eggs," she added, with a smile.

"No one's keeping him there," Ryan pointed out.

"I know, that's what's so weird about it. He hasn't set foot off the estate in more than a decade."

"Why do you think that is?"

"He's scared, I think. Of being hounded by the press, and also of people finding out the real guy is nothing like the legend. All this publicity around Lauren Rose isn't helping, either."

"Which leads to the more important question: Do you think he's innocent?" Ryan's gray eyes fixed on her, forcing her to confront the doubts that had been plaguing her.

"Yeah, I do." She was surprised by the conviction in her voice.

"What makes you so sure?"

"It wasn't anything he said. In fact, the subject never came up. I just can't picture him pulling that trigger, not on purpose." Grant had seemed more hunted than hunter.

"You barely know him. You don't know what he's capable of."

"True, but I trust my instincts."

"What if they're wrong? Are you willing to take that risk?" He leaned forward, wearing that stern-dad look he sometimes got when she was sticking her neck out too far, like the time she'd gotten a little too nosy with an actor at a press conference over his reputed mob connections.

She felt a little flutter of hope. "If I didn't know better, I'd think you were worried about me," she said, her mouth quirking up in a little half smile.

"Just because we're not together, it doesn't mean I don't still care about you," he said, with a touch of defensiveness.

"Ryan . . ." Now she *was* reaching for his hand. "The reason I wanted to see you, it wasn't just to tell you about my father. I wanted you to know how much I've missed you."

"I've missed you, too," he said quietly.

"You mean it's not too late?"

"If you're asking if my offer's still open, the answer is yes." His tone remained guarded.

The flutter became a surge of hope. "I still have some stuff to figure out. Are you willing to wait?"

"Maybe," he said slowly, not taking his eyes off her face. "It depends on how long a wait it would be."

Tears of frustration welled in Stevie's eyes. How she wanted to reassure him! But she couldn't mislead him. If all she could offer was honesty, she owed him that much at least. "I can't make any promises," she said.

"Just promise to keep an open mind."

Her heart soared. "Does that mean we could go back to the way it was before?"

"No, but I'd settle for a long engagement."

She saw the longing in his eyes, which made it all the more difficult to say what she had to say. "I can't. It wouldn't be fair to you. You want kids, and I don't know if or when I'll ever be ready for that."

"You feel that way now, but—"

"Ryan, listen to me," she said, not letting him finish. "You can afford to wait, but I can't. Why do you think Franny's in such a burning rush? After a certain age, it's not an option."

"You're a long way from that," he said.

"Maybe not as long as you think."

He withdrew his hand and sat back. "In other words, nothing's changed." The warmth in his face was cooling as rapidly as the coffee that sat before him, scarcely touched.

"I'm sorry." A tear slipped down her cheek.

Ryan, with a loud scrape that caused her to flinch, abruptly pushed his chair back and rose to his feet. "Look, I'm happy you found your dad. Let's leave it at that, okay?" He pulled out his wallet, and tossed some bills onto the table. "That's for the coffee." He started to go, then paused, turning slowly to face her. In his starving-poet's face a tug-of-war was going on, between blind desire to take what she had to offer and the knowledge that it wouldn't be enough. At last, he said gently, "Be careful, okay? He may seem like a nice guy, but there could be another side to him. You could end up getting hurt."

"Don't worry I'll be fine. I cover the headlines, I don't make them." She aimed for a brave smile that fell short of its mark.

"And just what kind of field day will the tabloids have when they find out you're his daughter?"

"I'll cross that bridge when I get to it. First, I have to find out for sure if he's innocent." Not just for her own satisfaction, but to put to bed the hornet's nest of rumors and speculation that had made a virtual prisoner of Grant.

"And how do you propose to do that?"

"I have my sources." Actually, just one so far: Keith Holloway, a former colleague at KNLA who was writing the definitive biography of Grant Tobin. He'd spent years researching it and presumably knew everything there was to know about the dark chapter involving Lauren Rose. If anyone could supply Stevie with the facts or at the very least point her in the right direction, it was Keith. Besides, he owed her for the six-figure deal Franny had gotten him.

"Just watch your back, that's all I'm saying," Ryan cautioned once more.

"Ryan . . ." she began, but he was already walking away.

Stevie started to get up, then sank back down in defeat. What was the use of going after him? It wouldn't change anything. Better to let him go. Let him find a nice woman who wanted kids. She only wished with all her heart that woman could be her.

Stevie hadn't known Keith Holloway all that well when he was at KNLA. He'd covered mostly hard news and there wasn't much overlap between that and her beat. But they'd kept in touch after he left. When he'd told her he was writing a book, a biography of Grant Tobin—apparently Keith had been a big fan of his music since he was a teen, back when others his age were into heavy metal and Seattle grunge—it hadn't meant that much at the time. But all that had changed with the discovery that she was Grant's child. Which was why she'd hooked Keith up with Franny and why, when she'd heard about his book deal, she'd called to suggest they get together for a celebratory drink. She already knew from talking to him that he thought Grant had gotten a bum rap, but not why. Did he know stuff that wasn't in the police report? Something that might ultimately exonerate Grant if he were to be charged with attempted murder.

"Nice place," she commented, as she stepped into the living room of his condo—not unlike her own, only cozily furnished and with a view of Santa Monica Bay. It was done in cool beiges and blond wood, with bold fabrics and vintage posters on the walls. "If you ever decide to take up interior decorating, I could use some help."

"Thanks, but I get enough grief from my mom for being single without her thinking I'm gay," he said with a chuckle, as she took a seat on the sofa. "What can I get you to drink?"

"White wine, if you have it."

He fetched a bottle from the kitchen, leaving Franny to ponder his remark. If he was still single, she didn't think it was for lack of opportunity. Keith, though not classically handsome, had a Matt Lauer-ish appeal that made him irresistible, if the collective female pulse in the newsroom was any indication. He was balding, like Matt, but kept his dark hair cropped close to his head, which made you focus on his thick-lashed brown eyes and killer smile instead. He was, in the words of Liv Henry, the kind of man who could make you forget you were married.

"Well, here's to your book deal," Stevie said, after he'd poured them each a glass. She lifted hers.

"It wouldn't have happened without you. You're the one who hooked me up with Franny." He sank into the leather club chair facing the sofa, looking a bit dazed still by his windfall despite the grin he wore. "I can't thank you enough." He added with a wry look, "Now all I have to do is write the damn book."

She followed his gaze to the room beyond, his office from the looks of it, where she could see through the open door piles of papers and folders covering the desk and floor, and a wall stuck with scribbled Post-its. "How's it going so far?"

"Slow." He picked up a paperweight off the table beside him, idly toying with it. "I thought researching it would be the hard part. But it's winnowing it all down into something that makes sense that's the real challenge." The Lauren Rose paperwork alone filled one whole box, he said.

Stevie's pulse quickened. "Anything that'll come as a surprise?" She kept her tone nonchalant.

He cocked his head, smiling at her. "If I told you, you wouldn't buy the book."

"I might," she said, smiling back. "It depends."

"On what?"

"On whether or not I'd be getting my money's worth."

He eyed her intently. "Why do I get the feeling you're not just asking out of curiosity?"

Stevie put her wineglass down on the coffee table and sat back, folding her arms over her chest. "Okay. I'll give it to you straight. I need your help."

"Anything," he said without hesitation.

"I need to know everything you know about the night Lauren Rose was shot."

His smile faltered a bit but remained in place. He set the paperweight back down on the end table and leaned forward, elbows on his knees, to fix her with a keen gaze. "Maybe you should start by telling me why it's so important."

"If I tell you, you have to promise to keep it confidential. At least until the book comes out."

"Okay."

"What would you say if I told you Grant had an illegitimate child?"

"I'd say prove it." He sounded more than a little skeptical.

"You want proof? You're looking at it."

His jaw dropped. "Are you saying—?"

"Grant Tobin is my father," she finished for him, taking a moment to relish the dumfounded look on his face before continuing, "Don't feel bad—there's no way you could've known. I didn't know myself until a few months ago."

"How did you find out?"

"My mom finally came clean."

"So all that time he never tried to see you?"

"He didn't even know I existed. At least, that's what he told me, and I believe him."

"You've met him?" Keith's eyes gleamed like those of a hound picking up a scent.

She nodded. "He's not what you'd expect," she told him. "He's actually kind of sweet, in an offbeat sort of way." She'd been to see him twice more since that first visit, and each time she'd come away more convinced of his innocence. Nonetheless, she'd need more than her instincts to go on.

Keith leaned forward, all ears. "Did he ever mention Lauren Rose?"

"No, and I haven't asked. I'm waiting for the right moment."

"I'm not sure how much help I'll be," Keith said, frowning slightly as he sat back. "I spent months interviewing everyone connected to the case, and never really got to the bottom of it.

The only one I haven't talked to is Lauren herself. Lauren and Victor."

"Victor?"

"The keeper of the gates."

"Big tattooed guy with shoulders out to here?" She spread her arms wide. She'd known him only by his nickname, Gonzo, short for Gonzalez. "He didn't strike me as the chatty type. In fact, I got the impression he'd be just as likely to break your arm as give you a hand."

Keith acknowledged this with a grim smile. "The one time I tracked him down I wasn't sure I was going to get away in one piece." Keith didn't rattle easily, so it must have been pretty scary. "The one thing I did manage to find out, from one of the maids, was that Victor was there the night Lauren was shot. There's a good chance he saw the whole thing go down."

"That's not what he told the police." According to the report, Grant's bodyguard had stated that he'd been bringing the car around to drive Lauren back to her place when he heard the shot. By the time he got to her, she was sprawled, unconscious, in a pool of blood.

"I know. But the maid claimed, to me at least—she was too scared to say anything to the police—that he didn't take the car out of the garage until *after* he called 911."

"So you think he's covering for Grant?"

Keith shrugged. "Your guess is as good as mine. There are only two people we know for sure were in the room that night. One of them is Grant, who's sticking to his story. The other is Lauren, who hasn't exactly been in a position to tell her version."

"Until now." Stevie felt a ripple of unease in the pit of her stomach. Word had it that Lauren was making good progress with her speech therapy. The only thing that remained to be seen was how much she remembered about that night.

"Are you sure you're prepared for it, if turns out he's *not* as inno-cent as he seems?" Keith asked in a quiet voice.

Stevie thought for a moment, then nodded, smiling thinly. "I've spent most of my life in the dark as far as my father's concerned. Believe me, anything's better than not knowing."

Chapter Four

Knock 'em dead, boss," said Inez as Jay was breezing past her on his way to the conference room.

He paused for inspection. "Is my tie on straight?"

She half-rose out of her chair to give it a tweak. "It is now." Her gaze dropped. "Let's just hope they don't notice you're wearing navy socks with brown shoes."

In the six years he'd been with Beck/Blustein, he couldn't remember a day that Inez hadn't been looking out for him. Two parts administrative assistant and one part nursemaid, she had a mouth that far exceeded her diminutive size—the top of her bleached-blond head barely came to his shoulder—and drawers stocked with items for every contingency: Band-Aids, breath mints, shoe polish, lint remover, and, for dire emergencies, a fifth of Glenlivet. It wouldn't have surprised him right now if she pulled out a pair of socks.

He continued on his way, down the corridor walled with laminated glass, on the other side of which he could see his coworkers on the phones or at their computers, and here and there in groups of two or more, bent over drafting tables or seated around tables in the smaller conference areas. All part of the ebb and flow of daily life here at Beck/Blustein, except that this wasn't just an ordinary day, as the steadily growing knot in his stomach was reminding him. The two Starbucks coffees he'd grabbed on his way to work hadn't helped, either. Now, on top of an upset stomach, he had heartburn.

It was the same before every presentation. Never mind that he'd been at this for more than a decade; Jay couldn't walk into a pitch meeting without that spike in blood pressure and tumbling in his gut, thinking that this time for sure he'd be unmasked, his true identity revealed: a Wisconsin farm boy who wouldn't know a bright idea from a bucket of slop.

He knew his fears were unfounded. But they were like the bone in his left foot that he'd broken ice-skating when he was nine and that had never healed properly, leaving him with a crooked toe: a legacy of his childhood. Growing up, whatever he did, it was never good enough. His dad never yelled at him or hit him, but Jay would feel his displeasure all the same, radiating off him like the chill off the re-frigerated truck in which the stainless-steel canisters of milk were carted off each day to the creamery. Every morning, as he headed out to the barn to help with the milking, he'd feel the same knot in his stomach he did now. At school it would abate—schoolwork was the one thing he *was* good at—only to return later in the day as he trudged home up the long, dusty hill from the bus stop.

It had been a shock, when he got to Princeton, to discover that he was no longer the smartest kid in the class. Being the star pupil and valedictorian of his class at Woodrow Wilson High hadn't pre-pared him for the rigors his college classmates who'd gone to elite prep schools seemed to take in stride. He'd had to struggle to keep up, each day like three down with long yardage and a minute to go in the game. By the time he'd caught up, he'd forgotten how to stop running.

He strode into the boardroom with minutes to spare, pleased to find his team all assembled—chief designers Darren Block and Jay's good buddy Todd Oster, who'd worked with him at Saatchi & Saatchi; his multimedia guy, Michael McCort; writers Phoebe Kim and Sebastian Beccera. They were standing in readiness, as alert as any military corps.

"*Irasshaimase.*" Jay welcomed the Uruchima executives as they filed in, shaking hands and greeting everyone by name, even re-membering to ask after Mr. Uruchima's wife, whom he'd heard was in ill health. A quick survey of the long cherry table satisfied him that Inez had seen to every detail: Neatly laid out at every place was a Mount Blanc pen and a copy of the material they'd had printed and bound. Refreshments included steaming pots of green tea in addition to thermoses of coffee, delicate rice cookies from Takashimaya along with the usual bagels and sweet rolls.

If his parents with their old-fashioned values had drilled one thing into him that had stood him in good stead in the workplace, it was that the personal touch, increasingly rare in today's fast-paced world, was often what made the difference between success and failure. It had helped land him more than one account and kept many of their existing clients from going to another agency when their numbers were down. And from the smiles and mur-murs of approval as the Uruchima executives helped themselves to the refreshments, he knew it was appreciated by present com-pany.

His pulse quickened. If they landed this account, it would be the jewel in Beck/Blustein's crown—bigger than Jacques-Bênoit Cosmetics and Performance Sporting Goods put together. Uruchima Motors, fast approaching Honda, Toyota, and Nissan in terms of U.S. sales, needed an innovative campaign to launch their new hybrid SUV, the Roughrider, and Jay believed their agency was up to the challenge.

He gave a short, punchy introduction, followed by a PowerPoint presentation outlining their main thrust. Until recently, he reminded them, the demographic for SUVs had been primarily families and young men in the eighteen-to-twenty-five age bracket, but new market research showed that a growing number of urban, white-collar males were buying them. Monster SUVs were the new status symbols—Viagra on wheels—though, with sales down due to high prices at the pump, what made the Roughrider so attractive was that it got in excess of thirty miles to the gallon. As Jay was listing the cities he saw as prime targets, he saw Mr. Uruchima's right-hand man nod slightly. So far, so good. Now all he had to do was bring it home with the demo for the sixty-second television spot they were proposing.

At the click of the mouse, an image filled the screen, showing a computerized rendering of a man standing at an airport baggage carousel, thirties, nondescript, wearing a business suit and holding a briefcase. He was surrounded by equally nondescript-looking counterparts, all dressed more or less alike and looking equally bored with their lives.

With each subsequent click the spot unfolded: The man searching in vain for his bag amid the identical black suitcases spewing onto the carousel, only to come across a small, gift-wrapped box, his name on it, containing a set of car keys. He looks mystified but intrigued. Next, he's shown climbing into the shiny new Roughrider SUV parked outside. Then streaking down a dirt road in the middle of nowhere, his briefcase flying out the window, followed by his suit jacket and tie, as the Roughrider disappears over the forested horizon trailing a plume of dust. The tag line reads: LIFE IS A GIFT. DON'T WASTE IT.

The lights came up, and in the ensuing moment of silence Jay's stomach did a slow somersault. The Uruchima executives all wore the same flat, unreadable expression, and it suddenly occurred to him that he might have offended them. To some extent the Japanese viewed conformity as a virtue. They might not have taken kindly to the suggestion that there was something less than desirable about it.

The silence was broken by Yoshiko Imurakami, the lone female of the bunch, a doll-size woman with sleek, shoulder-length hair. "What are we looking at in terms of budget?" she asked. Her English was flawless, and he remembered that she'd gone to Yale before getting her master's in economics from Harvard.

He indicated the page in the printed material where it showed a breakdown of the projected cost. "As you can see, we have bids from several Canadian production companies we've worked with in the past. It's more cost-effective to shoot there—no unions to jack up fees. Also, the exchange rate is in our favor. You'd end up saving quite a bit."

The hint of a smile creased Mr. Uruchima's lined face. Clearly the older man was impressed by Jay's attention to the bottom line. He rose, a slight man who nonetheless projected an aura of power, and his executives immediately followed suit. "Thank you, Mr. Gunderson. It has been most interesting," he said, shaking Jay's hand on his way out. "You will be hearing from us soon."

Jay flashed his best, west of the Mississippi grin. "Thanks for your time, Mr. Uruchima. I really hope we can work together. I think we'd make a great team."

"Way to go, dude. You really outdid yourself." Todd Oster, a huge, bearded bear of a man who'd have looked more at home in a lumberjack shirt and Red Wing boots than in the four-hundred-dollar suit he wore, high-fived him on the way back to their respective offices.

"Congratulate me when we have the account," Jay said.

Inez looked up from the keyboard she was hammering on as he walked in. "How'd it go?" she asked.

He knew better than to indulge in the usual ad-man hyperbole with her—she'd see right through it—merely commenting, "No one seemed to notice my socks. I take that as a good sign."

She gave him a thumbs-up and went back to her furious assault on the keyboard, pausing only long enough to call after him as he was stepping through the door to the inner office, "Oh, by the way, Franny called."

He paused in the doorway. "Did she leave a message?"

"No, but she wanted you to call her as soon as you got out of your meeting," Inez informed him without looking up.

Jay's heart was pounding as he reached for the phone on his desk. An urgent message from Franny could mean only one thing. "What's up?" he asked when she came on the line.

"Nothing much. I just called to see if you were doing anything after work."

He felt some of the tension go out of him. "Um, let's see . . ." He consulted his calendar. "Looks like we're having dinner with some friends." Friends of Vivienne's, that is; he had yet to meet them. "Why?" he asked, ever so casually.

"I was hoping we could meet for a drink."

"I think I can manage that. I don't have to be at the restaurant until seven."

"Great. Paddy's, around six?"

"See you then." He hung up, wondering if her casual tone had been just a cover. Was there something she wanted to tell him? Something too important to say over the phone?

His heart lurched at the thought.

So far, the baby thing hadn't been a huge issue. Other than the weirdness of having to masturbate into a plastic cup with a waiting room full of women just down the hall, the worst of it had been Franny's obsessing over *not* getting pregnant. The first two attempts were a wash, and she was convinced it was because her eggs had passed their expiration date. It didn't help, either, that Vivienne had conceived on their first try. The doctor had assured Franny it wasn't unusual, that these things can take time, but she was convinced she'd missed the boat, a dried-up old lady at the age of thirty-six.

But what if the third time had proved to be the charm?

At six on the dot he arrived at Paddy's, on the corner of Third and Eighteenth, a few blocks from his office. The faded gilt lettering over the door read SHAUGHNESSY'S TAVERN, but everyone called it Paddy's after its owner, Paddy Shaughnessy, a ruddy-faced older man with billowy white hair who greeted Jay warmly, gesturing toward the table where Franny sat sipping a beer and signaling to the bartender that Jay would have the same.

"Well, isn't this a nice surprise," Franny remarked, as Jay pulled up a chair.

"It's not as if you weren't expecting me," he said.

"You're usually late. I figured I had at least ten more minutes of looking mysterious and alluring."

Jay glanced about the tavern's darkened interior. Its woodwork was stained a deep nicotine, the walls hung with framed eight-by-tens of famous patrons from another era. These days it was just the regulars, who at the moment looked as likely to pry themselves from the baseball game they were watching on the TV over the bar as of getting up and dancing a jig. "If you're looking to get picked up, you're in the wrong place," he said, with a grin. "Unless you're into old guys and a married man about to become a dad."

"You can say that again."

"What?"

"The part about becoming a dad."

As Jay sat there staring at her with an idiot smile on his face, the world seemed to narrow to a single pinpoint. The bartender thumping his beer down on the table might have been a moth flitting in and out of his field of vision. "Franny . . . are you . . . is it . . ." He was suddenly at a loss for words.

She nodded, a corner of her mouth tipping up in a lopsided smile. "Yep. It's official. My doctor just confirmed it." Her smile broadened into a grin. "I don't know about you, but speaking for myself, I think it's worthy of a toast." Franny clinked her bottle against his, and he saw that it wasn't Guinness she was drinking but root beer. "Here's to our kid. Seriously, I couldn't have done it without you." She spoke with a wry tone, but her eyes searched his face anxiously, as if for signs of a belated attack of cold feet.

It hit Jay then and the floor seemed to roll away from underneath him. This wasn't just a favor he was doing a friend. Franny was pregnant . . . with his child.

"Wow," he said, slowly shaking his head.

"I know. It hasn't quite sunk in for me, either," she said. "I keep waiting for Monty Hall to step out of the wings and tell me my real prize is a brand-new washer-drier combo."

"Which you'll need. Unless you plan on camping out at the laundromat."

Franny reached across the table to take his hand. It was a warm day, even for June, and in her flowered sundress, with her cheeks flushed and her hair twisted up in a haphazard knot, tendrils corkscrewing down around her ears, she looked like she had in college.

His mind traveled back to the day they'd met. He'd been sitting on the steps of Firestone Library poring over the fall schedule, trying to decide which classes to register for, when he'd looked up to find a pretty, brown-haired girl standing a few feet away, chewing on her lower lip, her brow furrowed as if she were concentrating hard, or angry with herself.

Without thinking, he'd stood up and walked over to her. "Excuse me," he'd said. "But I couldn't help noticing you look a little lost."

"You got that right. Only it's not me that's lost," she'd replied in disgust, explaining that she'd misplaced her wallet, with all the spending money she had for the semester.

"Maybe someone turned it in. Have you checked at the proctor's office?" he'd asked.

She'd cocked her head, eyeing him curiously. "You're not from around here, are you?" she'd said, her Brooklyn accent lending her an air of streetwise authority.

"Is it that obvious?" he'd replied, with a laugh.

"Where I come from, you lose something, you might as well kiss it good-bye."

"In Grantsburg, whoever found it would take out an ad."

They'd exchanged smiles, and Jay had urged, "Come on. It's worth a try. The worst that can happen is it'll be a wasted trip."

Franny had hesitated a moment, then shrugged. "Yeah, why not?"

They'd started off in the direction of the proctor's office before he'd remembered to introduce himself. "Jay Gunderson." He'd paused to stick out his hand.

"Franny Richman." She'd worn a faintly bemused expression, as if trying to decide whether he was for real.

At the proctor's office she'd been amazed to discover her missing wallet waiting for her, its contents miraculously intact. Afterward they'd wandered over to the student center, where they'd gotten to know each other over coffee and crullers. When Jay had finally glanced at his watch he'd been surprised to see that two hours had passed. From that day on, they'd been inseparable.

"Listen, I want you to know I meant what I said before," she was telling him now. "You don't owe me a thing. I'm not going to twist your arm into coming to every soccer match and parent-teacher meeting. You'll have plenty of that as it is."

"Who says you'd have to twist my arm?" he replied, somewhat defensively. No matter what, it was still his kid.

"What I mean is, I don't want you to feel obligated."

He put on a mock aggrieved face. "Hey, it's me, remember? I thought we agreed that this wasn't going to change anything." It would defeat the purpose if they had to go from finishing each other's sentences to monitoring every word. "So are we good?"

"Yeah." She let out a breath, and some of the tension seemed to go out of her as well. "It's just that it's a little weird, you know. I've never been pregnant with my best friend's kid."

"You've never been pregnant, period."

"True."

He squeezed her hand reassuringly. "Let's take it one step at a time, okay?"

She nodded, though her expression remained pensive. In the dim light, her dark eyes seemed to take up her whole face. "No regrets?"

"None." It wasn't a lie exactly—he *was* happy, mainly for Franny—and if he had concerns, it was only natural. She didn't have to know he worried that this baby would affect more than their friendship, that it would put a strain on his and Vivienne's relationship as well. "Hey, what's a little DNA between friends?"

"Speaking of which, I hope he, or she, inherits your nose." Franny had always thought hers was too big, though in Jay's opinion it suited her face perfectly. "Long legs would be nice, too."

He laughed. "Aren't you getting ahead of yourself? It doesn't even have fingers or toes yet." He remembered Vivienne's first sonogram; it had looked more like a thumbprint than anything human. Not until the doctor told them the sex had the baby become real to him, a boy, for whom they already had a name picked out: Stephan, after Jay's grandfather.

"Hey, you know me. I'm already looking at schools," Franny joked.

"Just promise you won't become a vegetarian and ban me from entering your apartment if I have so much as a single cat hair on me." These days, with Vivienne on health watch, their loft felt more like a Zen monastery than a home.

"I don't know about cat hairs. But anyone who comes between me and my pork chops better be prepared for a fight," Franny mock-growled.

"I'll drink to that." He hoisted his beer.

Her smile faded. "Look, I know we've been over this ad nauseam, but now that it's not just a theoretical kid, I can't help worrying that it'll get in the way of you and Viv." It was as if she'd read his mind.

"Viv'll be thrilled," he assured her. "It was her idea, remember?"

Some of Franny's concerns were justified, though. It was complicated with her and Vivienne. Going all the way back to the guy Franny had been so crazy about when she and Vivienne roomed together after college. Vivienne had done nothing to encourage him, but she felt responsible nonetheless for his and Franny's breakup. Part of the reason she was doing this, he suspected, was to right an old wrong and become the kind of friend she'd always hoped to be, the kind he and Franny were.

"Still." Franny continued to eye him anxiously. "Promise you'll tell me if I'm ever stepping on anyone's toes." She frowned, her fingers tightening around his.

"Cross my heart, hope to die." He drew an invisible X over his heart.

She released his hand and sat back, her gaze turning inward—a look he'd come to recognize as that of the secret universe a woman entered when she became pregnant. One with its own language and customs and rhythms, from which men were, for the most part, excluded.

He felt an instant of panic, then the old Franny resurfaced. In a voice that made him breathe a little easier, she said, "Okay, now that that's settled, I want to hear all about your meeting. Every detail."

"Your friends were nice," Jay commented as he and Vivienne were leaving the restaurant later that evening.

She smiled indulgently, tucking an arm into his. "How would you know? You hardly said two words to them all evening."

He cast her a chastened look. "Sorry. Guess I was a little preoccupied."

Throughout the meal all he'd been able to think about was Franny's news. He hadn't even had a chance to tell Vivienne. By the time he'd gotten to the restaurant, she'd been immersed in talking to her friends. It wasn't the kind of thing you could just work into the conversation. *Oh, by the way, I just found out I have another one on the way.* He could only imagine what Rob and Melissa's reaction would have been. On the other hand, he'd better get used to seeing some dropped jaws because soon there'd be no hiding it.

There would be the matter, too, of explaining it to their parents. Vivienne's weren't a problem—they were European; nothing shocked them. But his own . . . They were simple farm people with no frame of reference for a situation like this. How was he supposed to break it to them? *Mom, Dad, listen, you know how you were always on me about grandkids? Well, you're getting two for the price of one.* His father would scratch his head and give him that *look,* the one that said, *Son, I don't know what kinds of wickedness you folks get up to in New York City, but out here we have such a thing as family values.* His mother, a staunch Baptist, was under the impression he still regularly attended Sunday services (which he hadn't exactly gone out of his way to disabuse her of), and would ask apprehensively if he'd spoken to his pastor about it. Anything not sanctioned by the Bible or the Christian Family Council was, in her mind, suspect.

"Is something the matter?" Vivienne's voice broke into his thoughts. "You're a million miles away."

He brought his attention back to her. "Sorry. I was just thinking."

"About what?"

"Franny." He paused in the middle of the sidewalk, turning to face her. "She's pregnant." He kept his voice neutral, waiting to see how she'd react, if she'd be okay with it now that it was an actuality.

Vivienne's face lit up. "Really? That's wonderful!" She looked even more radiant than usual, her cheeks flushed, her glossy black hair shimmering in the glow of the neon sign overhead. An evening out with friends always had this effect on her. "Why on earth didn't you say something?" she scolded lightly. "All that time we were chattering on about Rob and Melissa's new apartment, you were keeping this to yourself."

"It wasn't exactly dinner conversation."

"Your trouble is, you think everyone's as provincial as your parents." She gave his arm an affectionate little squeeze as they continued on their way. "Anyway, it's not as if it's a deep, dark secret."

He shrugged. "Guess I'm still getting used to the idea."

"You've had six months, isn't that long enough?" she teased, placing a hand on her rounded belly.

"I never thought I'd be fathering more than one child at a time."

"Well, this isn't just about you. And Franny's going to need all the support she can get."

They were strolling along Second Avenue, near St. Mark's Place, the muggy air blessedly cooled by the breeze blowing in off the East River. The East Village wasn't like it used to be when he and his friends had taken the train in from Jersey on weekends, he thought. No longer an affordable ghetto for the fringe element, its grunge and graffiti had given way to high-end housing and a chain store on every other block. The Starbucks crowd was moving in, pushing out the starving artists and musicians. These days you saw more tanning-salon tans than tattoos. Jay decided he preferred the East Village of his college days. Progress had a way of making him feel middle-aged.

Or maybe it was just impending parenthood. Friends with kids had warned that it was all-consuming and they'd been right. He and Vivienne talked of little else. Shopping excursions were generally baby related. And he'd spent the past two weekends painting the nursery and assembling the crib. But what he hadn't been prepared for was just how deeply it would affect him. He felt as if a wonderful gift had been bestowed on him, the chance to give his own son the kind of childhood he hadn't had.

Would he feel the same way about Franny's baby?

Later, at home in bed with his wife snuggled up against him, he was still wrestling with it. Franny wanted him to be a part of their child's life, and Jay wanted that, too. But how exactly would it work? Would they be a family of sorts? Or would this kid grow up feeling less loved than Stephan?

Vivienne reached for his hand, placing it on her belly so he could feel the baby kick.

"Feels like a foot," he said with a smile, never ceasing to get a little thrill each time. "That, or a knee."

"Face it, we've got a future NFLer on our hands. Forget onesies, this kid's going to need a helmet and knee pads."

"I was the same way. My mom used to joke that she should get a bulk rate from our family doctor, with all my sprains and stitches."

"I didn't know you were such a daredevil."

"I wasn't, really. It was just normal stuff." In school, he'd tried out for every team. Luckily for him, he'd turned out to be a natural athlete, excelling not only in football but in wrestling and lacrosse.

"Let's hope Franny's baby is a girl then. We'll have enough gray hairs worrying about Stephan."

One of each, he thought. Yes, that would be nice. In the darkness, he indulged in his first real smile of the day. He was drifting off to sleep a few minutes later when Vivienne murmured in his ear, "Babe? I forgot to tell you, the Kleins invited us for dinner on Friday."

"The Kleins?" he echoed groggily.

"From Lamaze. You know, the photographer and his wife. The ones having twins?"

"Oh, right." He remembered chatting with them after class the other night. Now he asked grumpily, "Is there a law that says just because we're all in this together, we have to socialize?"

"What a thing to say. They're very nice people."

"I'm sure they are. That's beside the point." Jay sighed, wide awake now. "Look, I've got nothing against Kleins, but I wouldn't mind a quiet evening at home for a change."

"We'll have plenty of that once the baby comes."

From the tone of her voice, he could tell she was sulking. Vivienne was used to getting her way. He supposed it wasn't her fault. As the late-in-life daughter of wealthy parents, she'd been denied nothing growing up. Home had been a luxury apartment off the rue du Faubourg St.-Honoré. School had been Le Rosey in Switzerland, where she'd palled around with the sons and daughters of royalty and heads of state. She was fifteen when she'd caught the eye of a modeling scout, and before long she'd been strutting down Paris runways and posing for *Vogue* magazine. She might have been just another pretty face, but she was too smart for that, so after a few years she'd put her modeling career on hold to attend Columbia. When they'd met, she was two years out of college and trying to reestablish herself in a business where twenty-three was considered over the hill.

It was around the time he'd gotten hired at Saatchi & Saatchi. He'd gone over to see Franny's new apartment and Vivienne had answered the door—the most gorgeous creature he'd ever laid eyes on. He'd been dumbstruck, scarcely able to form a coherent sentence. But he'd quickly recovered his wits, and once they'd struck up a conversation, he'd found her easy to talk to. After several more visits, he'd gotten up the nerve to ask her out, sparking an on-again, off-again affair that would have him chasing her for the next ten years.

Jay still thought himself the luckiest man on earth. He just wished Vivienne would be content to spend an evening at home more than once or twice a week. After a hard day's work, all he wanted was a home-cooked meal and some quiet time alone with his wife.

Once the baby's here, she'll settle down, he told himself. Until then, he'd just have to be patient.

He wrapped his arms around her, whispering, "You looked amazing tonight, by the way."

"Flattery will get you nowhere," she said, but he could tell she was thawing.

"Actually, I had somewhere a little more specific in mind." His hand traveled down under the covers.

She inched away from him. "Better not."

"The doctor said it was okay," he reminded her.

"I'm not taking any chances." She added in her sultriest voice, "I could give you a little something to help you sleep, though."

But Jay wasn't interested in sexual favors. He wanted Vivienne. It had been so long . . .

He rolled onto his back with a sigh. "Thanks, but I should get some shut-eye. I have to be up early. Dan wants to go over the buy schedule for the Welltrek campaign before we meet with their execs."

It occurred to him then that she hadn't asked how the Uruchima presentation had gone. He wondered if she would say something now—she knew how important it was to him—but she only yawned and rolled onto her side, murmuring, "Okay. 'Night, babe."

Chapter Five

Franny paced the lobby of the Sherry Netherland Hotel, waiting for Keith Holloway to appear. She was curious to meet him. From their conversations on the phone and what she'd read of his book so far, he seemed an interesting guy, one who'd seen his share of the dark side of humanity yet who hadn't lost his sense of humor. Would he be any different in person? With some of her authors, the person was a far cry from the persona. Like Linus Munson, the bestselling horror novelist with his many phobias, or the almost pathologically shy Beth Hubbard, who wrote sexy historical romances under the pen name Amanda Breckenridge. The evening would be a long one if Keith turned out to be as boring as his depiction of the seventies rock-and-roll scene was thrilling.

An elevator slid open and an attractive, thirtyish man dressed in jeans and a blazer stepped out. He spotted her and walked over. "You must be Franny. Hi, I'm Keith."

"You look different from your photo," she said, shaking his hand. Handsomer was what she'd meant.

"Usually when someone tells me that, I associate it with a bad blind date," he said, smiling down at her. He was tall, over six feet, and well-built in a natural, outdoorsy sort of way, his face tanned, except for the paler squint lines that radiated from the corners of his brown eyes.

Franny laughed. "I've had my share of those, too."

Keith apologized for being late, explaining that his flight had been delayed and that he'd only just checked in.

"No problem. I made the reservation for eight-thirty to give us extra time," she told him as they started toward the exit.

Over dinner in the Grill Room at the Four Seasons, she gave him an idea of what to expect at tomorrow morning's meeting with the publisher. "You'll love Eric. I couldn't have chosen a better editor for you. Did I tell you he used to work for *Rolling Stone*? And don't mind Gretchen. She'll talk your ear off, but she really knows her stuff when it comes to marketing. The main thing is, they're all really excited about this book. They have high hopes for it."

"There's a new wrinkle." He dropped his voice. "Have you talked to Stevie?"

Franny nodded. "I know about her and Grant, if that's what you mean."

"Who else knows?"

"Only a couple of other people. She wants to keep it under wraps for now. I don't have to tell you that the press would be all over this. The last thing she needs is to have paparazzi trailing her everywhere she goes."

"This thing with Lauren Rose could complicate the situation, though," he pointed out. "If she ends up pressing charges, Stevie could be visiting Grant behind bars."

"She seems to think he's innocent," Franny said.

Keith sipped his wine thoughtfully, looking out over the well-oiled machine that was the Grill Room at peak dining hour, its waitstaff gliding about with maximum efficiency without seeming to hurry, bearing meals under silver domes that would arrive piping hot at the tables. "Let's just say there's no real evidence that he isn't. On the other hand, from everything I've heard, he's an odd guy. Even Stevie says so. And it's common knowledge he had a drinking problem at one time."

"Do you think he still does?"

"All I know is that he checked into Sierra Tucson a few months after the whole thing with Lauren went down," he told her. "Whether or not he's stayed sober, nobody seems to know."

"You don't think Stevie's in any danger, do you?" Franny felt a flutter of unease at the thought.

"From what she's told me, I doubt it. Though it could be hard on her emotionally, if she finds out he's lying."

"She's tough. She can handle it."

"You've known her awhile, I gather," Keith remarked, taking a bite of his duck confit.

"Since college. We met at a rally." Franny smiled at the memory. It was an antiapartheid rally, back when Nelson Mandela was still in prison, and there'd been this one girl with shocking red hair and wrists jangling with bracelets who'd shouted louder than all the rest, waving her placard like a broadsword when the police showed up.

He asked where they'd gone to college, and that led to a discussion about her career. He was a good listener, and better yet he seemed to get her somewhat morbid sense of humor. Before long, it started to feel more like a date than a business dinner. Certainly if this *had* been a blind date, Franny wouldn't have been silently cursing whoever had fixed her up. He was, in fact, exactly the kind of guy she always hoped the strangers she occasionally flirted with online would turn out to be but never were. Intelligent, considerate, and good-looking enough to make her wish she'd worn something sexier than the conservative business suit she had on.

"What about you?" she asked. "What made you decide to go into the news business?"

"Easy," he said. "I sucked at playing guitar."

She smiled at him. "So you weren't kidding when you said you dreamed of becoming a rock-and-roll star?"

"I did more than dream. I actually had my own band. The Neon Conspiracy." He made a face. "Pretty terrible, I know. Needless to say, our big break never came. All we ever did was play local gigs." Franny thought she saw a touch of regret in his smile, even after all these years.

"Don't feel bad. I once took tap-dance lessons, but couldn't keep from tripping over my own feet," she confided.

"My uncle was the general manager of a small cable station at the time," he went on. "I started working there after school, carrying coffee and running errands, that kind of thing. In college, when I was trying to decide on a major, I chose communications because it was the only subject I knew anything about. I never looked back. Until just recently."

"What made you decide to write a book?"

"I guess it's my way of living out that old fantasy," he said.

"Do you ever miss the action?" she asked, recalling the few times she'd visited Stevie in the newsroom; its frenetic pace made publishing look sleepy in comparison.

He shrugged. "Once in a while, when there's breaking news. But I don't miss the hours. Now I get up with the sun every morning, whereas before all I did was occasionally come up for air."

"I know what you mean. I never used to go anywhere without a manuscript," she told him. She'd read on planes, in restaurants while waiting for her lunch date, even on the john. "Then one day it hit me that if I didn't slow down, I'd end up an old lady with nothing to show for my life except a bunch of dedications in books collecting dust on a shelf."

"Realizing it is one thing," he said. "The hard part is making a change."

"For me, it was more a question of my biological clock deciding for me." She felt her cheeks warm. She hadn't meant to get so personal.

"Meaning you're carrying something other than manuscripts these days?" he guessed, his eyes twinkling.

Franny nodded, feeling the warmth in her cheeks spread. "I'm due in February."

"Congratulations." He lifted his wineglass. "You and your husband must be thrilled."

"No husband. It's just me."

"Then you're one step ahead of me. Looks like I'll have to wait until I'm married."

"Any prospects?" Franny kept her voice casual.

"At the moment, no." He held her gaze a beat longer than normal. "I was pretty serious about this one woman awhile back. The trouble was, I was working so many hours, I was never around long enough to be any kind of a husband, much less have kids."

"So you want kids?"

"I come from a big family, so, yeah, I've always wanted one of my own," he said, as if there were nothing unusual about it.

Is this guy for real? Franny wondered. She felt her pulse quicken. It was all she could do to remind herself that this was *business*, not a date.

After dinner they strolled along Park Avenue, where the daffodils and tulips along the meridian had given way to bright clusters of impatiens. When Keith gave her his arm as they were crossing the street, it seemed only natural that she hang on to it once they'd reached the curb.

At his hotel, she found herself reluctant to part from him. Only the thought of tomorrow's meeting kept her from taking him up on it when he suggested they continue their conversation in the bar. If she didn't get to bed soon, she told him, she'd be no good the next day. Even so, back at her apartment, she had trouble getting to sleep. In place of the tiredness that dragged at her these days, she felt energized, her mind playing over every detail of the evening with Keith. Had she only imagined that he seemed interested in her, too? And what if he were? It would be unprofessional of her to date one of her authors. Awkward, too, considering her present condition. Not to mention the fact that he lived four thousand miles away. Nonetheless, when she at last drifted off, she was counting frequent-flier miles instead of sheep.

The meeting the following morning went well. Everyone was as charmed by Keith as she had been. They discussed a marketing plan, which would include a book tour and major media appearances. The fact that Keith was an old hand at TV wasn't lost on Gretchen Hensler, the marketing director, who was like a kid with a new toy. At lunch, she sat next to him, adopting a proprietary air that caused him and Franny, at one point, to exchange a knowing smile. She'd be even more excited, Franny thought, when Keith revealed the juicy tidbit he was keeping mum about until Stevie gave him the green light.

He and Franny had dinner again that night, at a little bistro near his hotel, where this time he insisted on treating her. Afterward, back at the hotel, he invited her up to his room for a nightcap. Franny knew what she was letting herself in for, unless she'd misread the signals, and as she rode up with him in the elevator, she felt something rising in her as well. Something she hadn't felt in a long time: hope.

She was standing at the picture window in his room, taking in the nighttime view of Manhattan twinkling with a million lights, a view she never tired of however long she'd lived in this city—it represented everything she'd sought to achieve through the years, everything she'd longed for living in the cramped Brooklyn apartment she'd shared with her mother and Bobby—when Keith came up behind her, circling her with his arms. She could see his ghost image superimposed against hers in the darkened glass. Her breath stopped and for a moment she couldn't move, then she turned slowly to face him. His eyes were shining with the city's reflected glow as he leaned in to kiss her gently on the lips.

"I've been wanting to do that all night," he murmured in her ear.

"That makes two of us." She put her arms around his neck and leaned into him, kissing him back.

Before she knew it, they were on the bed, limbs tangled together, feverishly exploring each other with their hands and mouths. It was Keith who drew back first, his face flushed and his shirt untucked. "I hope you don't think all I'm after is a one-night stand," he croaked.

"Fat chance. Don't forget, I still have a fifteen percent stake in you," she quipped. "That is, if you still want me as your agent."

"I wouldn't have it any other way." He wrapped a hank of her hair around his finger, using it to draw her in close. "The only question is whether or not we should expand on that theme."

"What exactly did you have in mind?" Franny's heart was wobbling strangely in her chest and she felt weak all over.

"How would you feel about a bicoastal relationship?" His mouth curved in a seductive little smile.

"I wouldn't know," she replied cautiously. "I've never been in one before."

"I'm making another trip out next month. I'd like to see you again."

"You're really serious about this?" She drew back to eye him askance. In her experience, when a guy seemed too good to be true, it was usually the case.

"Why should it came as a surprise?"

"For one thing, I'm pregnant."

"You thought I was just buttering you up when I said I love kids?" He nuzzled her neck, drawing little circles on her earlobe with the tip of his tongue.

"I'll bet you say that to all the ladies."

"Only the ones with a bun in the oven."

"You really know how to sweet-talk a girl," she said with a laugh.

"I mean it." His tone turned serious. "I want to see you again."

Franny hesitated a moment before replying. Not because she had reservations. She was merely reflecting on the irony of this happening after she'd pretty much given up hope of ever meeting anyone. Why now, when she'd be shopping for maternity clothes, not sexy lingerie?

But if Keith was game, then so was she.

Breaking into a grin, she said, "You're on, mister."

Chapter Six

Don't look so tense." Jay nudged Emerson playfully with his elbow. "It's a perfume launch, not an inaugural ball."

"I look tense?" The thought made Emerson even more anxious. This wasn't just *any* perfume launch. It was for one of Jay's biggest accounts.

"A little," he said, in a way that meant a lot.

"What I want to know is why *you're* so relaxed." She brushed a piece of lint from his lapel.

He grinned. "Easy. I hired you to do all the worrying for me."

"Well, at least you know you're getting your money's worth."

She did a quick survey of the restaurant. Le Epiphinie's gilded rotunda and Swarovski crystal chandelier glittered, and posters of the Sheer ad mounted on foam core, showing a model dressed in the barest shimmer of silk and holding a finger to her lips, with the caption, SHEER . . . I WON'T TELL, IF YOU DON'T, were everywhere she looked. On the flat-screen TV over the bar, the Sheer TV commercial ran on a continuous loop, and in the dining area waiters circulated trays of drinks and canapés while models passed out perfume samples.

The place was packed, with more people arriving every minute. Better yet, the press was here in force. Emerson had made sure of that by inviting names worthy of being mentioned in Page Six, prevailing on the ones with whom she had personal relationships.

Across the room, she spotted Louisa Upchurch chatting with Dana Greenway, the buyer from Bergdorf's. Emerson had known Louisa since she was a little girl, back when Marjorie had belonged to the Cosmopolitan Club. Yet the woman who used to fawn all over her mother at club functions and constantly seek out her advice, about everything from fashion to hired help, had stopped calling and visiting once word of Marjorie's reduced circumstances had gotten around. It had been years since Marjorie had seen or heard from her or any of her other so-called friends, except for the handful who'd paid duty calls when she'd first become ill. Her only visitors these days were the few old college friends she'd kept up with, and only on the rare occasions when they were in town.

"I should go see how Vivienne's doing," Jay said, eyeing his wife, across the room.

From the crowd of fashionistas gathered around her, though, it didn't appear Vivienne was in need of rescuing. She was the belle of the ball in a short gold halter dress with a plunging neckline that showed off her gloriously rounded figure. Even pregnant, she managed to make the working models around her look gawky by comparison.

As Jay made his way toward her, tall and handsome in his Armani suit, the buzz around him seemed to heighten, heads turning his way and people leaning in to each other to whisper, wearing admiring looks. He was the golden boy of the evening, the genius behind it all. Yet the one person who should have been most attentive was oblivious. But Vivienne had always been that way, Emerson reminded herself. *She* was used to being the center of attention. Even when other women flirted with Jay, she scarcely took notice. Emerson didn't doubt she loved him, but it was a distracted kind of love.

Franny appeared at Emerson's side just then, slightly out of breath from having battled her way through the crush by the entrance. "Sorry I'm late. I couldn't find anything to wear." She lifted her blouse to show off the fly on her black velvet jeans, held together with a large safety pin. "At this rate, in a few more weeks I won't even be able to fit into my fat clothes."

"Remember how big I was with Ainsley?" Emerson recalled. "I felt like the white whale in *Moby-Dick*."

"The most elegant whale on Park Avenue," Franny assured her, turning to scan the crowd. "Have you seen Jay?"

"He was here a minute ago," Emerson said as her gaze strayed to the TV screen over the bar, on which a naked woman was climbing out of bed, wrapped only in a satin bedsheet. "What do you think of his ad? Is that sexy, or what?"

"It's been so long since I had sex, I wouldn't know," Franny said with a mock sigh.

"What about your hottie in L.A.?" Emerson arched a brow.

Franny broke into a grin. "We're breaking bicoastal records for dirty e-mails."

"When do you see him again?"

"He's flying out in a couple of weeks."

Emerson wondered if Jay had been apprised of this new development and how he'd feel about another man's raising his child, if things got serious between Keith and Franny. She started to ask about it, but just then she spotted Ivana Trump, making an entrance worthy of Mae West, swathed in blond mink that matched her signature upsweep. Excusing herself, Emerson quickly headed off in that direction.

Once she'd made certain that Ivana had been photographed with all the VIPs, she stopped to have a word with her assistant, Julie, stationed near the entrance checking names against the guest list as latecomers trickled in. Most of the A-listers who'd RSVPed had arrived, Emerson was pleased to note, and for the first time all evening, she allowed herself to relax a bit. She'd done her job. Now Jay could simply bask in the glow of his success.

She made it through the rest of the evening on autopilot. No one would have guessed her mind was elsewhere. She chatted with the right people, and made certain no photo op was missed. She sang Jay's praises to the Jacques-Bênoit execs (though it was obvious she was preaching to the converted). Finally, when she was satisfied that everything was under control, she slipped away as the party was winding down, leaving Julie to take care of any last little things that needed to be attended to.

Outside, she hailed a taxi. As the cab slalomed its way up Park Avenue toward her mother's, she told herself she was merely being a good daughter, but she knew it was just an excuse. The fact was, she'd been dropping by a lot lately, often at night when she was reasonably sure her mother was asleep and she'd have Reggie all to herself. They'd sit and talk, and she'd tell him about her day while sipping the one whiskey and soda she allowed herself at the end of a hard night's work, and he in turn would fill her in on what was happening in school or recount some anecdote about Marjorie that made her seem more charmingly eccentric than difficult.

She just hoped her mother didn't become suspicious. Marjorie liked him well enough, but if she saw him as an obstacle to her goal of finding a suitable second husband for her daughter, he'd be gone as soon as she could think of an excuse to get rid of him. She still hadn't given up on the idea of Ed Stancliff upstairs as her future son-in-law. Emerson shuddered at the thought, pushing it aside to concentrate instead on the image of Reggie greeting her at the door when she arrived, his smile like a porch light left on, drawing her in from the dark.

"You know, I can't remember a time when I didn't think of parties as work." With a sigh, Emerson slipped off her high heels and propped her aching feet on the ottoman in front of her. "When I was growing up, it seemed like my mother was always entertaining. I spent my girlhood dodging wet glasses and funny uncles. And here I am all these years later, doing just that."

"At least you're getting paid for it," Reggie observed with a smile. He was seated on the sofa across the room, one arm hooked over the back in a way that outlined its muscled contours.

"True," she acknowledged, wincing as she massaged her instep. "Though I can think of easier ways to make a living."

"Would you choose differently, if you had to do it all over again?" he asked.

She settled back in her chair, thoughtfully sipping her drink. "Who knows? I used to like to sketch. Maybe I could've become an artist."

"Perhaps you'll have that satisfaction someday. When you see your daughter's paintings in a museum," he said, his smile broadening.

"Wouldn't that be something," she said, warming at the thought. They were in the small sitting room off the library, where the sound of their voices wouldn't disturb Marjorie, who was asleep. "Whatever she ends up doing, I want it to be the thing that makes her happiest."

He must have heard a note of wistfulness in her voice, for he asked, "And have *you* found such happiness?"

"Let's just say spin-doctoring is what I was born and bred to do."

She paused, wondering whether or not to go on. In past conversations, she'd only alluded to her childhood. But the hour was late, and the whiskey and soda, along with Reggie's soothing presence, had loosened her tongue. She found herself explaining, "I was brought up to believe I'd been born with a silver spoon in my mouth. It wasn't until after my dad died that I found out we were broke. Oh, sure there was always money for a new dress or a chair at some society fund-raiser, but not enough to pay the bills or even to tip the doormen at Christmas-time." She felt the old shame well up in her even now, recalling the times she'd had to look the other way to avoid meeting Nacario's eyes. Though he'd never treated Marjorie any less courteously from those who tipped him handsomely.

Reggie nodded, taking it all in with a thoughtful expression. "Where I come from, being poor is nothing to hide," he said. "Not that you could keep your neighbors from knowing just how many goats you had or how good your crop was that year," he added, with a chuckle.

"Believe me, we'd have been better off if the only thing we'd had to worry about was goats." She indulged in a laugh, feeling lighter somehow.

With her ex-husband she'd been a chameleon, weaving herself into the fabric of Brigg's life as she had into her mother's as a child, only belatedly waking up to the realization that he loved her for precisely that reason: because she was a reflection of him. But with Reggie, there was no pretense; she could just be herself. She found that more reassuring somehow than all of Briggs's wealth.

She regarded him now, the way the room's shadows brought out the slanting angles of his cheekbones and the way the lamplight on his skin made it gleam like polished teak. She wished there was some way of closing the gap between them. She wanted to feel him beside her, the heat of his body pressed up against hers. The thought caused her cheeks to warm and she had to avert her gaze so he wouldn't guess what was on her mind.

They talked about other things, Reggie making her forget her troubles with his tales about his own family and the conflicts that occasionally arose from too many people all under one roof—sisters and brothers, aunts and uncles and cousins, trooping in and out all day, bringing eggs from their hens, a basket of freshly dug yams, or the latest tidbit of gossip.

"How often do you get to see them?" Emerson asked.

"Not often enough to suit my mother. She is busy making plans for when I am home for good," he said, with a bemused shake of his head. "She even has a wife picked out for me."

Emerson felt a little inner jolt. "Someone you know?"

He nodded. "My cousin's wife's sister. Her name is Patience."

"And is she? Patient, I mean." Emerson tried to make light of it, but inside a lump of dread was forming.

He eyed her uncomprehendingly for a moment. Then understanding sank in and his face relaxed in a smile. "It's not what you think. We e-mail each other, but we're just friends. My mother will be disappointed when she learns her intended daughter-in-law is secretly engaged to another man."

Emerson grinned, a little too broadly. "She and my mom have something in common." She told him about Marjorie's trying to fix her up with Ed Stancliffe. "She's determined to see me remarried before she . . ." She caught herself, and went on, "While she's still around to make sure it's someone who won't get me banished from the *Social Register*." Reggie didn't know what that was, so she explained, blushing a little, about the directory that was updated every year, with all the names of the socially prominent, and how when a blue blood married outside the ranks, he or she was automatically deleted. She was quick to add, "It's pure nonsense, of course. I never took it seriously."

"It's the same everywhere," he said with a shrug. "Even in my village, it's all about who your grandfather and great-grandfather were."

"My mother used to love to boast about her son-in-law," she said. "Me? I didn't give a damn that he could trace his family all the way back to the *Mayflower*. Looking back, I think the main reason I married Briggs was to get away from my mother."

"Did it work?" he asked with one eyebrow cocked, as if he already knew the answer.

"You can see for yourself." She sighed, gesturing around her. "Just when I think I've gained some ground, she finds a way to reel me back in again." She dropped her gaze, embarrassed by the admission. "I guess that makes me sound pretty weak."

"Strength often lies in one's ability to bend," he said softly.

She looked up at him, smiling a little. "How did you get to be so smart?"

"From listening to *my* mother." He held her gaze, his green-gold eyes bright amid the shadows. "So this Mr. Stancliffe, is there any hope for him?" He cast a meaningful glance up at the ceiling.

Emerson laughed. "Not as long as I have any say in it." Was it her imagination that Reggie looked relieved? "Anyway, I'm not sure I want to get married again. Divorce has a way of curing you of your ideals."

"Perhaps it is only that you haven't met the right person," he said in a quiet voice, giving her a look that was like a current of electricity crackling between them.

She saw now, in his frank gaze, that whatever she was feeling, Reggie was feeling it, too. The knowledge brought a sudden lick of flame from the glowing coal at her center.

Not knowing how to handle it—she'd never been in a situation quite like this—she turned her gaze to the window, looking out at the traffic backed up along Park Avenue, like strings of Christmas lights. After a moment she heard the creak of footsteps and when she looked up, Reggie was standing over her. He smiled and held out his hand, and in that instant he might have been asking her to dance. The heat in her belly bloomed, spreading through her, and in some distant part of her mind she could almost hear the music. But then she realized he was only offering to freshen her drink.

"You don't have to wait on me," she said somewhat sharply, not needing any reminders of who paid his salary. "Anyway, it's late, I should be going." She glanced at her watch, astonished to see that it was half-past midnight.

The whiskey must have gone to her head for she wobbled a little as she hauled herself to her feet, prompting Reggie to catch hold of her elbow, to steady her. Their eyes met again, and for a long moment they remained locked in that stance, neither of them moving. The top button of his short-sleeved shirt was undone, and she could see a pulse beating steadily in the hollow at the base of his throat. Then slowly, ever so slowly, he brought his hand to her cheek, letting it rest there a moment before bending his head to kiss her.

Emerson closed her eyes and gave in to the swirl of sensation brought on by the pressure of his lips against hers. They were soft and full, gentle yet insistent. In response, she wound her arms around his neck, tilting her head back and parting her lips as the kiss deepened.

"Jesus," she breathed, when they finally came up for air.

"I'm afraid Jesus had very little to do with it." Reggie gave a low, throaty chuckle.

In a shaky voice, she asked, "So what now?"

He drew her close, whispering into her hair, "That's up to you."

The thought of Marjorie loomed. If she let this go any further, there would be hell to pay. It might even push her mother into an early grave. *Can I live with that?* Emerson wondered.

At the same time, she knew that if she were to give in to her mother yet again, she'd spend the rest of her life regretting it.

She couldn't let that happen. She'd sacrificed too much as it was.

She took Reggie's hand and led him over to the sofa, where they sank down, arms twined about each other. She brought his hand to her mouth, kissing its upturned palm, before guiding it to her breast. Slowly, he unbuttoned her blouse, each button a small seduction in itself. She moaned softly in her throat, sensations she hadn't felt in a long, long time dancing like sparks beneath the shell of ice she'd built around herself, thawing it in warm trickles.

Lost in the rapture, she felt as if she were being rudely awakened from a dream when she heard Marjorie's voice call peevishly from down the hall, "Reggie! *Reggie!* Where are you?"

They both leaped up, hastily rearranging their clothing. Emerson put a finger to her lips, signaling to Reggie to stay quiet—her mother didn't have to know she was here. He nodded in understanding, giving her one last lingering look before turning away and stepping out of the room.

Emerson waited another minute, and when she was sure the coast was clear, she snatched up her high heels, holding them in one hand as she padded out into the hall. *The story of my life. Thirty-six years old and still tiptoeing around my mother*, she thought, disgusted with herself, as moments later she slipped out the front door, easing it shut behind her.

In the days to come, Emerson thought of little else but Reggie. Over and over, she mentally replayed their interlude, and in her imagination they didn't stop at kissing. Fearful of where it would lead, she began restricting her visits to daylight hours. Not that it kept her from mooning over him like a lovesick teenager.

After a week, she'd had enough and resolved to settle it once and for all. She'd heard enough about Reggie's classes at school to have some idea of his schedule, and one blustery day, when she was between appointments, she tracked him down at NYU. No way was she going to have this conversation where her mother might overhear.

She spotted him as he was strolling out of the lecture hall where his advanced biology class was held. He was with several other classmates, all of them talking animatedly among themselves. In his snug-fitting jeans and button-down shirt, amid the younger students with their shapeless clothing and untamed hair, sprouting iPod wires from their ears, he might have been one of the professors. But while they appeared to defer to him, they also seemed to accept him as one of their own. One in particular, a pretty, petite girl with big brown eyes and riotous black hair, was hanging on his every word, clearly fascinated . . . or perhaps enamored.

Emerson felt a dart of envy. At her mother's, it was easy to fool herself into thinking it was just the two of them in their own little bubble apart from the rest of the world, but now she was reminded that Reggie had a life apart from her and Marjorie—one in which he was surrounded by fresh-faced young women unencumbered by all of her baggage.

He caught sight of her and broke into a grin, jogging over to where she stood. He looked surprised to see her, asking in his deep, melodic voice, "Is everything all right?"

"Fine," she said. "Listen, do you have a minute?"

"My next class isn't for another hour," he said.

"I'm sorry to ambush you like this," she said as they strolled in the direction of Washington Square. Amid the swirl of students barreling past with their backpacks, she was reminded of when she'd been a student at Princeton. It seemed like a hundred years ago.

"Any visit from you is a welcome one," he assured her. There was nothing in his face to indicate anything other than delight.

"It's just that I didn't want to have this conversation at my mother's," she explained.

He darted her an odd look. "Is this about the other night?"

She came to an abrupt standstill, feeling herself warm under his solemn gaze. "Listen, I just wanted you to know, I . . . I don't regret what happened. But I think we should cool it. For now. This isn't such a good time."

"Because of your mother?"

"Yes."

He nodded, and said softly, "I see."

"*Do* you?" she asked, pleading with him almost.

"I think so."

"Believe me, this isn't how I want it to be. It's just . . ." Emerson gave a defeated sigh, her shoulders drooping. "She's so sick and it would only upset her. Not that she doesn't think highly of you," she hastened to add. "It's just that she . . . well, you know how it is."

"It is your decision, of course," he said, but in his sea-water eyes that contrasted so vividly with his dark skin, she read an entirely different message.

"It's not, really. It's just how it is," she said weakly.

He shrugged again, as if the distinction were lost on him. "That is one way of looking at it."

"What other way is there?"

"Perhaps you are giving her too much power."

She thought of all the sacrifices she'd made for Marjorie, and knew that what he was saying was true. She had created a monster. One that would eventually devour her. At the same time she felt helpless to change it. A bit defensively, she replied, "I think I know my mother better than you do."

"But does she know *you*? Does she know what's in your heart?"

Emerson fell silent. His words had pierced her to the core. *No, she doesn't know me,* she answered silently. If Marjorie were privy to what was in her heart right now, she'd be horrified.

When they reached Washington Square, with its magnificent arch that graced the Fifth Avenue entrance, Emerson said, "I should get back to work." Even so, she lingered, reluctant to leave him. "You'll call me if you need anything?"

He got the message, that she would go on curtailing her evening visits, and nodded, wearing a grave look. "Of course."

"When you see my mother, tell her . . ." *What? That she's responsible for ruining my life?* "I'll be by on Saturday."

Emerson felt almost ill. There was a heaviness in her chest and her throat was tight, as if she were coming down with something. When Reggie drew her to him, not in a lover's embrace, but as if she were a patient in need of ministering, she felt too weak to protest.

She made no move to pull away until the sound of a horn honking jolted her back into reality. But before she could step back, he inclined his head toward her, his mouth closing over hers in the gentlest of kisses. A kiss more volatile, in its own way, than if he'd thrown her to the ground in a fit of passion. For as she was hurrying away in search of a cab, she knew that if her mission in coming here today had been to nip this in the bud, she'd not only failed miserably but managed to become even more deeply enmeshed.

Chapter Seven

The morning meeting had begun with the managing producer, Jules Hanratty, taking them through the breaking news of the day—a car crash in Glendale that had resulted in at least one confirmed fatality, flooding in Covina and a wildfire in Simi Valley, a marine killed by a suicide bomber in Iraq. Business as usual, in other words.

If they didn't inure themselves to the onslaught of bloodshed and mayhem that flowed in each day, Stevie knew, they'd end up burning out, or worse, getting an ulcer. So she sat blank-faced like everyone else, nibbling on a doughnut, as she listened to Jules fill them in on the gang shooting in Compton that had resulted in one death and two arrests.

Jules was wrapping it up when the news director, Jerry Fine, interjected, "What about the rash of carjackings in Huntington Park? We should do a story on that." A former naval officer, with a square jaw and close-cropped gray hair, Jerry liked to boast that he ran a tight ship. Only Stevie knew what a pussycat he was underneath. "Give it to Lisa," he said, referring to Lisa Blankenship, who was currently filling in as a coanchor for the five o'clock.

There was some discussion of the body that had been found in a Dumpster on Melrose, the victim of an apparent overdose, though homicide hadn't been ruled out. "I have a call into the ME's office," said Liv Henry. "The toxin screens weren't available last time I checked." An elongated exclamation point of a woman capped with frizzy brown hair, she sat with one bony leg crossed over the other, her foot jiggling compulsively as she spoke. The joke in the newsroom was that Liv didn't just drink coffee, she was on an IV drip.

They moved on to the flooding in Covina. "I think the story is storm fatigue. Sewers are screwed up. Water can't drop to normal levels," said Stan Lowry, who produced the weather segments. He took a bite out of his doughnut, sending a shower of crumbs down the front of his shirt.

Bubbly, blond Megan Johnstone, the lifestyles producer, suggested doing a piece on the gypsy look for her next fashion segment, and was given a sharp reminder by Liv not to use the word "gypsy"; it might cause offense.

Stevie, the lone reporter of the bunch, allowed to sit in on these meetings only because technically she was listed as the entertainment producer, was the last to put in her two cents. Throughout the meeting she'd been mulling over the ethical bind she was in. The only one who knew about her and Grant was Jerry, whom she'd sworn to secrecy. He was her "rabbi" at KNLA and understood the delicate nature of the position she was in; he was prepared to sit tight until the time was right for her to come forward. But Stevie couldn't lose sight of the fact that right now there was no bigger story than Lauren Rose's Lazarus-like rise from near death. Every day brought new tabloid headlines, with public interest showing no sign of waning. If Stevie didn't act soon, one of the rival stations would get wind of her bombshell and beat KNLA to the punch.

And now there was an added wrinkle.

"Diane Sawyer's got an exclusive with Lauren Rose," she announced. She'd just gotten it from a pal in the ABC newsroom.

"I didn't know she could even speak," commented Megan.

"Apparently so," said Stevie. Lauren's doctors had been tight-lipped about her progress, so most of what was in the news was hearsay and speculation. "They're taping it at the rehab center."

"Diane wouldn't be doing it if she didn't have the goods," interjected Jules.

"I wonder if the DA's involved," said Stan, idly brushing crumbs from the front of his shirt.

Stevie felt a little inner shudder at the thought. She kept her gaze on the tabletop in front of her, covered in a graffiti-like overlay of old coffee rings and cigarette burns, from the days when smoking was still allowed in the building. "Nobody knows anything yet," she said, struggling to keep her voice neutral. "We shouldn't jump to conclusions."

"Come on, everyone knows the guy's guilty as sin," scoffed Casey Beltran, who ran the assignment desk. Meaning Grant, of course.

Heat climbed into Stevie's cheeks. She couldn't defend Grant without raising suspicion, so she said nothing. Also, there was still that tiny grain of doubt: What if he *was* guilty?

She was grateful when Jerry intervened. "In case you haven't heard, there's such a thing as innocent until proven guilty in this country," he said pointedly to Stan. "Let's not forget the man was never even charged."

"Only because the lone eyewitness in the case couldn't communicate. Until now." Liv looked up from jotting something on her legal pad, wearing an ominous look.

"*If* she has something to say, we'll know soon enough. Until then, let's keep speculation to a minimum," Jerry shot back, darting Stevie a veiled look.

The meeting adjourned and minutes later Stevie was back in her pod, banging out copy for the piece she was doing on the multimillion-dollar business of marketing dead celebrities. But she couldn't stop thinking about Grant and what the ABC interview might mean for him. The more she got to know him, the harder it was to imagine him as a menace to society. But there was no question that if he *had* intentionally gone after Lauren, he'd shot to kill. No one put a bullet through someone's head with the idea of merely wounding the person.

If only she could talk to Ryan about it, this whole thing would be easier. He'd help her sort through the mixed emotions she was feeling and advise her on what to do. But she hadn't seen or spoken to him in weeks, and if she were to phone him now, it would only make it that much harder. With the pain of missing him a constant ache, she didn't need any reminding that he was no longer in her life.

She blinked back tears, pushing the thought of Ryan from her mind as she bent once more to her task. After she'd cut and filed her piece and done the noon broadcast, she was out the door. Her day had started at five A.M. and she was beat, but it wasn't over yet. Earlier in the week she'd volunteered to help her mother paint her bedroom and she couldn't back out at this late date, so instead of to the soft couch and stack of magazines that waited for her at home she headed to Nancy's.

Half an hour later she was pulling into the driveway behind her mother's old Ford pickup, piled with cartons of art supplies that Nancy hadn't yet gotten around to unloading. Nancy was in the kitchen peeling a cucumber when Stevie walked in.

"Hi, honey. I thought we'd have some lunch first," she said, looking up to smile at Stevie.

"You didn't have to do that, Mom." Stevie dropped a kiss on her mother's check. It looked like she'd gone to a fair bit of trouble. There was a quiche cooling on the counter along with a loaf of freshly baked bread. "I could have picked up something on the way."

"If you're going to help me paint, the least I can do is feed you. Will you hand me that?" Nancy used the peeler in her hand to indicate the knife on the counter near Stevie. "I hope you're hungry. I made enough to feed the entire neighborhood."

"I'm sure the neighbors will appreciate it," Stevie said dryly, knowing that whatever wasn't eaten would be wrapped up and delivered to someone down the road. The close-knit community of potters, weavers, and glassblowers had become a surrogate family of sorts, and they depended on each other for everything from candles and batteries during power outages to, twice, battling flames to save each other's houses when wildfires swept down from the surrounding hills.

"Why don't you set the table while I finish making the salad. Everything else is ready." Nancy waved distractedly toward the big oak table in the sunny dining nook. The table had been salvaged from an old garment factory that was being torn down, and Nancy had refinished it herself, leaving its dings and scars, which she said gave it character.

Stevie murmured in assent, but made no move toward the cupboard where the dishes were kept. Instead, she slid onto a bar stool and leaned forward to prop her elbows on the counter, watching her mother begin slicing the cucumber she'd peeled. This was what she remembered best about her childhood: hanging out in the kitchen with her mother after school. When Nancy wasn't in her studio, she always had something cooking. In summer, she'd make things with the vegetables and fruit from her garden out in back. At any given moment there were half a dozen jars containing sprouts in various stages of growth on the sill. The air always smelled of something baking or ripening or bubbling on the stove.

The years they'd lived in the Valley, Stevie had had to contend with other kids at school who'd made fun of her "hippie" clothes and her "lesbo" friend. (Sukie Foster wasn't a lesbian, but she'd sported a tattoo on one arm and dyed her hair a different color every week.) The only thing that had gotten her through those difficult years was having a safe place to retreat to at the end of each day. If Nancy had occasionally embarrassed her by showing up for parent-teacher conferences in clay-spattered overalls and rattling around town in their old VW Bug emblazoned with left-wing and pro-feminist stickers, her unconditional love and the haven she'd provided had more than made up for it.

Try as she might, Stevie couldn't picture her mother as the aimless drifter she'd once been. "Tell me about the night you and Grant . . . um, you know," Stevie found herself saying now. "I still don't know the whole story."

Nancy paused in the midst of her slicing, color rising in her cheeks. "There's not much to tell."

"You met at a concert, right?" Stevie prompted.

Nancy used the back of her wrist to brush aside a wisp of the curly reddish hair that was always trailing down in her eyes, hair once a rich auburn that had dulled to the color of old pennies. She was gazing sightlessly ahead, wearing a distant look. "They were playing the Fillmore that night, Astral Plane and Pink Floyd and some other bands you probably never heard of," she began at last, in a soft, almost girlish voice. "My friend Phoebe knew some guy who traded us a pair of tickets for some hash." She hesitated, darting Stevie a questioning look, as if to ask, *Are you sure you want to hear this?*

"Go on," Stevie urged.

"The place was mobbed when we got there. You could hardly

move," Nancy continued, almost as if talking to herself. "When Astral Plane started to play, everyone went wild. Grant . . . it was like he was on fire, burning up the stage. You couldn't even see his hands, his fingers were flying so fast over those strings." Her lips curved in a small, remembering smile. "That's when he spotted me. I was right up front, just below the stage, and for a second our eyes met. At first, I thought maybe I'd imagined it, but after the set one of the roadies came over and asked if I wanted to go backstage and meet him."

"What was he like?" Stevie asked, eager to know more.

Nancy brought her gaze back to Stevie, and the wild child she'd been faded into the calm, clean-scrubbed face of Stevie's mother. "Nice, polite," she said, with a shrug. "Just a guy from Omaha. Nothing like he was onstage. To be honest, I don't know that I would have gone back to his hotel with him if he hadn't been who he was." She gave a rueful smile, reaching across the counter to briefly lay a hand against Stevie's cheek. "But I'm glad I did because look what came out of it."

"Yeah, a pain-in-the-ass daughter who can't leave well enough alone," Stevie quipped, her voice gruff with emotion.

"Speaking of which, are you making any headway?" Nancy asked, referring to the informal investigation Stevie had been conducting.

"I spoke with the maid," she reported as she slid off the stool and headed over to the cupboard to grab some plates. She'd gotten the number from Keith. Luce Velasquez had been less than forthcoming at first, partly due to the fact that she didn't speak English all that well, but she'd opened up some when Stevie tried communicating in her rusty high school Spanish. "She told me the same thing she told the police, that she heard the shot, but by the time she ran downstairs the gun was on the floor next to Lauren and Grant was half out of his mind with hysteria. Which means either he's a really good actor or it happened just like he said. Frankly, at this point, I don't know what to believe."

"Is it so important that you know?" Nancy asked.

Stevie paused on her way to the table, turning to face her mother. "Whether or not my father's capable of murdering someone? Yeah, it does matter. It matters a lot."

Nancy regarded her thoughtfully, a mixture of emotions playing over her delicate-featured face, as if her brief foray into the past had stirred up more than just old memories.

"The truth isn't always what it's cracked up to be," she said at last, with the air of someone who'd faced some hard truths of her own.

The night the Diane Sawyer interview finally aired on *Prime Time Live*, after a week of tantalizing promos, Stevie was so keyed up she could hardly sit still. The week before she'd tapped all her sources at the network, trying to get a bead on what might be in store. But ABC was buttoned down tighter than the Pentagon. There wasn't so much as a drip, much less a leak. No one, maybe not even Diane herself, knew what Lauren was going to say.

The intro was agonizingly long, and Stevie fidgeted on the living room floor where she sat, the plate of food she'd earlier put in the oven to warm forgotten. Diane was her usual cool, studiedly empathetic self as she provided the back story for the three people on the planet who didn't already know it. It was accompanied by grainy footage of Grant in concert with Astral Plane and of him being interviewed at a long-ago press conference. There were photos and video clips of Lauren Rose as well, growing up in Michigan and as an aspiring young actress, along with a clip from a sitcom pilot that had never aired, in which she'd had a bit part. It was followed by B-roll footage of Grant's estate, shot from outside the gates, looking like a medieval fortress, high up on a hill partially screened by tall trees. Only Stevie and a handful of others were privy to what went on behind those gates, and at the moment she wasn't too sure how much even she knew.

Diane talked about the mystery that had shrouded the near fatal shooting from the beginning. The only thing they knew for certain was that Grant and Lauren had at one time been romantically linked. The extent of which was unknown, but it was well established that she'd been an overnight visitor at the mansion on numerous occasions.

After the commericial break, Lauren was shown working with her physical therapists at the rehab center where she'd been holed up for the past six months. It was the first time Stevie, or anyone, had seen anything more than old photos and footage, and she was struck by how altered Lauren was, almost unrecognizable from the pretty, vivacious young actress she'd been. Twelve years in a coma had left her wasted, the muscles in her legs so atrophied she was able to take only a few, wobbly steps at a time. Yet her face was oddly unlined, that of a very old baby. Had it not been for her once lustrous chestnut mane gone gray and cut short in a utilitarian bob, it might have seemed that time had passed her by while she slept. Only her pale aqua eyes were the same; they gazed with disturbing intensity from the hollows of her face.

The camera moved in for a close-up, and Stevie felt herself tense. What secrets lay behind those eyes? What revelations about to unfold? As Lauren sat facing Diane in the rehab center's lounge, Diane gently led her down that path, Lauren answering each question slowly and haltingly, like someone learning to talk again after a stroke, her speech slurred. Then, at last, it came: the money question.

"There's been a lot of talk about what really happened that night." Diane spoke in a hushed, confidential voice, leaning forward slightly in her chair. "Many people have a hard time believing it was an accident, as Grant claims. They seem pretty convinced he tried to kill you. What would you say to those people?"

A tight shot of Lauren showed her frowning, as if she was trying to recollect, or was perhaps haunted by the memory. Stevie was sweating now, almost as if it were *her* in the hot seat. Then, in her halting voice, Lauren began, "What I remember about that night . . ."

Summer

O gather me the rose, the rose,
While yet in flower we find it,
For summer smiles, but summer goes,
And winter waits behind it.

For with the dream foregone, foregone,
The deed foreborn forever,
The worm Regret will canker on,
And time will turn him never.

So were it well to love, my love,
And cheat of any laughter
The fate beneath us, and above,
The dark before and after.

The myrtle and the rose, the rose,
The sunshine and the swallow,
The dream that comes, the wish that goes
The memories that follow!

—WILLIAM ERNEST HENLEY

Chapter Eight

There's a lot of interest in this one, Myron." Franny, in her office on the twenty-eighth floor of the William Morris agency, paced back and forth in front of her desk, the phone to her ear. "I'm only giving you first crack because I think you guys would do the best job with it."

Myron Lefkowitz, her favorite editor at Random House, chuckled at the other end of the line. "What, you think I don't know you'd drop me like a hot potato if you got a better offer?"

"So make me an offer I can't refuse."

"First novels don't sell," said Myron.

"It could be the next *Da Vinci Code*."

"From your lips to God's ear."

"When was the last time a manuscript kept you up half the night?"

"It's good. I'm not saying it's not good. But a first-time author?

You and I both know it's a crap shoot." Myron wanted it; she could smell it. But he was being canny.

"There's always room for that one breakout book," she reminded him.

"I don't like to put all my money on one horse."

"Myron, I'm telling you, if you pass this up, you'll regret it."

"Okay, here's what I'll do. Three-fifty, and that includes foreign. Believe me, you won't get a better offer."

"Four hundred," she countered. "We keep foreign, you take book club and audio."

They went back and forth for a while longer, hammering out a deal that would be weeks in contract negotiations before it was finalized. As soon as she got off the phone, she called the author to give him the good news. An art history professor at William and Mary, Terry Lockhart probably made less in one year than what it would cost just to print the book. He was speechless when she told him she had an offer on the table for a two-book deal, for close to a million dollars.

Her stomach was rumbling by the time she wrapped up the morning's business. These days she felt as if she were eating, not just for two, but for an entire regiment. Yet it didn't bother her a bit that she'd outgrown even her roomiest clothes. Never in a lifetime of despairing over every extra pound would she have thought she'd revel in being fat.

Franny realized that for the first time in her life she was truly happy. Oh, there had been moments here and there when she'd known a kind of contentment, but it never lasted very long. There was always some crisis at work or a bad breakup or a deal that fell through. But these days when she got up in the morning, she actually found herself looking forward to the day. She sang in the shower and walked with a bounce in her step.

Keith, of course, had more than a little to do with it. Her L.A.

hottie, as Emerson liked to call him, had become a fixture in her life, if only a long-distance one. She picked up the phone now to give him a call. It had been a couple of days, and she found herself missing him.

"Hey, you," she said, when he picked up. "This is your agent calling."

He chuckled. "So is this work-related?"

"Did you have something else in mind?"

"Hmmm . . . let's see. Depends on how kinky you want to get at the office."

"The last woman here to get propositioned filed a sexual harassment suit," she informed him.

"Uh-oh. Then I better keep my hands to myself."

"You'd need pretty long arms otherwise."

He heaved a mock sigh, as if bemoaning the miles between them. "Which reminds me, have you booked your flight yet?"

"I was going to do it today." She was flying out to visit him next month, but she'd been so busy at work and preoccupied with the baby the rest of the time, she hadn't had a free moment to call her travel agent. "I just hope you'll still recognize me when you see me."

"It's only been a few weeks." He'd flown out for a long weekend in June. "How much bigger could you be?" She pictured Keith at the other end, with his bare feet propped on his cluttered desk, wearing jeans and his faded Black Sabbath T-shirt.

"Let's just say pantyhose is no longer an option."

"That just means there'll be more of you to love."

They bantered back and forth a few minutes longer before a glance at her watch reminded her of the weekly staff meeting she'd be late for if she didn't hurry. "Gotta run," she told him. "I'll call you tonight. Are you going to be around?"

"Where else would I be? I have a slave-driver for an agent."

She grinned. "I'll tell her to cut you some slack."

"Miss you, babe."

"Me, too."

"It won't always be like this. One of these days, we won't have to take out second home loans to pay our phone bills." He spoke teasingly, but she caught an undercurrent of seriousness.

For several moments after she hung up, she sat lost in thought, the meeting forgotten. More and more lately their talk had been straying into the future tense. There was only one problem: If she and Keith were to get married, she'd have to be the one to relocate. His elderly parents, who lived nearby, depended on him too much for him to consider moving. Careerwise, she could swing it; she could transfer to the agency's Beverly Hills branch. But that still left Jay. He'd made it clear he wanted to be an active part of their child's life. How could she deprive him of that?

She hated, too, the thought of being so far away from him. It was bad enough that she'd hardly seen him since he'd taken on the Uruchima Motors account. If he wasn't working, he was rushing home to Vivienne or to a Lamaze class. Franny understood, of course. His wife and child *should* be his top priority, especially with Vivienne due any day. Still . . . Each milestone—the first time she heard the baby's heartbeat and felt it kick, her elation when she'd gotten the results of her amnio showing everything to be normal— she'd found herself wishing Jay were around so she could share it with him.

Franny shook off those thoughts and gathered up her notes for the meeting. She was heading out of her office when the phone rang. Her assistant, Robin, called after her, "Franny! It's Jay." From her tone it sounded urgent.

Franny raced back to her desk and snatched up the phone.

"I'm at the hospital. They just took Viv into surgery." Jay

sounded as if he were trying not to panic. The baby's heart rate had dropped suddenly, he explained, so they'd been forced to do a C-section.

"Hold tight. I'm on my way," she told him, slamming down the phone.

She was hurrying down the hall when she bumped into Hannah Moreland. Hannah was carrying a stack of bound galleys for one of her authors' books. "Hot off the press. Isn't it gorgeous?" she said, thrusting out the topmost one for Franny to see. Her smile faded as she took in Franny's expression. "Something wrong?"

"I won't know until later. Right now I have to get to the hospital," Franny told her, continuing on toward the elevator.

Hannah fell into step with her. "Isn't it a little soon for that?" She was Franny's closest friend at work, and had been the first in the office to know about Franny's pregnancy. Ever since, she'd played mother hen, sharing everything from tips on combating morning sickness to maternity clothes.

"It's Jay. His wife's in labor."

Hannah's heart-shaped face creased with concern. "Everything okay?"

Franny shook her head. "Apparently there's some sort of problem with the baby."

"I'm sure it'll turn out okay. It usually does," Hannah assured her, a touch too heartily. "Mattie came out feet first and we thought we were going lose him, but look at him now. Keep the faith." She patted Franny's arm as she took her leave, giving her a sympathetic look.

Franny could only pray Hannah was right, that she'd arrive at the hospital to find everything okay, little Stephan safe and sound in his mother's arms.

✼   ✼   ✼

Jay had never been so scared in all his life. Throughout Vivienne's pregnancy he'd joked about being an old hand at this. Growing up on a farm, he'd helped deliver calves on more than one occasion when an extra hand was required. But this was entirely different. This was his child. His son. Who at this very moment might be taking his first breath . . . or last. While Jay could do nothing but sit and fret.

Thank God Franny was on her way. She'd calm his fears and make this tightness in his chest go away, so he could breathe normally again.

Jay rose from his chair in the visitors' lounge and headed over to the vending machine for a cup of coffee he didn't want or need. Once more seated, he let the steaming Styrofoam cup warm his chilled fingers as he stared sightlessly ahead.

His thoughts strayed to his own father, who'd been a mostly silent presence in his life, simply treading the groove worn through the years from house to barn. Up each morning while it was still dark to feed and milk the cows, seven days a week, three hundred sixty-five days a year. Everett Gunderson was most often described as a man of few words, as if that were a virtue, but to Jay, growing up, his father's silences were a kind of torment. He could never guess what was behind that stern visage, and so he was forever filling in the blanks. Was he a disappointment to his dad? A son who'd preferred books to farming and who'd sought to escape at the earliest opportunity. His mother had told him that they'd wanted more children. If he'd had brothers or sisters, there would have been someone to inherit the farm. Someone with whom his father could talk about herd size and milk prices and rumen pH.

All Jay knew was that he didn't want to be the kind of dad his father had been. He wanted his son to grow up knowing he was loved. All he needed was to be given that chance. . . .

The first part of the labor had gone smoothly. How could things have gone so badly awry so quickly? One minute he was coaching

Vivienne with her breathing and massaging her lower back, and the next she was being whisked off to the OR. The doctors and nurses had done little to assuage his fears, they'd been too busy seeing to Vivienne. But from the concerned looks on their faces he knew it was serious.

Now he glanced up at the clock on the wall over the nurse's station, surprised to see that it was almost noon. Any moment now, he told himself, Dr. Leavitt would emerge from the OR to inform him that everything had gone well, and mother and son were both fine. He kept his mind focused on that thought as he stared vacantly ahead, the minutes ticking by.

Please, Franny, get here soon, he mouthed silently. If ever he'd needed his best friend, it was now.

Franny emerged from the elevator on the fifth floor and quickly located the visitors' lounge, where she found Jay hunched over a steaming Styrofoam cup, staring into space.

"Jay."

He jerked a little at the sound of her voice, as if startled, then he looked up at her, his face flooding with relief. He lowered the cup onto the floor and rose to greet her. Wordlessly, she put her arms around him. He clung to her for a long moment before drawing back. "She's still in surgery," he informed her in a voice scratchy with exhaustion.

"The baby?"

He shook his head. "No news yet." His shirt was creased, and his hair rumpled, as if from his nervously running his fingers through it. He looked as if he hadn't slept in days.

"What went wrong?" Franny asked gently.

Jay sank back down in his chair and she settled into the one beside it. "I wish I knew. She was doing great," he said, absently scrubbing his stubbled jaw with an open hand. "We got to the hospital around nine. The doctor said she still had a ways to go, but everything looked fine. Then all of a sudden it wasn't fine." He looked up at Franny with red-rimmed eyes, as if seeking reassurance.

"She'll be okay, you'll see. Don't forget what great shape she's in," she reminded him. "All that health food and yoga, the kid's going to come out doing handsprings."

Jay gave a hollow laugh. They'd teased Vivienne often enough about the extremes to which she'd gone. Though at the moment it seemed more ironic than amusing.

They sat in silence, Jay gripping Franny's hand tightly, until the doctor appeared, a heavyset, gray-haired man in scrubs. His expression was grim as he took Jay aside. From where she sat, Franny couldn't hear what he was saying, but she could tell from Jay's expression that the news wasn't good.

When Jay returned to her side, his face was drained of color and his eyes wore a strange, unfocused look. "Jay, what's wrong? Is Viv all right?" Franny cried, jumping to her feet.

"She's fine," he said, in an odd, flat voice.

She let out a breath. "Thank God."

He met her gaze then, and she saw a terrible anguish dawning in his face. "The baby . . . ." His voice cracked. "He didn't make it."

It was as if the floor had dropped from underneath her: Franny felt as if she were plummeting downward in midair. "Oh, God. Oh, Jay." She didn't know what to say. How did you console someone after such a loss?

He didn't rail or cry out. He just stood there, his chest rising and falling rapidly, as if he were having trouble getting enough oxygen. "I should go to her," he said at last, in that same dead voice.

Franny placed a hand on his arm. "I'll be here when you get back."

He gave her a small, grim smile, and with obvious effort straightened his shoulders and set off down the corridor.

*   *   *

Jay felt as if he were moving underwater. Nurses and orderlies floated by, the blatting of the PA system like the roaring of distant surf in his ears. *It's got to be a mistake*, he told himself. *The doctor got her mixed up with another patient. Happens all the time.* When he got there, Vivienne would be sitting up in bed with their baby in her arms.

But when he reached her side, she was stretched on her back on a gurney staring up at the ceiling, looking like a casualty of war, her face waxen with bruised-looking hollows under her eyes. He spoke her name softly, and she turned toward him.

"It's okay, Viv. I'm here." He took her hand, squeezing it gently.

"Jay." Her voice was a hoarse rasp. "I've been trying to tell them, but they won't listen. They think I'm crazy."

"Why would they think that?" he asked gently.

"I keep telling them it's all a mistake. There's nothing wrong with the baby," she went on, as if he hadn't spoken.

His heart constricted in his chest. "Viv . . ."

"*Please.*" Her fingers tightened around his. "You've got to tell them. They'll listen to you."

"Shhh. You should get some rest," he soothed, stroking her hair.

But she was too agitated. "I know he's okay. I *know* it." Her eyes shone with feverish brightness. "Jay. Please. Tell them to bring me my baby! *I want my baby!*"

Jay stood there not knowing what to say as he struggled to maintain a grip on his emotions. But she must have seen it on his face, the hopelessness, for she began to weep, tears running down her temples and into her tangled hair. He tried to comfort her, but she pushed him away, batting weakly at him with her fists. The sounds emerging from her throat weren't even human; they were those of a wounded animal. It was all Jay could do to remain strong, for her sake, and not collapse under the weight of his own grief.

"Viv . . . we'll get through this. We still have each other," he choked out.

"Bring me my baby!" she cried, her voice rising on a hysterical note. *"I want my baby!"* She struggled to get up off the gurney, lashing out at Jay when he tried to stop her.

A nurse came running, and together they managed to subdue her. Even after the resident on call had given her something to calm her, she continued to thrash and rail until the sedative took hold. "Please, Jay," she pleaded in a cracked whisper, even as her eyelids grew heavy.

"Shhh. Get some sleep," he whispered in her ear as he bent to kiss her on the cheek.

After Vivienne had drifted off at last, Jay looked up to find a pair of gentle brown eyes regarding him with compassion. The nurse, a tall, angular black woman with elaborately braided hair, reached over to touch his hand, asking gently, "Would you like to see him?"

Jay thought for a moment, then shook his head. "No. Not just yet." Later, when Vivienne was herself again, they'd face it together.

As he retreated into the hallway, he was recalling the look on his wife's face as she was being wheeled into surgery. Vivienne had appeared more stunned than scared: She'd done everything to ensure the perfect pregnancy. This wasn't supposed to be happening to *her.*

But all those measures, he realized now, were like amulets used to ward off evil spirits, merely serving to lull them into a false sense of security.

As he made his way back to the lounge, he could see Franny right where he'd left her, in her red dress that stood out like a beacon amid the drab hospital decor. He felt a wave of relief sweep over him. As if he were far out at sea, struggling to stay afloat, and had spied land.

*   *   *

"How's she holding up?" Franny asked, eyeing him with concern. Right now, it was Jay who looked close to the breaking point.

"They gave her something to help her sleep," he answered in a hollow voice.

"Do you need me to do anything?"

He shook his head. What was there to do? How could she possibly make this better? "This wasn't supposed to happen," he said.

"I know." Franny swallowed against the lump in her throat.

"She was fine. Everything was fine." He sank onto the sofa across from the vending machine, where a man about their age, possibly a new dad, was fumbling for change.

Franny sat down next to Jay, her throat tight with the tears she was holding back. "I lie awake at night sometimes, thinking of all the things that can go wrong, but you're never prepared for something like this."

"So what now?" He turned his ravaged gaze to her.

"You pick up the pieces. You move on."

"I'm not sure I can."

"I know it's hard to believe right now, but you will. Trust me." After her brother's death, so soon after losing her mother, Franny had felt equally bereft. "You still have Vivienne. And me. I'll be with you every step of the way." Just as Jay had been for her, after Bobby died.

"Where would I be without you?" His red-rimmed eyes were filled with such gratitude and affection, it was all she could do not to crumble then and there.

"Exactly where I'd be without you—lost," she said, reaching for his hand.

Chapter Nine

The saddest thing in the world had to be losing a child, Emerson thought, choking back tears as she watched the miniature coffin being lowered into the ground. If it were Ainsley . . .

She glanced over at Jay, flanked on either side by Vivienne and his parents. Over the past few days he seemed to have aged ten years. His face had a grayish cast and his shoulders were bowed, as if under a tremendous weight. In contrast, Vivienne appeared strangely remote, a ghostly projection of the vibrant woman she'd been, as if she might have drifted away like so much smoke had Jay not been supporting her with his arm. The only time Emerson had seen her react all day was at the church when Franny had gone to comfort her and she'd visibly stiffened, as if being around Franny, big with Jay's child, was more than she could bear. Luckily, Franny hadn't noticed; she'd been too distraught.

In fact, a passerby witnessing the scene at the gravesite might have taken her to be the grieving mother. Franny's face was swollen and blotchy from weeping—she couldn't cry without looking like she had the measles—and she swayed a bit on her feet.

Stevie, standing beside her, blinking back tears of her own, reached for Franny's elbow, as if to steady her. In her plain black dress adorned only by a simple gold necklace, she looked uncharacteristically somber.

Emerson recognized the minister, a stocky, dark-haired man with thick glasses that kept sliding down his nose, as the one who'd officiated at Jay and Vivienne's wedding, in happier times that seemed light years from today's tragic proceedings. After the minister had spoken the final blessing, Jay stepped forward, grim-faced, to pitch the first shovelful of dirt into the grave. As it fell against the coffin with a hollow thud, Vivienne's face contorted and she let out a low, anguished cry.

Emerson was relieved to see Vivienne's father, a distinguished-looking man with thinning silver hair, step forward and put an arm around her waist, supporting her. He and Vivienne's mother, a striking Lebanese woman who must have been a great beauty in her day, had flown in from Paris and were staying with Jay and Vivienne for the time being. But Emerson couldn't help wondering how Vivienne would manage after they were gone.

Her gaze fell on Jay's parents. Everett Gunderson was built like Jay, lean and rangy, with the same arresting blue eyes. In his Sunday suit, with his stiff iron hair slicked down, he looked ill at ease in this unfamiliar setting. Beside him stood Jay's mother clutching a worn leather Bible, a trim, white-haired woman with her son's fine features and fair complexion, whose prettiness had faded like something left out in the sun too long. They looked as if they wanted to do more, but didn't know quite what was expected of them.

After the last prayer was read, everyone began drifting back toward the parking lot. The day was humid and overcast, the ground underfoot soggy from all the rain that had drenched the area over the past couple of weeks, making it difficult for Emerson to walk in her high heels. In place of a traditional wake, Jay had informed them earlier, it would be just family and close friends. He hadn't said as much, but she guessed it was because he didn't think Vivienne was up to anything more.

By the time Emerson arrived at their loft half an hour later, Vivienne was resting in the bedroom and Jay was occupied with both sets of parents. Emerson joined Franny and Stevie in the living room, where they sat sipping coffee and nibbling on the cookies that had been set out.

"I just wish there was something we could *do*." Franny cast a forlorn look across the room at Jay, who stood talking to his dad and father-in-law while the two mothers busied themselves in the kitchen.

"Like what?" asked Stevie.

"Like, I don't know, pack up the nursery or something," Franny tossed out. "Can you imagine what it must be like for them every time they walk in and see all those baby things?"

Emerson felt a fresh wave of empathy at the thought—the crib all made up, the picture books and stuffed animals lining the shelves, the cute little outfits tucked away in drawers. Even so, she hesitated before replying, "We could always offer."

"Friends don't just offer. They roll up their sleeves," Franny said with a note of impatience.

Emerson and Stevie exchanged a look. Emerson knew then that she wasn't alone in thinking maybe this wasn't the best time for Franny to be around Vivienne. It must seem a cruel irony to Jay's wife, another woman bearing his child after she'd lost her own.

"Even friends need to know when to back off," Stevie said gently.

Franny slumped back in her chair. Emerson knew it pained her to see Jay suffer so, when there was nothing she could do to make it better. But Franny was also smart enough to see the wisdom in what Stevie was saying, and after a moment she gave in with a sigh.

"What really sucks is that I can't even get drunk," she said.

"That doesn't mean *we* can't." Stevie said, shooting a glance at Emerson.

Emerson shook her head. "Count me out. I'm going straight home after this." It was the nanny's night off and she'd have trouble getting a babysitter on such short notice. Besides, she didn't feel like sitting around in some bar, growing more morose with each drink. "In fact, I should get going pretty soon," she said, with a glance at her watch. "I promised Karen I'd be back no later than five." To Franny, she added with a smile, "Don't be fooled into thinking your nanny works for you. It's actually the other way around."

"In that case, it's a good thing I won't be needing one." Franny explained that she was going to try to work from home, for the first year or two at least.

"Well, I hope you have better luck than I did." Emerson had tried taking a year off after Ainsley was born, and within six months she'd been climbing the walls. Much as she loved her daughter, she'd been forced to admit she wasn't cut out to be a full-time mom.

Stevie turned to Franny, wearing a mysterious look, as if she knew something Franny didn't. "I can think of one person who wouldn't mind sharing diaper duty with you." Meaning Keith, of course.

A flush rose to Franny's cheeks. "We'll see," she said with a shrug. She'd been disappointed in love too many times to wear her heart on her sleeve. "We've only known each other a few months."

"For some people, that's long enough." Stevie looked sad, and Emerson wondered if she was thinking about Ryan.

"On the other hand, you could know someone all your life and still have it not work out," Emerson said. She and Briggs had traveled in the same circle; their mothers had been in the same class at Chapin; they'd even helped out at several fund-raisers together before they started dating. Yet, in the end, they'd had little else in common.

"Right now, all I can think about is getting through the next few months," said Franny, placing a hand on the mound of her belly. "If marriage is in the cards, it'll have to wait."

"It could be sooner than you think," said Stevie.

Franny's eyes narrowed. "Do you know something I don't?"

"Nothing specific," Stevie hastened to assure her. "But you don't have to be a mind reader to know the guy's crazy about you."

Franny's face lit up for a moment before giving way to a troubled look. Her gaze traveled once more to Jay. Emerson guessed she was thinking about the impact it would have on him, especially now, if she were to move to L.A. "Or maybe just plain crazy," she quipped. "Can't you just picture us on our honeymoon? The two of us taking turns walking the floor at night with a screaming infant."

"From what I know of Keith, I don't think he'd mind," Stevie said. "He's a good guy. He'll make a good dad."

The wistful note in her voice prompted Emerson to ask, "Speaking of which, how's it going with Grant?"

Stevie's gaze dropped to the coffee cup she was holding on her lap. "I don't know. I haven't been to see him in a while," she answered quietly.

Emerson knew it had been a blow when the *Prime Time* interview aired. Lauren didn't recall much of what had happened before she was shot. Her memories of that night were like strobe flashes in a dark room, she'd said. Only one image stood out clearly: a hand holding a gun pointed at her head. The rest was all jumbled together in her mind: an angry, shouting voice . . . the insignia of a rose twined around a crucifix . . . the sound of glass shattering. None of which proved anything, but as far as the public was concerned, Grant had been tried and found guilty. Stevie, though perhaps not as quick to rush to judgment, was nonetheless finding it more difficult to believe in his innocence.

Franny retrieved the cup and saucer now tilting precariously on Stevie's lap and placed it on the coffee table in front of them. "Don't you at least want to hear his side of the story?" she asked.

"What good would it do?" Stevie replied darkly.

"Maybe there's more to it than you know," Emerson said. In her line of work, unless you got it from a direct source, it was generally open to interpretation.

Stevie gave a helpless shrug. "Maybe, but whenever I broach the subject, he clams up."

"So that's it? You're giving up on him?" Franny eyed Stevie in disbelief.

Stevie brought her head up, her expression a mixture of hope and despair. "I didn't say that. I mean, he's still my father." She let out an audible breath. "I just needed to give it a rest, you know?" She looked anxiously from Franny to Emerson, as if seeking their permission.

Emerson patted her on the knee. "It's okay. We're with you no matter what."

When it was time for them to go, Jay saw them to the door, hugging them each a little harder than normal, Franny hardest of all. "Thanks, guys," he said, his voice hoarse with emotion. "I don't know how I'd have gotten through these past few days without you."

"Anything you need, all you have to do is pick up the phone," Emerson told him.

Franny brought a hand to his cheek, her eyes searching his face. "Are you going to be okay?"

He nodded, as if he wasn't too sure but wanted to put on a brave face. "Viv's parents will be here until the end of next week, and mine aren't leaving until Monday." He darted a look at his parents, across the room talking to his in-laws, adding, as if he felt the need to explain, "Their neighbor's looking after the farm. Dad doesn't want to take advantage."

"I'm sure they'd stay longer if they could," Emerson said.

"If there's anything I can do . . ." Franny started to say, but he was already shaking his head.

"Thanks," he said, "but I think we need some time on our own to sort things out." A look of despair crossed his face, as if he were wondering how he and Vivienne would ever put the pieces together again, then he mustered a small smile and said without much conviction, "We'll be okay."

Out on the street, the women said their good-byes and headed off in separate directions, Franny to her apartment and Stevie to her hotel, leaving Emerson to wonder in her car, on the way uptown, how she was going to keep from smothering Ainsley with kisses when she got home. For the thought uppermost in her mind all day was, *What if it were my child?*

As it turned out, she didn't have to face an evening of putting on a cheerful front for her daughter's sake. When she arrived home, there was a message from Briggs on her answering machine asking if he could have Ainsley for the night. It seemed his parents were in town and wanted to take the whole family out to dinner.

Normally Emerson would have objected—he wasn't supposed to have Ainsley until the weekend, and besides, it was a school night—but she was so drained, she knew her daughter would be better off with Briggs, so she called him back and told him it was okay.

By the time he arrived, she'd changed out of the dress she'd worn to the funeral into an old terry robe. When they were married, she'd taken pains never to dress sloppily around Briggs—one of Marjorie's most firmly held beliefs was that a wife must remain alluring to her husband at all times—which was no doubt what prompted him to remark with concern, "You're not under the weather, I hope?"

"Do I look sick?" Emerson snapped.

Briggs drew back with a hurt look. "I was only asking."

"I'm sorry. It's been a rough day," she said, with a sigh, pushing a hand through her hair.

Why was she such a bitch toward him? If anyone deserved to be bitter, it was Briggs. The divorce had been her idea, after all. At the time, he'd claimed to be perfectly happy in the marriage she'd found so stultifying. If she found him irritating, it was only because he made her feel like a rotten person for disliking someone so harmless.

The irony was that the very qualities that had made Briggs so annoying when they were married made for a compatible ex-husband. He had a stiff upper lip and a backbone that wilted at the mere hint of a confrontation—he'd cross the street to avoid an unpleasant exchange. Looking at him now, not yet forty and already grown stodgy, with his expanding waistline and brown hair carefully combed to cover his bald spot, she wondered what on earth she'd ever seen in him. A few years from now, he'd be wearing plaid golf pants and talking of buying a place in Palm Beach.

"Ainsley all set to go?" He peered down the hall.

"She's getting her stuff together," Emerson told him.

"How's your mom?" he inquired politely, as he lowered himself into one of the matched pair of Hepplewhite chairs flanking the antique chest in the foyer.

"Not great, but we'll know more after her next test results," Emerson informed him. What she didn't tell him was that Marjorie's cancer was so advanced, any further treatment at this point was merely palliative.

Briggs made a sympathetic face. "Be sure to give her my best."

"I'll do that."

There was a brief pause, then he cleared his throat to remark, "I understand you hired a new nurse. Ainsley seems to have taken quite a liking to him."

Emerson felt herself grow warm at the mention of Reggie. "More importantly, my mother seems to like him, too."

They exchanged a small, knowing smile. Briggs had always gotten along well with Marjorie, but he knew how difficult she could be.

"How's . . . um . . . Shelby?" Emerson momentarily blanked on his new wife's name.

"She's fine. She says to say hello."

"And your parents, do they like living in Florida?" They'd moved to Fort Lauderdale the year before, after her former father-in-law retired.

Briggs brightened. "Dad says it's the best decision they ever made. Everything's walking distance. And he gets in his eighteen holes a day."

Emerson stifled a yawn. "Sounds ideal."

Just then, Ainsley came charging down the hall, her Mary Janes clacking on the tiled floor and the Barbie backpack she clutched in one hand flopping at her side. "Daddy!" She threw her arms around him as he was getting up, sending him toppling back into the chair.

"Whoa there, pardner." He scooped her up to deliver a loud smack to her cheek. "What's that you've got there?" He eyed the doll protruding from her backpack. "Don't tell me Samantha's coming, too?"

Ainsley nodded vigorously. "Look. We're twinsies." She twirled to show off her plaid jumper that matched the one her doll had on. Emerson had taken her shopping just last week at American Girl, Ainsley's favorite store in the world.

Now she bent down to kiss her daughter good-bye. "Remember your manners. Don't forget to thank Grandma and Grandpa." She'd never known them to visit without bringing armloads of presents.

Watching her daughter head out the door holding tightly to her father's hand, she felt unexpectedly bereft. Normally on the nights Ainsley was with her dad, she savored the time alone, taking a long, luxurious bath before curling up with a book or watching TV. But with the day's events so fresh in her mind, she knew it would be a long evening, with only her sad thoughts to keep her company.

On impulse, she picked up the phone and punched in her mother's number. But instead of Reggie, a strange, Hispanic-sounding woman answered. No, she didn't know where Reggie was, she informed Emerson; she was only filling in for the night. Emerson experienced a twinge of anxiety. It wasn't his regular day off, which meant either he was out sick or . . . An even worse thought occurred to her: Could Marjorie have become suspicious and sent him packing? Emerson had struggled to maintain a friendly distance, but her mother had a sixth sense when it came to such things.

Retrieving her Palm Pilot from her handbag, she found Reggie's cell number. "I just called to make sure you were all right," she said, when he picked up. She kept her voice light as she explained that she'd become concerned when she called her mother's and he wasn't there.

"I'm not sick. Just studying for exams. Though at the moment I'm not sure which is worse," he added with a low chuckle.

"I'm sorry. I didn't mean to disturb you."

"Believe me, it's a welcome distraction."

She carried the phone into the bedroom, and stretched out on the bed. "Well, if you feel like taking a break, I could use the company." She smiled lazily up at the ceiling. In some distant part of her brain, a voice was cautioning, *Are you sure you know what you're doing? Once you start down that path, there's no turning back,* but she ignored it.

There was a brief pause at the other end. "Do you think that's wise?" he asked.

Emerson went very still, her heart bucking up against her ribs. Had he changed his mind? Decided she wasn't worth the risk of losing his job? "You're right, dumb idea. Forget I mentioned it." She kept her tone breezy.

"I was thinking of Ainsley," he said quietly.

In her relief, she let out an involuntary little laugh. "Oh, I see. Well, you can put your mind at ease." *On that score, at least.* "She's spending the night at her dad's."

"In that case, my studies can wait."

She gave him her address, her heart pounding as she hung up. It would take him an hour at least to travel from Sheepshead Bay, so she used the time to take a long bath, then rub herself from head to toe in scented oil before getting dressed. Not wanting to appear too obvious, she settled on a plain bra and panties that didn't scream Victoria's Secret. A pair of jeans, with a cream silk blouse and pearls, completed the outfit.

But when Reggie finally showed up, she wasn't prepared for the sight of him standing in the doorway, tall and dignified, his hair jeweled with droplets of the rain that had begun to fall outside. The breath went out of her and she could barely manage a hello. She couldn't remember the last time she'd been this nervous on a first date, not since high school.

"I hope you don't mind staying in," she said, taking note of his suit and tie.

"Not at all." Reggie smiled as he stepped over the threshold, his frank gaze leaving no doubt that he'd known exactly what to expect.

"What can I get you to drink?" she asked, leading the way into the living room. "I have beer and wine, and I think a bottle of whiskey somewhere."

"Wine would be nice." He sank down on the sofa, his gaze traveling around the living room. She hadn't gotten around to redecorating since the divorce, and now she found herself seeing it through his eyes: the formal antiques and heavy Jacquard drapes, the pieces of Steuben crystal on the mantel. But if he felt ill at ease, it didn't show.

She fetched a bottle of chilled white wine from the fridge, her hand trembling slightly as she poured them each a glass. But before long they were chatting easily, just like all those evenings at her mother's. She told him about the new account she'd just landed, for a chain of fitness spas. And he amused her with a story about Marjorie's teaching him to play gin rummy and how furious she'd been when he beat her the second round.

Not wanting to spoil the mood, she held off telling him about the funeral until the bottle was nearly empty and she was feeling the effects of the wine. Reggie listened with furrowed brow, as if he understood what it was to lose a loved one. After she'd finished her sad tale, he told her about his baby sister who'd died when he was eight. "My mother was beside herself with grief," he recalled, his eyes glistening even now at the memory. "For days, she refused all food and drink. All she could do was weep and cry out my sister's name."

"But she got over it?" Emerson asked.

"In time."

"I hope my friend's wife is as strong as your mother." It was the first time she'd voiced her fear that Vivienne, like a bright ornament that had shattered, might not bounce back.

"It helps to have caring friends," he said, lightly touching the back of her hand.

"I'm not sure how good a friend I've been," Emerson confessed, taking another sip of her wine. "I've been so caught up in my own life, I haven't had time to focus on much else."

He nodded in understanding. "You have your mother to think of."

"True." The wine had loosened her inhibitions and now she looked him in the eye. "But maybe I've allowed myself to get *too* caught up."

For a long moment, neither of them spoke. Then Reggie set his glass down on the coffee table and took both her hands in his. "What is it you're saying?" he asked, his eyes searching her face.

"I'm not sure," she said, her fears creeping back in.

"We don't have to do this," he said softly.

When she gave no reply, he moved his hands up her arms to her neck, cupping her head lightly as he leaned in to kiss her. In that instant, with her eyes shut, she was aware only of his warm breath against her face and the pleasant, spicy scent of his aftershave. Then his mouth closed over hers, and she felt the last of her resistance slide into the warm sea opening up inside her. It was as if she'd been given permission somehow, and now all the feelings bottled up over these past weeks came pouring out. She loved this man. She loved everything about him: the sound of his voice, the feel of his skin against hers, the taste of him on her mouth.

Before she knew it, she was on his lap. She could feel how aroused he was, and that excited her even more. Yet when he started to unbutton her blouse, she captured his hand and pulled it away from her, whispering in his ear, "Not here." She got up, drawing him to his feet. *If we're going to make love*, she thought, *I want it to be on the bed.* Not the sofa, feeling like a teenager sneaking around behind her mother's back.

In her bedroom, she left the lights off and they undressed in the dark. Reggie removing her clothes first, taking his time, each button and hook a small seduction in itself. Finally he knelt to pull her jeans down over her hips, pausing here and there to kiss and caress her in places that hadn't felt a man's touch in so long, it was like the first time ever.

When she was naked, she undressed him as slowly as he had her, getting acquainted with his body, its muscled planes and hollows. In the darkness, each sensation was heightened, an exquisite note held. There was only the heat of their bodies, the velvety feel of his skin against hers. She heard the muffled chink of his belt buckle hitting the carpeted floor, then they were stepping over the clothes puddled at their feet as they felt their way toward the bed.

They lay down facing each other, and Reggie drew her in close, sinking his teeth lightly into her shoulder and whispering, "You taste sweet, like melon."

"I've never been compared to a melon before," she said, with a laugh.

"It is a good thing, trust me."

Their lovemaking was full of similar revelations. For Emerson, it was like learning to swim all over again, when before, with other men, all she'd done was tread water. Blood rushed in her ears and her breath quickened, coming in soft bursts as she rocked against him, matching her rhythm to his. When she came at last, it was so intense she almost lost consciousness. *Sweet God in heaven*, she thought as the wave of blackness receded, leaving a twinkling of stardust behind her closed eyelids in its wake. So this was what Franny and Stevie had been talking about all these years. It wasn't like with Briggs, when she'd always drop off to sleep afterward. She felt charged, ready to take on the world.

The question was, could she take on Marjorie?

What are you afraid of? she asked herself. *She can't hurt you.* But Emerson knew better. She knew her mother would stop at nothing to get her way.

She pushed the thought from her mind, murmuring, "That was nice."

"For me, too." Reggie's voice was a throaty rumble against her ear.

"It's always been hard for me with . . . with other men," she confessed.

"Then it's a good thing I'm not like other men," he said, stroking her hair.

"That you most definitely are not." She smiled to herself.

"And you," he traced the curve of her ear with his fingertip, "are like no other woman I've known."

"So where do we go from here?"

After a moment of silence, he said, "That's up to you."

She lifted her head to peer at him in the darkness. "Please don't take this the wrong way, but I think it would be better if my mother didn't know. For now, at least."

His chest rose and fell in a deep exhalation. "And when she does find out?"

"I'm hoping she won't." She didn't dare say it aloud: Her mother might not live that long.

She could see Reggie struggling with his emotions. He wasn't the type to sneak around. But finally he acquiesced with a slow nod, saying, "I will do as you wish."

What she *wished*, Emerson thought with frustration, was that she could shout her love from the mountaintops. But for now, she'd have to settle for whispering it in the dark.

Chapter Ten

"Another late night, bud?" Todd Oster stuck his head into Jay's office as he was leaving for the day.

Jay looked up from his drafting table, surprised to see that it was dark outside. He'd been so absorbed in his work, he hadn't noticed. He scrubbed his face with an open hand, blinking until his bleary vision cleared and Todd's bearded, mountain-man face swam into focus.

"It's this damn design," he said. "Something's not quite right, but I can't figure out what it is."

Todd crossed the room to peer over his shoulder. "Looks more like a box of chocolates than a breakfast cereal." He gave Jay an affectionate punch on the arm. "Either you're losing your touch or you could use a break. Knowing you, I'd say the latter."

When Jay had made the move from Saatchi & Saatchi to the smaller, edgier agency of Beck/Blustein, he'd brought Todd with him to head up his design team. They worked well together, and Jay considered him a valuable asset. But Todd had also proved to be a good friend, the only one here with the balls to give him exactly what he needed during this difficult time: compassion along with the occasional swift kick in the rear.

"That bad, huh?" Jay eyed the sketch, one of several concepts they were working on as part of their multimedia campaign for Heartland Mills.

"I've seen worse." Todd shrugged. "Listen, why don't you let me buy you a drink. You look like you could use one."

"Nah. I should be getting home." There was nothing Jay would have liked better than to stop at Shaughnessy's on the way, but he was late enough as it was.

"Another time then. Come on, I'll walk out with you." Before Jay could protest, Todd had snagged his suit jacket from the back of his chair and was handing it to him.

"Okay. I can take a hint." Jay stood up, arching his back to release the kink in his spine.

He and Todd took the elevator down to the main floor. They were making their way across the nearly deserted lobby when Todd inquired, a bit too casually, "How are things at home?"

"All right. We're taking it a day at a time." Jay kept his tone neutral.

"I think that expression was coined by AA. You haven't taken up drinking, have you?" Todd's bearded face creased in a smile.

"It's always an option," Jay said.

"Seriously, you okay?" Todd wasn't letting him off the hook so easily. "No offense, buddy, but you haven't exactly been at the top of your game lately. If there's anything I can do . . ."

"I'm fine, really." Jay spoke more sharply than he'd intended. "Things aren't great, I admit, but they could be a lot worse," he added, even as a voice inside him asked, *Oh really? And just how could they be worse?*

"Yeah, you could be going through a divorce," Todd muttered, referring to his own current situation. "Hell, if it weren't for the kids—" He broke off, wearing a contrite look. "Sorry. That was stupid of me."

"It's okay. You don't have to tiptoe around me." Jay preferred the occasional gaffe to those who monitored their every word, fearful of saying anything that would remind him of his loss.

As if he could forget.

The revolving glass door deposited them on the sidewalk, where they were met by a blast of hot, muggy air. August in the city. He ought to be used to it by now, but after all these years he still missed breathing in air that smelled of new-mown hay instead of exhaust and rotting refuse.

"Later, bud." Todd clapped Jay on the shoulder before heading off down the street.

Jay stood there for a moment, watching his friend stride along Third Avenue. He almost envied Todd going home to his semi-furnished bachelor pad. Todd could be as miserable as he wanted; he didn't have to pretend to be cheerful for his wife's sake. And if it was another night of takeout, at least he could enjoy it without his stomach being in knots.

Jay felt a stab of guilt, resolving to be more patient with Vivienne.

It was tough, though, chattering on about his day while she sat like a zombie, barely responding. Not even the antidepressants she was taking seemed to be working. She slept most of the day, and had lost so much weight it was scary. Even more worrisome, she'd lost all interest in socializing. Whenever he suggested getting together with friends, hoping it would cheer her up, she'd merely shake her head, saying she wasn't up to it.

Yet if he grew frustrated at times, he had to keep reminding himself that it was harder for her than for him. He hadn't carried their baby inside him for nine months.

And, of course, the thing that went unspoken—he had another child on the way.

The thought of Franny brought a fresh helping of guilt. He'd been keeping her at arm's length lately. It was simply too painful for Vivienne to be around her. The few times Franny had dropped by, it had been so uncomfortable she hadn't stayed long. Franny was trying her best to not take it personally, he knew, but how could she not feel rejected? In a matter of weeks, she'd gone from a close family friend to a virtual pariah.

He wanted to make it up to her somehow, but how? He was already sliced so thin, any more and he'd crumble.

He took a cab home, getting out on the corner of Broadway and Twenty-fifth. Approaching his building, he was pleasantly surprised, when he glanced up, to see the lights on in their loft. Vivienne must be up and about. A good sign.

Coming in through the door, he called more brightly than usual, "Viv! I'm home!"

No answer.

He walked into the bedroom to find a half-packed suitcase lying open on the bed. He stared at it, not comprehending, until Vivienne emerged from the walk-in closet with an armful of clothes, dressed as if to go out. "Jay . . ." She halted, a guilty look coming over her face.

"What's all this?" He gestured toward the suitcase.

"Please, don't be angry," she said in a small voice. "It was Maman. She insisted I come."

"Why didn't you say something before?"

"I only found out today. She'd already booked the ticket."

"You could have discussed it with me first," he said in a hard voice.

153

"I was afraid you'd try to talk me out of it." Vivienne's eyes filled with tears. She sank down on the bed, the clothes in her arms sliding to the floor in a heap. "I can't do this anymore. If I don't get away, I . . . I don't know what will happen."

She looked so distraught, his heart went out to her despite himself. He took a step toward her. "And you thought I wouldn't understand? Am I really that insensitive?"

"No, of course not." She dropped her head into her hands, kneading her temples as if she had a headache coming on. "It's just . . . we're both hurting. Being around each other is only making it worse."

"It's hard when you keep shutting me out."

"I know. It's not your fault." She looked up at him with red-rimmed eyes. Her face was pale, the skin stretched too tight over her cheekbones. "Don't you see? You can't fix this. You're too close to it yourself." She sighed. "Maman's right. It's time for me to go home."

"I thought this was your home."

"Please, Jay, don't make this any harder."

He eyed her for a long moment, wondering if *his* feelings had factored into her decision at any point. But what was the use of arguing? Her mind was clearly made up. He released the pent-up air in his lungs, sinking down beside her on the bed. "How long will you be away?"

Her thin shoulders lifted and fell. "Until I'm better. Until I can find a reason to get up in the morning."

"I have a better idea," he said, taking a wild stab. "Why don't I take some time off from work? We'll take that trip to Greece we've always talked about. You'd like that, wouldn't you?"

She started to cry, her mouth working in soundless misery.

Jay used his thumb to wipe away the tears running down her cheeks. "Babe, I know it's been hard, but running away isn't going to help. I need you. We need each other."

She shook her head. "You don't need me, not like this. I know what you think, that it's time I snapped out of it. I can see it in your eyes. But I *can't*, Jay. I've tried and tried, and each day it gets a little harder because I see *you* moving on."

He winced inwardly, knowing there was more than a grain of truth to what she was saying. Even so, he reminded her, "I lost a child, too."

"But you still have Franny's." She gave a harsh laugh. "God, when I think how arrogant I was! Imagining we could all be one big happy family. You, me, Franny, our kids." Her eyes that had been dead for so long blazed to life like a struck match.

"No one could have predicted this," he said.

"It's like I'm being punished," she went on, as if she hadn't heard him.

"For being a good friend to Franny?" She wasn't making any sense.

"Oh, I'm a good friend, all right."

The bitter irony with which she spoke made him ask, "Viv, is there something you're not telling me?"

She rose abruptly to her feet. "I have to go. I'll miss my flight." She hastily finished packing and zipped the suitcase shut.

He walked her to the door, feeling as if he were in a play for which he hadn't rehearsed his lines. There was so much he wanted to say—*Don't go. I love you. I'll miss you*—but the words wouldn't come. Instead, all he could manage was "Call me when you get there."

He must have looked bereft, for she brought her hand to his cheek. "Don't be sad, *chéri*. It's better this way, really. You won't miss me as much when I'm gone."

It wasn't until the door closed behind her that the meaning of her words sank in. For in a way, hadn't she already left him?

✳ ✳ ✳

In the weeks that followed, Franny made it her mission to see that Jay didn't spend his every waking hour either at work or moping around the loft. On weekends when the weather was nice, they went for long walks, stopping here and there to poke around in shops or grab a bite to eat. If it was raining, they went to a movie or a museum. And when her monthly appointment with her obstetrician rolled around, she insisted Jay accompany her.

Listening to the baby's heartbeat for the first time, his eyes lit up and a huge grin spread across his face. It was the first real smile she'd seen in weeks, and it warmed her. Her old friend whom she'd missed so much was gradually returning to the land of the living.

"How can you stand not knowing?" he asked as they were leaving the doctor's office. He still couldn't get over the fact that she'd opted not to be informed of the baby's sex.

"Shouldn't there be a few surprises left in life?" she said, placing a hand on her belly, where at the moment their baby was doing what felt like the mambo. "Anyway, we'll know soon enough."

"Just promise me one thing: If it's a boy, you won't name him after your uncle Moishe."

She flashed him a grin. "Why not? I always liked my uncle Moishe."

"Tell that to our kid when he's getting the shit kicked out of him in school."

Franny tucked her arm into his as they strolled along Madison Avenue. "How about buying a pregnant lady lunch?"

"Sure. What's your pleasure?"

"Anything, as long as there's lots of it. I'm starved."

Franny took it as a good sign that he hadn't insisted on getting back to work or even glanced at his watch. He was making progress. Either that, or he was going out of his way to make up for all the doctor's appointments he'd missed. She'd assured him over and over that she was a big girl and didn't expect him to hold her hand throughout her pregnancy, but knew he felt bad that he hadn't been there for her.

They walked several more blocks before ducking into Le Pain Quotidien, where they were able to snag a table for two. Their waitress brought them a basket of crusty bread still warm from the oven, and Franny fell on it as if she hadn't eaten in a week.

"I really shouldn't, I know," she said, as she was buttering her third slice. "Dr. Stein will have to weigh me on a freight scale next time."

"You're eating for two," Jay reminded her.

"It feels more like three. If I didn't know better, I'd swear I was having twins." Jay's expression clouded over briefly, and she placed her hand on his arm, saying gently, "I know it's not the same as with Stephan. I don't expect you to be as excited with this one."

Jay pulled himself out of his funk to give her a smile. "Believe me, when this kid is born, I'll be passing out cigars."

"You don't smoke," she reminded him.

"You're missing the point."

"Which is?"

"I plan on being a hands-on dad."

Franny warmed at the thought, a mental picture forming of Jay with a Snugli strapped to his chest, their baby's fuzzy head poking up from it. Then the thought of Keith intruded.

"While we're on the subject, there's something you should know," she broached, feeling uncomfortable all of a sudden. "Keith and I . . . um, it looks as though I might be moving to L.A."

Jay blinked and sat back. "So it's official?"

"Not yet," she said. "But I think he's getting ready to pop the question."

"That's . . . well, that's great. I'm really happy for you." Despite his words, he looked crestfallen.

"Don't break out the champagne just yet. He hasn't asked . . . and I haven't accepted."

Why was she talking this way? She'd be crazy not to marry Keith.

"Do you love him?" Jay's gaze held hers for a beat too long, sending her stomach into free fall.

"Lately, I don't know if it's my hormones or my heart talking." All she knew was that these past few weeks she'd been feeling confused where before she'd been 99 percent sure about Keith. Could it have anything to do with Jay, all the time they'd been spending together? The thought was so disconcerting, she quickly pushed it out of her head. "I'll know more when I see him. Did I tell you I'm flying out there for my birthday?"

"The doctor says it's okay to travel?" Jay eyed her with concern.

"You heard him. I'm as healthy as a horse. As big as one, too," she added, smiling as she glanced down at her belly.

"There's always a risk," he said, frowning. She knew he was thinking about the baby he'd lost.

"I don't have to go, if you'd rather I didn't." The words just popped out, and immediately she wanted to kick herself. What on earth had gotten into her? She and Keith had been planning this for weeks.

"Nothing doing." Jay straightened his shoulders, rearranging his features into a reasonable facsimile of a smile. "You're not changing your plans because of my stupid fears." He reached for her hand, bringing it to his mouth to deliver an affectionate kiss. Innocent enough, yet the brush of his lips against her skin sent a mild jolt through her. She drew back, confused.

What was going on? Why was she feeling this way?

Throughout the meal, it was all Franny could do to act as if nothing were out of the ordinary, as if she weren't noticing how the sunlight streaming in through the windows brought out the glints of gold in his hair or the way his eyes crinkled at the corners when he laughed. How was it she'd never before been struck by how beautiful his hands were? It was as if the friend for whom she'd felt nothing but affection all these years had morphed into a complete stranger. Someone with whom she felt as self-conscious as if this were a first date, hoping she didn't have onion breath or a piece of lettuce stuck to her teeth.

"How about we walk off some of this food?" she suggested, after they'd finished eating and were on their way out the door. She told herself that if she kept on pretending everything was fine, this temporary insanity would sort itself out eventually.

They set off in the direction of Central Park, only a few blocks away, Franny remembering when her mother used to take her and Bobby there on nice days in the summertime. They'd ride the F train from Kings Highway all the way to Fifty-seventh Street, nearly an hour-and-a-half trip. In the park, Mama would spread a blanket over the grass in some shady spot to eat the picnic lunch she'd packed. Central Park was for *everyone*, she'd say, in a tone that suggested she had just as much right to it as the Upper East Side ladies for whom she did alterations at Bergdorf's. And now, strolling along a path under the canopy of trees, Franny took perverse pleasure in the sight of tourists and picnickers and moms pushing strollers catching the same cool breezes as the homeless people in their shabby clothes.

They walked until Franny grew tired, then settled on a bench overlooking the boat pond, where ducks glided alongside model sailboats powered by handheld remotes. It was so shady and peaceful where they sat; Franny was scarcely aware of the other people strolling by. Nor did anyone pay particular notice to them, except an older woman who smiled at them in passing, no doubt mistaking them for a couple expecting their first child.

When Jay reached for Franny's hand, it was no different from countless times he'd done so. So why now was she so acutely aware of his fingers curled about hers? She watched him from out of the corner of her eye, taking in his relaxed expression. If he had any idea of the new and alarming shift in her feelings toward him, there was no sign of it.

"This is nice," he said, looking up at the trees. "You can almost forget you're in the city."

Just then the silence was pierced by the distant wail of a siren. "Home sweet home," Franny said with a wry smile.

"Where I come from, if your neighbors live less than a mile away, it feels crowded." Jay toyed with a leaf he'd picked up off the ground, gazing out at the pond.

"Try living in Brooklyn," she said. "You sneeze and twenty people say gesundheit!"

He turned to look at her, smiling in a way that made her heart go wobbly all of a sudden, like the model sailboat out on the water that had just capsized. "Funny, isn't it? We come from such different backgrounds, but we always see eye to eye."

"Yeah, I know." She kept her voice light. "And here we are having a kid together."

"Yeah. God must be having a good laugh right about now."

She knew from the bitterness of his tone that he was thinking about the son he'd never know.

"Have you talked to Vivienne lately?" she ventured, after a bit.

"For what it's worth," he replied, wearing an odd, tight expression.

"You sound angry."

"Maybe I am. But you have to admit it's a pattern with her." He was referring to all the times Vivienne had disappeared on him in the past. Back when they were dating, just when things would start to get serious, she'd always find an excuse to go abroad, often for months at a time.

"Did she give you any idea when she'd be back?"

He shrugged. "Your guess is as good as mine."

Franny gave his hand a little squeeze. "Look, I'm sure it's as hard on her as it is on you. She didn't ask for this, either."

He let out a breath. "I know. It's just . . ." He shook his head. "I feel as if I've been abandoned."

"She'll be back. Give her time."

In the meantime, you still have me, she added silently. She'd go on doing her best to cheer him up. Wasn't that what friends were for? If she was on shaky ground at the moment as far as her own feelings were concerned, Jay would remain none the wiser. It would be like in college, before they fell in with Stevie and Emerson. Just the two of them.

Make that three, she thought, feeling the baby start to kick.

Chapter Eleven

Pulling up to the gates at Grant's estate, Stevie's stomach was in knots. It had been weeks since her last visit and she wasn't sure why she was here now. It wasn't to satisfy her curiosity; she already had a pretty good idea of what kind of man her father was: the kind who'd try to kill someone then lie to the police. If Stevie didn't know exactly how it had unfolded, it was easy enough to fill in the blanks. In the version he'd given the police, they'd had too much to drink and Lauren had grabbed the gun, and it had gone off when he'd struggled to take it from her. But Stevie had since learned, along with the rest of the world, that it hadn't happened that way, at least not according to Lauren. Stevie guessed they'd gotten into a fight, and it was Grant who'd reached for the gun. The rest was history.

So why had she come? She didn't quite know. Maybe to find out if she wanted anything more to do with him. Or to see if he wanted anything more to do with her, given how she felt. The only thing she was certain of was that she owed him an explanation, and the chance to come clean. She smiled thinly at the thought as the gates opened and she was waved through. There was an almost cosmic irony in not being able to go public with what could be the biggest scoop of her career.

When she arrived at the house, she was met at the door by Victor. The bodyguard-slash-houseman was no friendlier than on her previous visits; in fact, if anything he was even more hostile. "He's out back." He jerked his head toward the hallway leading to the patio. As usual, he was wearing a suit and tie, which made a weird contrast to the tattoos snaking up the sides of his thick neck and shaved skull.

"I know the way." Stevie started to walk past him but he moved quickly to block her path. She waited for him to step out of the way, but he didn't budge. Looking into his eyes, as he stood there with his arms crossed over his steroid-enhanced chest, was like trying to see though a limousine's polarized windows: flat, gray, impenetrable. In an attempt to lighten the mood, she cracked, "All right, just one more dance, then I really have to go."

Victor's broad face remained impassive. "He's expecting you."

"Probably because I phoned to let him know I was coming." A note of impatience crept into her voice.

"It's been a while. He figured you were pissed at him or something."

"What gave him that idea?"

"You're a smart girl, you figure it out."

"I needed some time to sort things out, is all." Why was she explaining herself to this thug? It wasn't as if it was any of his business. "Now, if you'll excuse me . . ."

This time he didn't try to stop her. He merely murmured in his throaty growl, as she was brushing past him, "I wouldn't bring it up if I were you. He's a little touchy on the subject. It might set him off." She didn't have to ask what subject he was referring to.

Was he protecting his boss . . . or warning her? Somehow, despite Lauren's conflicting version of events, Stevie couldn't see Grant as a threat. Before this whole business, it had been just the usual rock-star stuff: trashed hotel rooms, wild parties, drunken binges. The man she knew, though peculiar in some ways, struck her as basically harmless. Whatever had set him off that night, she suspected it had been an aberration as opposed to any kind of pattern.

Still, you never knew . . .

She found Grant stretched out on a chaise longue by the pool with his nose buried in a book. He sat up at her approach, putting his book down on the table beside him and pushing his sunglasses up onto his head. She thought he looked pleased to see her. Even so, he greeted her somewhat cautiously, with an exaggerated drawl that bordered on parody. "Howdy, stranger."

"Hey, Grant." She spoke mildly, but her heart was pounding.

"Hot enough for you?"

"It's supposed to rain later on, at least according to the weatherman."

He glanced up dubiously at the clear blue sky. "I'll take your word for it."

She looked down at her shadow, stretched across the quarry paving stones like an accusing finger. The words balled in her throat wouldn't come. "How have you been?" she asked instead.

"Okay. You?"

"Working too hard, but what else is new."

"Help yourself." He gestured toward the cabana, where a pitcher of lemonade stood on the tiled wet bar. Years of exposure to the sun had left his skin the color and texture of cowhide. In his baggy swim trunks, with his gray ponytail snaking down his back, he might have been an aging beach bum.

"Thanks." She walked to the bar and poured herself a glass, carrying it over to the pool, where she slipped out of her shoes and rolled up her pant legs, lowering herself onto the edge. As she dipped her legs into the water, her reflection rippled on the surface, seeming to mock her in some way. *Some father and daughter reunion*, she thought. A burned-out rocker with a past and a woman who couldn't seem to embrace the future.

But today wasn't about forging bonds. She had to find out, from Grant's own mouth, what had *really* happened the night Lauren was shot. Or how could she ever learn to trust him?

"You're probably wondering why you haven't heard from me in a while," she ventured after a bit.

"Yeah, well. I know you've got better things to do than to hang around keeping your old man company." His tone was nonchalant, but she sensed he was hurt. "Besides," he added, with a dry chuckle, "If I get lonely, I can always catch you on TV."

She put her glass down and turned to face him. "The thing is . . ." She swallowed hard and heard a clicking sound in her ears. "We need to talk."

He remained very still. With the sun at his back, his face was in shadow. All she could make out were the unhappy lines of his mouth. "I guess I don't have to ask what about," he said.

"No, I guess not."

His lips curved in a mirthless smile. "Funny, ain't it? Phone's been ringing off the hook these past few weeks. Every reporter in the universe has been trying to get hold of me — except you."

"I'm not here as a reporter. I'm here as your daughter."

"So you want to know if your old man's the Antichrist, like everyone's saying?" He gave a bitter laugh.

"I'm not casting any stones. At least, not until I've heard your side of the story." She could see from the obstinate set of his shoulders that this wasn't going to be easy. "The *real* story. Not just what you told the police."

His eyes narrowed. "You think I was lying?"

"Frankly, I don't know what to think anymore."

Abruptly, he got up off the chaise and padded over to the bar, reaching underneath and pulling out a bottle of vodka. He poured a hefty slug into a glass and downed it.

"I thought you quit drinking," Stevie said, feeling a brush of unease.

"I did." He poured himself another one and knocked it back in one swallow.

She got up and walked over to him. "What are you so afraid of? I already told you, this is off the record."

He stood there frowning, as if lost in thought. She saw something dark in his eyes that she didn't like the look of and felt a light chill skim her over, raising goose bumps. "Whatever's done is done. Talking about it ain't gonna help," he said in a hard voice.

She recalled Victor's warning and once more felt a brush of unease in her belly. "It would help *me*," she said quietly.

"What, knowing your old man's a fuckup?"

"If you are, that makes two of us." She seized the bottle from his hand as he was getting ready to pour himself another drink, placing it out of reach. "You want to know why my boyfriend dumped me? Because I wouldn't marry him, even though I'm crazy about him. So you see, I'm as fucked up as you. I don't know if it was growing up without a dad or because I inherited your genes, but either way, I'm damaged goods."

His frown deepened. "I thought this was about Lauren."

"It is. But it's all wrapped up in who *I* am, too. I didn't just grow up without a father. I invented one to take his place. This prince who was going to show up one day and whisk my mom and me off to his castle." Stevie fought down the lump swelling in her throat.

"If it was nothing more than a stupid fantasy, where does that leave me?"

In the scowl Grant wore she caught the dull gleam of something deeper, frustration perhaps. Or regret. After a long, tense moment, he sighed. "You want the truth?" He came around to where she stood, scooting onto a bar stool facing her. "Okay, I'll tell you. I don't know what happened. I was so out of it, I could've mowed down an entire village and I wouldn't remember." He went on in a slurred voice, "We'd been drinking and doing blow all night. We were both pretty high. The last thing I remember was taking our clothes off and going for a dip in the pool." He squinted toward its shimmering blue expanse, as if half-expecting the youthful Lauren Rose to rise dripping from its depths. "The next thing I knew she was lying on the floor inside the house, bleeding." He brought his gaze back to Stevie, and she saw from his ravaged eyes, those of a man haunted by a memory he couldn't quite recapture, that he was telling the truth. "I don't know. Maybe I did pull that trigger. Maybe I'm the danger to society they say I am."

"Is that why you quit drinking?" Stevie asked, looking pointedly at the empty glass in his hand.

He eyed the bottle longingly before lowering his glass onto the bar. "I haven't touched a drop since. Until today. *That* much I can swear in a court of law."

"I believe you," she said, after a moment.

"What, about the drinking, or what happened with Lauren?"

"Both." She gave him a stern look. "What I still don't get, though, is why you lied to the police."

"Your old man's a coward, that's why. I didn't want to spend the rest of my life behind bars." He glanced around him, smiling a little as if at the irony in it: He'd merely traded one prison for another.

"I'm glad you told me." It wasn't what she'd expected, but she'd learned through the years that the real story seldom was.

"So I guess this is it then. The part where you say sayonara, it's been nice knowing you." His bloodshot eyes were sorrowful. He looked as if he'd aged years in the span of a few minutes. "Sorry your long-lost dad turned out to be such a disappointment."

Stevie thought about her mother's struggle to get sober, with the help of AA; how Nancy had likened it to clawing her way up the face of a cliff with her bare hands. The person Nancy had been back then was nothing like the one Stevie knew. Maybe it was that way with Grant, too; his dark side only came out when he drank. Not that he was entirely blameless. But neither had he been in his right mind.

Abruptly she came to a decision. "Get dressed," she told him.

"What for?" He blinked at her in confusion.

"Go on, you heard me. We're going for a little ride." She took him by the elbow, pulling him off the stool and marching him toward the house. Hopefully the effects of the alcohol would wear off some by the time they arrived at their destination.

"You still haven't told me where you're taking me," he protested.

"I think it's about time you met my mother," she said.

The visit with Nancy went surprisingly well. Other than her initial shock at how altered he was, she'd welcomed him as if they were old friends. Within minutes she was bustling about the kitchen, putting on a pot of coffee.

When it was brewed she poured some into a mug and plunked it down in front of Grant. "Here, drink this. You'll feel better."

"Yes, ma'am." He cast her a faintly sheepish look.

"Stevie tells me you don't get out much." Nancy settled into the chair opposite him at the table while Stevie took the one at the end.

He nodded, as if ruminating on it, before replying, "Yeah, it's been a while."

"Well, I'm glad you're here. You like zucchini?"

"Uh, sure." He spoke hesitantly, as if not quite sure why she was asking.

"Good. I'll send you home with some." She nodded toward the fresh-picked zucchini on the kitchen counter. "This time of year I have more than I know what to do with. Try it stir-fried, with a little basil and olive oil. I find what works best with most food is to keep it simple."

"I'm not much of a cook," he confessed.

"What *do* you do with yourself all day?" Her eyes crinkled with something close to amusement. In the jeans and man's button-down shirt she had on, both liberally streaked with clay, she looked anything but the starstruck flower child he'd once singled out of the crowd.

"Read, mostly," he said blowing on his coffee before taking a careful sip. "I never finished school, so I have some catching up to do."

"I make pots," she told him, nodding in the direction of her studio out back.

"So I hear." He sat back, stretching his legs out in front of him. "You any good?"

"I make a living at it." Nancy was too modest to mention that her ceramics fetched top dollar in high-end galleries across the country. "What about you? Writing any new songs these days?"

"Hell, no, I haven't in years. Though I still pick up my guitar from time to time. The old 'caster hasn't let me down yet." His face relaxed in a smile. Nancy seemed to have a calming effect on him, as she did on most people.

"I remember the night you played the Forum," she recalled. "I thought a riot would break out after that last number. No one wanted to believe it was the final stop of your farewell tour."

"You were there that night?" Stevie asked her, surprised that this was the first she was hearing of it.

Nancy smiled at her. "You were, too."

"I was?" Stevie sat up straighter.

Her mother nodded. "You were only three at the time, that's why you don't remember. I'd pawned my grandmother's brooch to pay for the tickets. But it was worth every dime. We witnessed history that night." Nancy smiled faintly as she stared off into space, toying with the end of her braid.

"It was Stark," Grant explained, referring to bassist Rick Stark. "He was sick of me bagging out on gigs. He gave me an ultimatum, either clean up my act or he was throwing in the towel."

"And did you?" Nancy looked at him with her unwavering gaze that on more than one occasion had forced a confession out of Stevie the times she'd gotten into trouble as a teenager.

His shoulders slumped, and he slowly shook his head. "Can't say that I did. Not until it was too late. Guess a lot would've turned out different if I had." He glanced over at Stevie wearing a look of profound regret.

"It's never too late," Nancy said, placing a work-roughened hand over his. Not as if they'd ever been intimate, but as if he were a wayward soul she'd taken in. "In fact, I was just thinking about taking in a meeting when Stevie called. Would you care to join me?"

Stevie was pretty sure AA had been the furthest thing from her mother's mind until now. Nancy regularly attended meetings but nothing short of an emergency—or, in this case, a seminal event— could pry her away when she was in the middle of work.

Grant thought for a moment, as if weighing his options, then nodded slowly. "I'd like that."

The following morning Stevie had a hard time concentrating on her work, her thoughts were so wrapped up in yesterday's strange turn of events. When it was time for her six-thirty A.M. broadcast, she was so preoccupied she almost missed her cue. Only her years of experience kept her from flubbing it when the cameras rolled to her.

"He's number one with a bullet," she began, switching into autopilot as the words scrolled down the monitor. "The rapper known as Fifty Cent once again killed the competition with his album *Blood in the Streets*. This week, he's number one with a bullet, selling twice as much as his nearest competitor, Jay-Z." B-roll of the rapper strutting down the red carpet at the Grammys, then she was segueing into "Next, Brad Pitt is Down Under this week, making nice with the crowds who turned out for the premiere of his new movie *American Original*, costarring Gwyneth Paltrow . . ."

Stevie flew through the rest of her segment, until the floor director's voice in her earpiece cued, "That's a wrap."

On the way back to her pod, she checked in at the assignment desk. She was covering the Russell Crowe–Nicole Kidman press conference at the Peninsula in less than an hour—they were in town on a press junket promoting their new picture—and she needed to line up a crew. Luckily, she was able to snag Matt O'Brien, who'd just come in. While he was assembling his gear and lining up a truck, she ducked into the break room to grab a quick bite. She hadn't eaten all morning; she'd been in too big a rush as she was leaving for work.

Liv Henry walked in as she was tearing open a bag of chips. "Hey, nice work on the Andrews piece."

It was a moment before Stevie realized Liv was referring to her obit on silent-film star Verna Andrews, who'd passed away over the weekend. The piece, which had aired on Sunday, had been in the can—standard practice with older and ailing celebrities, one that might strike the uninitiated as ghoulish but saved reporters from having to drop what they were doing and dash to the newsroom when the sad news came.

"Thanks," she said, unused to receiving compliments from Liv.

"I looked for you at the screening last night," Liv said, pouring herself a cup of coffee. "I must have missed you."

"Which screening was that?" Stevie asked distractedly. She got invitations to so many she couldn't keep up with them all.

"For your boyfriend's new picture." Liv wore a look of studied innocence, but Stevie could tell from the quickness with which her gaze slid away that she wasn't just being chatty.

"*Ex*-boyfriend." She kept her tone mild, not wanting to give Liv the satisfaction of knowing how much it still hurt to hear his name.

"Oh? I didn't know you two had broken up."

"Months ago. I'm surprised you hadn't heard." Stevie nonchalantly crunched down on a chip, concentrating hard to keep from choking as she swallowed it.

"That explains it."

"What?"

Stevie was already kicking herself for falling into the trap even before Liv answered, "The woman he was with." Liv tore open a packet of sugar and dumped it into her coffee. "I thought maybe it was his sister."

"He doesn't have a sister." Stevie spoke more sharply than she'd intended.

"Oops." Liv flashed her a sympathetic little smile. "Come to think of it, they did seem awfully cozy."

"If he's seeing someone, it's fine by me," said Stevie, a bit too blithely.

"That's the attitude." Liv gave her a you-go-girl pat on the arm before sailing out of the room with her steaming mug.

As soon as she was out of sight, Stevie dropped her uneaten chips in the trash can and collapsed into the nearest chair. Her appetite had vanished along with any hope of a reconciliation with Ryan. It shouldn't have come as a shock that he was seeing someone. He'd made it pretty clear that he had no intention of waiting around for her to come to her senses. Nonetheless, she felt as if she'd been kicked in the stomach. He hadn't even sent her an invitation to his fucking screening. Somehow, that's what hurt most of all.

That afternoon, she phoned Franny from her car on the way home from work. They hadn't talked in a while and Stevie wanted to firm up plans for when Franny was in L.A.

"How's Junior?" she asked.

"Doing gymnastics at the moment. At this rate, I'm not sure which of us is going to get to the delivery room first."

"Where are you?" Stevie could hear traffic noises in the background.

"In a cab on the way to my Lamaze class. Like I can even bend over, much less get down on the floor," Franny groaned.

"Is Em with you?" Emerson was Franny's labor coach.

Franny hesitated before answering. "Um, well, the thing is, there's been a slight change in plans."

"How so?"

"I have a new coach."

"Who, the cabbie?" joked Stevie.

"No, Jay."

"Wow. When did that happen?"

"Don't act so surprised. He *is* the father, after all."

"But I thought . . ."

"I know. Me, too." Franny rushed ahead, not letting her finish. "But it was his idea. He says he's ready to move on."

"Does Vivienne know about this?"

"He hasn't said. Who knows if she'll even be back by then."

"Poor Jay. It hasn't been easy for him."

"He has his down days," Franny acknowledged. "But lately more up than down."

"Knowing you, you had something to do with it." Franny was no doubt cooking him meals and nagging him into getting out more. But there was something else, too, something in her guarded tone that was making Stevie's reporter's nose twitch. She knew better than to try and get it out of Franny over the phone; she'd have to wait until she could quiz her in person. Which reminded her . . . "Listen, if you don't have any plans for the Sunday you're in town, my mom's having a barbecue. You and Keith are invited."

"Sounds like fun. I'll check with him, but as far as I know we're free."

"You guys won't be off in some romantic hideaway?" she teased.

Franny laughed. "In my condition? Marine World is more like it."

"Seriously, how's it going with you two?"

"Great. He says he can't wait to see me." Franny didn't say how excited she was to see him.

"Any idea what he's getting you for your birthday?" Stevie asked.

Franny was silent a moment. "From the hints he's dropped, I have a feeling it's coming in a small box."

Stevie sucked in a breath. "You think he'll pop the question?"

Her mind traveled back to when Ryan had asked her to marry him. All morning the thought of him with another woman had been throbbing in her head like an infected tooth. She should have seen it coming. He hadn't returned any of her calls and the one time she'd run into him at a function, he couldn't get away fast enough. Even so, in the face of all evidence to the contrary, she'd nursed the tiny hope that she could win him back. More and more lately, she'd been thinking that marriage wouldn't be such a bad idea after all. She still wasn't quite ready to take that leap, but it didn't seem so scary anymore. Maybe the trick was not to look down.

"It's a definite possibility, though I'm not holding my breath."

Franny sounded less than ecstatic about the prospect for some reason. Puzzled, Stevie was about to ask if she was having second thoughts when Franny announced that her cab had arrived at its destination. She said a hurried good-bye and hung up.

Leaving Stevie to wonder what possible hope there was for her if Franny, the Cinderella in search of Prince Charming to her Typhoid Mary of Commitment, was getting cold feet.

Chapter Twelve

Y ou're looking a little peaky, dear. You really should think about hiring extra help. You're working much too hard." Marjorie peered at Emerson in the grainy light of the waning afternoon.

"I'm fine, Mother. Nothing a good night's sleep won't cure," Emerson said with a cheeriness that had nothing to do with their sad little meal on TV trays in the living room. Sleep was a thing of the past these days. Between work, caring for Ainsley and her mother, and juggling her schedule to snatch stolen moments with Reggie, she was running on empty.

"Nonsense. You're stretched too thin. In my day, women stayed home to look after their children." Marjorie's gaze drifted to Ainsley, who'd finished eating and was on the floor putting a puzzle together.

Like you did with me? It was all Emerson could do not to give in to the derisive laugh swelling in her throat. What she recalled was a succession of nannies, until the money ran out; after that, the only adult she could rely on was Nacario. What did it say when you got more affection from the doorman than your own mother?

"Honestly, Mother, I wouldn't know what to do with myself," she said.

"God knows you made out well enough from the divorce," Marjorie went on, as if she hadn't spoken. "However you feel about Briggs, you can't say he hasn't been generous." Marjorie was fond of reminding her of Briggs's wealth.

"True," Emerson agreed. No, Briggs didn't stint, especially with Ainsley. But she saw no point in pursuing the subject. "More chicken?" she asked, though her mother had scarcely touched what was on her plate.

It was painfully apparent she was going downhill. Her skin had a waxen cast, and the shawl she was swathed in couldn't disguise how skeletal she'd become. Still, Marjorie clung to the false hope that she'd be back on her feet in time, only joking about her imminent death as a way of warding off her fears. You had to admire her for it, Emerson thought. No one dictated to her mother, not even the Grim Reaper.

"Thank you, dear, but I don't seem to have much of an appetite these days." Marjorie carefully folded her napkin and placed it on her tray. "It's no wonder, the way that new girl is always shoving food at me."

"She has a name, Mother. It's Chanel." Emerson could barely contain her impatience. Marjorie's last day nurse had finally thrown in the towel, and the agency had had to scramble to replace her on such short notice. They were lucky to have gotten anyone at all.

"As if anyone with an ounce of class would be named after a fashion label," Marjorie sniffed.

Emerson bristled. These days, she was more sensitive than usual to such remarks. "You named me after my grandfather," she said dryly. "Lots of people would think that was strange."

"That's entirely different."

Just because that's how our kind does it? Emerson had been dealing with the same convoluted logic all her life. Rules ordinary people lived by didn't apply to them. But she didn't dare get into it with her mother, lest she accidentally let the cat out of the bag about Reggie.

Wasn't it bad enough that Ainsley had almost walked in on them the other day? Her nanny had brought her home early after Ainsley had thrown up at Callie Whittaker's birthday party. Poor Reggie had had to hide out in the bedroom while Emerson hustled Karen out the door, then tended to Ainsley. By the time she'd gotten her cleaned up and into bed, he was gone.

Now Ainsley was running over to them. "Grandma, look, I got all the pieces!" She held up the puzzle Marjorie had bought her, or rather had Nacario pick up at the store. Lately she'd been prevailing on him for all kinds of errands that went well beyond his duties as concierge. Yet he refused the tips Emerson tried to press on him, saying it was between him and Mrs. Fitzgibbons—never mind that Marjorie had no money of her own.

"What a clever girl you are!" Marjorie leaned forward to hug Ainsley, her shawl slipping off her shoulders and revealing a collarbone so prominent it was all Emerson could do not to wince.

Ainsley beamed. "I read the book you got me, too. Reggie helped me with the hard words."

Marjorie reflected on this for a moment before saying sweetly, "You've certainly been spending a lot of time with Reggie, haven't you?"

Ainsley nodded vigorously. "He's my friend."

"That's nice, dear. But we mustn't forget he's an employee."

Emerson felt the mouthful of potatoes she'd just swallowed push its way back up her throat. It was history repeating itself, Marjorie attempting to poison Ainsley's mind just as she'd tried to do with her.

"Ainsley can be friends with whoever she likes," she said, a bit too sharply.

Marjorie cast her a long, speculative look, and Emerson realized too late she'd tipped her hand. Oh, God. Why did she have to bite? Why couldn't she have let it go and explained to Ainsley later on that her grandmother had old-fashioned ideas about some things?

"It looks like Ainsley's not the only one with a new friend." Marjorie went on studying her with those cool, assessing eyes.

Emerson's face went hot and panic rose in her, beating like the wings of a captive butterfly. Her mother suspected something. She was almost sure of it. "Of course, we're friendly. I'm over here all the time. Who else is there to talk to?" Not until the words were out did she realize her gaffe.

But it was too late to take it back. Flags of color appeared on Marjorie's cheeks and she seemed to shrink into the mound of pillows at her back. She looked like a baby bird without its feathers, tiny and vulnerable.

"I meant when you're asleep." Emerson tried to smooth it over.

But her mother wasn't buying her flimsy explanation. "I'm sorry I'm such a burden to you," she said in a small, hurt voice.

"I didn't say that."

"If you'd rather not come, just say so. No one's holding a gun to your head."

Emerson blew out an exasperated breath. "I'm sorry, Mother. That came out wrong. It's just that I'm a little stressed at the moment."

"You're overworked, is all." Somewhat mollified, Marjorie seized the chance to drive home her earlier point. "If you'd stop being so stubborn and find someone to live-in . . ."

Emerson tuned out the rest. She felt a headache coming on. Why couldn't she have been honest with her mother? But it was useless, she knew. If she'd told her about Reggie, it would only have made matters worse. Marjorie's doctors had warned that her heart, weakened from the chemotherapy and radiation, could very well give out if subjected to any undue stress. *How would I feel*, Emerson wondered, *knowing I was responsible for robbing her of what little time she has left?*

No, there was only one person she could talk to right now. Someone who wouldn't judge her or make her feel guilty. "Why don't you see what's on TV while I take some of this food down to Nacario?" she said when her mother had finally run out of breath. She picked up their trays and carried them into the kitchen. Leaving the washing up for later on, she made up a plate and carried it down in the elevator.

"Ah, *chiquita*, you know the way to an old man's heart," Nacario said, peeling off the tin foil to eye the leftovers as if this were a gourmet feast.

"I still don't see why you have to work weekends," she said as they settled on folding chairs in the box room where the staff took their breaks. He certainly had enough seniority to assign this shift to one of the more junior employees.

He shrugged. "Jamal and Ernesto, they have young children at home." Nacario's were grown, the four eldest with families of their own and the two youngest off at college. "Besides, I'll be retiring soon enough."

She smiled and shook her head. Nacario had been talking about retiring for years. "I'll believe it when I see it."

"Soon it won't be up to me to decide." He pressed a hand to the small of his back, wincing a little. "My spirit is strong, but the body is not so willing these days. There's no getting around it, *chiquita*. I'm old. There comes a day when even the most stubborn man has to face that fact." In that instant, as he sat there hunched over the plate of food balanced on one splayed knee, he *did* look old. But his familiar face, even with its sagging jowls and the pouches under his eyes, was all the more dear to her because of it.

"If I know you, you'll be doing chin-ups while your buddies are being pushed around in wheelchairs," she said with a laugh. Even so, she felt a touch of unease.

"God willing." He rolled his eyes heavenward as he made the sign of the cross. He was digging into his food when he paused to inquire about her mother. "I haven't seen her in days. I hope she hasn't caught that flu that's been going around."

"No. Just this latest round of chemo—it's really knocked her out." On nice days the day nurse usually took her out to get some air, but lately Marjorie hadn't been feeling up to even that.

"And how have *you* been, *chiquita*?" he asked, eyeing her as if he sensed something was on her mind.

"Either miserable or happier than I've ever been in my life, depending on when you ask," she said with a sigh. She lived for the stolen hours with Reggie, when he was between classes and Ainsley at school, but then there were the days when they were apart, when she'd long for him and feel angry at Marjorie for forcing them to sneak around. Taking note of Nacario's puzzled expression, she explained, "I've been seeing someone, and let's just say my mother wouldn't be too happy if she knew."

"I take it she wouldn't approve of this man?"

Emerson smiled thinly. "Actually, it's Reggie." It felt good to let the secret out, if only to Nacario.

"Ah." Nacario nodded slowly, taking it in. "This is a delicate matter, I agree."

"If my mother found out, it would kill her."

"Meanwhile, you are the one who is suffering," he pointed out.

"I've looked at it from every angle, and I can't see a way out."

"Are you sure it's only your mother that's holding you back?" His gaze was gentle but probing.

She thought for a moment before reluctantly acknowledging, "I suppose a part of me is afraid of making another mistake. And we're so different—on the surface, at least."

"True love knows no obstacles," he said, no doubt thinking of his wife, whom he'd married when they were just sixteen. They'd arrived in this country penniless, speaking no English, and with a baby on the way. Forty years later they were still very much in love.

"From your lips to God's ear, as my friend Franny would say." Though in Emerson's experience, love rarely conquered all. With a sigh, she rose to her feet. "I should be getting back. My mother will wonder what's keeping me. Don't worry about the plate. I'll come back for it later on." It was no use telling him, she knew. The plate and flatware would be delivered to their door sparkling clean before the day was out.

She hugged him, resting her head on his shoulder a moment before drawing back. "Thank you," she said.

"He's a good man. You chose well," he told her.

As she rode up in the elevator, Emerson thought about all the bumbling first dates and blossoming relationships Nacario had witnessed through the years. He'd been there to listen and when need be provide a shoulder to cry on, but until now he'd always kept his opinions to himself. The fact that he'd given Reggie his approval meant a great deal to her.

Now if only she could get her mother to see it the same way. . . .

*   *   *

The following Thursday, Emerson was leaving the office at the end of the day when her cell phone rang. It was Reggie. Her heart leaped at the sound of his voice, but just as quickly fell when he told her why he was calling. There was something he needed to talk to her about, something urgent he couldn't tell her over the phone. From his tone she guessed it wasn't good.

"I'm on my way home," she told him. "Why don't you meet me there? Ainsley will be at a play date until dinnertime."

By the time he joined her half an hour later, she'd worked herself into a state, convinced this was it, he was going to break up with her. He was tired of sneaking around, he'd say. If she couldn't see him openly, he had no choice but to end it. It took her completely by surprise when instead he pulled a folded letter from his back pocket and wordlessly handed it to her.

Reading it, Emerson felt the blood drain from her face. "It says your visa has been revoked. This can't be right. It has to be some mistake." She shook her head in disbelief. "They don't even give a reason!" Just some governmental gobbledygook that made no sense.

"Apparently they don't have to." He spoke with the bitter resignation of someone used to the byzantine ways of the INS.

"But they can't do this! You haven't done anything wrong!"

She looked up to find Reggie smiling sadly. He looked as if he'd run the whole way, his face lightly sheened with perspiration and dark half-moons of sweat standing out under the arms of his shirt. "You forget I don't have the same rights as you."

"Okay, so you weren't born in this country, but that doesn't mean they can just throw you out without an explanation," she went on, growing more indignant by the moment.

"It appears they can."

"We'll fight this. We'll get a lawyer."

He shook his head. She knew what he was thinking: He couldn't afford a lawyer and was too proud to let her pay.

"But . . ." She started to protest, but he put a finger to her lips.

"There is another way." He eyed her gravely, and she understood at once what he was getting at.

For a wild moment she seized upon it. Of course! They'd get married. That would solve everything.

Just as quickly she realized it would only complicate matters. She had her daughter to think of. Much as Ainsley adored Reggie, it would be wrong to spring it on her without warning. And she didn't even want to consider the consequences where Marjorie was concerned. Whatever anyone else might think, she knew the threat of imminent death was real. She couldn't have that on her conscience. She was having a hard enough time dealing with the guilt Marjorie had heaped on her in her lifetime.

"Oh, Reggie. I wish it were that easy." She put her arms around him, burying her face against his shoulder and breathing in his strong, earthy scent. "If it were a year from now or even six months . . ." She lifted her head to search his face for some sign that he understood, that he didn't hate her for being weak. "I'd marry you in a heartbeat if I had only myself to think of."

"I know. I was wrong to suggest it," he said gently.

"We'll fight this," she vowed again through gritted teeth. Suddenly she was all business. Reggie might lack the resources, but she knew her way around the system. In her line of work, she dealt with government agencies all the time. Okay, so it was mainly just booking public rooms for parties, but from the red tape involved, it might as well be lobbying Capitol Hill. She wouldn't let Reggie's pride stand in the way either. This was too important. "I'm calling my lawyer." Henry would be able to recommend someone who specialized in immigration law. "Don't worry about the money, you can pay me back."

But Reggie was shaking his head, looking stricken. "It's too much to ask. It could take years."

"You're not asking, I'm offering." She spoke briskly, brooking no argument. "If you're going to live here, you might as well get used to the fact that in this country, it's not always the man taking care of the woman. I get to take care of *you* some of the time." She took him by the arm, steering him over to the sofa. "Now sit tight while I call Henry. . . ."

Fall

They say only fools fall in love, and that's okay.
Been fallin' all my life, so I'm goin' that way.
I may be a fool, and I'm no saint.
I done wrong, pretended to be what I ain't.
Broken some hearts, bitten off more than I could.
Left before the sun was up, stayed longer than I
  should.
But I know one thing and it's true:
I need you.
It's a long way to the ground.
All I ask, babe, please, is catch me on the way
  down . . .

— "HEART OF CLAY," BURN IT UP (1974 ALBUM BY
                                   ASTRAL PLANE)

Chapter Thirteen

Close your eyes," Keith ordered.

Franny did as she was told. "Can I open them now?" she asked after a few seconds.

"Not yet."

"The suspense is killing me."

It had been ever since she'd arrived in L.A., the Friday before. In the days since, each time Keith cleared his throat or let his gaze linger on her a beat too long, she'd wonder, *Is this it? Is he going to ask me to marry him?* Only a short while ago, having him pop the question would have been her heart's desire. And why not? He was wonderful and caring. Best of all, the fact that she was pregnant with another man's child didn't make her marked-down goods in his eyes the way it would with some men; amazingly he viewed it as a plus. In short, he was everything she'd ever wanted in a man. There was just one problem: Marrying Keith would put a continent between her and Jay.

Now the moment of truth had come. Today was her birthday, and she knew that it was now or never. Listening to the rustle of paper—something being lowered onto the table, where she sat—she felt as if her heart would explode.

"Okay, you can open your eyes now," Keith said.

Franny opened them to the sight of a large gift-wrapped box tied with a pink satin ribbon. Her first thought was that it was too big to be a ring. A strange mixture of disappointment and relief washed over her. "You shouldn't have," she said, grinning up at him.

"Nothing's too good for the birthday girl."

"What's in it?" she asked, giving the box a little shake.

"If I told you, it wouldn't be a surprise."

"I'm not so big on surprises."

"Why not?"

"They're not always the good kind."

"I'm pretty sure you'll like this one." He smiled at her, looking adorably scruffy in his jeans and Lakers sweatshirt, unshaven and barefoot.

"Okay, here goes." Franny couldn't decide whether it was the baby or butterflies making her stomach flutter as she gingerly untied the bow. She pried off the lid and dug through layer upon layer of tissue paper, only to discover the box was empty. "What is this, some kind of joke?" she asked, smiling up at him in puzzlement. "I know I said I didn't want anything for my birthday, but isn't this going a little far?"

Wordlessly Keith drew a small velvet box from the pocket of his sweatshirt. "I told you it was a surprise." He lifted the lid to reveal a diamond ring that flashed in the sunlight pouring in through the large picture window overlooking the bay. He sank down onto one knee before her, asking solemnly, "Franny Richman, will you marry me?"

Franny immediately burst into tears.

Keith gathered her in his arms, not an easy feat considering how much of her there was. With a laugh that was more of a hiccup she said, "If you were hoping to get laid out of this, I'd have settled for a foot rub."

He drew back with a grin. "Shoot. You mean I went to all this trouble for nothing?"

"What can I say? I'm a cheap date."

"And I'm a guy who knows a bargain when he sees one. I figure I'll be getting two for the price of one." He placed a hand on her belly, which formed a fuzzy mound in the borrowed terry-cloth robe she had on, his expression turning serious. "That is, if the answer is yes."

Franny dried her tears on a napkin. How could she not love this guy? He was cute, smart, funny, and he loved kids.

The thought of Jay intruded, but she pushed it aside. Whatever she was feeling for him right now, it wasn't love. Not *that* kind of love. It was just that her emotions had somehow gotten tangled up in his being the baby's father.

She blew her nose into the napkin, saying with a wobbly smile, "In that case, mister, you've got a deal." A chance like this came but once in a lifetime. She'd be crazy to pass it up.

"You won't regret it. I promise." He wriggled the ring onto her somewhat swollen finger.

"My mother is rolling over in her grave right now," she said, with a teary laugh.

He arched a bow. "Because she wouldn't want a goy for a son-in-law?"

"You're talking about a woman who thought a Christmas tree was one step from hanging a crucifix on the wall."

"Mine goes all out—theme sweaters, plastic Santas, reindeer on the lawn, the works. And guess who has to put up all those outdoor lights each year?"

"What am I getting myself in for here?" Franny asked with a mock groan.

"A guy who adores you. Plus a lifetime of mind-blowing sex." He rose to his full height, pulling her to her feet and wrapping his arms around what was left of her waist.

The sex *was* good, she thought. At least as good as it could be given her swollen state—these days, their lovemaking felt more like a Jacques Cousteau special on the mating habits of whales.

All at once her elation faded and she thought of all that she'd be giving up. Not just Jay, or the chance for her baby to know its father. Her whole life was in New York; she'd be leaving behind a job, friends, not to mention Zabar's and the Carnegie Deli.

Keith must have sensed something, for he drew back wearing a look of consternation. "You're not having second thoughts, I hope."

"Are you kidding? Until the swelling goes down, you'd need a hacksaw to get this ring off my finger." She gave it a little tug to demonstrate that it was on tight. But her lighthearted words did nothing to dislodge the tiny pebble that had settled in the pit of her stomach.

She was heading off to the bathroom—lately, it seemed as if she had to pee every five minutes—when Keith said, "Hold on. I have something else for you." He disappeared into the next room, reappearing moments later with another gift-wrapped box. "It'll have to wait until after the baby comes, but I couldn't resist."

She unwrapped it to find a lacy silk teddy from Victoria's Secret, in a size that might have fit her when she was around ten. What did he think, that she was going to magically shrink to a size two after the baby came? But she thanked him anyway, adding, "Just don't expect me to be able to squeeze into this anytime soon." Even at her smallest, she'd have been lucky to fit it over one thigh.

They spent the rest of the morning calling everyone with the good news. Keith's parents made all the right noises, though given the slightly cool reception Franny had gotten from them, she suspected it had more to do with her willingness to relocate than anything else. His three sisters, all married themselves, seemed genuinely thrilled, however. And Emerson equally so.

"Have you told Stevie yet?" she asked, after Franny had filled her in.

"We're having lunch at her mom's. I thought I'd wait until then."

"What about Jay?" A cautious note crept into Emerson's voice. She was no doubt thinking that a move to L.A. would have long-lasting repercussions as far as their child was concerned.

Some of the wind went out of Franny's sails. "Not yet. It can wait till I get back." She didn't want to tell him over the phone.

"By the way, I had dinner with him the other night," Emerson reported.

"How did he seem?" Franny worried that in her absence he'd revert to his old habits.

"A little out of sorts, to be honest."

Franny felt her chest constrict. "I'm sure he misses Viv."

"I don't think that was it."

"What then?"

There was a brief pause at the other end, then Emerson said, "I could be wrong, but I think their marriage is in trouble."

Franny had suspected as much herself. Even so, she asked, "What makes you think so?"

"It wasn't anything he said. Mainly it's what he *didn't* say. He barely mentioned her the whole meal."

"Can you blame him?" Franny quickly rose to Jay's defense. "He's hurting, too. And it doesn't seem as if she's in any hurry to get back."

"You know Viv." Emerson was referring to her penchant for disappearing.

Franny knew that Emerson had never particularly cared for Vivienne, though she tried her best for Jay's sake. Emerson's heart had genuinely gone out to her after she'd lost the baby, but it was obvious now that her charity was starting to grow thin. Maybe Vivienne's self-centeredness reminded her of her mother's . . . or she didn't consider her a good match for Jay. Probably a little of both, Franny guessed. Either way, she decided it would be best to change the subject. She'd had her own issues with Vivienne in the past and didn't want to say anything that would make her appear unsympathetic.

She asked instead how it was going with Reggie.

Emerson filled her in on the latest chapter in her ongoing soap opera. So far, they'd come up against a brick wall in trying to get his visa reinstated, but she had a lawyer on it, supposedly one of the best in his field, and she was confident he'd get to the bottom of it.

"I'm sure it'll work out," said Franny, hoping she was right.

"I'm counting on it. But, listen, don't let me rain on your parade." Emerson spoke with forced cheer. "Congratulations again. Oh, and by the way, happy thirty-sixth. With all the excitement, I almost forgot it was your birthday."

"I wish I could say the same," Franny replied with a laugh, remembering when getting older was cause for celebration. Now each advancing year made her want to turn back the clock.

After she got off the phone, she showered and got dressed for the barbecue at Stevie's mom's. She'd told Stevie in advance that she didn't want a big fuss made over it being her birthday, but Stevie had said it was too late, she already had a surprise in store. As soon as Franny and Keith pulled up in front of Nancy's house, Stevie came dashing out to meet them.

"So what's the big surprise?" Franny asked as they were on their way into the house.

"You'll see," Stevie said mysteriously, hooking an arm through Franny's.

But inside, Franny could see nothing out of the ordinary. Just people milling about, and Nancy in the kitchen stirring something on the stove. She gave Franny a peck on the cheek and greeted Keith warmly, introducing them to the other guests, most of them neighbors.

Afterward Franny was pressed into service cutting up celery for the potato salad while Keith husked the corn. In all the confusion, she scarcely noticed when Stevie slipped out the back door.

Moments later she looked up at the sound of the door banging shut to find Stevie walking toward her, accompanied by an older, weather-beaten man in jeans and flip-flops and sporting a gray ponytail. "Guys, there's someone I'd like you to meet," Stevie said, sounding shy all of a sudden. Even from across the room, Franny could see she was blushing. "Franny, Keith, this is my dad."

The ear of corn Keith had been husking slipped from his hand, landing on the floor with a thud. He looked as astonished as if it were Jim Morrison risen from the dead. But he quickly recovered and stepped forward, thrusting out his hand. "Mr. Tobin, it's an honor."

"I know only one Mr. Tobin and that was my dad," the man said. "Please, call me Grant."

"Nice to meet you." Franny wiped her wet hand on her pant leg before shaking his hand. "I've heard a lot about you."

"I'm sure you have," said Grant, with a rueful look that spoke volumes.

Within minutes he and Keith were deep in conversation at the other end of the room. Grant had to know that Keith was writing a book about him. She'd seen the initial guardedness on his face when they were introduced, but whatever reservations he'd had seemed to have abated. Knowing Keith, he was jiving with Grant on his favorite subject: rock and roll. Even if Grant remained gun shy about being interviewed, the two would never run out of things to talk about.

"So this is your big surprise, huh?" Franny commented to Stevie as they were carrying platters of food out to the picnic table. "And all this time I thought it was a birthday cake."

"There's that, too," Stevie said, shooting her a wry glance.

"So did you have to twist his arm to get him to come?"

"You could say that. I told him Keith was the only one who could set the record straight and unless he wanted to spend the rest of his life trying to live down the rumors, he'd better come meet him."

"Sounds more like bribery to me."

"Whatever, it worked. For some reason, he listens to me."

"Maybe because you're his daughter."

"Maybe." Stevie seemed to ponder that fact as she set out plates and napkins.

"So have you two worked it out?" Franny knew Stevie was still troubled by his dark past.

"Let's just say we've arrived at an understanding," Stevie said. "I know he's far from perfect but I also know he's trying, in his own way. And he knows I'm not going anywhere."

"It's a start," Franny said.

"Yeah, I guess it is." Wearing a small smile, Stevie tipped her head back, momentarily basking in the sunshine filtering through the trees. Overhead, smoke from the barbecue rose in a thick gray plume and nearby insects attracted by the food darted and spun.

The meal was as delicious and eclectic as Franny had come to expect from Stevie's mom. In addition to hamburgers and sword-fish steaks, there were tofu dogs and veggie burgers for the nonmeat eaters, which included husband and wife glassblowers and the man

Nancy was currently seeing, a yoga instructor who'd recently converted to Buddhism.

When the table had been cleared, Nancy brought out a cake with candles on it and they all sang "Happy Birthday." While she passed out slices, Stevie poured the champagne—sparkling cider for Franny, Nancy, and Grant—and everyone lifted their glasses in a toast to the newly betrothed couple. Franny sat there grinning, feeling self-conscious about being the center of attention. Or maybe it hadn't quite sunk in that she was engaged. Each time she looked down at her left hand and saw the diamond ring glittering on her finger, it came as a mild shock.

Her gaze fell on Grant, and she thought about Stevie's growing up not knowing her dad. Franny wondered if one day her child would feel the same way about Jay, that he was a father in name only. Was she doing the right thing in moving so far away? And what about Jay? How did you tell a guy who'd lost one child that he was about to lose another?

It was several days after she returned to New York before Franny got up the nerve to phone Jay. But any apprehension she'd felt vanished at the sound of his voice. He seemed happy to hear from her and they chatted just like old times. When he told her he had a belated birthday present for her, she didn't hesitate to invite him over.

Seeing him walk through the door, his hair windblown and cheeks flushed from the outdoors, she felt for the first time since she'd gotten back that she was truly home. In one hand was a shopping bag full of Chinese takeout and in the other a gift-wrapped package. He handed her the gift, saying, "It's a little late, but they say the best things in life are worth waiting for."

She opened it to find the Victorian brass carriage clock she'd admired in an antiques store on one of their jaunts. "Oh, Jay." For a moment she was speechless. "It's beautiful. I can't believe you re-membered."

"Of course," he said as if it was only natural that he would. "Anyway, I never properly thanked you, so this is partly to let you know how much I appreciate everything you've done." Just then the clock chimed, and they shared a smile that seemed to contain a world of unspoken sentiment.

"Don't be silly. What are friends for?" Franny set the clock down on the small cherry cabinet she'd inherited from her grand-mother, where it looked perfectly at home. "There. Now I'll think of you whenever I look to see what time it is."

"Is that supposed to be a hint?" he said, referring to his chronic tardiness.

She kissed him on the cheek, relieving him of the shopping bag. "Another way of looking at it is that from now on I won't be so annoyed when you're running late."

He laughed. "Fat chance."

Watching him shrug off his suit jacket, she fought an impulse to smooth his windblown hair—a sisterly gesture that wouldn't have seemed so sisterly given how her heart was racing—peering into the bag instead. "I hope you didn't get any of those fried dumplings. You know I can't resist them, and the last thing I need is to put on any more weight."

"You can have the chicken and broccoli," he said.

He went into the kitchen, scooping a handful of clean flatware from the dishwasher before reaching into the cupboard above it for some plates. He knew where everything was in her apartment, sometimes better than she did. Once, after she'd spent fifteen min-utes searching for her missing corkscrew, he'd found it still in the cork of a half-drunk bottle of Chardonnay in the fridge. Now, watching him pry open containers and dump their steaming contents into bowls, Franny thought that a stranger catching a glimpse of them through the window just then would have assumed he was her husband.

"Here's to getting older," he toasted, clinking his glass against hers when they were seated at the table about to dig into their feast.

"And hopefully wiser," Franny said.

They spent the rest of the meal catching up on everything that had happened while she was gone. Jay told her all about the TV commercial he was working on for Uruchima Motors—they'd been so pleased with the job he'd done on the Roughrider, they'd given him the account for their newest sports car, the Wasp. Franny, for her part, only lightly touched upon her trip to L.A.—the places she'd gone, the people she'd seen—not wanting to drop her bombshell in the middle of dinner. For the same reason, she'd taken off her engagement ring and tucked it away in a drawer.

"What's the latest from Viv?" she ventured at last.

"I spoke to her last week. She's doing better."

"Did she say when she was coming home?"

"She was a little vague about that." His expression tightened. "To be honest, Viv and I don't have much to say to each other these days."

Franny thought back to what Emerson had said and wondered if their marriage really was in trouble. It certainly looked that way. "I imagine it's a little like dancing around the five-hundred-pound gorilla in the room," she said in Vivienne's defense.

"I suppose so." With a visible effort, he brightened. "But listen, you didn't invite me over to watch me wallow in self-pity."

Franny couldn't help feeling a twinge of sadness, knowing that evenings like this one would soon be coming to an end. They'd always be close, but somehow it wouldn't be the same.

She waited until they were curled on the sofa in front of the TV with bowls of ice cream that she finally broached the subject she'd been avoiding all evening. "Jay, there's something I should have told you before."

"What?" He turned to her with an expectant look.

"Keith's asked me to marry him."

Slowly, he lowered his spoon into his bowl. "And?"

She swallowed hard. "I told him yes. Look, I know we agreed you'd help raise this child, but . . ." She let the sentence trail off.

"That'll be kind of hard with me living on the opposite coast," he said quietly.

"You're not mad, are you?"

"No. Just . . . you caught me off guard." He shook his head as if to clear it, mustering a small, strained smile. "So you decided to go for it after all?"

"He offered to make an honest woman of me. How could I refuse?"

"In that case, I guess congratulations are in order. When's the big day?"

"We haven't set a date yet. I'm not making any more major decisions until after the baby's born."

"As long as you love him, that's all that matters."

Franny didn't say anything. She knew she ought to assure him that she *did* love Keith, that he was the best thing that had ever happened to her, but for some reason the words wouldn't come. Right now, Jay didn't need any more reminding that another man would be raising his child. She brought her head to rest on his shoulder. "Are you going to be all right with this?"

"If it's what you want, I'm all for it," he said, with forced enthusiasm.

"It's not what we talked about, I know, but things don't always work out the way you plan."

"Tell me about it." She heard the bitterness in his voice, and immediately felt bad for reminding him of his loss. But he rallied, saying, "We'll work something out. I have a lot of frequent-flier miles racked up."

"Whatever happens, our kid will grow up knowing who his dad is," she promised.

Jay nodded, looking less than convinced. He was smart enough to realize their child would nonetheless grow up calling another man Dad. He smiled in resignation, bringing a hand to her cheek. "You've waited a long time for this. You deserve to be happy."

"I just wish . . ." She broke off, looking away.

"You wish what?" He put a hand under her chin, bringing her head around to meet his gaze.

"Nothing," she lied.

She studied his face as if to memorize it, his prairie sky eyes and mouth that turned up at the corners even when he wasn't smiling. She felt like Dorothy saying good-bye to the scarecrow: *I'll miss you most of all.*

When he leaned in to kiss her she scarcely realized what was happening. As she sat there, too shocked to move, there was only the warm pressure of his mouth, the tip of his tongue playing lightly over hers. A lazy heat curled through her like smoke and before she knew it, she was responding, parting her lips and winding her arms around his neck.

All the while, her mind spun, unable to grasp what was going on. This was Jay . . . *her* Jay?

"What was *that* all about?" she gasped, when they finally drew apart.

"I don't know." He looked equally shaken.

Confusion quickly gave way to embarrassment. It was a freak thing, she told herself. All that talk about being separated had gone to their heads.

She pulled away, saying in an unsteady voice, "I think maybe we've been spending too much time together. It . . . it might be a good idea if we didn't see each other for a while."

"You're probably right," he said unhappily, reaching up to smooth his thumb lightly over her cheek, a move that set off an avalanche in the pit of her stomach.

"We can't let this get in the way of our friendship." Even as she spoke, she knew her words were hollow. Right now, what she wanted most of all was for him to kiss her again.

He sat in silence for a moment, his eyes searching her face. At last he seemed to come to some sort of resolution, and rose to his feet a bit unsteadily, saying, "I guess I should be going."

She saw him to the door, not kissing him good-bye as she normally would. A deep awkwardness had set in and she was suddenly desperate for him to leave. At the same time, she was equally desperate for him to stay. As he was heading out onto the landing, she called after him, "Jay." He paused and turned to face her: a tall, fair-haired man, in a creased blue suit and tie that hung askew, who in that moment appeared scarcely older than the boy she'd first encountered all those years ago on the steps of Firestone Library. "Just for a little while, okay? Until we . . ." What? Develop amnesia? "Until we get our heads straight."

He nodded, giving her a slow, sad smile, then turned on his heel and was gone.

Chapter Fourteen

No! Don't put me on hold!" Emerson cried into the phone. But the woman at the other end apparently didn't care that Emerson had been getting the runaround for weeks and had heard every song in the Muzak repertoire, for the line went silent. Damn! It was all she could do not to slam down the phone in frustration.

Greg Purcell hadn't gotten much further. The only thing the immigration lawyer had accomplished so far was to get a six-week extension on Reggie's visa while the matter was being investigated. But at least it would buy them time, which they desperately needed.

When at last the caseworker came back on the line, Emerson was informed that Mr. Okanta's case had been transferred to another department. She was put through to a supervisor's voice mail and she left a message along with her phone number, though she didn't expect a call back anytime soon. In any event, it would just be more reshuffling of the deck.

No sooner had she hung up than her new secretary clomped into her office with a stack of pink message slips. Jenna dropped them on her desk, saying, "I didn't want to interrupt you while you were on the phone." Today's outfit was a shapeless plaid skirt, crew-neck sweater at least three sizes too big, and black tights with clogs. A recent Sarah Lawrence graduate, Jenna was under the mistaken impression that what had been acceptable attire on campus was equally acceptable in the work world. Emerson made a mental note to take her shopping when all this was over. Jenna might have graduated summa cum laude, but she clearly needed a lesson in Fashion 101.

Emerson leafed through the message slips while sipping coffee gone lukewarm: Woody Reichert from Oasis Records—she was promoting an event for one of their artists; Janelle Rusk from HarperCollins, wanting to know about a press release; Bill Schnei-der, manager of the Tower Records store that was hosting the Oasis event. All stuff she should have followed up on sooner. Instead, she'd spent the better part of the morning in the seventh circle of hell known as government bureaucracy. In fact, these past few weeks, a lot more than she cared to think about had been relegated to the back burner.

With a sigh, she dropped the slips in her in-box. They'd have to wait until later. She had a meeting at eleven with the principal at Ainsley's school and, if she didn't hurry, she'd be late. Grabbing her purse and dashing out the door, Emerson wondered what Mrs. Ballard wanted to talk to her and Briggs about. It must be fairly serious to schedule a meeting. Was Ainsley falling behind in school? Was it even possible to flunk second grade? Guilt, the bane of her existence, crept up on her with the stealth of an assassin. If there was something going on with Ainsley, shouldn't she have noticed it herself?

Outside, the car she'd hired was waiting at the curb. Luckily, traffic was light and at five past eleven they were gliding to a stop in front of the school. Tall, ivied brick walls enclosed the campus and Episcopal church beyond, accessed by a wrought-iron gate that was kept locked after hours. Stepping through it onto the campus dotted with trees, mostly bare now, Emerson felt her anxiety abate somewhat. Whatever it was, how bad could it be?

Inside, the school was sunny and welcoming, with colorful paintings and class projects taped to the painted brick walls and the happy sounds of children drifting from the classrooms. Emerson was ushered into the principal's office, where her ex-husband, always annoyingly punctual, sat chatting with Mrs. Ballard, a heavyset, grandmotherish lady who favored seasonal sweaters like the green cardigan patterned with jack-o'-lanterns that she had on now. "Sorry I'm late," she apologized, casting a weak smile at Briggs as she sank into the chair beside him. "I hope I didn't miss anything."

"Not at all," Mrs. Ballard assured her. "Your husband and I were just . . ." She let the rest of the sentence trail off, as if remembering that Emerson and Briggs were no longer a couple, and resumed her seat behind the desk. "Thank you both for coming. I hope you know I wouldn't have asked you here in the middle of the day if I didn't feel it was important."

She began by reiterating what they already knew, that Ainsley was an excellent student, that her reading scores were at the fourth-grade level and she showed a real aptitude for art. And until recently she'd been sociable and fun-loving as well. Here, Mrs. Ballard's brow furrowed. Emerson felt herself tense up as the older woman went on to explain that lately Ainsley had been withdrawn and that she cried at the drop of a hat. It was so unusual for her that Mrs. Ballard felt it warranted sharing her concerns. Had either of them noticed a change in her behavior? she asked.

Emerson felt a renewed attack of guilt. *My fault*, she thought,

I'm a bad mother. She hadn't been spending enough time with her daughter lately. By the time she got home at the end of each day, she was usually so exhausted she could hardly see straight. And, let's face it, her thoughts were so taken up with Reggie she hadn't been able to focus on much else. When she wasn't slipping off to be with him, she was making calls on his behalf. If Ainsley was feeling neglected as a result, was it any wonder? What made it even worse was that it had somehow escaped Emerson's attention. Sure, there had been some incidents recently, a few temper tantrums and periods of moodiness, but she'd simply chalked it up to growing pains.

But if Briggs shared her poor opinion of her mothering, he refrained from airing it. Instead, he surprised her by confessing, "I'm afraid I've been remiss, Mrs. Ballard. You see, I've been working such crazy hours these past weeks that when Ainsley's with me, it's usually my wife who looks after her." His firm had recently merged, he explained, and his workload was twice what it normally was. "I don't know if that's what's bothering her, but there could be a connection. You know how little girls are. They want their daddies all to themselves." He smiled, clearly not wanting too big a deal made of it.

Emerson could have kissed him just then. But it wasn't fair to let Briggs shoulder all the blame. "I should have been paying closer attention myself," she said.

"Have there been any changes in her routine? Or in *your* routines? Other than work-related, that is." Mrs. Ballard's brow furrowed as she glanced from Emerson to Briggs.

"Well, there's my mother, she's quite ill," Emerson offered.

Mrs. Ballard eyed her with sympathy, asking, "Are she and Ainsley close?"

"Yes, of course." It wasn't strictly true—even before Marjorie got sick she was always too busy with her committees and various social events to spend much time with Ainsley—though if her mother had a soft spot, it was for her grandaughter. "But my mother's been sick for some time. Ainsley's had time to adjust."

"May I make a suggestion then?" The principal sat back in her chair, her pudgy fingers forming a steeple under her chin. "Perhaps Ainsley would benefit from seeing someone."

"A therapist, you mean?" Emerson experienced a little inner jolt. Was it really that serious?

"Our school psychologist has put together a list of names . . . ," Mrs. Ballard went on, so sincere and well-meaning that Emerson wanted to strangle her.

"Thank you, Mrs. Ballard, but we'll take it from here." Briggs politely but firmly cut her off, smiling pleasantly as he rose to his feet. "We appreciate all your efforts and we'll certainly look into it." He put out his hand. "In the meantime, if anything else comes up, please don't hesitate to let us know." Standing there so erect, he looked almost statesmanlike with his wire-rimmed glasses and herringbone jacket the same tweedy brown as his hair.

He swept out of the office, leaving Emerson to totter after him in her four-inch heels, wondering, *Who was that masked man?* She couldn't recall her ex-husband ever being that assertive when they were married. She hadn't even known Briggs was capable of it.

He paused outside, waiting for her to catch up. "We need to talk," he said.

"Now's as good a time as any." She pointed to the bench adjacent to the church, at the other end of the campus. It was a bit chilly to sit outdoors, but it would be private enough.

Briggs glanced at his watch and nodded. Out of long habit she took his arm as they strolled along the pathway to the church.

"I should have seen this coming," she said, when they were seated. "It's these damn hours. Between that and my mother . . ." *Reggie, too,* she added silently.

"Before we start blaming ourselves, we should find out what, if anything, is wrong," Briggs said in a more measured tone. "How do we know it's not something school-related?"

"She adores Mrs. Frey." Ainsley was always saying she wanted to be just like her teacher when she grew up.

"Maybe one of the other kids then. You know how they can be."

"She's always gotten along well with her classmates." Emerson tried to think of anything that had happened at school recently that might have upset her, but the only thing that came to mind was Ainsley's best friend, Hillary, being out sick for a whole week.

"Something at home then?" he ventured cautiously, darting her a look. Briggs was always careful not to pry into her private life, but she could see the question in his eyes.

She agonized for a moment before concluding that it would be wrong to keep it from him. If it involved Ainsley, he had a right to know. "Actually, I've been seeing someone," she confessed, shivering a little in the cool air. She kept her gaze fixed on a sparrow hopping along the courtyard that bordered on the church, a sturdy red brick structure dating back to the nineteen hundreds.

When she looked over at Briggs, he was wearing an expression so carefully neutral, she knew it masked something deeper. But whatever he was feeling, he kept it to himself, saying only, "I'm surprised Ainsley hasn't mentioned it."

"She doesn't know yet. At least, I'm pretty sure she doesn't." Emerson thought of the time Ainsley had almost walked in on them and her face grew warm. "I've only had him over when she's not around. Still, it's possible she might have picked up on something."

"She's old enough now to know you have a life outside her," Briggs said gently. "Don't you think it would be best if she met this man?"

"She already knows him. In fact, they're good friends." She

turned to him with a wan smile. "It's Reggie, my mother's night nurse."

Briggs knew all about Reggie; these days Ainsley talked of little else. Still, it had to come as a bit of a shock. In her world, though prejudice was openly frowned upon, very few of the people she'd grown up with dated outside their race. But when her eyes searched Briggs's face, she saw nothing to indicate anything other than mild surprise.

"In that case, I should think she'd be delighted," he said. "She seems to think the world of him."

Emerson was grateful to him for not making her feel any worse than she already did. It struck her then that if he hadn't been what she'd wanted in a husband, she hadn't given him much of a chance. Perhaps if she'd been more honest from the beginning he'd have loved her for who she was. She wouldn't have had to wear herself out with all her efforts to please him that, in retrospect, she saw were mostly of her own and Marjorie's making.

"Ainsley's not the problem, it's my mother," she said. Emerson didn't have to spell it out; he'd spent enough time around Marjorie to know she'd disapprove of such a match. "Also, there's a new wrinkle." She explained about the problem with Reggie's visa.

"I know someone who might be able to help," Briggs said, frowning in thought.

"Seriously?" She perked up.

"Remember Brad Whittier? He was in my class at Buckley." She shook her head. The name was vaguely familiar, but she couldn't put a face to it. "He's a state assemblyman now, very tight with Pataki, I understand," Briggs went on. "Anyway, he owes me. A few years ago, I helped his stepdaughter get into Yale. Whenever I run into him, he always mentions it. If I asked him to, I'm sure he wouldn't mind picking up the phone."

"You'd do that?" Emerson eyed him in amazement.

He smiled thinly. "Don't look so surprised. I'm not such a bad guy, you know."

"I never thought that," she said, blushing a little.

"Just the wrong guy then." His smile gave way to a look of resignation. "It's all right. I'd like to think we're past all that. In fact, it would be nice if we could be friends. For Ainsley's sake."

"Not just for Ainsley." She reached for his hand, giving it a light squeeze. "Look, I know you don't have to do this, and I'm truly grateful."

"Actually, I have an ulterior motive," he said, a corner of his mouth turning down in a wry smile. "I know you've always thought I was . . . how shall I put it . . . a bit of a wimp? It would be a matter of personal pride if I could redeem myself, if only belatedly."

She broke into a grin. "Are you kidding? If you pull this off, I'll have a bronze statue erected in your honor."

Several days later, he called her at her office. "How's Ainsley?" he asked.

"She seems okay, but it's hard to tell. I still don't know if it's just growing pains, or if something's really bothering her," Emerson said. She'd tried having a heart to heart talk with her daughter but hadn't made much headway. "Franny gave me the name of a therapist, an author of hers who wrote a book on children of divorce. I spoke to the woman over the phone, but I didn't want to make an appointment without discussing it with you first. In fact, I was just about to call you."

"Sounds like a good idea," he said. "Do you need me to be there?"

"Not for the first appointment. She'd like to see Ainsley alone."

"You'll fill me in afterward then?"

"Of course."

There was a pause at the other end, then Briggs said more cautiously, "Listen, I have some news about your friend."

"Oh?" Her heart began to pound.

"Brad made some calls."

"And?"

"They referred him to Homeland Security."

Emerson was so taken aback she let out an involuntary little laugh. "That's the craziest thing I ever heard. What, do they think he's a terrorist?" Even so, she could feel the blood draining from her face.

"They didn't say. Brad's looking into it." There was another long pause, then Briggs asked in a grave voice, "Em, how much do you actually know about this man?"

"I know he's not a terrorist!" she cried.

"I'm not saying he is. I'm just wondering if there's something in his past that you don't know about."

"I'm sure he has nothing to hide. I know what kind of person he is!" She realized she was practically shouting and glanced at the door to the outer office, relieved to see that it was shut. Getting a grip on herself, she said in a more even tone, "All right. If it'll make you feel any better, I'll talk to him. I'll see if he can think of any reason he'd be on a watch list."

"I think that would be wise. For *all* our sakes," Briggs added ominously.

Emerson hung up feeling as if she were going to be sick to her stomach. She knew in her heart that Reggie was innocent of any wrongdoing. Nonetheless, a small voice in her mind whispered, *It wouldn't be the first time you were fooled into thinking a man was someone he wasn't.*

With a heavy hand and an even heavier heart, she picked up the phone once more, this time to punch in Reggie's number. She arranged to meet him after work, at a Village trattoria where they were unlikely to be spotted by any of her mother's aquaintances.

She arrived just before dark to find him waiting for her out front, wearing a thin overcoat and blowing on his hands to warm them.

"Why didn't you wait inside? You must be freezing," she scolded lightly, as they made their way into the restaurant.

"I was afraid you wouldn't find me so easily." He smiled, gesturing toward the mob scene at the bar. *This* was the Reggie she knew and loved, Emerson thought, a man who understood that it was more about the little, everyday courtesies than any grand gestures.

"My treat this time," he said, when they were seated at their table with menus.

"That's sweet, but really, it isn't necessary. I can write it off as an expense." They both knew it was just an excuse, that the real reason she insisted in paying every time was that she was conscious of his limited resources.

He shook his head. "No, I insist. Otherwise, I shall feel like a kept man." They argued a bit more before she finally gave in. She knew better than to get in the way of his pride.

"When you called, I thought at first it was bad news," Reggie confessed, after they'd ordered and were sipping their drinks.

"What made you think that?" she said, growing uncomfortable all of a sudden in the cozy restaurant filled with bright chatter and delicious smells.

"I don't know. Something in your voice." He shrugged. "But clearly I was wrong. Anyway," he glanced around him, smiling, "I don't see anyone coming to arrest me."

He'd only been joking, of course, but she felt something twist in her gut nonetheless. Only long practice at putting the best face on things kept her from blurting out what was on the tip her of her tongue.

"Do I need a reason to see you?" she asked, lightly running her fingertips over the back of his strong, callused hand. "It's been almost a week. I've missed you." Lately she'd been rushing home from work each day to be with Ainsley, so she hadn't had a moment to herself.

"In that case, we shall have to make up for lost time," he said, smiling at her in a sultry way that sent a surge of warmth spilling down from the pit of her stomach. She could almost feel his hands stroking her skin, teasing her body into loosening its inhibitions . . .

Then the chill of reality set in. Her mind traveled back to her conversation with Briggs. There was no getting around it. She had to ask Reggie if there was anything in his past that might have raised a red flag. If there was even a grain of truth to those accusations, it was her duty to find out.

"Actually, there *is* something," she began, the gravity of her tone letting him know there was another reason she'd asked to meet him. Instantly, he grew alert, his dark eyes, glittering in the candlelight, fixed on her. "A friend of my ex-husband's made some calls on your behalf. Apparently there's been some kind of misunderstanding."

"What kind of misunderstanding?" Reggie frowned in puzzlement.

"Your case has been referred to Homeland Security."

He appeared as dumbfounded as she'd hoped. "I don't understand," he said, shaking his head. Then his eyes widened in dismay. "You can't think . . ."

Emerson wanted desperately to deny it, but she couldn't. She had Ainsley to think of. And her mother. Suppose, just suppose, he *had* been involved in some suspicious activity back in Nigeria. Even if he himself would never harm them, it could expose them to a potential threat. Nonetheless, she felt as if she were plunging a knife into his heart when she asked, "Can you think of any reason you'd be on a terrorist watch list?"

"No. There is no reason." He spoke firmly.

The expression on his face alone should have been the only answer she needed, but she couldn't leave it at that. There was too much at stake. "Maybe something that happened a long time ago that you forgot about?" she pressed, hating that she had to do this.

"I wouldn't forget a thing like that."

"But there must be *some* reason."

"In my country, there has been much bloodshed through the years, for reasons that seldom make sense." He spoke softly, enunciating each word. "My people know it's pointless to ask why. The question always is *how*. How do we get beyond this? But sometimes there is no getting beyond it, and I can see that this is one of those times." He rose to his feet, holding himself perfectly erect. No king had ever looked so dignified. "Please give your mother my regards and tell her I regret that I can no longer care for her."

"No! You don't understand!" Emerson jumped up, catching hold of his sleeve. But it was obvious from the deeply wounded look he wore that he had understood her perfectly.

He removed himself from her grasp, tenderly, regretfully almost, taking a step back. "I wouldn't wish for you to be concerned about her safety, so I think it's best that I go."

With that, he turned on his heel, leaving Emerson struggling to catch her breath in a room suddenly devoid of oxygen.

Winter

My love for Linton is like the foliage in the woods. Time will change it, I'm well aware, as winter changes the trees—my love for Heathcliff resembles the eternal rocks beneath—a source of little visible delight, but necessary.
—EMILY BRONTË, *WUTHERING HEIGHTS*

Chapter Fifteen

Jay was in the war room with Todd Oster and the rest of his design team going over the Concept jeans ad when Inez buzzed him on the intercom.

"Jay, it's Franny on line two."

He picked up, pleasantly surprised to hear from her. These days it was unusual for her to call unless it was about their Lamaze class. Outside that, they'd gotten together only occasionally over the past few months, always with other people around; most recently for Thanksgiving dinner at Emerson's and a book-launch party for one of Franny's authors. They kept up the facade that nothing had changed, but a certain self-consciousness had crept into their conversations, neither of them willing to acknowledge the elephant in the room.

"Hey, what's up?" he asked.

"Are you in the middle of something?" The familiar sound of her voice brought a tug of longing. He missed their old camaraderie. And recently, he often found himself wishing, despite all his careful reasoning, that it could be more than that.

"Nothing that can't wait," he said, ignoring the arch look Todd shot him.

"I just thought you'd want to know that I'm having contractions." Her tone was deliberately casual, but he could hear the veiled anxiety in her voice.

Jay felt his heart kick into high gear. "Jesus." He did a quick mental calculation. "But you're not due for two more weeks." He lowered his voice so the others wouldn't hear.

"Tell that to the baby," Franny said.

"How far apart are the contractions?"

"Ten minutes or so. Too soon to be pushing the panic button."

Too late for that, Jay thought. "Shouldn't you be at the hospital?"

"No way," she said, reminding him of what their Lamaze teacher had cautioned against. "I'd only be stuck there for hours while every intern in the joint took turns poking me like I was a Thanksgiving turkey."

"But you *did* speak to the doctor?"

"I just got off the phone with him," she said. "I think I caught him in the middle of a golf game. Either he meant it when he said I had plenty of time or he didn't want to lose his putt."

"I don't see how you can joke at a time like this." He was mildly dismayed to hear his father's dour voice coming out of his mouth.

"What else am I going to do? It's too late to back out, so I might as well enjoy the ride." He knew she was only cracking jokes as a way of relieving her anxiety. "Though try me when I'm pushing a watermelon through a straw; I might not be laughing then," she said, quoting one of the other women in their class who'd given birth twice before.

A new, panic-driven thought occurred to him. "Please tell me you're not at work." Knowing Franny, it was entirely possible.

"What, you think I'm nuts? Just because I'm in no hurry to get to the hospital, it doesn't mean I want my baby delivered by the office boy."

Our baby, he mentally corrected her.

"I'm on my way over," he said.

"I'm telling you, it's too—" She broke off with a groan. As soon as she'd caught her breath, she gasped, "Ooh. That was a doozy. Okay, so maybe I wouldn't mind some company after all."

"I'm hanging up now. I'll phone you from the cab." He was already reaching for his coat.

Five minutes later he was in a taxi racing across town. It had begun to snow outside, a wet, sleety snow that pelted the windshield. But despite the cold he was sweating profusely under his heavy overcoat in the unheated cab. *You're worrying needlessly*, he told himself. What could go wrong? Franny was healthy and the pregnancy normal.

But hadn't the same been true of Vivienne?

When he arrived, Franny met him at the door in her bathrobe and fuzzy slippers, her hair gathered up in a top knot from which dark curls spewed like a geyser. "That was fast," she said, letting him in. "Did you ski over?"

He shook the snowflakes from his overcoat before tossing it onto the coat rack. "Just about," he said, recalling how the taxi had gone into a skid as they were making the turn onto Bleecker.

"How about a cup of tea?" She was quick to add, "I promise it's not herbal."

Ignoring the offer, he said nervously, "Shouldn't you be . . . I don't know . . ."

"Thrashing around in bed biting on a leather strap?" she finished for him. "I guess that comes later."

"Why don't you sit down while I get *you* some tea," he said, steering her into the tiny, overstuffed living room—Franny could never throw anything out—that right now, with the snow drifting down outside the windows that looked out over the momentarily pristine white landscape of Perry Street, made them seem like the last two people in the world.

"No thanks. I'm supposed to stay on my feet, remember?" She began pacing back and forth across the room, her slippered feet working the worn oriental carpet into little furrows. Then all at once she doubled over, clutching her belly and gasping, "Quick. What time is it?"

He consulted his watch. "Twelve past the hour."

"That's six minutes since the last one," she said, straightening with an effort. She waddled over to the sofa, her hands pressed to the small of her back, and collapsed onto it, panting, a light sheen of perspiration making her forehead gleam in the winter-pale light.

"That's it, we're going. Get dressed while I have them bring the car around." In the taxi on the way over, he'd had the foresight to call his car service. She started to protest but he cut her off, saying firmly, "You can argue all you want on the way to the hospital."

"When did you get so bossy?" She mock-glared at him as he hauled her to her feet.

"This isn't my first time, remember?"

They exchanged a solemn glance. How could she forget?

Franny took a quick shower and threw on her maternity jeans and an oversize sweatshirt emblazoned with a bucking bronco that he recognized as one he'd brought her back from a long-ago trip to Montana. With it stretched over her belly, she looked like the world's most rotund rodeo queen. As he helped her on with her coat, she peered out the window at the falling snow. "How bad is it supposed to get?"

"They're saying a foot. But we should be all right. The worst of it won't be till tonight." He grabbed the bag he'd packed while she was in the shower. Vivienne's had been ready weeks in advance, but with the baby coming early, Franny hadn't had a chance.

Outside, he held onto her elbow, steering her over the slippery pavement to the car waiting at the curb. The only one available had been a stretch limo, and as they climbed in, Franny said, "I thought you were taking me to the hospital.

"I am."

"Then why do I feel as if we're on our way to the prom?"

Jay grinned at her. "I would have gotten you a corsage but there wasn't time."

"Some date you turned out to be."

"I'll make it up to you when all this is over," he promised, momentarily forgetting he was a married man and that Franny was engaged.

She doubled over with another contraction. This time, she held tightly to Jay's hand, grimacing, until it had passed. Jerking her head in the direction of the glass divider, through which they could see the back of the driver's head, she muttered, "I wonder if he charges extra for delivering."

"I'd rather not put that one to the test."

Traffic along Eighth Avenue was bumper to bumper, slowed by the snow covering the roadway in slushy tracks. The contractions were coming every five minutes now; he'd been timing them ever since they'd left. And, unlike Vivienne, who even in hard labor had remained ladylike, Franny was making plenty of noise, grunting and huffing.

"It's all your fault," she panted between contractions, shooting him a fierce look. "If you hadn't signed on for this, we'd be at Shaughnessy's right now, kicking back with a couple of beers."

"As I recall, you had to twist my arm," he said, with a smile.

"I didn't have to twist very hard. Oooohhh." She doubled over once more.

Jay massaged her back, murmuring encouragingly, until she straightened again, looking as if she'd exploded out of a cannon, her face crimson and her curls corkscrewing in every direction. "It's really happening, isn't it?" she said in a hushed voice. "We're having a kid."

He placed a hand on her belly. "I have a feeling he's destined for great things. With our genes, how can he miss?"

"Let's get through this first before we start putting aside money for Harvard."

"Actually, I sort of had my sights set on our alma mater. If we—" He broke off, seeing her suddenly freeze as a stricken look came over her face. "Franny, what is it? Are you all right?"

"I think my water just broke." She looked down at a wet patch spreading over the crotch of her jeans.

He grabbed a baby blanket from the zippered bag and used it to pat her dry as best he could. They were both breathing hard, and Jay's heart was racing. He held Franny in his arms the rest of the way, murmuring over and over in her ear that everything was going to be okay.

At St. Vincent's, she was whisked into a wheelchair and trundled off to the elevator, Jay holding her hand as he jogged alongside. Luckily, the semiprivate room to which she was assigned was unoccupied so Franny was spared having to listen to another woman's anguished howls. Hers alone were enough to bring the roof down.

"You're not leaving, are you?" she called plaintively as he was being hustled out of the room so the doctor could examine her in private.

"I'll be right outside. You think I'd leave this to amateurs?" he teased.

The nurse in attendance responded dryly, "Your wife's in good hands, I assure you."

Jay and Franny exchanged a wry look. Neither bothered to set her straight.

Franny knew now what it would have been like for Fay Wray to give birth to King Kong's baby. If this monster of a kid pushing its way out of her weighed under ten pounds, she thought through her fog of pain, her hips must be smaller than she'd thought. When all this was over, she ought to be able to fit into Paris Hilton's bikini.

"Come on, Franny. Give us a little push," she heard Dr. Stein urge through the roaring in her ears.

"I'm giving birth to King Kong's baby and you want *little?*" she growled. No way was this kid going out the same way it came in. She arched her back, her whole body clenching with the pain as it mounted to a monstrous pitch, a sound that was scarcely human emerging from between her clenched teeth: "Grrrnnnaaaaarghhhh . . ."

"You're doing great, Franny. Almost there." Jay smoothed away the strands of hair stuck to her sweaty forehead. The sound of his voice had a soothing effect, like the shot they'd given her earlier to dull the pain.

"I'll believe it when I see it," she groaned.

"Just a few more pushes. You can do it. I know you can." His voice was gentle yet insistent.

Another tsunami of pain ripped through her, and she cried out. For a moment she almost wished she hadn't gotten herself into this. What was being childless compared to being split open like a ripe cantaloupe? But there was no way out; at this point it was damn the torpedoes and full speed ahead.

Franny bore down with all her might, every muscle in her body quivering.

"I see the head!" crowed the nurse.

Through the rushing noise in her ears, Franny heard the doctor say, "All right, Franny, you can ease up now." She fell back gasping, but no sooner had she caught her breath than he was urging, "Okay, just one more big push." From this angle, all she could see of Dr. Stein between the V of her spread legs were the fuzzy ends of his gray hair poking from under his surgical cap. If she were to rip out every one of those hairs at once, she thought, he still wouldn't know what *real* pain was.

Then she was pushing again, with no other thought than of dislodging this *thing* inside her.

She felt something warm and wet slip out between her thighs, and the pain abruptly eased. Dr. Stein was holding something up, but when she lifted her head to get a better look, all she could make out through the sweat pouring down her forehead and into her eyes was a vaguely flesh-colored bundle smeared from head to toe with what looked like Noxzema.

"A girl!" Dr. Stein cried.

Franny blinked and the bundle materialized into a tiny, perfect infant.

"Mr. Gunderson, would you care to do the honors?" The doctor extended a pair of scissors to Jay.

Jay stopped gazing rapturously at their newborn long enough to cut the umbilical cord, then Franny was cradling the tiny, warm bundle against her breast, her baby's rosebud of a mouth rooting for her nipple. "Smart girl. She knows just where to go." She beamed up at Jay, whose face was wet with tears.

"She's perfect," he said, in a voice soft with wonder. He stroked a tiny, wrinkled foot with his fingertip.

"We did good." No, better—they'd produced a miracle. "Look, she has your eyes." Eyes the blue of a prairie sky in haying season. "And my nose." Her mother would have been proud, even though Franny had wished for a nice straight one like Jay's.

"Not much hair, though." Jay fingered the pale tuft on top of the baby's crown.

"It'll grow," she said.

Jay's happy expression briefly dimmed, as if he were remembering that he wouldn't be around to see that happen. Franny reached for his hand, holding on tight, determined not to let anything spoil this moment. As they huddled together, gazing in awe at the tiny girl with her father's blue eyes and the Richman nose, theirs was an unbroken circle.

Chapter Sixteen

I t's almost enough to make me want another one." Emerson gazed down at the baby, asleep in her cradle.

Stevie peered over her shoulder. "I notice you said 'almost.' Though I have to admit, she is pretty cute." Ruth Jaden Richman, named after Franny's grandmother, was the image of Franny, her face squinched in determination as she held a tiny fist tucked under her chin.

When Franny had announced that she was having a naming party for Ruth, traditional for Jewish girls in lieu of the ritual circumcision for boys, Stevie had immediately booked a flight. Keith had flown out as well, as had Jay's parents, seeming somewhat dazed by the unorthodox arrangement that had resulted in this grandchild.

The only one absent was Vivienne. Stevie wondered if she was ever coming home. Jay must have wondered, too, because he'd apparently moved on and was in the process of building a life without her. These days, all he could talk about was the baby. Stevie couldn't help noticing, too, his new protectiveness toward Franny and the way he'd reacted when Keith had shown up. Jay went out of his way to be friendly, but it seemed forced, as if he secretly resented Keith. And from the proprietary way Keith acted with Franny whenever Jay was near, it was obvious he'd picked up on it, too.

"If only they stayed this little forever," Emerson said, with a sigh. "Just wait until she's older. You'll be worn out trying to keep up with her."

"I have a ways to go until then," said Franny. "Right now my biggest worry is diaper rash." She bent down to smooth Ruth's blanket, looking like a Fra Angelico madonna with her curls framing a face made radiant by motherhood.

"I'm surprised you've had to change even one diaper, the way Jay hovers over her," Stevie teased. Franny shot her an odd look, making her wish she'd kept her mouth shut. Jay's role in all this was clearly a sensitive subject.

"He's like any proud papa," Emerson said, quick to smooth it over.

"Except he knows it's not for keeps." Franny spoke quietly, gazing down at Ruth.

"He'll still see her," Emerson said. "And when she's older, she can fly out to visit him."

"I know. But it won't be the same." Franny looked sad.

"Have you set a date yet?" Stevie asked, knowing that Keith was getting antsy.

"Please." Franny sank into the rocker, landing on a squeeze toy that let out a muffled squeak. She extracted it from under her and tossed it onto the floor. "I'm exhausted enough as it is without having to pack up all my things and move to the other end of the continent. I can't even think about that until Ruth is at least sleeping through the night."

She glanced around the alcove off her bedroom that she'd painted a pale yellow and stenciled with characters from nursery rhymes. It was so small, there was room only for the wicker cradle and matching dresser, and the padded rocker she sat in.

"You'll love living near the beach," Stevie told her. "Think of how much fun you'll have building sand castles with Ruth. Not to mention all those romantic moonlit strolls on the beach," she added with a sly smile. An image formed in her mind of her and Ryan, on their first date, walking along the beach at night, the surf rolling in over their feet.

"The most romantic thing we've done lately is watch *Sleepless in Seattle*," Franny said. "And I fell asleep halfway through."

"Shouldn't we be whispering?" Emerson asked in a hushed voice, as the baby stirred in her sleep.

Franny smiled and shook her head. "This one? She'd sleep through rush hour on the Bruckner Expressway." She was as relaxed about this baby as Emerson had been fretful with Ainsley. "Though when she lets loose you wouldn't believe the set of lungs on her."

Stevie shot Franny a bemused glance. "Gee, I wonder where she gets that."

"Luckily, she's good most of the time," Franny said. "And when she does cry, Jay's there to pick her up."

Stevie and Emerson exchanged a look. Ever since Franny had brought Ruth home from the hospital, Jay had been practically living at her apartment. He slept on the sofa bed, but still it struck Stevie as awfully connubial for a married guy and a woman engaged to another man.

But what did she know? The only guy she'd ever really cared about she'd let slip through her fingers. She thought of Ryan once more and felt a dull ache. It had lessened somewhat with time, and even that made her sad, because it meant she was letting go. Something he'd done months ago if the rumors she'd been hearing, not just from Liv, were true.

It had been sweet torture going to see his new film, about the joint efforts of a community led by a charismatic minister to rebuild their West Virginia coal-mining town that had fallen on hard times, aptly titled *With These Hands*. She'd half-hoped to find it saccharine, or worse, moralizing, but instead she'd been deeply moved, as much by the knowledge that she'd once shared a life with someone so gifted as by his portrayal of his subjects. She wasn't surprised when it earned him his second Oscar nomination, and with the Academy Awards ceremony just weeks away, she was secretly rooting for him to win.

If only I'd had as much faith in our relationship, she thought.

If he'd still cared enough to hear it, she'd have told him that things had changed. *She* had changed. She had a better understanding now of why she'd been so terrified to walk down the aisle. It wasn't because she feared Ryan wouldn't make a good husband, but that she'd make a lousy wife and mother. What did she know about keeping house? She'd grown up in a household where there was never enough money and they'd had to move from one funky rented place to another. In the absence of a father, the only men in her life had been teachers at school who'd taken an interest and helpful neighbors who'd pitch in when a fuse needed changing or the car wouldn't start.

The men Stevie had dated when she grew older proved just as transient. It wasn't until Ryan that she'd let her guard down and started to believe it could be different with him. Until push came to shove, that is.

It was only recently that she'd started to believe marriage wouldn't be so bad after all. Grant had been the key. For the first time in her life she knew who she was and where she'd come from. Out of that had come the realization that there was no such thing as an ideal dad . . . or an ideal relationship. It was about taking the bad with the good; accepting that there would be days when everything about the other person rubbed you the wrong way.

But she would probably never get a chance to tell Ryan all that. He'd moved on. And so should she.

With a small sigh, she joined her friends as they trooped out into the living room, where the other guests were gathered. The naming ceremony was brief but meaningful. Emerson and Stevie, as joint godmothers, took turns holding Ruth as the rabbi intoned the Hebrew blessings and Franny and Jay each made a little speech. There were blessings said over the wine and challah as well, then platters of food were brought out—bagels and cream cheese and four different kinds of smoked fish along with various salads and condiments and the noodle pudding Franny's aunt Bella had made. Stevie loaded up her plate and carried it over to where Emerson sat, in the corner by the bookcase. The room was so crowded there were no other seats, so she had to perch on an arm of the chair.

She inquired about Reggie and learned that things were still at a stalemate. The only good news was that, with the investigation dragging on, he'd been granted another extension. Though as far as Emerson was concerned, he might just as well be in Nigeria. She hadn't seen him since their breakup and there was no sign of a reconciliation in the offing. Despite her best efforts to look as if she were having a good time, she appeared forlorn, sitting there perfectly upright with her legs crossed at the ankles and a teacup and saucer balanced on one silk-stockinged knee: a portrait of a woman quietly suffering beneath her carefully composed facade.

"Don't you think he's overreacting a bit?" Stevie commented. "I mean, it's not like you accused him or anything."

"I questioned his integrity. It's the same thing."

"You had no choice. You said so yourself."

"I know what I said, but I was wrong."

"I hate to ask you this, but are you a hundred percent sure he's *not* a terrorist?" As a reporter, Stevie knew you sometimes had to dig to get all the facts.

"If he is, I'm in the wrong profession," Emerson said. If reporters dealt in facts, publicists knew all there was about spinning them and could spot a fake from a mile away. "Anyway, a terrorist would've taken out my mother while he had the chance," she added, smiling faintly. "No one without the patience of a saint could've put up with her as long as he did."

"So he's gone from a terrorist to being a saint?"

Stevie's effort to lighten the mood had no effect. Emerson sat sipping her tea, looking off into the middle distance. "No, a saint would have returned my calls. He's hurt and he wants me to know it," she said. "Besides, even if he decided to forgive me, unless a miracle happens and the State Department intervenes, what good would it do?" Her eyes glimmered with unshed tears. "I should have married him while I had the chance. Now it's too late."

Stevie's gaze swept the room, but nobody seemed aware of the quiet drama taking place in their corner. The other guests stood chatting with one another or helping themselves to the food. Franny was talking to her friend Hannah Moreland, from work. Jay was sharing a few laughs with his buddy Todd. Across the room, Jay's mother was deep in conversation with the rabbi. While within earshot of where Stevie and Emerson sat, several women from Franny's Lamaze class exchanged their own hair-raising tales of childbirth.

Stevie brought her gaze back to Emerson. "I guess that puts us in the same boat," she said, thinking of Ryan.

Emerson turned toward her. "So what do we do now?"

"As opposed to spending the rest of our lives kicking ourselves, you mean? When I have it figured out, I'll let you know." Stevie stabbed with her fork at a piece of creamed herring. "How's Ainsley taking it? From what you've told me, she and Reggie were pretty close."

"She keeps asking why he had to go away, why we can't see him. Try explaining to a seven-year-old that it's because her mother is ten kinds of idiot."

"Aren't you being a little hard on yourself?"

"Okay, make that eight kinds of idiot." A corner of Emerson's mouth turned up in a halfhearted smile.

"She still doesn't know about you two?"

Emerson shook her head. "I don't think so."

Stevie leaned into her, putting an arm around her shoulders. "You'll get through this. Life sucks sometimes. But the good news is, it keeps on going."

Emerson tilted her head up to look at her. "Are we talking about my love life or yours?"

Stevie shrugged. "Both, I guess."

The sun had come out, the showers that had been predicted nowhere in sight. The streets were blocked off from Highland to Orange, and the first of the limos was pulling up in front of the hospitality tent, where early arrivals sipped refreshments and schmoozed with one another while awaiting their turn to step through the metal detector and onto the red carpet lining Hollywood Boulevard. The world's media was out in force; TV crews packed the risers along the west side of the boulevard, the bigger stations and networks with their own ministudios, and print reporters were stationed across the way. It was some of the most valuable real estate around, each tiny plot as jealously guarded as oceanfront property in Malibu.

Stevie had an advantage in that she was among those in the first row, just behind the faux boxwood hedge, where she could snag celebrities as they passed by on their way to the preshow platform to be interviewed by the likes of Joan Rivers and Mary Hart from *Entertainment Tonight*. From where she was positioned, she could see the entrance to the Kodak Theatre, flanked by a two-story-high Oscar, and across the way the old Roosevelt Hotel where the very first Academy Award ceremony was held back when Hoover was in office.

On either side of her were CNN's Gunnar Swenson and MSNBC's Jeff Moody. She'd known both men for years and had even shared drinks with them on occasion after a hard night covering an event, but today it was every man for himself. No one would cut her any slack, and if either of them was to try to muscle in on her, they'd feel the business end of the no-nonsense shoes she had on under her vintage Mary McFadden evening gown.

Now the limos were pulling up one after the other, and the people in the hospitality tent had begun trickling out onto the red carpet. First among them Christian Slater with his date, and an unescorted Sharon Stone in a slinky, crystal-beaded gown. They made their way through the thicket of reporters calling out their names, amid a blaze of handheld lights and camera flashes. Stevie felt a flicker of sympathy for the nobodies on the arms of somebodies—if you've ever wondered what it was like to be invisible, she'd been told by one Hollywood wife, go to the Oscars—before she was swept up in it all, her only thought snagging the next celebrity sound bite.

Stevie all but lunged over the faux hedge to capture Brad Pitt's attention. He'd arrived solo, as godlike in person as on the screen, something that couldn't be said about every movie star. There were those with bad skin and heads too big for their bodies, women enviably slender on the screen who looked emaciated in person, leading men who couldn't have been much more than five feet tall.

The one thing they all had in common was star quality. Even the homely ones glittered, and the collective glow of so many in one place was nearly blinding. This was Stevie's twelfth year covering the event, and she never failed to be knocked out by it. It took all her experience to maintain her professionalism as she zeroed in on Nicole Kidman, ethereal in a gown made up of layers of pale rose chiffon, and moments later snagged Angelina Jolie as she was gliding past, trailing a black velvet train. It wasn't until she came face-to-face with the last person she'd expected to see that she momentarily lost her cool.

"Ryan! What are you doing here?" She fumbled with her mike, nearly dropping it.

"I'm up for an award this year," he reminded her.

"Right! Of course! Um, well, congratulations. I hope you win." In the blink of an eye, she'd gone from ace reporter to a babbling seventh-grader with a crush on her teacher.

"Thanks." In his tuxedo, tanned and fit, he could have been a Hollywood player. For what was a player without a tall, gorgeous blonde at his side? "I don't believe you've met my friend Kimberly." To Kimberly, he said, "This is Stevie. She works for Channel Seven."

Stevie flashed her a smile as faux as the hedge that snagged her dress as she leaned over it to shake her hand. "Kimberly, hi. Nice to meet you. Is this your first Oscars?"

Kimberly nodded in response. "But not my last, I hope." She cast a meaningful look at Ryan. "I keep telling Ryan we'll have to make room on the mantel for all his awards."

Stevie didn't think it was an idle comment. Ryan must have told her about them, and Kimberly was letting Stevie know that it was *her* tootbrush parked in his medicine cabinet now. Which meant that Stevie was still considered a threat. She might have taken some small consolation from that fact, if not for the way Ryan was glancing past her, as if anxious to move on. He couldn't have made it any clearer that she was yesterday's news.

Nonetheless, some streak of masochism in Stevie forced her to ask, "So you're living together?" She *had* to know.

Ryan looked distinctly uneasy. "Well, actually . . ."

"Just until I find my own apartment," Kimberly jumped in before he could finish. The way she was clinging to his arm, Stevie doubted she was in any hurry to find a place of her own.

"Kim worked with me on the movie," Ryan explained.

"We met on location," Kimberly said. "It was Ryan who convinced me to move out here." She gave Ryan's arm an affectionate squeeze, while he stood there wearing a strained smile, looking as if he'd rather be anywhere but here, bookended by his past and present girlfriends. "I was kind of stuck in my career, you know? You can only go so far at a university." She explained that she'd been working as a research assistant for a professor at WVU who was writing a book about the Marshall County coal-mine disaster of '24.

"I'm sure it's opened a lot of doors for you," Stevie murmured politely.

Including Ryan's. Clearly, he hadn't wasted any time.

"I just got hired at DreamWorks," Kimberly said, beaming.

"Where they actually have budgets for making movies," Ryan put in, with an ironic laugh.

Stevie turned to him. "You should be proud of your movie. It's amazing."

"You saw it?" He looked a little surprised.

"Twice," she confessed with a sheepish smile.

Out of the corner of her eye, she caught a glimpse of George Clooney as he headed past, but she made no move to grab his attention. *Now I know I've got it bad,* she thought, gazing helplessly after Ryan instead, as he strolled off arm in arm with his new girlfriend.

Chapter Seventeen

Jay waited outside the security gate at JFK, his heart thudding in his chest as he scanned the disembarking passengers streaming down the ramp toward him. When Vivienne had phoned the week before to let him know she was coming home, the news had brought mixed emotions. Not so long ago, he'd looked forward to this day. Now he wasn't so sure it was what he wanted. He'd been getting along just fine on his own. He'd even found a measure of peace, something he hadn't thought he would experience again anytime soon.

Franny and Ruth were responsible for that. It took him by surprise each time, the surge of love he felt whenever he looked at his daughter. What had started out as a favor to a friend had proved to be his own redemption. With Ruth had come renewed hope and purpose. These days his step was lighter and he often found himself smiling for no reason. And where he'd once put in long hours at work, often losing track of time, now when five o'clock rolled around, he was eager to be out the door and on his way to Franny's.

Then with a single transatlantic call everything had changed. What would Vivienne's reaction be when she laid eyes on his daughter for the first time? he wondered. Would she want Ruth to be a part of their lives . . . or would she keep her at arm's length? And how would Vivienne feel about Franny now that she was the mother of his child?

He craned his neck, trying to spot his wife amid the crowd. He'd only been playing house with Franny, he realized, making believe they were a family. The reality was, they were both promised to other people. And soon Franny and Ruth would be living three thousand miles away.

He felt his chest tighten at the thought. How would he handle his daughter growing up calling another man Dad? And Franny . . . how was he supposed to live without her? He'd become accustomed to seeing her every day, and if they'd fallen into a domestic routine, it was one he'd found comfortable. More than that, he was seeing Franny in a new light, as a woman, not just as a friend. These days even the casual brush of her fingertips brought an answering tug in his midsection, and at night when she kissed him good night on the cheek, it was all he could do not to follow her into the bedroom.

But he couldn't dwell on it. He had to let her go, for his sake as much as hers. He had his marriage to think of now. If there was anything left of it, he had to work on rebuilding it.

When he finally spotted Vivienne, he scarcely recognized her. The glowing woman walking toward him bore almost no resemblance to the ghost he'd said good-bye to all those months ago. She was still thinner than he would have liked, but her eyes sparkled and there was color in her cheeks. She strode down the ramp with a sense of purpose, a straw bag slung over one shoulder, her loose skirt swinging about her tanned calves.

His weren't the only pair of male eyes tracking her progress, he noticed, and as she stepped past the security gate and into his arms, he felt a swell of the old pride: *Eat your heart out, boys, she's all mine.* How had he, a farm boy who'd been poking along on a tractor while she'd been riding around in private jets and limousines, gotten so lucky?

"I can't believe it. You're actually here." He held on to her, breathing in her scent.

She drew back to smile at him. "Did you think I wasn't coming?"

"No. I just . . . never mind. It's great to see you. You look well."

"So do you."

"You got some sun."

"Our cottage was right on the beach," she told him. "All I did was lie around and let Maman fatten me up." She took his arm as they made their way toward the baggage area.

"I got your postcard." He hadn't even known she was in Majorca until it had arrived in the mail yesterday.

At the hint of reproach in his voice, she paused, turning to look at him. "I'm sorry, *chéri.* I know I should have phoned. It's just that every time, hearing your voice . . ." She let the sentence trail off. "Do you forgive me?" Her eyes searched his face, anxious for reassurance.

"Of course," he said. Why start off on the wrong foot?

They stuck to safe subjects as they collected her suitcases and made their way to the taxi stand. Vivienne talked about the friends she'd reconnected with in Paris, and how wonderful it had been to visit all her old haunts. Jay, in turn, told her about the campaigns he'd been working on, and how pleased the folks at Uruchima Motors were with the one for the Roughrider SUV; so much so, in fact, that Mr. Uruchima had invited Jay to visit him in Japan.

"Am I invited, too?" Vivienne asked a bit hesitantly.

"Sure. I just don't know when I'd find the time. It's been so busy at work." The truth was, he hadn't been able to bear the thought of being away from Franny and the baby that long.

He waited until they were back at the loft, relaxing over a bottle of wine, before he raised the subject they'd both been avoiding. "Would you like to see what she looks like?" he asked quietly.

She nodded, knowing he'd meant Ruth. He retrieved the latest batch of photos from his desk drawer and handed them to her. Wordlessly she studied them, her face carefully devoid of expression. "She's beautiful," she said at last, handing them back. She appeared composed, but he could feel the tension in her slight frame, held so taut it was almost quivering. "I'm happy for you. Franny, too."

"Her name is Ruth."

"What a lovely name—very old-fashioned."

"It was Franny's grandmother's."

"How is Franny, by the way?"

"A little overwhelmed, but other than that she's fine. She wants us to come for lunch on Saturday." He caught the glimmer of tears in his wife's eyes, and reached to comfort her, lacing his fingers through hers. "I'm sorry, Viv, I didn't mean to upset you."

"No, it's okay." She managed a tremulous smile. "It may not look it at the moment, but I really am better. I don't know that I'll ever be completely over it. I don't think that's possible. But I'm ready to get on with my life. *Our* life." She cast him a timidly hopeful look.

"I'm glad. For a while there, I wasn't sure." A lame response, he knew, but what did she expect? All those times he'd asked to visit her in Paris, she'd put him off, insisting it would only make it harder for her. How could he not feel rejected?

"Poor Jay. You must think I'm heartless." She brought his hand to her cheek. He knew her remorse was genuine, but he couldn't help noting the perfect picture she made, with her dark hair spilling over her slender shoulders, and the lamplight accentuating the curve of her cheekbone, where a single tear glistened like a dewdrop on a rose.

"I don't think that," he said. She wasn't heartless, just self-centered.

"You wouldn't have wanted to see me the way I was," she went on. "Even Maman and Papa couldn't look at me without shaking their heads."

I'm your husband! he wanted to say. Hadn't he vowed to love her in sickness as in health? But there was no point in reminding her of that. Besides, they'd suffered enough. If they were to make this work, he'd have to concentrate on rebuilding, not tearing down what was left of their marriage.

"Well, the change of scenery must have done you good. You look wonderful," he said, with a false heartiness so reminiscent of his father's awkward attempt to cheer him up at the funeral, when he'd reminded Jay in the same hearty tone that he would have other children, that he cringed inwardly.

"It won't be like before," she told him. "I know now it's possible to move on, even after something so terrible."

But Jay wasn't thinking about the baby they'd lost. In his mind, he was seeing the way Ruth's sweet little mouth puckered in anticipation of being fed and the way she looked just out of the bath, fat and pink and delicious. And her scent—if they could find a way to bottle it, there would be no need for antidepressants. All those things that had been denied Vivienne were his to enjoy. How could he not open his heart to her?

Impulsively he leaned over and kissed her on the mouth. The intensity of her reaction took him by surprise. With a low cry, she pressed up against him, winding her arms tightly around his neck and opening her mouth to his, not so much passionately as with a kind of desperation.

"I want to try again," she whispered when they drew apart. He'd assumed she'd meant *them*, so her next words took him by surprise. "I want another baby."

He sat back. "Are you sure it's not too soon?"

He felt her stiffen. Clearly it wasn't the response she'd expected. "I know we can never replace Stephan," she said. "But that doesn't mean I wouldn't love another child just as much."

Jay thought again of Ruth. Didn't Vivienne deserve to know that joy? But as tempted as he was to give in, he knew it would be a mistake. First, they needed to shore up their marriage.

"I don't think we should jump into anything just yet," he said.

"It's been six months," she reminded him. Her voice was cajoling, but the expression on her face said, *How can you deny me this?*

"You just got back. You don't think it can wait a week or two?" he said more gently. This wasn't the time for a conversation as important as this. They'd talk again in a few days, after Vivienne had rested up from her trip.

"*Mais oui, chéri.*" She recovered, saying lightly, "I didn't mean now, this minute."

But he knew Vivienne all too well. That was exactly what she'd intended, that he throw her down on the rug then and there. Not that his libido wouldn't have been happy to oblige. He'd been living like a monk these past months. But this wasn't just about satisfying his sex drive. Was he ready to stake his entire future on a wife who'd walked away when he'd needed her most?

At the same time, he didn't believe it was hopeless. Okay, so they didn't have a lot in common, but wasn't that true of a lot of couples? Look at his parents. He couldn't think of two people more unsuited to each other, his taciturn dad and his high-strung mother who dissolved into tears at the drop of a hat, yet they'd been happily married for more than forty years. Who was to say he and Vivienne wouldn't be just as happy in the years to come?

There was only one thing holding him back, and it wasn't uncertainty about what lay ahead. It was Franny. He couldn't stop thinking about her. How she looked in the morning just out of bed, with her hair a mass of curls, and cradling their daughter in her arms as she nursed her. They had more than a child together; they had a history. They fit together, pieces of a quilt made from snippets of cloth from various periods of their lives.

But dwelling on that wasn't going to do him any good. He had to concentrate instead on putting the pieces of his life back together. In time, the rest would fall into place. "We'll get there," he told his beautiful, broken wife, lightly stroking the back of her neck. "There's no rush."

"I need you to behave yourself today," Franny said, peering down into Ruth's scowling red face.

On any other day she wouldn't have minded the baby's being fussy, but today she was having Jay and Vivienne over for lunch and the last thing she needed was for Ruth to be the center of attention the entire afternoon. After what Vivienne had been through, she'd need time to adjust.

But Ruth apparently had other ideas. She'd fussed all morning, breaking into full-scale wails whenever Franny put her down. With Jay and Vivienne due to arrive any minute, Franny felt like crying herself. She was already so nervous, not just about how Vivienne would react but how it would feel being around Jay now that Vivienne was back, she was about to jump out of her skin.

She tried nursing her, but Ruth wasn't interested in food, either. "What, not good enough for you?" Franny cajoled, tickling the baby's feet to get her to latch on. "Do you know how many guys would kill to be in your shoes right now?"

Ruth's only response was to let loose with another wail. "Do you need to be changed, is that it?" Franny unsnapped the baby's fleece jumper to check her diaper, only to find it dry.

The only thing she wanted, it seemed, was to be held. Franny paced the floor, jiggling her up and down while she hummed a lullaby her mother used to sing to her when she was little. Oh, how Mama would have loved this baby! Franny understood now why she'd worked herself to the bone to give her children a better life and why she'd worried herself sick over Bobby. Franny felt the same way about Ruth.

At the moment, her entire life revolved around her daughter. Ruth consumed every waking hour, making sleep a thing of the past. On the plus side, it kept her from fixating on her current dilemma. Lately Keith had been pressuring her to set a date for the wedding. He didn't mind waiting, he'd said. He just wanted to be able to start making plans.

But how could she think about a wedding when she couldn't plan any further ahead than the next feeding? She knew deep down, though, that it was only an excuse. The real reason she'd been putting it off wasn't just because she was tired all the time or in no rush to pack up and move. It was Jay: She would miss him too much. Learning that Vivienne was coming home had come as a bit of shock—an unwelcome one, she was ashamed to admit. Her mind reeled back to the other day, when Jay had been taking care of Ruth while Franny ran to the laundry room downstairs to put a load of dirty clothes in the washer. She'd returned to find him on his cell phone.

"That was Vivienne," he told her when he'd hung up. "She's flying home on Tuesday." Jay had looked a little shocked himself.

"That's great!" Franny had cried, a bit too enthusiastically, after the moment of leaden silence that followed his announcement.

"Yeah." Jay had looked preoccupied, staring off into space.

"Jay, what is it?" she'd asked gently, touching his elbow.

He'd brought his gaze back to her, wearing a wan smile. "Nothing. It's just sort of unexpected, is all. I know that must sound strange, considering that for the longest time I was counting the days, but . . ." He shrugged, not finishing the sentence.

"It *has* been a while," she said. "But once you see her, it'll be like she never left." Franny was doing her utmost to convince herself that this was for the best, but her words rang hollow.

He'd nodded, looking equally unconvinced. "I'm sorry about dinner."

She'd remembered then that they had reservations at Nobu for next Tuesday, their first evening out since the baby—a sort of belated celebration. "Oh, that," she'd said, rushing in to cover her disappointment. "Don't give it a second thought. Besides, I'm sure Emerson will be relieved to hear we won't need her to babysit. She's probably already regretting the offer." Not that Emerson didn't adore Ruth, but she had so little free time.

Jay had eyed her with regret and something else—a touch of longing?—then Ruth had awakened from her nap, filling the gap of unspoken words that had opened between them.

Now, a week later, Franny was still at loose ends, trying to make sense of it all. And with Jay and Vivienne due to arrive any moment, she knew the toughest part was yet to come.

Ruth nodded off at last. But just as Franny was putting her down, the door buzzer shrilled, causing her to awaken with a start and let out a yell. When Franny answered the door, it was with a squalling infant in her arms and her breasts leaking milk down the front of her shirt.

"I'm sorry. She's usually down for her nap by now." Franny raised her voice to be heard above Ruth's wails. "Why don't you guys make yourselves at home while I get her to sleep."

"Maybe if I take her . . ." Jay stepped forward with his arms outstretched, but Franny shot him a warning look. The situation was awkward enough without his playing proud papa.

But Vivienne maintained her composure. "Anything I can do to help?" she asked brightly.

"I have a frittata in the oven," Franny told her. "Could you take it out when the timer goes off?"

She was in the nursery attempting to rock Ruth back to sleep when Vivienne appeared in the doorway. She hovered there for an instant before stepping forward, the picture of elegance in a maroon pencil skirt, calfskin boots, and a fitted blazer of a soft heather shade. Her hair was swept back in a chignon that showed off the diamond studs in her ears, the only jewelry she wore other than a gold bangle bracelet. Vivienne didn't need jewelry or makeup; she looked stunning just out of the shower. Franny, in her maternity jeans and blouse stained with milk and spit-up, felt lumpish in comparison.

Vivienne gazed down at Ruth, transfixed, shades of emotion chasing like clouds across the smooth planes of her face. At last she bent down to place a finger in one of the baby's loosely curled fists, and Ruth obliged by clamping down on it. Vivienne smiled, a slow-breaking smile tinged with heartache.

"She's looks just like Jay," she said softly.

"Would you like to hold her?" Franny asked.

Vivienne eyed her uncertainly. "Are you sure it's all right?"

"I should be asking you that," Franny said, eyeing Vivienne's expensive-looking blazer. "But if you don't mind a little spit-up, she's all yours." She transferred the baby into Vivienne's waiting arms. "Just watch her neck. She can't hold her head up yet."

Ruth immediately grew still, staring raptly up at Vivienne as if at an entirely new creature, one she'd never seen before. Vivienne couldn't take her eyes off Ruth, either. She examined every inch of her, peeling back the blanket to marvel wordlessly over each finger and toe. Seemingly oblivious to Franny's presence, she began to sing softly to Ruth in French, a melody as haunting as the expression on her face.

The oven timer pinged in the next room, and Vivienne came out of her daze, reluctantly handing the baby back to Franny. "I'll get it," she said, in an odd, tight voice, hurrying out of the room.

It was at least ten more minutes before Franny was able to get Ruth down for her nap. When she finally emerged into the living room, it was immediately apparent something was wrong. Jay sat slumped on the sofa, staring into space, and Vivienne was nowhere to be seen.

"She's in the bathroom," he said, his tone letting her know it wasn't just a call of nature.

"Is everything all right?" Franny asked, concerned.

Jay shook his head, letting out a sigh. "I was afraid of this." He dropped his voice. "But she insisted on coming. She said the longer she waited, the worse it would get."

"She's right, but that doesn't make it any easier." Franny perched on the arm of the sofa, placing a hand on his shoulder.

"I know. I guess it was too soon."

"We don't have to do this. You could come another time," she said, noting how drawn Jay looked, as if he hadn't been sleeping well.

"It seems a shame, after you went to all this trouble." He gestured toward the table, set for three.

"A fritatta? Please. Shaving my legs, now *that's* a big deal," she joked in an attempt to cheer him up.

He gave her a thin smile and rose to his feet. "I should see how Viv's doing."

He disappeared down the hall and moments later she heard voices speaking in low tones. Franny's heart went out to them both: Vivienne, who was being asked to do the impossible—move on in the face of her loss with her husband's baby to remind her every step of the way—and Jay, torn between his wife and his daughter. But it didn't change the fact that all this left Franny squarely in the middle, with nowhere to turn.

This is my doing, she thought. If she'd gone to a sperm bank like any normal person, none of this would have happened. They'd tried to fool Mother Nature and had gotten caught with their pants down, with Mother Nature getting the last laugh. On the other hand, if she'd done things differently, she wouldn't have Ruth. And how could she want that?

Jay reappeared a few minutes later, with Vivienne. She'd done her best to repair her face, but it was obvious she'd been crying. "I'm sorry," she apologized. "I guess I'm still a little jet-lagged."

"Do you need to lie down?" Franny reached out to touch her arm, and Vivienne flinched.

"No, I'll be all right," she said, in a strange, dead voice.

"Can I get you something to drink? Some tea? Or maybe a glass of wine." Franny was desperate to salvage the situation.

"Thank you, no," Vivienne said, casting a beseeching look at Jay.

He put his arm around her, saying, "We should be going."

Franny saw them to the door, assuring them repeatedly that it was no big deal, of course they could have a rain check. At the same time, she couldn't help thinking there was something more she ought to be doing. But what? She couldn't apologize when she'd done nothing wrong. Nor was it her place to inject herself into what was clearly a private matter. All she could do was stand by helplessly while two people she cared about suffered, knowing she'd unwittingly made it worse by allowing things to get out of hand while Vivienne was away. In playing house, she and Jay had played with fire, and now that fire was too big to put out.

Seeing the forlorn look Jay cast over his shoulder as he was walking out the door, she knew he felt the same way.

As soon as they stepped outside, Vivienne's mood seemed to lift. It was a nice day, milder than usual for this time of year, so instead of heading straight home they strolled along Bleecker Street, stopping at the Magnolia Bakery for cupcakes—his wife's one weakness when it came to food.

"You're trying to fatten me up, aren't you?" she said, licking the last dab of frosting from her finger.

"You could use a little meat on your bones," he said.

"I'm sorry about lunch." Vivienne's expression clouded over again.

"Don't worry about it. I'm sure Franny understands."

"I didn't think it was going to be so hard."

"I know."

"She looks so much like you. In the pictures it was hard to tell, but seeing her . . . it was a shock."

Jay felt a swell of paternal pride even as he replied, "She looks like Franny, too."

Vivienne strolled alongside him, not saying much. It wasn't until they were home, and he was warming up the slices of pizza they'd picked up along the way, that she came undone.

"It's all my fault," she said, burying her face in her hands.

He sat down next to her at the kitchen table, stroking her back. She was so thin, he could feel the sharp wings of her shoulder blades through her blazer. "No one's to blame," he soothed.

She lifted her head, her anguished eyes meeting his. "No, I should've been here. I was wrong to have stayed away for so long." She grabbed his hand, squeezing it so tightly she cut off the flow of blood to his fingertips.

Jay's heart lurched. Had she picked up on his new closeness with Franny? "You did what you had to do," he said gently.

"Oh, God," she said, beginning to weep.

"Viv, what is it? What's wrong?"

"I did a terrible thing," she choked out, tears running down her cheeks.

"It wasn't your fault," he reassured her once more. "You said yourself you weren't in your right mind."

"It's not just that."

"What then?" He eyed her in puzzlement.

She hesitated, clearly wrestling with some kind of decision. Finally, she said, "While I was in Paris, I met someone."

Comprehension sank in. "A man," he responded dully.

"It didn't mean anything, I swear! I wasn't in love with him. It was just . . . a way to escape. Please, Jay, you have to believe me." Her grip on his hand tightened.

He sat there, too stunned to process what she was saying; it was like gears gnashing in his head without engaging. Then, little by little, it began to sink in: All that time he'd been eating his heart out, worrying about her, Vivienne had been in the arms of another man. Of all the scenarios he'd pictured, that one never occurred to him. Not, he realized now, because he didn't think Vivienne capable of it—all those times she'd skipped out on him in the past, there had been vague allusions to other men. But that was before they were married.

He'd been raised to believe that one's wedding vows were sacred. Except for that one time he'd kissed Franny—a kiss that had surprised him as much as it had her—he never would have cheated on Vivienne. Not that he hadn't been tempted. All those nights lying awake on Franny's sofa bed, knowing she was in the next room, had been a kind of torture. It was only out of loyalty to his wife that he'd resisted the urge to go to her.

Now, as he sat there without moving a muscle, Vivienne appeared to be receding, as if he were looking at her from the backseat of a car as it was pulling away from the curb. At last, he disengaged his hand from her crushing grip. "I don't know what you want me to say." He felt cold all over. Even the sunlight warming the tiles at his feet left him chilled. His gaze wandered to the pot of African violets on the windowsill. Each week, while Vivienne was away, he'd faithfully watered it. And all that time . . .

"Say you forgive me!" Vivienne cried.

He slowly shook his head, bringing her back into focus. "You want forgiveness? For what, cheating on me . . . or being selfish enough to think you could get it off your conscience at my expense?"

She squeezed her eyes shut, as if in anguish . . . or in prayer. "I don't blame you for being angry with me. You have every right."

"I'm curious," he said, in an oddly unemotional voice that didn't match the dull drumbeat in his head. "Why *did* you tell me? If you'd kept it to yourself, I never would have known."

"But *I* knew. I didn't want it to come between us."

"So you think this will just blow over? Am I really that much of a pushover?" But he already knew the answer. Time and again he had gone out of his way to accommodate her at the expense of his own needs. Mostly because he'd wanted to please her, but also because it was easier than having her sulk.

"What I think," she said, pulling herself up straight to look him in the eye, "is that you're a good man. A good husband."

"You're right about that," he said coldly. "I wouldn't have cheated on *you*."

"Am I such a terrible person?" she said. Her eyes, shimmering with tears, seemed to fill her whole face.

It always came down to this, didn't it? Vivienne thought all she had to do was look at him a certain way and he'd melt. But this time it wasn't going to work. He saw clearly now how manipulative she was, how she used her charms to wrap him, and other men, around her little finger. No, she wasn't a terrible person, he thought, just a terribly spoiled one. All her life, she'd gotten her way. In her view, why should this be any different?

"I'm going for a walk," he said, pushing his chair back with a loud scraping noise that was like a gunshot. He saw Vivienne flinch.

"Jay . . ." She put out a hand to stop him, her eyes beseeching him. To do what? Stay . . . forgive her . . . try for another baby? It didn't matter. He was done.

He shook her hand off his arm. "No, not this time, Viv. I'm not rolling over. What happened to us was terrible, but we couldn't have prevented it. This is different. You made a choice. You wanted something to make you feel better and you took it. It's that simple."

"You don't understand. I was in so much pain!"

Something broke loose inside him and he roared, "Dammit, I lost a son, too!"

She shrank back, made small by the blast of his fury. "I know. I never said—"

"You weren't the only one suffering!" Blood rose to his head, swelling against his temples. "What about me? *My* pain. Didn't I deserve better than to have you jump into bed with the first guy who came along?"

"It wasn't about you," she said, shaking her head.

"Exactly." He eyed her coldly. "It's never been about me, has it? Not really. You married me because I adored you. But that's not the same as love, is it? So maybe I'm to blame, too. I guess I should have known better."

Vivienne's pretty, tear-streaked face crumpled. "You can't mean that. You're angry, I know, but—"

"I meant every word," he said, cutting her off. His fists flexed at his sides. He wanted to punch something, anything. "Honestly, Viv, did you think of me at all when you were fucking him?"

She winced at his crudeness, covering her ears with her hands. "Please, don't talk this way."

"Dammit, I want an answer!" He smacked a hand down on the table, causing her to jump and her hands to drop to her sides.

"No, you don't. You only want to punish me!" she shouted back, her eyes blazing.

As suddenly as it had come over him, his anger ebbed. He didn't want to punish Vivienne. What he wanted was for none of this to have happened. For Stephan not to have died and for her not to have run away to Paris. He wanted their marriage to be what it should have been.

He turned to go, announcing, as if to no one in particular, "I'll be at Franny's if you need me."

Vivienne jumped up and followed him to the door. "Franny. Of course." Her voice turned bitter. "Why do you need me when you have *her*?"

He swung around. "Are you suggesting . . . ?"

She didn't let him finish. "Yes, you've suffered. I know that. But you have another child. While I . . . I have nothing."

He felt a sort of pity for her then and part of him hoped that in time she'd know the joy he'd found with Ruth. But it wasn't enough to make him stay. "Good-bye," he said, as he let himself out. "Don't wait up for me."

Franny was just getting off the phone with Emerson when Jay appeared at her door without warning. She hadn't expected to see him again so soon, and one look at his face told her he hadn't come to retrieve an umbrella or jacket he'd accidentally left behind. If he'd been mugged on the way over, he couldn't have looked in worse shape, his face ashen, dark circles under his eyes and his hair disheveled. Even his coat seemed to hang awry on his lanky frame.

"Jay, what is it? What's wrong?" she cried.

Wordlessly, he took her in his arms, holding her so tightly she could feel the pounding of his heart against her rib cage. "It's a long story," he said. "First, I need to sit down."

In the living room, he sank down on the sofa and she brought him a cup of coffee. After he'd calmed down a bit, the whole story came out. About Vivienne's tearful confession, and how it had forced him to confront what he'd known in his heart for some time: that it was over between them. "I just didn't want to admit it," he said. "I think Viv must have felt it, too. Why else would she have cheated on me?"

"Oh, Jay. How awful for you." Franny's heart went out to him. She reached for his hand. "After all you've been through. Now this."

"I'll admit, I was thrown. But I suppose I should have expected it." He sounded more resigned than angry.

"If I were you, I'd want to put my fist through a wall."

"I nearly did." He smiled crookedly. "But a funny thing happened on my way over." He gazed at Franny in a way that made goose bumps break out on her arms. "I realized that maybe it was a blessing in disguise. I could finally admit how unhappy I've been."

"But I always thought—" She broke off, frowning. There was no denying that lately there had been some pretty visible cracks in his marriage. Not the least of which was their own growing attachment.

"Me, too," he said. "It wasn't until after the baby that I started to wonder if maybe the reason it all fell apart was because there had been nothing holding it together in the first place."

"But you loved her once."

"Yes," he acknowledged.

"What about Vivienne, does she love you?"

"I suppose, in her own way. But to tell the truth, I'm not really sure why she married me."

"*I* know," she said, speaking up in his defense. "You're kind and thoughtful, not to mention smart, funny, and good-looking." In short, everything a woman could want in a husband.

He smiled. "You left out sexy."

"I wouldn't know about that." Her cheeks warmed at the memory of their kiss.

"Maybe it's time you found out."

Franny felt the heat spread through her. Something was happening here. Something she'd secretly wanted to happen, but didn't know how to handle.

"Be serious," she said with a laugh. "You always went for the leggy blondes. Emerson was more your type than me."

"I'm completely serious." His frank gaze left no room for doubt.

"You're not thinking straight," she insisted nonetheless, growing panicky. "You just found out your wife cheated on you. Plus, we had a baby together. Even if it wasn't the old-fashioned way, that's enough to mess with anyone's head."

"If I was confused before, it's perfectly clear to me now." He spoke calmly, holding her gaze. "*You're* my family. You and Ruth."

Franny sat back, not knowing what to make of it all. "Are you sure you're not just saying this because of what happened with Viv?"

"You know me better than that."

Franny's heart was pounding so, the whole room seemed to reverberate with each beat. Questions she had no answer for swirled in her head. If they fizzled as lovers, could they ever go back to being friends? And what about Keith? "I know you, but I don't know *me*," she said. "In case you haven't noticed, I'm kind of a mess myself right now." Being a new mom had wreaked havoc with her hormones. How could she trust her feelings when she couldn't watch a stupid Hallmark commercial without reaching for a box of Kleenex?

"You don't look a mess," he said, as if he hadn't noticed her stained blouse and her stomach spilling over the top of her too tight jeans. "In fact, you've never been more beautiful."

"I'll bet you say that to all the girls."

He gave her a lopsided grin. "Just the ones I've knocked up."

She snorted. "You're a real charmer."

Franny jumped to her feet before they could wade in any deeper, carrying their coffee mugs into the kitchen, where she busied herself washing up. For once, she was sorry that Ruth was down for her nap. She could have used the distraction. Oh, God, why was her heart racing like this? Didn't it know better?

But what her heart knew was that this wasn't just a knee-jerk reaction on Jay's part. He'd clearly given it some thought. As had she. So why was she so skittish?

She wasn't aware that he'd crept up behind her until she heard him say, in a teasing voice, "You can run, but you can't hide."

The mug in her soapy hands slipped into the sink with a clunk. Slowly she turned to face him, her cheeks burning. "Jay, this is crazy, you know that, don't you?"

He arched a brow. "Crazy because you think I'm nuts . . . or because you feel the same way?"

"Both," she said.

He came to her then and wrapped his arms around her. "Franny," he murmured. Just that, her name.

Even as she clung to him, she went on shaking her head. "We can't do this. We can't pretend we're a family when we're not."

"Who's pretending?" He drew back to look at her, and if there was any doubt in her mind, she didn't see it reflected in his clear-eyed gaze. "The only thing I'm wondering is what took us so long."

"Maybe we were too close to the forest to see the trees," she said in a voice that was little more than a croak.

"Or too blind to know the difference."

"So where does that leave us?"

"This is the part where I kiss you."

He leaned in and his mouth closed over hers, not tentatively like the first time, but with conviction. She parted her lips, letting the tip of his tongue play over hers. It should have felt strange, but instead it felt like the most natural thing in the world, and at the same time deeply thrilling. She was vaguely aware of the edge of the counter pressing into the small of her back and the soap bubbles fizzing on her hands as they dried. From the apartment next door drifted the faint sound of a stereo playing, music that might have been the soundtrack to this weird movie she'd found herself starring in.

Jay drew back to whisper in her ear, "Proceed directly to the bedroom. Do not pass go, do not collect two hundred dollars."

"What, I don't get the hotel on Park Place?" she said, giving a shaky laugh.

In the bedroom, with Ruth sound asleep in her cradle, Franny undressed with her back to Jay so he wouldn't see her naked and change his mind before she could duck under the covers. But Jay wasn't having any of it. As she was reaching around to unhook her bra, he put his hands on her shoulders and turned her so she was facing him.

"Let me look at you," he said.

"They're huge, I know," she said, feeling self-conscious as his eyes dropped to her breasts. "It takes a little getting used to."

"Oh, I don't know. I think I can handle it." He smiled, bending to kiss first one, then the other.

She realized then that she had nothing to hide . . . or fear. They were still Jay and Franny, the same two people they'd always been. The only difference now was that their minds knew what their hearts had known all along.

They made love on the bed, with the sunlight streaming in through the blinds—Jay astonishing her at each turn, but no more so than her own body, which had been more or less dormant in that regard since giving birth but which now blazed to life with a roar. With each new place he explored with his hands and mouth, she was left gasping for breath and desperate for more. But where she'd always approached lovemaking like everything else in life, with gusto, she found herself taking her time, savoring each delicious sensation.

Oh, God . . . to think all these years there had been this amazing lover inside the man she'd thought of as her best friend. Was this *Jay* licking the tender hollow between her breasts and running his thumbs lightly over her nipples, making her shudder with delight? Kissing her there . . . and there . . . and, oh, sweet God in heaven, *there?* With her eyes shut and the languorous afternoon light warming her limbs, she could almost believe this was an erotic dream.

She explored every inch of him, from the mole behind his left ear to the little trail of golden hairs on his belly that disappeared into the thatch below, stopping to kiss and lick, until at one point he groaned, "You'd better stop, or I'll come."

"That's sort of the point." She said pulling herself up to nibble on his earlobe.

"No, you first." He pushed her onto her back, straddling her.

This time she didn't—couldn't—hold back. As he entered her, she arched back to take him in, wrapping her legs around him. Moments later they were coming together, Franny with an unbridled yell as she hurtled through the vast, star-spangled space behind her closed eyelids.

"Wow," she gasped, when she finally came up for air. "And to think I settled for a turkey baster when I could've had this."

He grinned. "You can't say we didn't make up for lost time."

"You're not sorry, are you?" she asked a little while later, as they lay snuggled together under the covers.

"You mean because of Viv? No." He turned to her. "How about you?"

She knew he meant Keith. She sighed. "I'm not sorry, no. It's just that I hate the thought of hurting someone who's been nothing but good to me."

She hadn't thought about Keith while they were making love, but now the unpleasant realization crept in: She'd have to break off their engagement. How could she marry him now? It wouldn't be fair to either of them. She was pondering her dilemma when Ruth awoke with a cry.

"I'll get her," said Jay, climbing out of bed. Minutes later he was back, holding a freshly diapered Ruth.

He'd no sooner handed her over than she latched on hungrily to Franny's nipple. Whatever had been bothering her before, she was all business now, nursing with a sense of purpose, her tiny fists kneading Franny's breast as she squinted up at her like a drunken sailor on shore leave.

"Now there's a girl who knows what she wants," Jay said. His smiling gaze met Franny's over their daughter's downy head. "One more thing she inherited from her mom."

She saw the question in his eyes and knew he needed to be reassured that *this* was what she wanted. But she couldn't make that promise just yet. Not until she'd resolved things with Keith. And that she would have to do face-to-face. She owed Keith that much.

"Let's hope she didn't inherit my big mouth along with that appetite," Franny said with a laugh, leaving thoughts of the future for another day. "Speaking of food, I don't know about you, but I'm starving. Which reminds me, I still have that frittata in the oven. . . ."

Chapter Eighteen

After they'd checked out the dinosaur skeletons in the main hall of the American Museum of Natural History, they wandered over to the culture hall. This section hadn't changed much from when Emerson's nannies had taken her here on rainy days when she was Ainsley's age: the same gloomy, semideserted corridors lit by the lunar glow from the dioramas of various primitive peoples. They paused before one of a polar bear rearing up, teeth bared as if to attack the life-size wax Eskimo brandishing a harpoon at it. The bear, its glass eyes dull and fur matted, looked as if it didn't care whether it ate or got eaten. Ainsley, too, seemed bored. She didn't perk up until they reached the African Peoples exhibit.

"Look, Mommy, A-F-R-I-C-A," she spelled aloud. "That's where Reggie's from."

At the mention of his name, Emerson felt a familiar loosening in her belly. She hadn't seen him in months, but that didn't stop her from thinking about him night and day. His graceful, long-fingered hands and how they'd felt against her skin, and his low, musical voice in her ear as they'd caressed each other in bed. She'd replay their conversations, marveling anew at his insights and his knowledge about a vast range of subjects. Now she was reminded of how he'd gone out of his way to be kind to her little girl.

"Why don't we go upstairs and look at more dinosaur bones?" she suggested, when Ainsley showed no interest in moving on.

"I want to see *Africa*," her daughter insisted.

"I don't know about you, but I've seen enough," Emerson said. She needed no more reminders that Reggie would be returning to his homeland any day now.

"But you *said*." Ainsley scowled up at her.

Emerson sighed. It had been a battle just getting Ainsley dressed this morning—she'd insisted on wearing the sparkly pink Hello Kitty sweatshirt she'd outgrown and that was now a size too small— and Emerson didn't want another meltdown. Since the meeting with Mrs. Ballard, Emerson had been making a concerted effort to spend more quality time with her daughter. That, along with the therapist Ainsley had been seeing, seemed to be helping. They hadn't been able to pinpoint what, if anything, was bothering her. But Ainsley *had* been less moody these days. It was just that today everything Emerson suggested seemed to rub her the wrong way.

"All right," she said, "but if we look at the whole exhibit, we'll be late for the planetarium." They had tickets for the two-twenty showing in the Rose Center across the street.

Ainsley lingered nonetheless, studying each diorama. She became entranced by one in particular, which depicted some sort of tribal ritual complete with feathered headdresses and carved wooden masks. Would Reggie wear funny things like that when he went back home? she wanted to know. Would he dance around the fire in his bare feet?

Emerson smiled, explaining that it wasn't like that in all parts of

Africa. Reggie came from a village where the people were more likely to wear the kind of clothes they saw on the streets of New York.

"Have you ever been there?" Ainsley asked.

"No, but he's told me what it's like."

"I wish he didn't have to go back. I wish he could be with us." Ainsley heaved the deep, unfettered sigh of a child who saw no reason to hide the fact that she was in mourning.

"Me, too," Emerson replied in a soft voice. Eyeing her ghostly reflection in the diorama's thick glass, she wondered what he was doing right now, if he was thinking of her.

Earlier in the week, she'd gotten word that his court appeal had been denied, which meant he'd run out of recourses. Soon he would be leaving, and she'd have to face the fact that she might never see him again. At the thought, she felt the sting of tears behind her eyes. If only they'd had a chance to say good-bye! She could have told him how much he meant to her, how he'd brought her back to life when she'd been as dead inside as those wax figures behind the glass. She could have held and kissed him one last time . . .

"Mommy, are you crying?"

Emerson touched her cheek and found that it was wet. She was about to make up some excuse about having something in her eye, but the anxious look on her daughter's face as she peered up at her reminded her so much of herself at that age, she decided to be honest instead. "I'm fine, sweetie . . . just a little sad about Reggie," she said, smiling through her tears.

"It'll be okay, Mommy." Ainsley wrapped her arms around Emerson, burying her face in the folds of her skirt. "Grandma said so. She said someday you'd see she did the right thing."

Emerson stiffened, a red light switching on in her head. "What did Grandma say exactly?"

Ainsley drew back, looking worried. "I'm not supposed to tell."

"You can tell me. I'm your mom."

"But . . ."

Emerson knelt down so she was eye level with her daughter. Ainsley looked both scared and a little defiant, like when she'd gotten caught doing something naughty. "Honey, whatever it is, Grandma shouldn't have asked you to keep it a secret. That was wrong of her."

"Are you mad at Grandma?" Ainsley's lower lip quivered.

"No, I'm not mad." *But I have a feeling I will be*, she added silently. "I just want to know what she said."

In a tiny mouse voice, Ainsley said, "I heard her talking on the phone with Aunt Florence." Marjorie's sister in Boca Raton. "Grandma told her she sent a letter saying some things about Reggie." Her eyes filled with tears. "Is it true, Mommy? Did Reggie do something bad?"

The red light in Emerson's head was pulsing now. "No, honey, he didn't."

"Then why did Grandma say that?"

Emerson closed her eyes for an instant, praying for the strength to keep from losing it. "I think it was because she didn't like that Reggie and I were friends." It was all she could do to maintain an even tone.

"He's *my* friend, too," Ainsley stated emphatically.

"I know, sweetie, but with us it was special. Like with Mommy and Daddy when we were married." *Enough pretending.* All that sneaking around was what had given Marjorie license to take matters in her own hands. It was time she started telling the truth.

"Is that why he was in your bed?"

Startled, Emerson rocked back on her heels. So Ainsley had seen them after all. She must have caught a glimpse through the doorway when Emerson was slipping out of the bedroom that day

264

she'd come home sick from Callie's party. More to the point, she was okay with it. She adored Reggie, so it was only natural her mother would, too. If Emerson hadn't been so upset, she'd have smiled at the irony of her seven-year-old's being wiser than she.

"Yes, honey," she said.

"Does Daddy know?"

"We talked about it. Actually, I think he'd like Reggie." She gave a small smile.

Ainsley frowned. "I thought Grandma liked him, too."

"I'm sure she does. She just didn't like that I was seeing him."

"Is that why he had to go away?"

Emerson nodded, for a moment not trusting herself to speak. "Something like that."

Ainsley eyed her in confusion. To her, there was only right and wrong, with no shades of gray in between. She didn't understand the complex strategies by which adults had to navigate the world. Someday she would, and when that day came, Emerson would mourn her loss of innocence.

But right now she had bigger concerns. Like Marjorie. It was high time Emerson confronted her, to hell with the consequences.

Somehow she made it through the rest of the afternoon. At the Rose Center, she dutifully oohed and aahed as the ersatz heavens were rolled out for their viewing pleasure. Afterward, she treated Ainsley to high tea at the Lowell Hotel, where they nibbled on miniature sandwiches and éclairs. All the while, Emerson was simmering inside as she rehearsed in her mind what she would say to her mother.

In the cab on their way home, she phoned Briggs to ask if he'd mind having Ainsley overnight. Something had come up, she told him. To her relief, he didn't press for details.

After she'd dropped Ainsley off at his place, Emerson could at last give in to the anger that had been throbbing inside her all day, like a blister about to burst. As she stepped through the glass door into the lobby of her mother's building, Nacario took one look at her and made the sign of the cross, muttering, "*Madre de Dios. Someone's in trouble.*"

"I think you can guess who," she said in a low, tight voice.

He shot her a warning look. "Don't forget, she's your mother."

"Not anymore," she said. "I'm officially resigning as her daughter."

"*Cuídate, chiquita,*" he called after her as she marched past him on her way to the elevator. *Be careful, little one.*

Reggie's replacement, an older woman named Sonia, met her at the door as she was letting herself in with her own key—Nacario must have called ahead to alert her. "Your mother's asleep," she informed Emerson in a hushed voice.

"Good." Emerson stepped past her. *She'll need to be plenty rested for what I have to say.*

"She's had a rough day . . . ," the nurse protested weakly, hurrying to keep up with her as she continued down the hall.

Which is about to get a whole lot rougher, Emerson thought.

Her mother must have been awakened by the sound of their voices, for she was sitting up in bed, powdering her nose, when Emerson walked in. "Darling! What a nice surprise. I wasn't expecting you until tomorrow." She took her eyes off the compact in her hand, her smile falling away when she saw the expression on Emerson's face. "What's wrong?"

"I think you know." Emerson's voice was cold.

"Really, darling, I'm not a mind reader. You'll have to be a little more specific." Marjorie's innocent look didn't fool her. Emerson hadn't missed the way her mother's gaze flicked toward the door, as if to make sure it was shut. God forbid the hired help should overhear.

"I found out something interesting today." Emerson stepped closer to the bed, her hands balled into fists at her sides and her whole body quivering with bottled-up rage. "I should have suspected as much, but I didn't think even *you* were capable of sinking that low."

"Darling, what in the world are you talking about?"

"*You're* the reason Reggie's being deported, aren't you? You made up those lies about him."

Marjorie went a shade paler, but other than that she remained the picture of innocence. "Honestly, I have no idea what this is all about. Whoever told you that must be confused."

Emerson gave a harsh laugh. "That's another thing. How dare you make my daughter keep your dirty little secret? For God's sake's, Mother, she's *seven*. You ought to be ashamed."

"You're one to talk." Marjorie dropped the pretense, arching a penciled-in brow in derision.

"What do you mean by that?"

"All that sneaking around behind my back. You think I didn't know?"

"What business was it of yours?"

"I should think you'd at least have had the decency—"

"Decency?" Emerson said, cutting her off. "Don't talk to me about decency! You don't know the meaning of it."

"No need to raise your voice. I might be dying, but there's nothing wrong with my hearing."

Emerson might have fallen for that trick in the past—Marjorie in her dying-swan mode—but no more. She was done handling her mother with kid gloves. "God, I can't believe what an idiot I was! All this time I've been waiting on you hand and foot, you've been stabbing me in the back. No wonder you don't have any friends left."

Marjorie collapsed with a gasp into the mound of pillows at her back. "What an awful thing to say." Emerson could see she was genuinely wounded.

But she was too angry to care. "Not that they were ever really your friends. Have you ever asked yourself why none of them ever visit anymore? Did it ever occur to you they were only interested in your social status?"

Twin spots of color appeared on Marjorie's cheekbones, over which the skin was stretched so tightly it was almost transparent, like bone china webbed with age. Yet she still had enough of the Kroft backbone to eye Emerson haughtily and in her best Upper East Side lockjaw pronounce, "At least *I* don't run around with the hired help."

"Too bad. It might have done you some good," Emerson said. "Your whole life you've been living in this bubble." She gestured to take in the once grand room, painted in the pastel shades of a Fabergé egg, with its chipped gilt and frayed velvet. "You're like the rest of them, you think all that matters is a pedigree. But you're wrong, Mother. And you know something else? I think you're jealous. You couldn't stand it that I'd finally found someone who made me happy. It reminded you of everything you'd missed out on. That's why you wrote that letter, isn't it?"

"The only thing I did was save you from making a fool of yourself!" Marjorie hissed. Her eyes glittered in the pale death mask of her face. "Do you have any idea what it would have done to your reputation if it'd gotten out that you were . . ." She faltered.

"Sleeping with a black man?" Emerson finished for her.

Her mother's eyes narrowed. "I can see it's rubbed off on you already."

"Or maybe I'm just sick of pretending to be someone I'm not. Sick of the lies, too. The truth is, you're a nasty, selfish old lady who doesn't know where her bread is buttered. If I didn't have my *reputation* to think of," she spat out, "I'd cut you off without a cent."

"Are you threatening me?" Despite her haughty tone, Marjorie looked frightened.

Emerson let her mother sweat it out for a moment longer before she replied in a remote, businesslike voice, "You can relax, Mother. I'll keep on paying the bills." If she were to cut Marjorie off, it would only give her an excuse to play the grand dame of martyrs. "But from now on, you won't be seeing me anymore. And that includes Ainsley."

"You'd do that? Take away my only grandchild? You know I don't have much time left . . ." Marjorie's voice quavered.

"After what you did to Ainsley, you don't deserve to see her," Emerson said, growing indignant all over again. Was that why Ainsley had needed a therapist? she wondered. Because of the secret she'd been told to keep and the even more despicable lie behind it? "But don't worry, we'll be at your funeral. Your *friends* won't suspect a thing."

She glanced at her watch on the way out the door. If she phoned Reggie now, she might still catch him before he went out for the evening. And maybe, just maybe, it *wasn't* too late for them. Suddenly she knew what she had to do. It was as if she'd been wandering around, lost in the wilderness, and the blast of fury she'd just unleashed had scorched a path clear.

"Where are you going?" Marjorie called after her plaintively.

"To do something I should have done a long time ago." Emerson paused just long enough to give her mother a last look before quietly but firmly shutting the door behind her.

On her way home, she tried reaching Reggie on his cell phone, but there was no answer, so she called his aunt and uncle's house. When the uncle informed her that Reggie was, in fact, at that very minute on his way to the airport, the shock of it slammed into her with the force of a blow. Oh, God. Why had she waited so long? Now she wouldn't even have the chance to say good-bye.

Even so, she knew she wouldn't be able to live with herself if she didn't at least try, however remote the chance of reaching him in time. She got the flight information from Reggie's uncle, and as soon as she'd hung up instructed the cabdriver to take her to JFK instead. Reggie's flight was in less than an hour, and as they hurtled across town toward the Triborough Bridge, she prayed for a miracle on the order of the parting of the Red Sea.

But the Red Sea, it seemed, was a piece of cake compared to I-495, where traffic was bumper to bumper. "Isn't there another route?" she called to the driver as they slowed to a crawl.

He shook his head, babbling something in broken English. Emerson had no choice but to sit back and stare helplessly out at the cars creeping along at a snail's pace ahead. A call to the airline only confirmed her fears: Flight 172 to Frankfurt was scheduled to depart on time. "Damn," she cursed under her breath as she hung up. The one time she could have used engine trouble or a fogged-in runway, everything was running like clockwork.

The traffic eased up when they hit the Grand Central Parkway, and she began to think that, with a little luck, she'd make it in time. Staring out the window at the illuminated billboards and road signs flashing by, she thought about all the time she'd wasted thus far. Had she ever really believed Reggie was a terrorist? Of course not. Concerns about Ainsley hadn't been the reason she'd been reluctant to marry him, either. No, her main fear had been of rocking the boat. A lifetime of trying to please her mother had left her ill-equipped to buck the inexorable tide that was Marjorie Kroft Fitzgibbons. Typical of her that even when she'd found the strength to do so, she'd waited until it was too late. Now, with the clock ticking, she felt like a contestant on a game show, not knowing if her prize would be a rosy future or a lifetime of regrets.

And even if she got there in time, it wasn't as if Reggie was going to just fall into her arms, saying all was forgiven. She'd all but accused him of being a terrorist. Would he ever trust her again?

She closed her eyes a moment and thought of the closeness they'd once shared. Two people who couldn't be more unalike on the surface, who were the same under their skins. She recalled Reggie's climbing into the Jacuzzi with her one time, how they'd giggled at the sight of their limbs, dark and pale, entwined beneath the sudsy surface. Afterward, they'd toweled each other dry, and Reggie had wiped the steam from the mirror so they could get a full view of themselves. Afterward they'd made love, right there on the rug still damp with their footprints. The memory brought a shudder of delight tinged with sorrow and she had to lean her forehead against the cool window glass until the heat in her cheeks abated.

After what seemed an eternity, they turned off the Van Wyck Expressway onto the airport access ramp. By the time they reached the international terminal, her nerves were so frayed she nearly jumped out while the cab was still moving. She shoved a wad of bills at the driver and raced for the curb, slaloming her way around piles of luggage and pushing her way through the revolving door into the terminal.

Inside, she scanned the electronic board listing gates and departure times. Flight 609 to Frankfurt was already boarding, she saw. Her heart keeping time with the pounding of her feet, she raced for the nearest white courtesy phone. Moments later she was stationed outside the security gate listening to his name being called out over the PA system and praying she wasn't too late. Each passing minute was a small death as she scanned the passengers streaming past, in the hope of spying Reggie. After several more minutes, when he didn't appear, flagging hope slipped over into despair. She pictured his plane taxiing down the runway, Reggie buckled into his seat, oblivious to her torment. Or had he simply chosen to ignore the page? Either way, she might never see him again, unless she decided to chase him all the way to Africa. Which would only have been an exercise in frustration, given the remote likelihood that he'd be allowed back into this country.

She was so overcome at the thought, she grew dizzy and had to lean back against the wall. She could already see what the rest of her life would look like, how every man she met would fall short of the mark. Why had she questioned him? She knew why, and that only made her more furious with herself.

She lingered nonetheless, until she was absolutely certain it was hopeless. When at last she turned to go, it was with a heart so heavy each step was like plowing her way through a snowdrift. She was trudging past the line of ticketed passengers that snaked toward the security gates when she heard a deep, masculine voice call out her name.

"Emerson!"

She whirled around and there he was, striding toward her with a backpack slung over one shoulder, tall and handsome in a blazer and button-down shirt amid a sea of hoodies and sweatpants and jeans, wearing a grin so dazzling it was like looking straight into the sun.

Reggie caught up to her, enveloping her in a crushing embrace and lifting her off her feet—not an easy feat given that she was almost as tall as he. When he set her back down, they were both grinning from ear to ear.

"I thought you'd left!" she cried breathlessly.

"I very nearly did," he said. "When I heard my name, I was afraid it was the authorities coming to arrest me."

"Why would they want to arrest you?"

"Perhaps for an act of terrorism I couldn't recall having committed?" he speculated with a twinkle in his eye, causing her to blush.

"What kept you from getting on that plane?" she asked.

"I thought there was a possibility it might be you."

"And you were willing to take that risk?"

"For you, yes."

"So you're not angry with me?"

"I was, at first. Perhaps not so much angry as hurt." His expression turned serious.

"Is that why you didn't return any of my calls?"

"I thought it would be easier," he explained with a grave nod. "If there was no trust between us, how could it ever be as it was? What I didn't count on was how hard it would be. I've spent every day of these past months wishing for a chance to put all this behind us. Now that you're here . . ." His voice trailed off, and in that moment he looked sad.

He must think I've come to say good-bye, she thought.

"Oh, Reggie. I'm sorry. I never should've questioned you, even for an instant," she rushed to reassure him. "It was my mother. I just found out *she's* the one who wrote that letter to the INS."

Reggie eyed her in confusion. "Why would she do such a thing?"

"Somehow she found out about us. She figured it was the only way to keep me from marrying you."

"I see." He nodded slowly, taking it in. "And what gave her the idea you intended to marry me?"

"She must have read my mind. I did . . . I do . . . want to marry you. That is, if *you* still want to," Emerson said, eyeing him hopefully.

He shook his head, causing her heart to plummet. "Not if it's for the wrong reasons."

"You think I'd marry you just so you can get your green card? I may have almost broken a leg getting here, but I'm not *that* crazy." She seized hold of his hands, gazing up at him. "What I want is to wake up every morning for the rest of my life next to the man I love."

She saw a light come on in his eyes. "There's still the matter of my legal status," he reminded her.

"We can work all that out later. Once we're married, they'll have to give you your green card."

He broke into a grin. "In that case, it had better be soon or the authorities *will* come after me."

"What about tonight? If we rent a car and drive to Maryland, we won't have to wait. We can get a license right away and have a justice of the peace marry us."

"Only a foolish man would turn down such an offer," he said, wrapping his arms around her and bending to kiss her on the lips, a kiss that said more than any wedding vows.

"I love you," she murmured.

"Even though I have no money?"

"I wouldn't care if all you had were the clothes on your back," she assured him.

"Which, in fact, happens to be the case." Reggie explained that the suitcase containing most of his belongings was on the plane. "So, you see, I am entirely at your mercy."

"Well, then, we'd better hurry, because I'm not sure how much longer I can keep my hands off you," she said, tucking her arm through his as they made their way to the escalator.

Chapter Nineteen

D o you want me to take her?" Stevie asked somewhat hesitantly.

Franny, rummaging in the overflowing diaper bag slung over one shoulder while she held the baby cradled in the other arm, glanced up at her. "No, it's okay," she murmured distractedly. "Dammit, where did I put that thing . . . I know I packed it. There it is." She straightened, brandishing a tube of ointment. "Cradle cap. It's almost gone, but I wanted to be sure."

"I never knew babies came with so much equipment," Stevie said as she helped Franny unload her luggage off the baggage cart, which included a car seat and portable crib in addition to a large suitcase. The last time Franny had visited, all she'd brought was a single carry-on bag. "Did you have to reserve a special cargo hold for all this stuff?"

When Franny had phoned to let her know she was coming, Stevie had worried about her condo's not being equipped for a baby, but it looked as if Franny had brought everything but the kitchen sink.

"You don't know the half of it." Franny rolled her eyes. "Try getting around on the subway with a stroller at rush hour. Or nursing in public without making some dirty old man's day. Believe me, poopy diapers are the least of it." But she sounded cheerful enough, despite the long trip.

Stevie strapped the car seat into the backseat of her Firebird while Franny nursed Ruth up front. It was hot out on the parking lot's tarmac, and by the time Stevie had wrangled the last buckle into place, she was drenched with sweat. Franny lowered a drowsy Ruth into the car seat, and minutes later they were off, the air conditioner going full blast. Stevie felt as if she'd run a marathon and they hadn't even made it out of the lot.

And yet . . . the thought of having a child of her own someday didn't freak her out as it once had. Either she was mellowing with age or being around Ruth was having an effect on her. Not that she'd be shopping for maternity clothes anytime soon. Not with Ryan, at any rate. She felt a dull ache at the thought, knowing that the next time she ran into him and his girlfriend, she might very well be congratulating them on something other than an Oscar.

"So you're really going through with it?" Stevie asked as she was merging onto the freeway. When Franny had told her that she was breaking up with Keith, it hadn't made sense at the time. It was only after she'd thought it through that she'd realized it must have something to do with Jay. She'd first noticed it at the naming party, when the rabbi was saying the blessing, the way Franny and Jay had looked at each other, as if they were the only two people in the room. If Stevie had been paying closer attention then, she'd have known what anyone with eyes in their head could see: that they were in love.

Franny sighed, squinting against the glare as she dug around in her purse for her sunglasses. Even with the few extra pounds she had yet to lose and a stain that might have been spit-up on her blouse, she'd never looked more radiant. "I'm just not sure this is the right time for me to be thinking about getting married," she said. "I just had a baby. That's enough of a change without pulling up stakes and moving all the way to L.A."

"So this has nothing to do with Jay?" Stevie darted her a look, taking note of the color rising in Franny's cheeks.

"What gave you that idea?" Franny hedged, the color deepening.

"You still haven't answered my question."

Franny was quiet for a moment, as if contemplating her answer. "If I tell you, you have to promise not to make a big deal of it," she said at last.

"Okay, I promise."

"We had sex."

"*What?*" Stevie was so thunderstruck, she nearly drove the Firebird into the breakdown lane.

"It was just the one time," Franny was quick to add. As if that made a difference.

Stevie shook her head, incredulous. "Wow. I can't believe it. You and Jay."

"We *did* have a baby together," Franny reminded her.

"Donating sperm is one thing. This is something else altogether."

"I don't know how to explain it. Everything changed after I got pregnant. Then when Vivienne went away . . ." Franny let the rest of the sentence trail off.

"How long have you felt this way?" Stevie wanted to know.

"For a while, but we didn't do anything about it until after he found out Viv cheated on him."

"I gather it's over between them." Stevie knew as much from talking to Jay.

"That's what *he* says. But they've been together a long time. Besides, you know Viv. She's not used to losing." Franny frowned, looking troubled as she stared out the window at the other cars zipping by.

"I thought she was going back to Paris." Jay was staying at a hotel in the meantime.

"I'll believe it when I see it."

"Let's say she does. Where does that leave you and Jay?"

"To be honest, I'm not really sure." Franny's frown deepened. "Remember in *When Harry Met Sally* after they finally did it and couldn't look each other in the eye? It was like that with us. The next day we didn't know how to act around each other. We don't know if we're friends or lovers, or some weird in-between."

"Isn't it possible to be friends *and* lovers?" Stevie asked, thinking of her and Ryan.

"Maybe, if you start out that way. Also, there's Ruth. That sort of complicates things."

"How so?"

"I can't help thinking none of this would've happened if it hadn't been for her."

"Who knows?" Stevie said. "Maybe you guys have been in love with each other all this time and just didn't know it. What is love, anyway, except two people wanting to be together all the time?" Franny and Jay certainly fit that description.

"Maybe you're right." Franny sounded dubious.

"So how was it? The sex," Stevie asked after a moment, when it became clear Franny wasn't planning to say any more on the subject.

"Good," Franny answered, sounding embarrassed. This from the same woman who hadn't been able to stop talking about Keith.

"That's it? Just *good*. I want details!"

Franny's lips curved in a sly little cat smile. "Let's just say he knows stuff he didn't get out of the *Farmer's Almanac*."

That was all Stevie could get out of her. After another failed attempt to satisfy her curiosity, she moved on to another topic. "So how's the blushing bride?" she asked, in reference to Emerson.

"So far, it hasn't been much of a honeymoon," Franny said. "You heard about her mom?"

"Yeah, tough break." Apparently when Marjorie learned of the elopement, she'd taken a turn for the worse and ended up in the hospital with a case of pneumonia. Now Emerson was faced with the impossible choice of forgiving the unforgivable . . . or turning her back on her dying mother.

"She's still in intensive care. For a while there, they weren't sure she was going to pull through."

"Poor Em." Stevie's sympathies lay entirely with her friend. It was hard to feel sorry for Marjorie after the dirty trick she'd pulled. Still, these past months with Grant had taught the importance of having a relationship with one's parent, even if that parent was less than perfect. "I wonder how she'll feel after her mom goes. I know she's pretty fed up with her right now, but still it's her mother."

"For her own sake, she needs to make peace," Franny agreed. They'd exited off the freeway and were cruising along Santa Monica Boulevard. "Whatever's eating you, it doesn't end when you bury someone. If anything, it gets worse, because it's too late to get it off your chest."

"Was that how it was with your mom?" Stevie knew that Franny and her mother, though close, had often clashed. Probably because they were so much alike. Esther was a pistol, like Franny.

"In some ways. I mean, I loved her and all, but you couldn't tell her anything. She always knew best. If I said I wasn't hungry, she'd insist I eat. If I said I was hot, she'd tell me to button up. She did the same thing to Bobby. I used to think it was why he went crazy." Franny gave a dry little chuckle. "I just hope I do a better job with Ruth." She looked over her shoulder at the baby asleep in her car seat, her expression tender.

Stevie glanced in the rearview mirror. "From the looks of it, you're doing just fine."

"Talk to her in thirty years," Franny said, with a laugh.

Franny phoned Keith as soon as she got to Stevie's. Earlier, he'd been a bit taken aback when she'd told him she was staying at Stevie's, until she'd explained that it was a lightning business trip—tomorrow she was having lunch with a producer who was interested in film rights for one of her author's books—and that Stevie was babysitting. She arranged to meet him at his place afterward. The sooner she got this over with, the better. All day the thought of what lay ahead had been like a dry-swallowed aspirin stuck in her throat.

The following morning, after she'd showered and gotten dressed, she assembled everything Stevie would need for Ruth—Pampers, baby wipes, bottles, scalp ointment, and several changes of clothing. Watching her lay it all out, Stevie fretted aloud, "What do I do if she cries?"

"If she's hungry, give her a bottle," Franny instructed. The night before, Stevie had been horrified when Franny used a breast pump to express her milk, pronouncing it positively barbaric.

"What if that's not it?" Stevie hadn't been this nervous since doing her first on-air interview.

"You know how to change a diaper, don't you?"

Stevie gave her a blank look.

"It's not brain surgery." Franny demonstrated, changing the still dry diaper she'd just put on Ruth. "If she's still fussing after that, she might need to be burped." She showed Stevie how to do that, too, but it did nothing to ease Stevie's anxiety.

"What if I do it wrong?" she asked.

"She'll survive. Babies are pretty indestructible."

On the drive to Beverly Hills in Stevie's borrowed Firebird, her thoughts turned to Jay. She couldn't help worrying that he'd change his mind and go back to Vivienne. She knew how seductive Vivienne could be. After that long ago business with her ex-boyfriend, Brian, when Franny had cooled toward her, Vivienne had knocked herself out to work her way back into Franny's good graces, calling regularly to ask for advice and bringing her thoughtful little gifts, even presenting her with a beautiful cashmere sweater on her birthday, until finally, Franny had come around. Jay would be even more susceptible. He was her husband, after all. And no matter what she'd done, he'd be inhuman not to have feelings for her.

Her lunch with Avery Freeman, from Greenlight Productions, took place in the Polo Lounge at the Beverly Hills Hotel, where movie deals made over seared foie gras and Rémy Martin were a matter of course. Universal was keen on making the picture, he told her; it all hinged on whether they could line up a big name to star in it. Without that, Franny knew, the deal wouldn't get off the ground. They discussed terms and the possibility of a movie tie-in. It was Franny's first grown-up lunch since giving birth and she found herself enjoying it. It felt good to sit in a nice restaurant wearing a dress and high heels after schlubbing around in nothing but jeans and baggy sweatshirts stained with spit-up, discussing something other than Pampers versus Huggies and what worked best with diaper rash.

The mood ended as soon as she was back in the car. Would Keith be angry when she told him? she wondered on her way over to his place. Or would he pull on her heartstrings, causing her to weaken? It wasn't that she didn't love him, after all, just that she loved Jay more.

She couldn't quite put her finger on why. Sure, she'd known Jay longer, but it was more than that. Their friends were fond of joking that they'd been separated at birth, and it wasn't far from the truth. Jay was her psychic twin. He understood her in a way even her own kin hadn't. He knew that at parties, when she was at her most loquacious, it was because she was feeling insecure. He always took her hand whenever they were walking along a subway platform, for though she'd never voiced it, ever since her brother's death she'd had nightmare visions of being sucked under the wheels of an oncoming train. Whenever she was at her bluest and the phone would ring, nine times out of ten it was Jay calling to cheer her up. And now there was an added wrinkle: the sex. Which had been incredible. She couldn't even think about it now, or she wouldn't be able to look Keith in the eye.

Yet as soon as she walked in through the front door, Franny was reminded all over again of why she'd fallen for him. On the kitchen counter that opened onto the living room was a bottle of champagne chilling in an ice bucket, beside it a vase holding a dozen long-stemmed red roses. Her heart sank. This was going to be harder than she'd thought.

"Nice touch," she said, with a lightness that belied the knot in her stomach. "But isn't it a little early to be celebrating? I don't even know yet if I have a deal."

"In that case, we'll just celebrate the fact that you're here," he said, taking her in his arms. In the snug-fitting jeans he had on, with his shirtsleeves rolled up, he might have been a candidate for *People*'s sexiest bachelors. But he must have sensed something was wrong, for he drew back to eye her with concern. "Everything okay?"

"Sure, fine. I'm just a little jet-lagged," Franny said. How could she do this with him gazing at her as if she was Nicole Kidman? Maybe it would be easier after she'd had some champagne, she thought, as he popped the cork and poured them each a glass. She wasn't supposed to drink while she was nursing, but she supposed it wouldn't hurt just this once.

She sank down next to him on the sofa, the invisible aspirin in her throat now the size of an Alka-Seltzer tablet. Eyeing the framed watercolor over the mantel that she'd given him for Christmas, she felt a wave of sadness. She'd bought it with an eye toward both of them enjoying it in the years to come. But looking at it now, it might have been a painting in a museum.

The first glass of champagne went down easily as they chatted about her meeting and the progress he was making on his book. She didn't protest when he poured her another one. Before she knew it, they'd killed the entire bottle, and she was feeling decidedly lightheaded. When she finally got up the nerve to say why she was here, it came out, "Keith . . . there's somethin' I haf to tell you."

"Whoa there. Better slow down." He pried the nearly empty glass from her hand. "When was the last time you had anything stronger than root beer?"

Franny giggled, realizing she was ever so slightly sloshed. "I don't drink. Ish bad for the baby," she told him.

"I don't know about the baby, but I think it's kind of cute," he said, smiling. "I've never seen you drunk before."

"I'm no sush thing!" she declared, rearing back in indignation.

"Okay, inebriated then," he amended with a laugh. "Remind me to hold the liquor on our wedding night."

Oh, God. This was turning into a nightmare. What the hell could she have been thinking, drinking so much? She shook her head in an effort to clear it, struggling to form a string of coherent words around a tongue that felt swollen twice its normal size. "You don't want to marry me, trush me. I'd make a terrible wife."

"I disagree. In fact, I wouldn't change a thing about you," he said, gazing at her in bemusement.

"This is all wrong. I can't marry you," she tried again, enunciating each word as if for the hearing impaired.

"Why don't I make you some coffee," Keith said, rising to his feet.

"No! Wait!" She lunged to grab hold of his arm as he started toward the kitchen, slipping off the sofa and onto the floor in the process.

He helped her back up. "Sit tight, I'll be right back."

She stood up to go after him, but the room began to spin, causing her to plop back down again with a groan. How the hell had she managed to screw things up so badly? Maybe this was God's way of telling her not to look a gift horse in the mouth. Who was she to throw away a perfectly good man? She, who didn't exactly have guys standing in line.

Jay didn't count. He was . . . he was . . . she didn't know what he was. Not a boyfriend exactly, and not just a friend. She buried her head in her hands, letting out another groan. From somewhere in the distance she heard a trilling, but it was several moments before she realized it was her cell phone. She rummaged amid the jumbled contents of her purse, half of which ended up on the floor, before she managed to fish it out.

"Help! I don't know what to do!" It was Stevie, clearly at her wits end. In the background, she could hear Ruth wailing at the top of her lungs. "She won't take the bottle. She wants *you.*"

"I'm on my way. I jush have to find the keys." Franny began hunting in her purse for the keys to Stevie's car as a fit of hiccups quickly turned into a fit of giggles.

"Are you *drunk?*" Stevie demanded.

"Course not!" Franny cried, adding with another giggle, "Well, maybe a little."

"You'd better let Keith drive then."

Franny realized with a sinking heart that the speech she'd

planned would have to wait. You didn't break up with the designated driver when you were three sheets to the wind and had a hungry baby to rush home to. Besides, whatever she said, he wouldn't take her seriously. He'd just think it was cute.

Keith reappeared moments later carrying a steaming mug. "Who was that?" he asked. Franny explained the situation and he instantly took charge, assisting her to her feet and steering her out the door, an arm firmly around her waist.

"You're a good man, Keith Holl'way," she told him when they were in Stevie's car, zipping along the road on their way to the freeway. She patted his knee, smiling at him blearily. It wasn't his fault he'd chosen a woman who didn't know her own mind.

Chapter Twenty

After dropping Franny off at the airport the following day, with a hangover bigger than all her luggage combined, Stevie decided, on an impulse, to drive over to Grant's. She'd taken the day off, and besides, there was something she needed to discuss with him. It seemed her frequent visits to the mansion hadn't gone unnoticed. The news community was abuzz with the rumor that she'd managed to wrangle an interview with the elusive Grant Tobin. She'd have to publicly set the record straight, and soon, or risk having someone else get the real scoop. The tricky part would be getting Grant to agree to it. He was like a skittish horse when it came to the press. Complicating matters was the rumor that the DA's office was calling for a reopening of the investigation in the Lauren Rose case.

Cruising north on I-405, she speed-dialed his number, and was surprised when Grant himself picked up. She'd been expecting to get Victor. "Hi," she said. "So you're answering your own phone these days."

"Victor's in the gym," Grant explained. Among the mansion's many deluxe features was a fully-equipped gym, where the only person Stevie had ever seen work out was Victor. One reason the guy was built like a Sub-Zero. "What's up?"

"Nothing much. I just thought I'd swing by if you weren't busy."

"I don't know. I'll have to check my calendar," Grant said in a dry voice.

Half an hour later she was pulling into the drive. The day was chilly, and she shivered as she stepped out of the car, wishing she'd worn a heavier jacket. In the far-off distance she could see Mr. Mori riding around on his tractor-mower, its drone so faint it might have been that of an insect. Grant's housekeeper, Maria greeted her at the door.

"Mr. Grant say make yourself at home," Maria said as she showed her in, explaining that he was on the phone. A short, round lady with an open, smiling face, she'd been with Grant for years and was more family member than live-in help.

Stevie thanked her and wandered around for a few minutes before a muffled clanging sound drew her to the stairs leading to the gym on the floor below, where she found Victor on his back bench-pressing what looked to be at least three hundred pounds. She waited until he'd finished his reps before approaching him. The re-opening of the Lauren Rose investigation would mean more interviews with the household staff, Victor chief among them. Now that they were getting along a little better these days—she'd made a concerted effort to be friendly—she wanted to feel him out a bit, see if he knew anything he hadn't told the police that might shed some light on what had happened during the time of Grant's blackout that long-ago night.

He spotted her and rose from the bench, breathing hard and drenched with sweat. "Hey," he said, lifting a hand in greeting.

"What are you up to?" She nodded toward the barbell he'd been pressing.

"Three-fifty," he said with a shrug, reaching for the towel slung over the top of the weight rack and using it to mop the sweat dripping from his forehead.

"Wow. You must work out a lot."

"One of the perks of the job." He grinned at her, a flash of teeth that did nothing to take the chill from his demeanor. He tossed aside the towel and reached for a free weight, one heavy enough to have put Stevie's back out, lifting it with ease, his biceps swelling with each rep.

"My idea of a perk is an extra vacation day," she said.

He glanced at her without breaking his rhythm. "You don't get much time off, do you?"

Pretending not to notice the faint suggestion in his tone that these visits of hers were somehow work related, she said, "In Hollywood even the dead don't sleep." Victor shot her a quizzical look, and she explained that dead celebrities were cash cows for their heirs. Though it was the living ones, she said, who kept her busiest.

"You like digging up all that dirt?" It was more a statement than a question.

She watched a dribble of sweat make its way down one scarred cheek. "I'm not in the business of exposing celebrities' secrets, if that's what you mean."

"That so." He gave her an arch look. "What about old rockers?"

"If you're suggesting that this is all part of some grand scheme," she said, jerking her chin upward to indicate the floor above, where Grant was presumably still on the phone, "you couldn't be more mistaken." What did Victor think, that she planned to make a circus sideshow of her own father?

"Yeah, I know, you're only making up for lost time with dear old dad."

She bristled at his tone. "Something like that."

"You know who he's on the phone with right now?"

"No, who?"

"His lawyer."

It dawned on her then what this was all about: Victor must think she was after Grant's money. That her plan all along had been to butter him up so he'd put her in his will. And the only reason it could possibly matter to Victor was if *he* was angling for the same thing. She played dumb, though, not wanting him to suspect that she was on to him.

"It must be important. He's been on a long time." She spoke casually, as if she had no idea what it was about, which in fact she didn't.

"I wouldn't know. It ain't my business." With a grunt, the houseman heaved the weight in a last curl that caused his face to contort and the veins on his bulging biceps to pop out.

She'd never before seen him without a long-sleeved shirt, and now she wondered if he was on steroids. You didn't get monster muscles like that just from working out at the gym. She moved in for a closer look, fascinated and repelled at the same time. That's when the tattoo on his forearm came into focus: a rose twined about a crucifix, complete with the head of a Jesus figure, its thorns forming the crown on Christ's head. It seemed familiar somehow, and after a second it came to her: In her *Prime Time* interview, Lauren Rose had spoken of a crucifix and a rose, a scrap of memory she hadn't been able to place in context.

Now the mists were clearing. She understood why Victor treated her like a party crasher and why he'd been so hostile the one time she'd asked him about that night. She recalled, too, the maid whose story had conflicted with Victor's. Maybe, she thought, he knew more than he'd let on.

"Nice tattoo," she commented, pointing at his arm.

"Thanks." It didn't escape her notice when he subtly shifted position so it was obscured from view.

"I knew a guy once who had the whole U.S.S. *Constitution* tattooed on his chest," she said. "Though I imagine it must have hurt when he had it done."

Victor grunted in response.

"You must have a pretty high tolerance for pain," she went on. "Or maybe you just like inflicting it."

His blood-engorged face darkened further and he dropped the weight to the floor with a resounding thud. "What are you getting at?" he growled, swinging around to face her.

"I'm just wondering if you know more about Lauren Rose than you're telling." As she met his cold gaze, she felt a chill skitter up her spine. But what was he going to do, take her out in broad daylight with Grant and the rest of the staff within shouting distance? She backed off nonetheless when he took a step toward her, not liking the look on his face.

"What business is it of yours?" he said, his dark eyes glittering with menace.

"You know that Grant thinks he's the one who pulled that trigger?" she told him.

"How do you know he didn't?"

"It's possible," she said, nodding thoughtfully. By his own admission Grant had been so high that night, he probably wouldn't have noticed if a 747 had crash-landed in his backyard. "But I'm guessing he didn't."

"Then it's like he said." Victor reached for his towel once more, patting his face dry. "Anyway, there were no eyewitnesses. Plus, the only fingerprints on the gun were hers."

"Whoever did it could have wiped theirs off before putting it in her hand."

"Like you said, anything's possible," Victor said, with a shrug.

"Just for the sake of argument, if they were *your* prints, is that what you would have done?"

He shot her a derisive smile and shook his head. "No way. I ain't fallin' for that, lady. You may be good at getting people to talk, but I ain't no Hollywood whore looking to get my picture in the papers."

"Maybe you'd rather tell it to the police," she said.

He gave her an odd, calculating look. "I already told them everything I know."

"There's talk that they're reopening the investigation. I think they might be interested in having a look at that tattoo." Stevie gestured toward his forearm. "Lauren seems to recall something about a rose and a crucifix. Who knows, maybe there's a connection."

"They can't prove nothing." He looked worried nonetheless.

"Maybe not. But I'm sure they'd want to talk to you even so." She fumbled in her shoulder bag for her cell phone.

Victor flicked a nervous glance at it as she pulled it out. "You're full of shit."

"Try me."

"What's in it for *you*, a fucking exclusive?" He sneered.

"Let's just say I have a vested interest in setting the record straight." Stevie punched a button on the phone. She had the number for the LAPD on speed dial—you never knew when you were going to need a sound bite about a celebrity who'd met with either the wrong arm of the law or a questionable death—and now she scrolled down until she got to it. Her finger was hovering over the Send button when Victor snatched the phone from her hand, tossing it onto the bench that still bore the sweaty outline of his torso.

"I don't need the cops crawling all over me. They give me enough heat as it is," he said. Stevie recalled something in the old clippings she'd perused about Victor's having a record—something gang-related in his youth.

"Okay, so tell me what you know." She retrieved her cell phone and tucked it back into her bag.

Victor frowned, as if mulling it over. "Off the record?" When she didn't respond, he gave a harsh laugh. "What the hell. You can't prove nothing anyhow. You start talking shit about me, I'll fucking sue your ass. I'll say you're one crazy bitch who's out to get me."

Stevie didn't bat an eye. "Why would I be out to get you, Victor?"

"*She* was."

"Who?"

"Who do you think? The bitch who started all this."

"Lauren."

"Yeah, her. She's not what you think, all innocent and like. She had it coming."

"Had what coming?"

He was looking straight at her but his eyes were vacant, as if he'd retreated to some other plane, a dark one that existed only in his mind. "She was playing him." Meaning Grant, no doubt. "She was playing both of us, making out like it was really *me* she wanted. Fucking cocktease."

"So you and she had a thing?" Every nerve ending in Stevie's body was quivering, like when she was closing in on a big story.

He shrugged again, which she took to mean yes.

"Does Grant know?" she asked, zeroing in.

"He was so shit-faced most of the time, he couldn't find his own dick," Victor sneered.

Fine way to talk about your employer, Stevie thought. But keeping this bottled up for so long had clearly had a corrosive effect. Since she knew Grant hadn't kept him around all this time for his sunny personality, she could only suppose it was out of gratitude. For years, it had been Victor who'd picked him up whenever he was passed out, cleaning him up and putting him to bed. And apparently he'd done more than that; he'd also taken care of his boss's girlfriend's sexual needs. Still, that didn't explain why Victor would put a bullet through Lauren's head.

"You were in love with her, weren't you?" she said, as comprehension sank in. "You couldn't stand it when you found out she was using you, and you wanted to teach her a lesson."

"It wasn't like that." He dropped heavily onto the bench, staring off into the middle distance, still wearing that vacant look. He appeared to be wrestling with himself, but apparently the need to come clean outweighed his sense of self-preservation. "I loved her, yeah. But all I was trying to do was get her to see she'd be better off with me. I coulda got hold of some money"—Stevie didn't have to guess where—"we woulda been okay. Not rich, but we woulda had enough to get by. Only she laughed in my face. Said it wasn't money she wanted from me. The way she looked at me, like I was a toy she was tired of playing with . . . I just . . . I don't know . . . something came over me and I snapped. I knew where he kept his gun. I only wanted to shake her up a little, make her see she couldn't get away with treating me that way. Only . . ." He dropped his head into his hands, clutching his forehead.

"The gun went off," she finished for him.

His silence told her all she needed to know.

Stevie knew the rest of the story. In the end it had turned out to be the oldest in the world: a love triangle gone awry. Leaving Victor to his own tormented memories, she turned and walked away. As she passed through the doorway on her way to the staircase, she reached into her shoulder bag and groped for the tape recorder she'd surreptitiously switched on earlier when retrieving her cell phone, thumbing the Off button.

Chapter Twenty-one

"Quiet on the set!" Todd Oster yelled through cupped hands, for the benefit of no one but the cars whizzing past. He turned to Jay with a grin. "I've always wanted to do that."

They were standing on the corner of Park and Thirty-ninth, overseeing the crew that had been hired to shoot the TV commercial for the new Uruchima Wasp sports car. The ad would show the Wasp zipping through the Park Avenue tunnel, part of a sixty-second spot that would begin airing in the spring. The entrance to the tunnel had been blocked off to traffic, where the director, Doug Chen, was conferring with the driver of the process car, with its camera mounted on top that would track the Wasp as it made its way through the tunnel.

To those who'd never spent a day on a shoot, Jay thought, it must seem like exciting work. Mostly, though, it involved a lot of standing around waiting while the crew set up shots. Normally he was glad for any excuse to spend the day away from his desk; it was just tough luck that it had to be Sunday, the only day they could get a permit to block off traffic to the tunnel.

Jay glanced at his watch for the dozenth time, wondering where Franny was right now. He hadn't heard from her since she'd left for L.A., so for all he knew she'd changed her mind about breaking up with Keith. An image flashed through his mind of the two of them in bed together, and something twisted in his belly. For the past two days he'd been a nervous wreck, cursing his idiocy in letting her get on that plane without having told her exactly how he felt: that he loved her, in every way a man can love a woman. By the time she got back, it might be too late; she might have deemed Keith the better bet. Why settle for a man newly estranged from his wife when you could have one without all that baggage?

He tuned back in to hear Todd saying, " . . . so I was telling Kapinsky, if we don't get a bonus out of this, I'll settle for an employee discount." Todd ran his hand lovingly over the Wasp's hood. Hornet yellow, with sleek, low-slung lines reminiscent of the classic Corvette, the car had already attracted a fair bit of interest. Several passersby had jokingly asked if they could take it for a test drive. "Man, think of the places you could go with this baby."

"You planning on taking a trip?" Jay asked, smiling.

"Who said anything about a trip? I'm talking about getting laid." Ever since his divorce, Todd had been on the prowl. "Women," he snorted. "I used to think that all they wanted was a nice guy, the kind who gives foot rubs and remembers to take out the trash. But you know what the last one I went out with said when I took her back to my apartment?"

"What?"

"That she couldn't see dating a guy with a rusty refrigerator."

"Serves you right for buying it at the Salvation Army."

"Like I had a choice. After Christy cleaned me out, I could barely afford a toaster oven."

"I don't know why you even need one. All you ever eat is take-out."

"Go ahead and laugh," Todd replied good-naturedly. "A few months from now, when you're in the same boat, it won't seem so funny." Hunched inside his parka, his hands wrapped around a steaming Styrofoam cup, he looked like a bear just emerging from hibernation.

Jay felt a ripple of unease as his thoughts turned to Vivienne. He hadn't seen her since the night he'd walked out. When he'd returned from Franny's the following day to pack his suitcase, she hadn't been home. There had been only a note from her saying he didn't have to worry about finding another place to live because she was going back to Paris, this time for good. Thinking it would be only a matter of days, he'd been staying at a hotel near his office. But just this morning, when he'd called to let her know that he'd be dropping by later on to pick up some of his things, there had been no mention of her leaving for Paris. In fact, she'd sounded strangely upbeat.

"I won't be eating reheated takeout out of a rusty refrigerator, that's for sure," he joked, not wanting Todd to guess what was really on his mind. "Ramen noodles is more my speed."

"Seriously, bud, I know what you're going through." Todd clapped a hand over Jay's shoulder, eyeing him with concern. "When Christy and I split up, it was a kick in the gut. It gets better, though. If it weren't for the kids, I'd say it was the best decision I ever made."

Jay could have told him that his current mood had less to do with Vivienne than with Franny, but that would have required a lengthy explanation, so all he said was, "Thanks. I'll keep that in mind."

It was several more hours of take after take by the time they wrapped. It had consumed the better part of the afternoon to get what would amount to fifteen seconds of usable film, but all in all it was a successful day. Jay declined Todd's offer to buy him dinner, heading back to the loft instead to pick up some things. In the taxi on the way over, he tried Franny once more on his cell phone, but all he got was her voice mail. Damn. Was there a reason she wasn't returning his calls? Was it like what she'd said about wanting to deliver the bad news to Keith in person? Was she planning to do the same with him?

When he walked in through his front door, his mind occupied with thoughts of Franny, it came almost as a shock to find the living room softly lit with candles and the dining room table set for two. In the kitchen, Vivienne, wearing a slinky hostess gown that showed off her figure, was putting the finishing touches on the supper she'd prepared.

She looked up at him and smiled. "Surprise."

"It's quite a surprise, I'll say that." Jay's tone was flat.

"I hope you haven't eaten already." She gestured toward the still crackling roast she'd just pulled from the oven. "Everything's ready. I just have to warm the sauce."

A knot formed in his belly. "Viv—"

"I got the recipe from Maman," she went on in a rush, not letting him get a word in. "I know how much you love roast beef."

"It looks good," he noted without much enthusiasm.

"It's wonderful to see you. It's been so lonely here without you these past few days." She paused in the midst of stirring something on the stove to cast him a meaningful look, one that made her appear at once vulnerable and seductive. Whatever tears she'd shed, she was on a mission now and, from the gown she had on, through which the outline of her body was visible, he didn't have to guess what it was.

Few men, he thought, would be immune to her charms. Vivienne's lay not only in her beauty but in the sexuality that radiated from her like heat from a fire. Even now, as he stood there eyeing her dispassionately, he could appreciate how enticing she was, the graceful lines of her body beneath her gown and the way her hair caught the light as she moved about the kitchen. Once it had had the desired effect on him. Each time she'd return after a long absence during which he'd been left wondering why he wasted his energy on a woman who collected men's hearts the way other women collected pieces of jewelry, the process of wooing him back would begin all over again. But not this time. He was done.

"You shouldn't have gone to all this trouble," he said, meaning it.

"It was no trouble at all," she replied airily, bending to pull a warmed baguette from the oven. "Besides, after all those restaurant meals, I thought you could use something home-cooked."

"That's not what I meant." His voice softened. He could see the effort she'd put into it. Even so, he said, "Viv, I can't stay. It would be wrong for us both. You don't need a husband whose heart isn't in it. And you've made it pretty clear yours isn't either." She was just lonely and scared right now. That wasn't the same as love.

Vivienne's eyes filled with tears. "You don't mean that. You're just upset with me."

"I was, yes, but not anymore," he said. "I've had some time to think it over, and I realized something—it was over even before you cheated on me. I knew it deep down, after all those months, when you didn't come home."

"No, *chéri!* It's not true!" A spoon clattered to the counter as she put out a beseeching hand.

"It is for me," he said quietly.

"It's because of Franny, isn't it? You've been with *her* all this time." Vivienne's voice rose, growing shrill.

He didn't reply, letting his silence fill in the blank.

Her eyes narrowed. "So I'm not the only one who was unfaithful."

"It's not the same."

"Why, because you *love* her?" Her mouth twisted as she spat out the words. "Because you had a baby with her?"

"Nothing happened. Not until . . ." He let the rest of the sentence trail off.

"I'm sure it wasn't for lack of trying on *her* part." Bitterness crept into her voice. "I'll bet she was over here every day reminding you of everything I couldn't give you." Even in her anger, Vivienne looked glorious, her skin flushed and her eyes afire, like some beautiful creature in the wild. "What she's conveniently forgotten is that she wouldn't have that baby if it weren't for me. I did it because I wanted her to be happy, not so she could steal my husband!"

"Whatever your reason, it was a good thing." Vivienne's one selfless act. He placed a hand over hers, letting her know that whatever else she'd done, he would always be grateful for that.

"I wanted her to see that I could be her friend, too." Tears filled her eyes, making them shimmer. He realized then that, for *all* her mad socializing, Vivienne had few real friends, none of them female, just the gay men who were drawn to her like bees to honey.

"She's always liked you," he said.

"Not like it is with you and Em and Stevie. She *tries*, for your sake, but it's not the same," she went on in a choked voice. The saucepan on the stove bubbled on unnoticed, steam rising from it in wisps to caress her woebegone face. "She's never really forgiven me for Brian."

"From what you've told me, there was nothing to forgive." Besides, it had been a long time ago. Hadn't the statute of limitations run out? Still, something in her expression made him ask, "Is there more to the story than Franny knows?"

"What are you implying?" Vivienne said.

From the way her back went up, he could tell she was withholding something. All at once, it made sense. He eyed her narrowly. "You fucked him, didn't you?"

"Oh, so now I sleep with every man I meet?" she shot back.

"Answer the question."

"All right, yes! I slept with him!" she cried, throwing up her hands in frustration. "He followed me to Paris. He told me it was over between him and Franny. What was I supposed to think?"

He understood now why she'd been willing, no, eager, to go to such extraordinary lengths for Franny. It had been a way to right an old wrong. "You should have kept in mind that Franny was your friend," he said, filled with contempt for this woman he'd once loved. "Whatever he said, you knew she'd be hurt. That's why you didn't tell her."

"It was only that one time! After that, I told him I couldn't see him anymore."

"It didn't mean anything, is that what you're saying?" he said, echoing her words from the other night.

She rushed to explain, "What happened with Claude was different . . . I wasn't myself."

"You're wrong about that." In his mind he could hear his mother saying, A *leopard never changes its spots*, and his mouth stretched in a mirthless smile. "You've always been true to yourself, Viv. My mistake was believing you could change." Not waiting to hear any more of her tortured explanations, he took a last look at the feast she'd prepared and said, as he was turning to go, "Thanks, but I'm afraid I've lost my appetite."

* * *

In the cab on the way home from the airport, Franny stared out the window at the pouring rain, absorbed in her thoughts. Fortunately, Ruth had slept most of the way, giving her a chance to reflect on everything that had happened over the past few days, none of which had turned out quite the way she'd expected. Now she looked down at her daughter, slumbering in her car seat, and felt envious of her blissful ignorance. Ruth didn't have to fret over things yet to come or know the heartache of having to hurt someone. She didn't have to wonder if her dreams would come true . . . or come crashing down around her ears.

Franny tried to summon the courage to call Jay. He'd left several messages while she was away that she hadn't returned. There was so much to tell him, but at the moment, exhausted from the trip and still nursing a hangover, she didn't think she could get it all out in any kind of coherent fashion . . . or face whatever it was he might say to her. Finally, she worked up the nerve, but decided to low key it for the time being. There would be ample opportunity for a more serious conversation later on.

"To think I left sunny California for this," Franny said.

Jay glanced out his office window at the rain streaming down outside. "How was your trip?" he asked as casually as he could with his heart in his throat.

"Uneventful. Ruth slept most of the way. The flight attendants couldn't get over what a good baby she was. They should have seen her reenactment of the *Exorcist* the other day." No mention of Keith. "Poor Stevie. She's probably making an appointment to have her tubes tied as we speak." She explained that Ruth had refused to take the bottle she'd left with Stevie, howling at the top of her lungs until Franny showed up to nurse her. "I just hope we haven't created a monster. Who knows where it could lead. We'll give her a tricycle and she'll demand a Ferrari. Or hold the tooth fairy for ransom."

Jay chuckled in spite of himself. "I think the tooth fairy is safe for the time being. We still have a few more years." Years in which he prayed he would get to watch Ruth grow up.

"Easy for you to say, you're not the one who has to listen to her scream."

He knew she'd meant it facetiously, but he couldn't help wondering if he was, in fact, destined to be a long-distance dad. It was all he could do to keep from asking outright how it had gone with Keith. The only thing that kept him from doing so was that he wasn't sure he wanted to hear the answer. What if it was bad news? At least this way he could go on hoping a little while longer. He asked instead if he could stop by on his way home from work, and when Franny begged off, pleading exhaustion and asking if he could come the following evening instead, he tried not to read too much into it.

The next day was the longest of his life. Mr. Uruchima arrived unexpectedly from Japan and insisted on taking Jay and his whole team out to dinner. There was no way he could refuse, so he phoned Franny and told her not to expect him. All that night and into the following day, he merely went through the motions, his mind on Franny all the while. By the time Thursday rolled around, he needed a drink to brace himself for the crushing news he now felt certain lay ahead, so he let Todd twist his arm into going to Shaughnessy's for a beer after work.

Forty minutes later he was standing outside Franny's door, letting himself in with the spare key she'd given him after Ruth was born. He walked in to find her sitting on the sofa in the living room, nursing Ruth, looking impossibly sexy, with her blouse unbuttoned and her curls spilling over her full breasts. He took his time hanging up his coat, while willing his erection into submission, before he crossed the room to drop a kiss on her cheek.

"Looks like she's recovered from her ordeal," he said, fingering the downy tuft on top of Ruth's mostly bald head.

Franny rolled her eyes. "You think *she* had it bad."

"I take it you're referring to Keith." Jay sat down next to her, his heart bucking against his rib cage.

She nodded, shifting Ruth to her other breast. "Let's just say getting drunk didn't help."

"Uh-oh." He smiled knowingly. Franny never could hold her liquor.

"He had to drive me back to Stevie's," she explained. "Try breaking up with a guy when you're three sheets to the wind. I might as well have been talking to him in Farsi."

"But you *did?* Break up with him, I mean." She might only have intended to, he thought, then changed her mind after Keith had performed heroically.

"I—," she started to say, but Ruth let out a cry just then and Franny stood up to burp her. As she paced back and forth, patting the baby on the back, Jay found new meaning in an old expression—he felt as if the suspense were literally killing him.

Ruth let out a loud burp, and Franny disappeared into the next room to change her and put her down for the night. It seemed hours, not minutes, before she reappeared, her cheeks flushed and her hair tousled, seemingly unaware that the top two buttons of her blouse were still undone. He thought of all the opportunities they'd missed through the years, swapping jokes and sharing confidences when they could have been making love. It seemed absurd that he'd never noticed before how sexy she was.

Even so, the old patterns were hard to break. He felt the lure of the familiar, the safe, as Franny flopped down next to him on the sofa, propping her stockinged feet on his lap. He thought how easy it would be to fall back into that comfort zone. No risk of heartbreak, no turning down a road from which there was no return. They wouldn't have to wonder what came next. They'd know already.

Jay cleared his throat. "So?"

Franny met his gaze, and he knew from the look on her face that he wasn't the only one who was scared. "You first," she said.

He eyed her in puzzlement, not sure what she wanted to hear. Then it dawned on him. "You want to know if I've changed my mind about Viv?"

"Have you?" she asked, eyeing him anxiously.

Jay shook his head. "Not a chance. It's over." He considered telling her about Viv's most recent confession and decided there was no reason Franny had to know.

She closed her eyes and put her hand over her heart, as if to say a silent prayer of thanks. When she opened them again, she was smiling. "Okay, my turn. Yes, I'm officially unengaged. It was pretty bad, but Keith took it well, when I finally sobered up enough to tell him. I think mostly because he was in shock."

Jay struggled to hold back the grin that was fighting to break loose. "No regrets?"

"I feel terrible about it, if that's what you mean."

"But you're not not sorry?"

Franny's eyes widened as comprehension sank in, and she bolted upright, pulling her legs in against her chest. "You can't think . . . oh, Jay . . . no, of course I'm not sorry *that* way."

"So I guess this means you're stuck with me." He grinned and reached for her hand, bringing it to his mouth and unfolding her fingers one at a time to kiss each one.

She looked both happy and bewildered. "There's just one thing. How are we supposed to go from being best friends to being lovers? I'd hate it if we started acting weird around each other." Her fingers tightened around his. "I don't want us to lose what we have."

"We won't. It'll just get better."

Her expression remained faintly troubled, though. "You know how we're always saying we can read each other's minds? Well, it's no joke. A lot of the time it's like we actually can."

"Franny, really, you're worrying about n—"

"Okay," she said, cutting him off. "What am I thinking right now?" She closed her eyes.

Jay was about to make some lighthearted remark, but she looked so serious, with her eyes screwed shut, he thought better of it and spoke from his heart instead. "You're thinking that we're a family— you, me, Ruth. We were even before Ruth, we just didn't know it." She opened her eyes, a tremulous smile forming on her lips. "In fact, I don't think it was an accident that we had her. I think it was meant to be—God telling us to quit stalling and get on with it."

"Warm, definitely warm," she said.

"How about now?" He drew her into his arms, stroking her hair.

"Any warmer, and I'll have to break out the fire extinguisher." She curled up against him, dropping her head onto his shoulder.

He put a finger under her chin, tipping her head up. "Okay, your turn. What am *I* thinking?" he murmured as he bent to kiss her.

She squeezed her eyes shut again, holding her teepeed fingertips to her temples as she frowned in mock concentration. "I'm seeing a bed with two people in it."

"Are they naked?"

"Yeah, I think so. It's a little fuzzy. I can't say for sure."

"Let me give you a hint." He kissed her again, more deeply this time.

Minutes later they were on the floor with half their clothes off. Jay was tugging off his jeans when Ruth let out a cry in the next room. Franny cursed and sat up. "I swear, she does this just to taunt me. If I were in front of the TV stuffing my face with Pringles, she'd have slept through the night."

"It's all right. I can wait," he said.

"I'm not sure I can." Frowning, she wriggled back into her jeans.

"What's the rush? We have all night."

"Stop being so understanding. You're making me look bad," she said with a laugh.

He smiled, brushing a stray curl from her forehead. "What are friends for?"

Chapter Twenty-two

Emerson, her eyes half shut and her hand in Reggie's, sat listening to the sublime music of the pianist onstage playing Chopin's Nocturne for Piano in E Minor, thinking, *This is how it must be for other people.* The contentment she felt must seem normal to those who hadn't grown up in a crazy, upside-down world where money earmarked for summer camp was spent on a table for that year's Costume Institute Ball, and where lavish dinners at the Four Seasons and Lutèce were followed by discreet visits to the Provident Loan Society, the pawnbroker for the rich. And how ironic that the thing she'd been brought up to view as social suicide, marrying outside your class, was what was making her so happy.

She glanced over at Reggie, who was gazing raptly at Emmanuel Ax up onstage. A lot of husbands fell asleep at concerts — Briggs used to jokingly refer to them as a "good nap spoiled." But Reggie loved classical music as much as she and relished any opportunity to see it performed live. Things she'd always taken for granted—concerts, Broadway plays, a night at the opera—were, for him, a rare treat.

He'd opened up a whole new world for her as well: neighborhoods she'd only driven through before, like Spanish Harlem, Greek Astoria, and Arthur Avenue in the Bronx. Together they'd explored funky shops selling exotic incenses and fetishes, and eaten at places she might have turned her nose up at in the past, like the Ethiopian restaurant where they'd feasted on a spicy stew, using chunks of flatbread in place of utensils.

Ainsley was blossoming as well. Having Reggie come live with them was, for her, like Christmas and Easter rolled into one. She'd attached herself to him like an appendage, and only his unflagging good humor kept him from begging off when for the umpteenth time she asked to be lifted onto his shoulders or sit on his lap, or have him carry her to bed.

The icing on the cake was Briggs's befriending Reggie. The day he'd invited Reggie to join him for a game of golf at his club, she'd been reminded once more of why she'd once loved Briggs: Under that stiff neck and even stiffer upper lip was good heart.

No, marrying Reggie had turned out to be far from social suicide. Sure, there had been some raised eyebrows, as well as those knocking themselves out to show how openminded they were. Like tonight at the intermission, when they'd bumped into Bunny Hopkins, a long-time acquaintance of her mother's. Bunny had been elaborately polite to the point of parody. But overall, Emerson had been pleasantly surprised by the reaction to her new husband, which was basically no reaction at all other than polite interest.

The one remaining sore spot was Marjorie. Emerson hadn't seen or heard from her since the night she and Reggie had eloped, and though in some ways it was a relief, the silence was more resounding than all of Marjorie's yammering. Emerson still got regular reports from her caretakers and had spoken to her doctor several times while she was in the hospital. She knew Marjorie was doing as well as could be expected, that she was eating a little something at every meal and moving her bowels regularly. And while Emerson would have protested aloud that she didn't owe her a thing, as she had the other day when Franny gently broached the subject, a sliver of guilt had worked its way in nonetheless, and was now festering.

It wasn't that Marjorie didn't *deserve* to be cut off. No judge or jury would condemn her for doing so. Nor was it that she missed her mother's company. It was more a vague sense of something being out of alignment.

She squeezed Reggie's hand, and he turned to smile at her, his gaze lingering, as if the sight of her were so captivating he had trouble tearing himself away. In his new suit, which she'd insisted on buying him, he was easily the most elegant man at the concert. *Yes, we make a fine pair,* she thought, looking down at their entwined fingers.

It would be months before they got through all the red tape with the INS, but at least Reggie was in no danger of being deported. After learning that the claims against him were false—Emerson had leaned on her aunt Florence to provide an affidavit to that effect—they'd determined that he wasn't a security risk, and were currently evaluating his application for citizenship. Emerson was confident it would all work out. No one who saw them together could possibly doubt their genuine love for each other. Besides, who would choose all the obstacles they'd faced, plus the ones still ahead, for any reason other than pure devotion?

A heartbreakingly beautiful rendition of Beethoven's "Moonlight Sonata" followed the Chopin nocturne. Finally, after the last encore, when the thunderous applause had died down, they rose to go, Reggie helping her on with her jacket. A gentleman of the old school, he never failed to open doors for her or pull out her chair. Once, when she'd teasingly accused him of spoiling her, he'd looked baffled.

Wasn't this how all men behaved? he'd asked. When she'd told him that he was the exception rather than the rule, he'd replied that it was only because those men hadn't had the benefit of Miriam Okanta boxing their ears.

Having met his mother, who, along with Reggie's father and two of his brothers, had flown over to attend the small reception at her apartment, Emerson didn't doubt that she'd raised her children with a firm hand. But if so, it was one tempered by warmth and good humor. A tall, handsome woman with a laugh as full-bodied as her figure, Miriam had managed to communicate to Emerson, despite her limited English, how pleased she was to have both a new daughter *and* a granddaughter.

Outside, it was cool and breezy. As they strolled arm in arm along Fifty-seventh Street on their way to Sixth Avenue to get a cab uptown, still under the music's spell, Emerson's thoughts turned to Franny and Jay. The only ones who had been surprised when they'd gotten together were Franny and Jay themselves. Now, as if to make up for all that lost time, they planned to make it legal as soon as Jay's divorce came through. Naturally, Emerson had offered her services in planning the wedding. The caterer she used for most of her events would give them a good price, and she knew an excellent florist who—

Her thoughts were interrupted by the trilling of her cell phone. As always, she felt a little flutter of unease, wondering if it was Ainsley's nanny calling to report some mishap or minor ailment. But it turned out to be her mother's nurse. Marjorie was on her way to the hospital, Sonia informed her. Apparently she was having trouble breathing, and Sonia had insisted, over Marjorie's objections, on calling an ambulance. Sonia sounded worried.

Hanging up, Emerson was torn between her unforgiving heart and her sense of duty, which was all tangled up in the old tug of yearning for her mother's love. But Marjorie had made her bed, she told herself, and now she had to lie in it. Emerson decided that a call to her mother's oncologist in the morning was all that was required of her.

Reggie, though, had other ideas. "We must go," he said.

"I can't." Emerson shook her head.

He eyed her gravely. "She could die."

"I would have thought you, of all people, would understand," she said, feeling slightly miffed that he wasn't on her side. Hadn't he suffered at Marjorie's hands, too?

"I understand only that she is your mother."

"For what it's worth," she said bitterly.

"Nonetheless." His jaw was firmly set; he wasn't taking no for an answer.

"Are we having our first fight?" she asked.

"There's no need for us to fight," he said calmly. "You know in your heart that what I'm saying is right."

The magic of the evening had vanished, and as they stood on the sidewalk with people streaming past them like eddies around a rock in the middle of a river, she felt as if she were at a crossroads. Part of her wanted to cry out at the unfairness of it. Why was she the one who had to turn the other cheek when it should have been her mother begging *her* for forgiveness? At the same time she knew that there was wisdom in what Reggie was saying, and that if she listened to her heart it would tell her the right thing to do.

She reached for her husband's hand. "Let's go."

It was long past visiting hours by the time they arrived at Lenox Hill Hospital, but the nurse at the desk in the oncology ward, recognizing her from previous visits, said they could have a few minutes. As Emerson walked down the corridor lined with carts and gurneys, holding tightly to Reggie's hand, it was only Franny's cautionary words echoing in her head—*When someone dies, your anger doesn't die with them*—that kept her from bolting.

Marjorie was propped up in bed when they walked in, almost as if she'd been expecting them. It had been weeks since Emerson had last seen her and she was shocked by the change in her appearance. There was almost nothing left of her except skin stretched over sharply protruding bones. Without her wig, the outline of her skull was visible through her wispy gray hair. Her eyes looked out at them from darkened hollows, and her chest rose and fell with the oxygen being pumped in through the tube in her nose.

"If you've come to watch me die, I'm sorry to disappoint you," she said, every other word punctuated with a labored breath. "My doctor tells me I'm not ready for the morgue just yet."

Emerson could only stand there staring at her mother. The sight of Marjorie so diminished seemed to have sucked all the anger out of her, leaving her strangely devoid of emotion.

It was Reggie who stepped forward to say, "I'm glad to hear that. How are you feeling, Mrs. Fitzgibbons?"

Emerson tensed, half expecting Marjorie to unleash a stream of invective, but she only said, "I'm still breathing, so that's something, at least. And how are you and your bride?"

"We're both well," said Reggie, as if taking no notice of her sarcasm.

"So married life agrees with you."

"Very much so." He briefly turned to smile at Emerson. "I hope we have your blessing."

Marjorie eyed him curiously, as if not quite sure whether to take him at face value. "I'm surprised it matters to you," she said. "I should think you'd want nothing to do with me."

He inclined his head slightly, as if acknowledging that he did indeed have a right to be upset with her. But when he spoke, his tone was gentle. "We didn't come to air our grievances."

Suddenly Emerson's hard-heartedness seemed small and petty in the face of Reggie's compassion. She realized now that it had been wrong of her to punish her mother by staying away. In a sense, hadn't it been just one more way of allowing herself to be controlled? It was only by letting go of her anger, as Reggie had, that she would be truly liberated. Also, deep down she knew that however misguided Marjorie's actions, she hadn't done it to be malicious. In her own twisted way, she'd thought she was doing what was best.

"Even so, I owe you both an apology." Marjorie spoke stiffly, as if defying them to accept it. "There, I've said it. You can go on hating me if you like, but I wanted you to know."

"I don't hate you." Emerson said, finding her voice at last.

"I know I haven't been much of a mother." Marjorie's expression softened a bit as she turned toward Emerson. "The truth is, you terrified me. Whatever I did, I was always sure it was the wrong thing. And that look you'd give me, as if you couldn't bear to have me touch you—" She broke off with a sigh. "After a while, it was easier just to leave you be."

Emerson's resentment rushed back in. "Are you saying it's *my* fault?"

"No, darling, of course not." Marjorie's hand, mottled with yellowing bruises left by IV needles, lifted, as if to reach out to her, before falling back onto the mattress. She shook her head, looking deeply tired. "All I'm saying is that things aren't always as black and white as they seem."

"You were never there for me when I needed you," Emerson said, choking back tears. "All you ever cared about was my marrying well, but that was only because of how it would reflect on you."

Marjorie arched a brow. "And what will you tell Ainsley if one day she accuses you of letting her down?"

"She knows I love her."

"And you think I don't love you?"

Emerson didn't know how to respond.

"You were right about one thing," Marjorie went on wearily.

"My friends haven't exactly been beating a path to my door, so I suppose that says something about the kind of person I am."

"It only goes to show how shallow *they* are," Emerson said, in her defense.

"Water seeks its own level." Marjorie sounded more resigned than bitter. "Oh, I don't doubt they'll all turn out for the funeral. Not because I was so beloved, but because it's expected of them. It's what we do, and there aren't many of us left. We have to stick together."

Emerson thought of the black, leather-bound copy of the *Social Register* gathering dust on a shelf in her mother's library, a directory of all the names of any note. People who were favored, not because they were smart, accomplished, or even necessarily rich, but simply because they'd had the good fortune to be born into the right families. However silly Emerson might think it, her mother's entire existence had once revolved around it. It was unbearably sad to think of her dying without having lived outside those bounds.

She sank down in the chair by the bed, feeling drained. "Mother, I wish you wouldn't . . ." she started to say.

But Marjorie waved aside her usual objection. "Nonsense, darling. We have to talk about it sometime. I think even my doctor would agree that the sooner we make funeral arrangements, the better."

"W-what did you have in mind?" Emerson stammered. It felt so strange discussing this.

"A horse-drawn hearse draped in black, mourners lined up three deep along Fifth Avenue, and a full choir to send me on my way," Marjorie replied without missing a beat. "But, darling, regardless of what you might think, I'm well aware of who's footing the bill, so in light of that, I'll settle for cremation and a nice memorial service. Really, it's the least I can do."

Emerson swallowed hard and forced a smile. "I'm sure that can be arranged."

They were getting ready to leave when Marjorie's gimlet eye fell on Reggie. "You want my blessing, you have it—on one condition. That you don't let her walk all over you like she did her ex–husband. She likes to think it was Briggs who ruled the roost, but don't believe it for a minute. She's my daughter, after all, much as she hates to admit it."

"I don't think there is any danger of that, Mrs. Fitzgibbons," he said, struggling to suppress a smile.

"Marjorie, please," she said, with an airy wave of her hand. "I think we're beyond formalities at this point, don't you? Just don't forget—" She broke off to suck in a breath, and Emerson braced herself, expecting to hear something along the lines of, *Don't forget your place.* But all she said was, "I can still beat the pants off you in gin rummy."

"I welcome the opportunity to prove you wrong," he said.

Marjorie closed her eyes, looking utterly spent. In a barely audible voice, she said, "We'll see about that. In the meantime, why don't you two run along and let me get my beauty sleep."

Emerson lingered a moment longer, watching as Marjorie drifted off to sleep, then she bent to plant a light kiss on her forehead, murmuring, "Good night, Mother. Sleep tight."

When the call came in the middle of the night that Marjorie had died quietly in her sleep, Emerson felt more relieved than anything, grateful that her mother wouldn't have to suffer anymore. They'd both been put out of their misery, in a way. She, in having made peace with Marjorie at the end. Now, instead of crying over a lost opportunity, she could truly mourn her mother.

And just as Marjorie had predicted, the society crowd all turned out for her memorial service the following week. The older members of the Cosmopolitan Club, represented by Bunny Hopkins and her ilk, mingled with the congregants at St. Thomas's Church (Marjorie would have been pleased to note several Mayflower descendants among them). Emerson's ailing aunt Florence flew in from Boca Raton, attended by her caretaker, a lovely Haitian woman named Eugenie. Nacario, too, came to pay his respects, as did Emerson's ex-husband and his wife.

Jay and Franny were there as well. And Stevie, for whom it hadn't been easy getting away, given her newly acquired fame as Grant Tobin's daughter, which had turned the tables on her, making *her* the focus of a media feeding frenzy. As Emerson sat listening to the minister read from Proverbs, flanked by Ainsley and Reggie on one side and her friends on the other, she felt enfolded by love. She may not have been born into the family she'd have chosen, but she'd done all right in making one of her own. In fact, she wouldn't have it any other way.

"Have you thought about where you're going to scatter the ashes?" asked Franny as they were pulling away from the church in the limo.

Emerson looked down at the urn cradled in her arms. As discreet and tasteful as Marjorie would have wanted, with a polished mahogany veneer, it was surprisingly light: the sum total of her mother's life. "One of her happiest memories was when she and my dad honeymooned in the Loire Valley," she said, smiling faintly. "I asked one of my clients who owns a vineyard if I could scatter her ashes there. That way every time we drink a bottle of wine from that year, I'll think of her. She'd like that."

"Scatter mine over a wheat field," Franny instructed Jay. "If I can't eat all the bread I want in my lifetime, it'd be nice knowing I'll be in all those loaves after I'm gone."

Jay tightened his arm around her shoulder. "No more talk about dying, please. I don't know about you, but I plan to be around a long, long time."

They were such a perfect couple, Franny with her curly head nestled against Jay's shoulder, it was hard to remember when they'd been nothing more than friends.

"Speaking of which, have you given any more thought to what kind of wedding you'd like?" Emerson asked.

"Isn't walking down the aisle alone enough of an ordeal?" joked Stevie. But the wistful look she wore told the real story. The other day she'd confided to Emerson that it had been the biggest mistake of her life not marrying Ryan.

"We haven't even officially announced our engagement yet," Franny reminded them.

"My mommy and Reggie got married. Now I have *two* daddies," announced Ainsley, who sat perched on Reggie's lap.

"Which means I have two lovely ladies to look after instead of just one." Reggie reached for Emerson's hand, lacing his fingers through hers. "And I owe it all to your grandmother. I wouldn't have met either of you if it hadn't been for her. I'm grateful to her for that."

"Good-bye, Grandma." Ainsley patted the urn. "Do you think she can hear me all the way up in heaven?" she asked Emerson.

Emerson felt the sting of tears behind her eyes. What she'd learned about losing someone close to you was that it wasn't necessarily the big, cinematic moments that set you off—the Bible readings and eulogies, the friends and relatives offering their sympathies—but the small reminders: a word, a gesture, a memento, like her mother's favorite teacup upended in the kitchen drainer or the familiar scent of violets that had come wafting from the closet when she'd been hunting for a dress for Marjorie to be cremated in.

"I don't know, sweetie," she said. "But if she can, I'm sure she's smiling right now."

Chapter Twenty-three

For Stevie, the weeks following Victor Gonzalez's arrest (and Grant's subsequent exoneration) were almost surreal. Overnight she'd found herself on the other side of the camera, dodging reporters and TV crews—some of the same people she'd worked alongside for years. Only because she was a veteran of the business was she able to negotiate the shoals, opting for a few select interviews merely to set the record straight, with KLNA naturally getting first crack, instead of allowing herself and Grant to be swallowed up by the media feeding frenzy. It hadn't been easy getting Grant to go along with it. He was still gun shy from his years of being under siege and she'd had to persuade him that in the long run it was for the best. As soon as the public's curiosity was satisfied, it would move on to the next scandal. There was always one waiting in the wings, and except for the brief flurry of interest that would come with the publication of Keith's book, Grant Tobin and Stevie Light would soon be yesterday's news.

Her life was just beginning to settle back into some semblance of a routine when a blind item in Page Six of the *New York Post* jumped out at her one morning as she was sitting at her desk in the newsroom, scanning the daily papers for items she could use:

... Just asking: What studio head recently separated from wife number three was spotted canoodling at a recent fund-raiser with a certain babelicious blond production assistant, last seen on the arm of an Academy Award–winning documentary filmmaker?

Her heart did a flying leap. It had to be Ryan's girlfriend, she thought. Who else fit that description? And blind items were often more reliable than official statements from publicists. But there was only one way to get the *real* scoop: from Ryan himself. How, though? She couldn't just pick up the phone and casually ask, "Oh, by the way, are you and Kimberly still together?" She'd come across as an old-boyfriend-obsessed loser.

It wasn't until the following morning, after a restless night with the tumblers in her head whirling, that an opportunity presented itself. Almost as if fate had decreed it, news came over the wires of the death of Delilah Jacobs, a former child actress who'd gone on to become a leading wildlife preservationist. It seemed Delilah's last film project, in 1999, when she was in her late seventies, had been a *National Geographic* documentary about her extraordinary life, produced and directed by none other than Ryan Costa.

Stevie spent the next twenty minutes at her computer feverishly hammering out a proposal for a package on the late Delilah Jacobs, which she fired off to Liv. In the wake of Stevie's new notoriety, the station had gotten its highest ratings ever, so Liv was on her best behavior these days. Even so, Stevie wasn't surprised when the producer e-mailed her back saying, *Who gives a rat's ass about some has-been actress???? A few lines will do.* She could have gone over Liv's head, but that would only have pissed her off and in the end made Stevie's life more difficult. Instead, she tracked Liv down in her office, working on her until she finally agreed to let her do the piece, mainly just to shut her up. Minutes later Stevie was scurrying off to the assignment desk to line up a crew, armed with a legitimate reason that didn't involve groveling to interview her ex-boyfriend. Face-to-face, it would be easy enough to find out what the score was and if there was any chance of rekindling *their* romance.

Briefly, she allowed herself to imagine what it would be like. Meeting Ryan for drinks or an early dinner at the little bistro around the corner from his studio, like in the old days. The way they'd play off each other, like jazz musicians riffing, feeding each other lines and laughing at inside jokes no one else would get. The lovemaking had been great, yeah, and there were times, especially at night, when she'd ache for him with a kind of hunger that was seldom satisfied by the quick-fix method she'd become quite efficient at. But it was the small, seemingly inconsequential moments that had provided the most lasting memories: his little ritual of bringing her coffee and the paper in bed on Sunday mornings; the nights they'd order Chinese takeout and stay in to watch a movie on DVD; the rides they'd take up the coast on nice days, with the top down on the Firebird and no particular destination in mind, just enjoying the sea breezes and sunshine.

Could that be hers again? Was it too much to hope for?

But when she called Red Gate Productions, it was only to learn that Ryan was out of town. Instead of an on-camera interview, she had to settle for a sound bite over the phone. Ryan gave a tribute to Delilah, whom he described as a grand old gal who'd been fonder of four-legged animals than the two-legged kind, and in the end it turned out to be a nice piece. But all Stevie could think of while she was cutting it was how businesslike he'd sounded. Whatever his status, it was clear he'd moved on as far as she was concerned.

It came as a pleasant surprise when he phoned the following day to compliment her on the piece. She was at the ABC studios, on the set of their hit sitcom *Baker's Dozen*, about a foster mom named Francine Baker and her thirteen kids, getting ready to interview the star, so she couldn't really talk. She asked if she could call him later on, then spent the rest of the morning obsessing. Had his call been just a collegial pat on the back, or was there more to it than that?

By all rights he should want nothing more to do with her. She was the one to blame for their breakup; when push came to shove she'd chickened out. And wasn't love all about taking risks? Look at Jay and Franny, and Emerson and Reggie. Each had taken an enormous leap of faith. It wasn't all a bed of roses for them, and there had to be times they missed single life. But wasn't it worth giving up those little perks—never having to reach for the milk carton and find it empty, getting to read in bed at night as late as you like, and blasting ABBA's *Greatest Hits* on the stereo without anyone rolling their eyes—when you got to come home at the end of each day to the one person you loved best in the world? Someone you could talk to about anything and everything. Someone who didn't mind giving you a back rub when you were too tired to have sex, and who said you were gorgeous, and meant it, when you were having a bad-hair day or your face was broken out.

"How did the interview go?" Ryan asked, when she phoned him later on.

"Fine, except we had to bleep out all the four-letter words." She explained that Jackie Ramone, the star of *Baker's Dozen*, had strong opinions on subjects ranging from politics to her pet environmental cause, and wasn't shy about expressing them. "I talked to some of the kids, too. The littlest one, who's so adorable on air, turned out to be a terror."

He chuckled. "In other words, just another day at the office."

"What about you? What are you up to these days?" Stevie kept her voice casual.

Ryan told her about his current film project, about the late, great jazz saxophonist, Gerry Mulligan. There was no mention of Kimberly or the blind item in the *Post*.

She, in turn, filled him in on the latest with Grant, and with her friends.

"So Franny and Jay finally got together?" he said. "I can't say I'm all that surprised. If ever two people were made for each other, it's them."

"I admit I didn't see it coming," Stevie said. "But, yeah, it makes perfect sense."

"Be sure to give them my congratulations. Em, too." He paused before adding, half jokingly. "Now that they're all squared away, I guess that makes you the odd man out."

Stevie wondered what he'd meant by it and was on the verge of asking point-blank if he and Kimberly were still an item when she heard a call-waiting beep and Ryan announced, "Oops. There's my other line." He put her on hold a moment, and when he came back told her, "I have to take this. Can we talk another time?"

Stevie took a wild stab, knowing she might not get another chance. "You free for lunch sometime next week?"

"Next week's no good. But I could do brunch tomorrow." His tone was brisk, businesslike.

"I think I could manage that." Suddenly she was having a hard time catching her breath.

"Ten-thirty at the Crow's Nest?"

"Great. See you then."

After she'd hung up, Stevie's heart was racing. She thought briefly about phoning one of her friends, but what was there to report? It was just brunch, not a declaration of undying love. Also, Jay, Franny, and Emerson were no longer available to chat at all hours; they had families. As Ryan had so succinctly pointed out, she was the odd man out.

Feeling at loose ends, Stevie wandered into the kitchen in search of something to nibble on. But going through her mostly empty cupboards only provided more evidence of her lonely existence. All she could find were a few cans of soup, a half-eaten package of stale tortilla chips, and a box of Cheerios. The refrigerator told an even grimmer tale, with its wilted lettuce, single shriveled carrot, and container of yogurt resembling a sixth-grade science experiment. The only thing she had lots of was the coffee she fueled herself with each morning before she jumped on the proverbial treadmill.

The following morning she rose early to shower and get dressed. On days when she didn't have to arrive at work camera ready, a touch of lipstick and mascara usually sufficed, but today she took her time applying her makeup and polishing her nails. She took equal care in choosing an outfit, settling at last on a pair of strappy sandal heels and her most flattering dress, a wraparound with a plunging neckline, which even when she was bloated with PMS made her look like she'd been living on salads for a week. The finishing touch was a pair of chandelier earrings she envisioned swinging sexily as she leaned close to whisper in Ryan's ear.

But any words of love would have to be shouted she realized as soon as she arrived at the Crow's Nest, a favorite brunch spot on the Santa Monica Pier, to find it packed. As for knocking Ryan off his feet with her sexy outfit, that hope ended when some bozo bumped into her as she was pushing her way through the crowd of people by the entrance, spilling half his Bloody Mary down the front of her dress. She was dabbing at it with a napkin when she looked up to see Ryan standing in front of her.

"It's not what you think," she said, noting his concerned look. She added with a grin, "Though there may be some bloodshed involved in getting to the front of this line."

She gestured toward the hostess station, where the harried-looking hostess was fielding requests for tables.

"I have a better idea," Ryan said. "There's a coffee shop down the way. Why don't we pick up something to go?"

Fifteen minutes later they were strolling barefoot along the sand with a bag of muffins and coffees to go, Stevie wrapped in the sweater she'd had the foresight to bring along. The sky was overcast and a chill wind was blowing in off the ocean, so they had the beach pretty much to themselves. The only other people they passed along the way were a young woman walking her dog and an old man using a metal detector to scavenge in the sand for loose change. Farther out, on the water, fishing boats glided like ghosts in and out of the fog.

"How's Kimberly?" she ventured after a bit, when it became obvious he wasn't going to volunteer the information.

"Kim and I broke up." His tone was matter-of-fact.

Stevie's heart leaped. "Oh? I'm sorry to hear that," she said as sincerely as she could with a grin tugging at her lips.

He shrugged. "It happens."

Stevie felt the tiny spark of hope she'd been nurturing send up a feeble flame. Feeling more kindly toward Kimberly now, she said, "Well, she seemed like a nice person."

"She is."

Stevie edged a bit further out onto the limb. "You don't sound too broken up about it."

"It was mutual. We both realized it wasn't going anywhere," he said, gazing out to sea. He looked like a modern-day Heathcliff, in his jeans and blazer over a vintage Mötley Crüe T-shirt, his curls wild from the damp ocean air. Good enough to wrap up and take home. Had it really been nearly a year since he'd last held her in his arms? Since she'd heard him say the words *I love you*?

"I can relate," she said.

He turned to glance at her as they strolled along the sand. "It wasn't like it was with us."

"How so?" she asked, her heart in her throat.

"I wasn't in love with Kim."

"Ah." Stevie shivered inside her sweater, wondering if he was speaking in the past tense regarding his feelings for her.

"What about you, are you seeing anyone?" he asked casually.

"No one in particular." The few dates she'd been on had been non-starters.

"I would've thought with all that publicity you'd have men beating your door down," he said with a smile.

"There was some interest," she acknowledged, recalling the flood of letters and e-mails she'd received at the station after appearing on *Oprah* with Grant. "Mostly the kind of guy you wouldn't want to be stuck talking to at a party much less go out on a date with."

"There's plenty of fish in the sea," he said.

"I'm not exactly looking."

He arched a brow. "Don't tell me you've given up on men?"

"Well, there *is* this one guy. An ex-boyfriend," she ventured, darting him a look. "Only I'm not sure he's still interested."

"Have you asked him?" Ryan said, playing along.

"I'm afraid to," she confessed. "You see, when we were together, I had my head so far up my ass, I couldn't see what was right in front of my nose."

"What was that?"

"That I'd be crazy not to marry him."

He came to an abrupt standstill, his bemused expression falling away. "What are you saying, Stevie?"

"That I was an idiot to let you go." Her eyes were watering, and not just from the cold. "After I saw you at the Oscars, I didn't sleep for a whole week. Do you have any idea how many TV channels there are? Over a hundred. I thought if I had to look at one more late-night lawn-product commercial, I was going to donate my set to Goodwill."

"And if you had it to do all over again?" he said, his eyes searching her face.

Stevie recalled how nervous she'd been the one time she'd babysat for Ruth, but they'd both survived, neither the worse for wear. Her fears about marriage and motherhood had been equally misguided. It wasn't some shiny prize that would become dulled and chipped with handling, she realized, but a nest you built a straw at a time.

She realized, too, that if she wanted a second chance with Ryan, she would have to be the one to stick her neck out this time. No more pussyfooting around; she had to go for the bold stroke. Struck by a sudden inspiration, she said, "Close your eyes."

"What for?" He eyed her with faint mistrust.

"Just do it."

After a moment's hesitation he complied. "You're not going to run out on me, are you?" he asked.

"You're going to have to start trusting me sometime, so you might as well start now," she said, as she began backing away. "Now keep them closed until I tell you to open them."

"All right, but this better be good."

"It will be, I promise," she called back to him as she raced toward the tide line.

A short while later she yelled through cupped hands, "Okay. You can open them now!"

Ryan didn't say anything at first; he just stared at the giant block letters traced in the wet sand along the tide line. "It's not that creative, I know," she said, as she walked back toward him, "but it was the best I could do on short notice."

"Is this some kind of joke?" he asked when he'd found his voice.

"Nope. But you better act fast. The tide's coming in." As she spoke, the surf rushed in to wash away the bottom half of the letters that spelled out MARRY ME.

Ryan set down the bag he was holding and walked to meet her, putting his arms around her and pulling her in close so that the top of her head fit neatly under his chin. "The answer is yes," he said in a strangely thick voice.

"That was quick," she murmured, holding him tightly with her cheek pressed up against his chest. "You don't want to at least think about it?"

He drew back with a grin. "I'm not as slow to make up my mind as some people I know."

"I'm sorry it took so long, but I plan to spend the rest of my life making it up to you."

"Does that mean kids?" he asked, eyeing her hopefully.

She swallowed hard. "That, too."

"So you're really serious about this?"

"I didn't say we should get started right away, but yeah," she said, thinking of how it had felt holding Ruth in her arms. "I've even become quite adept at changing diapers. Though I have to admit, that's my least favorite part."

He shook his head, looking both bewildered and bemused. "Honestly, Stevie, I never know what to make of you."

She smiled mysteriously. "Give it another fifty years or so. Maybe both of us will have me figured out by then."

Epilogue

Six months later

The Princeton chapel's carillon bells could be heard tolling across the campus on the day of Jay and Franny's wedding. It was the first week in October, and the clouds and rain of the week before had given way to clear skies and mild temperatures. Windows stood open in the ivied brick buildings, and students lolled on the lawn in front of Firestone Library, heads tipped back, luxuriating in this last, glorious gift of sunshine.

As Emerson and Stevie made their way up the chapel walk, dressed in identical pale green silk chiffon dresses tied with darker green sashes, Emerson thought back to her own student days. She remembered how nervous she'd been her freshman year walking into her dorm room for the first time, wondering what her roommate would be like, this girl from California with a boy's name, and if it was possible to room with someone for an entire year without them guessing you were an impostor. But within minutes of meeting Stevie, she'd known she had nothing to fear, and by the time they'd finished unpacking they were fast friends. Stevie Light, true to her name, was like lightning in a bottle, energizing everyone she came into contact with and keeping Emerson perpetually on the go. All these years later, she was still struggling to keep up.

"Slow down, will you?" she panted. "If I trip and go into labor, Franny will never forgive you." Franny was riding over in the limo with Jay's parents and Ruth, so Emerson had taken her car, forgetting that it was a long walk from the parking area to the chapel.

"Sorry." Stevie immediately slowed her pace, darting Emerson a sheepish look. "You okay?"

"I'm fine. Just a little out of breath." Emerson paused to rest, a hand on her belly. Had she been this big with Ainsley? She was glad Franny had seen the wisdom of going with an empire-waisted bridesmaid dress; she'd already had to let hers out twice. As for the shoes, dyed to match her dress, she should have done the sensible thing and worn flats.

"I just hope I look as elegant as you when I'm that far along," Stevie said.

Emerson stared at her, her mouth dropping open. "You're not—"

"No, I'm not." Stevie was quick to set her straight. "Ryan wanted for us to get started right away, but I told him I needed at least a year before I plunged into the deep end."

Their wedding, on a secluded beach in Pacific Grove, had been as low-key and untraditional as Stevie herself, with only close friends and family in attendance. The bride had worn a simple gown fashioned of vintage Irish lace, the groom a Hawaiian shirt and white jeans. Both were barefoot. But the real showstopper was when Grant Tobin showed up, toting his guitar. He'd written a song especially for the occasion, which he'd played for Stevie and

Ryan as they stood under a bower woven of twigs studded with seashells, the setting sun bathing them in a golden glow. His singing had been a little rusty, that of someone who'd been down roads few would ever travel, but somehow that made it all the more haunting. Emerson had glanced over at Stevie's mother at one point and seen tears rolling down her cheeks. It must have seemed a kind of miracle to her that a casual encounter in her free-spirited youth had led to this moment: her beautiful daughter and the stranger who'd fathered her sharing this special occasion.

Now Emerson turned to Stevie with a smile. "You know what they say, 'If you want God to laugh, make plans.'"

She, too, had planned to wait before having another child, at least until the dust had settled. But Mother Nature, it turned out, had other ideas. Soon after her elopement, Emerson's doctor had informed her that the two periods she'd missed that she had thought were the result of all the stress she'd been under, with Reggie's INS troubles and her mother's death, were in fact what Marjorie would have referred to as "a little stranger on the way." Reggie had been over the moon when she broke the news to him, and Ainsley was delighted by the prospect of a baby brother or sister. But it had taken Emerson a while longer to get used to the idea. Having another child had seemed like such a huge responsibility. Once the shock wore off, though, she'd relaxed. She hadn't done so badly with Ainsley, so there was no reason to think she wouldn't do all right with this one, too.

They resumed walking, at a slower pace. "Somehow I can't quite picture Grant as a grandpa," Stevie remarked.

"It would save on music lessons," Emerson pointed out.

"You're right about that. He'd have the kid playing the guitar before he could even talk," Stevie said, with a laugh.

"How are he and your mom getting along, by the way? They seemed pretty chummy at the wedding."

Stevie laughed at the suggestion in Emerson's voice that there was something going on with them. "They're just friends. They go to AA meetings together. Other than that, they don't have much in common."

"Except for you."

A corner of Stevie's mouth hooked up. "Yeah, well, there is that. Though Grant only takes my word for it that he was there the night I was conceived."

Despite her facetious remark, Emerson knew that Stevie had grown close to her father in the short time they'd known each other. Maybe not as close as if she'd known him all her life, but she was sensible enough to accept that in life, as Emerson herself had learned, you simply took what you could get and made the most of it.

At the chapel, they entered the vestry through a side door. For Emerson, it was like coming home. The home she'd made for herself here at Princeton, with her friends, light years from the fractured one in which she'd grown up. Peeking through the doorway into the sanctuary, where the pews, fashioned out of oak originally intended for Civil War gun carriages, were already half filled, her gaze was drawn to the Great East Window over the chancel. It depicted the love of Christ, the six smaller ones on either side the Psalms of David and the great Christian epics—Dante's *Commedia*, Malory's *Le Morte d'Arthur*, Milton's *Paradise Lost*, and Bunyan's *Pilgrim's Progress*. She was reminded of her own heritage, ancestors who included a pre–Revolutionary War hero and the secretary of state under James Madison—a Princetonian himself, memorialized in the Window of Law high up in the south clerestory. A heritage she could take pride in now that she was no longer held hostage by it.

She spied Reggie near the entrance with the other groomsmen: Franny's cousin David from Israel, Stevie's husband, and Jay's friend Todd from work. Seeing her husband, tall and dignified in his dark suit and tie, a sprig of clematis in his lapel, Emerson felt her heart take flight. Six months into her first marriage she'd been chafing at the bit, but with Reggie it just kept getting better. If God was smiling now, she thought, it was because the accident she'd always been sure was just around the bend had turned out to be a happy one.

Briggs showed up just then with Ainsley, who looked like a little princess in her frilly dress and patent-leather shoes, her hair in curls. She'd spent the evening before rehearsing her role as flower girl, and had been so wound up Emerson had had a hard time getting her to sleep and an even harder time rousing her earlier this morning. Luckily Briggs, who'd driven down from the city the night before, was staying at their hotel, so he'd volunteered to bring her over.

Emerson greeted them both with hugs and gave Ainsley the basket of rose petals she'd be scattering over the length of white cloth on the runner. "I know you'll do just great, sweetie," she whispered in her daughter's ear before dispatching them both to the pew in back where Ainsley would await her cue, and she resumed her own place in the vestry.

The tolling of the carillon bells had given way to a Bach cantata, played with enthusiasm by the organist in the choir loft, when she heard a rustling noise behind her and turned to see Franny stepping through the doorway, breathtaking in her fitted silk-taffeta gown that Emerson had helped her select, a bouquet of pink and white roses clutched in one hand. She was accompanied by Ruth, and Jay's parents, Everett Gunderson in a dark suit and tie looking more at ease than Emerson had ever seen him—mainly due to Franny's efforts, she suspected—and his wife, Yvonne, doing her best to keep the squirming toddler in her arms from crushing her corsage.

"I hope I didn't keep you waiting," Franny said.

"Like we could've started without you," said Stevie.

"Look at you. You're so beautiful." Emerson dabbed at her eyes with the hankie she'd had the foresight to tuck into her sleeve. Franny's gown suited her hourglass figure perfectly: cinched at the waist, with a sweetheart neckline that accentuated her full breasts. With her hair pinned up and her veil falling in soft folds about her face, she was a sight to behold.

"Thanks to you," Franny said. "If you hadn't gone with me, I'd still be at that bridal shop obsessing over what to wear."

"Don't forget, she's had lots of practice," Stevie teased.

"Which is more than I can say for you," Emerson replied, with a laugh. "You had to be dragged kicking and screaming down the aisle."

"I never want to have to go through *that* again," Stevie pronounced with a mock shudder. "So I guess this means Ryan's stuck with me."

"I don't see him complaining," Franny said.

From the choir loft came the first soaring notes of Puccini's "Chi il bel sogno di Doretta," sung by Franny's friend from work, Hannah Moreland, in her lovely soprano voice honed by amateur theatre productions. Emerson peeked into the sanctuary once more to find Jay standing at the altar with his best man, Todd Oster. The pews were mostly filled and the doors stood open, where moments from now the bride and her two bridesmaids would be making their entrance, preceded by Ainsley. Emerson, slipping an arm each through those of her two best friends, announced, "It's showtime, girls."

As the three women made their way back outside and along the path toward the front of the chapel, Stevie thought about the even longer journey it had taken to get where they were today. Take her own wedding, for instance. After all the drama leading up to it, she'd expected to be a nervous wreck, but instead, as she and Ryan had stood barefoot in the sand exchanging their vows, the sun setting over the ocean and the people she loved best looking on, she'd felt strangely at peace. Maybe it had something to do with Grant, knowing what it had taken for him to travel those few miles, more than her aunt Katherine's flying in from Hong Kong for the occasion. She had sworn she wouldn't cry—that was for dewy-eyed girls with hope chests who subscribed to *Bride's* magazine—but when he'd played the song he'd written for the occasion, she'd almost lost it. Good thing she'd had the excuse of the sun being in her eyes to explain why they were watering.

Then it was over, everyone clapping and cheering and rushing up to congratulate them. Afterward, there had been a barbecue on the beach, and when night fell they'd built a big bonfire and toasted marshmallows for S'mores. At one point, Stevie had noticed Nancy and Grant slipping off together. A short while later she'd spotted them strolling along the shore, their figures silhouetted against the moonlit sea. Briefly she'd entertained the fantasy that they would fall in love and get married. But Nancy had laughed at the idea when Stevie suggested it later on. They were just fellow survivors who, in time she hoped, would be good friends, she'd said. There was no more likelihood of their falling in love than of the Fillmore Auditorium of yore rising from the ashes.

Now, as they climbed the chapel steps, Stevie leaned in to murmur encouragingly in Franny's ear, "Trust me, you won't know what hit you until it's over."

"Don't listen to her. Enjoy every second of it," Emerson advised from her end.

In lieu of a father or close male relative to give her away, Franny had broken with tradition and was having her bridesmaids do the honors. Stevie could feel her trembling as they started down the aisle following the crooked trail of rose petals Ainsley had strewn, and wanted to pat her hand and whisper once more that it was going to be okay. But Franny's gaze was fixed firmly on Jay, at the altar, who even in his tuxedo looked as if he'd just hopped down off the back of a pickup, with his perpetually windblown hair and sun-kissed cheeks, and from the way Franny was beaming, it was clear she didn't need any reassurance.

As Franny made her way up the aisle, arm in arm with Emerson and Stevie, she was scarcely aware of the people around her. Here and there, a familiar face would emerge from the blur on either side of the aisle—her aunt Sadie and uncle Moe who'd flown up from Fort Lauderdale; Stevie's mom, Nancy; Jay's mother, in regulation mother-of-the-groom crepe de chine, holding Ruth on her lap. Franny blew Ruth a kiss, but she only gaped at her in open-mouthed wonder, as if she didn't recognize her.

Not for the first time, she wished her mother and brother could have been here. Esther might have grumbled a bit in the beginning about her marrying a goy, in a church no less, but the fact that it was Jay, whom she'd referred to as her Yiddisher son, convinced he'd been Jewish in another life, would have made it all right. And Bobby . . . well, he might have disrupted the proceedings somewhat with his odd behavior . . . but he, too, would've been happy for them.

She thought, too, of the last time she'd seen Jay standing at the altar in a tuxedo: when he was marrying Vivienne. Franny had been the maid of honor on that occasion. Now Vivienne was in Paris and the last she'd heard living with some Frenchman. And it was Franny walking down the aisle, dressed all in white, with a heart full of love and her mind as certain as it had ever been.

Then there was only Jay, his shining eyes the polestar keeping her on course. When she reached his side, he laced his fingers through hers, whispering, "You look amazing."

The chaplain spoke briefly but eloquently about the sanctity of marriage and the challenges they would overcome together in the years ahead. When it was time for them to exchange vows, Jay pulled a folded sheet of paper from his vest pocket. Clearing his throat, he began to read aloud: "Franny, you're my best friend and my soul mate. I didn't always know you could have both in one woman, but I do now. I also know that if the rest of our lives is anything like it's been up until now, we're in for a real adventure." He glanced up at her and they exchanged a smile, accompanied by a ripple of laughter from those who knew them best. "I can't imagine life without you. You make me laugh. You're always there when I need you. You keep me honest, and I know I'm a better man because of you. Best of all, you've given me our beautiful daughter. If I could have one more wish, it would be to spend the rest of my life with you at my side."

Franny's eyes filled with tears and she whispered, "How am I supposed to top that?"

The vows she'd written suddenly seemed inadequate. How could words alone express what Jay meant to her or sum up all the experiences they'd shared through the years? All the laughter and the tears; the sentences one of them would start and the other would finish; the long talks that had sometimes gone well into the night; the collective gallons of chicken soup she'd taken him when he was sick and the countless french fries he'd let her cadge off his plate; the chick flicks he'd endured for her sake and the football games she'd sat through with him; the bedcovers he let her hog and the toilet seat he always remembered to put down; the countless times he'd gotten up in the middle of the night with Ruth.

Jay squeezed her hand, whispering back, "You already have."

"A beautiful tale of loss, redemption and hope:
WOMAN IN RED IS A MASTERPIECE."
–Barbara Delinsky
"Her best book yet. Nothing short of brilliant."
–Luanne Rice
"Once you start this wonderful book, you won't be able to put it down."
–Kristin Hannah
WHO IS SHE?
WHAT TERRIBLE SECRET IS SHE HIDING?
WOMAN *in* RED
a novel
EILEEN GOUDGE
Vanguard Press A Member of the Perseus Books Group
Visit www.EileenGoudge.com to meet Eileen online.
www.WomanInRedBook.com